BAND OF MISFITS

An All-teen Short Story Anthology

Edited by Hannah Smith & Nicole Brouwer
Foreword by Kiersten White

Owl Hollow Press
in partnership with Teen Author Boot Camp

ISBN 978-1-945654-23-7 (paperback)
ISBN 978-1-945654-24-4 (e-book)

Publisher's Note: This is a work of fiction. Names, characters, places, and incidents are products of the authors' imaginations. Any resemblance to actual people, living or dead, or to businesses, companies, events, institutions, or locales is completely coincidental or fictionalized.

BAND OF MISFITS/ Smith, Brouwer. 1st ed.

www.owlhollowpress.com

To the amazing authors who have shared their stories.
May you always dream in blue.

CONTENTS

Foreword: Alone Together in the Infinite Blue

It's always been out there.

There's so much blue, more blue than you could ever explore. More blue than everyone who ever lived could explore. And that fact keeps most away. It's too big for them. Where would they even start? When the blue sparkles on the horizon, winking with promise, they feel nothing. When storms rage, they close their shutters. They don't want to peer into the tempest and see what's inside. When they dream, the blue doesn't call to them.

Some build boats and set out with high hopes, but before the afternoon is out they've returned. There wasn't anything out there. They were bored. It was hard work. They could only see blue. What were they supposed to do with so much blue? They're only one very small person. And there's so much to be done on shore.

Some tinker with their boats, tell anyone who will listen what adventures they'll have, how much they'll sail, what they'll bring back. How much better their boat is than yours. (They *really* need you to know their boat is better than yours.)

But they never actually leave the shore. They'd rather think about it than do it. Than face the reality of all that empty blue.

And it looks empty, from shore. Those who stay can't imagine what it could offer. They only see what their eyes tell them.

But you? You dream in blue every night. You catch yourself staring at it when you should be doing other things. You *feel* the blue out there, waiting.

You build your boat. You don't look at the other boats. You don't worry that yours isn't crafted the same, that it isn't as fancy or as big or as old as the others. It's yours. That's all it needs to be. And, when no one is watching, with no crowds to cheer you on, you tentatively set out. Alone. It's the only way to do it.

At first it *is* empty, like everyone said. Maybe you should have stayed on shore. The blue is so big, and you are so small. Your boat might not be good enough. You might not be strong enough, brave enough, clever enough to navigate and discover.

But then you take a deep breath, hold tight to the edge of your boat, and peer over the side. And you can never go back. Not now that you've seen: There are *worlds* down there. So much more than unbroken blue. So much more than you could ever have known.

You push forward. You sail until you leave the shore far behind. You work through familiar swells and comfortable shallows until you navigate to unknown territories, where the crystal depths reveal unimaginable life. You have to dive to see it. And dive you do. You emerge gasping and delirious. Joyful with what you bring back up with you. Every time you dive, you go deeper, farther. It's hard. It's worth it.

But still, it's just you. And as many times as you dive, as much as you discover, it's always

Just

You.

You range farther. You battle storms with overwhelming, white-capped mountains of waves. You tip. You flounder. You keep hold of your boat and yourself. And after the storms, something worse comes: Nothing.

Flat, glassy blue as far as you can see. Nothing to break the monotony of the sun, the glare of the blank reflection. You dive down, but the blue offers you no treasures. Nothing to explore, to get lost in. It's all one color. Empty. So are you.

You climb back into your boat and wonder what it was all for. All these worlds you carry in your boat, stalled out, dead in the water with you. It feels like there will never be another breeze, never another wave to ride, never a new wonder beneath. You'd even take a storm, just for *something* to happen.

You're alone, and nothing has changed.

When you're ready to give up, to go back to shore, to leave behind the blue forever, you see it—afar on the horizon. Not beneath the blue, but floating on top of the vast, lonely expanse. Another boat.

And when, at last, you make your way to each other, you pause, suddenly shy. You've been alone in this wonderland for so long. How can you share it? A tentative hello. A remark on the unremarkable weather. A pause.

But they're out here, too. In their own boat, so different than yours. It suddenly strikes you not as lonely, but as *glorious*. In that boat, they've seen things you never could. And in yours, you've seen things they never could. Now you are alone, together, in the infinite blue, with more colors and shades and depths than ever before.

"Do you want to hear a story?" you ask.

The relief and excitement on their face reflects your own.

"Yes," they whisper. "And I want to tell you one, too."

The Night the Ship Went Down

"**Y**ou cursed women win every game," one of the pirates around the table in the corner of the muggy tavern complained. Obscenities of agreement rose from around the group of drunken gamblers as cards were thrown down in spite. Captain Emberly Burnsfield of the ship *Calamity* splayed a royal flush, claiming the entire pot of winnings for her own.

"Tell me something I don't know." Emberly winked at the gathered men, most of whom were fellow captains. She took a long swig of her bitter drink, slamming the stein back down once she was satisfied. Her second-in-command, a dark-skinned woman called Shauna, pulled the grimy coins toward herself and her captain, counting them with her eager eyes.

"You should put your money where your mouth is for once," challenged the pirate who had complained before, his dark hair falling into his even darker eyes. The man was Captain Gavin of the *De la Rosa*, an expensive ship that could pass for one from the Spanish navy.

"For once?" Emberly gestured to the pile of loot in front of her.

Gavin clenched his jaw. "Stop acting like a child." He took a swig of his drink before setting it back down with a measured calmness that Emberly knew all too well to be false.

ADVENTURE ON THE HIGH SEAS · 11

"You're the one acting like a sore loser," Emberly said innocently, though she pursed her lips in an entitled sort of way.

"Enough! Both of you," one of the other pirates cut off the bickering pair. He was Captain Edwards, with a scraggly, grey beard and stormy eyes. "Come to an accord or scatter."

Emberly made a face at Edwards while he wasn't looking, and then rose her sea-foam colored eyes to Gavin's black-brown ones. "Well?" Emberly's tone requested an apology. "Why so glum?"
Gavin rolled his eyes. "You win everything. Your crew has the best luck that I've ever seen."

"You flatter me," Emberly said flatly.

"Let me finish." Gavin gritted through his golden teeth. "You win every game but you bet stolen coins and hide cards in your sleeves. You don't win for skill or honor, nor do you bet with any real consequence. I wonder if you have any honor in you at all?"

"I *live* by a code of honor." Emberly rose slowly and dramatically to her feet. "And if you think you haven't seen my crew's skill...then you haven't been watching close enough. Tell me, where is your pocket watch?"

Gavin felt his breast pocket, and then all of the other many pockets that lined and covered his trench coat. He rose to his feet when he came up empty-handed, bracing himself on the table and glowering at her. Emberly looked over her shoulder, smiling at a girl across the bar who leaned against a crackling fireplace, tossing a pocket watch up and down and matching her captains smirk.

"Honor indeed." The corner of Gavin's mouth twitched. "This is what I speak of exactly, this sort of inconsequential fun that you like to have. Do something real. Something that shows just how much of a *pirate* you are."

"And why should I jump at the chance to prove myself to you?" Emberly's eyes narrowed.

"No pirate would pass up the chance to prove their superiority," he said, which Emberly begrudgingly had to admit was true.

"Then what do you suggest?" Captain Edwards' calloused hand drifted to the flask on his belt as he too, rose from his seat. A moment of silence followed as Gavin thought.

"I have an idea," Emberly announced brightly, her thoughts sluggish and drunken, making her far too self-assured and far too thoughtless. "Calypso."

There were a few gasps from the lesser men at the table, and even Emberly's second tugged at her sleeve. She looked down at Shauna, but the surety that filled Emberly's eyes was enough to make the same overconfidence manifest itself in her second.

"Calypso?" Gavin asked. "You're bloody insane."

"Thanks." Emberly smiled. "We'll both set out on the morning tide to find Calypso's Island."

"It's not a matter of *finding* the island." Edwards face grew decidedly paler than when Emberly had last looked over at him. "There are maps in abundance to lead one there. But every crew that's been crazy enough to go looking for it have never returned."

"Then consider me certifiably mad." Emberly bowed. "Legend has it that whomever dares to seek out and find Calypso's Island will be granted one wish by the goddess herself. Think of it, ladies." Emberly spread her hands in front of her as if painting a picture. Several of her crew had gathered around her and were listening to the promise that she was making, all of them too drunk to realize what they were getting themselves into. "All the money we could ever dream."

"You must be joking," Gavin rubbed his forehead, trying desperately to comprehend what it was that Emberly was suggesting.

"Why would I be?" Emberly took another chug of alcohol, completely unbothered by the task she was setting for herself and her crew.

Gavin floundered for a moment. "And what's to stop you from changing your mind and running scared once you sober up come sunrise?"

"You said it yourself." Emberly shrugged. "Honor."

"You would be surprised how quickly honor fades to the background in the face of fear," Captain Edwards offered darkly.

Another one of the pirates from the table stood up with a toothless grin. "They should trade seconds."

"They would become hostages on the opposing ship." Gavin smirked, growing fond of the idea.

Emberly nodded in agreement. Shauna looked to her captain, her eyes worried. But they had made it through worse. This would be nothing compared to the countless feats that the *Calamity* crew had conquered.

"But what's on the table?" Gavin wondered aloud.

"Status…" Emberly answered. "As the best pirate on the sea. Not to mention, the first crew that finds Calypso will get their wish granted."

"One more rule," Gavin demanded.

"Fire away."

"We play fair," he looked Emberly in the eye.

"I'll do my best." Emberly's lips twisted into a wry smile.

Gavin sighed, understanding that this was the best he would get. He stuck out his hand for Emberly to shake. Emberly grinned and tapped her fingers on her chin as if deciding whether or not to take the bet she had placed. Her crew could do this in their sleep. And if it would seal the debate on whether she was the best pirate to sail the seas—then whatever was to come of them would be worth it. And not only that, they would gain more gold than they would know what to do with. More money than they could ever hope to spend.

"To a bet that counts?" Emberly looked up at Gavin through her lashes and placed her hand in his.

"To a bet that counts." Gavin shook her hand in promise. "We sail at first light…after we swap seconds, of course."

Emberly grinned, her crew smug and silent around her as she pulled her hand away first. She grabbed a drink off the tray of a passing barmaid and downed it in a few gulps, savoring the powerful fog in her mind as the drink filled her veins and made her invincible.

+

"Yo ho, m'ladies!" Captain Emberly chanted as she jumped down from the edge of the *Calamity*, her short hair blown back from her face by the wind coming off the salty sea. Her boots landed on the deck with a damp thud, her shirt billowing around her. The crew was shuffling about, setting things into place for a long and steady ride across the ocean. "We got a good start this morning but that's no reason to drag your feet!"

Emberly stopped herself from calling for Shauna, remembering that her second was not aboard her ship. She swallowed as she continued her waltz around the deck, coming to a stop in front of the hostage, Gavin's second-in-command, who was tied to the mainmast and looking all too unamused.

"How long are you going to keep me tied up, Emberly?" he asked.

Emberly bristled, standing up straight and ignoring the familiar pang in her head from the sunlight, the usual side effect of a night spent in a tavern. She narrowed her eyes at the man, with whom she had history. When Gavin had boasted the young man, shoving him toward Emberly's crew that morning, she had been none too pleased to see his impish face. Still she had bid Shauna farewell-for-now and kept a straight face as she welcomed the new hostage aboard. Now

Emberly smirked unkindly and crossed her arms over her chest. "That's *Captain* to you."

"Understood, *Captain* Emberly," he said with a not so innocent grin, his eyes alight with disrespect.

"Good job on the work we did before sunrise!" Emberly called out, keeping her gaze on the man in front of her. The crew cheered and laughed. "Speaking of, I wonder what's holding up Gavin and his crew? I thought we were sailing out on this morning's tide...not tomorrow's."

"What did you do to our ship?" The hostage's face tightened with skeptical exasperation.

"Who ever said we did anything to your ship?" Emberly mocked offense.

"I do wonder how their rudder is holding up though." Amelia approached to study the stranger. Amelia was Emberly's red-headed third-in-command, now taking Shauna's place while she was temporarily gone.

"The rudder?" The hostage tugged against his binds, the rope unnecessarily tight by the captain's request. "What have you done to the rudder?"

"A magician must never reveal her tricks," Emberly teased.

The hostage rolled his eyes—far too much like Gavin had the night before, which made Emberly stand a bit taller in displeasure. "You promised fair play!" he whined.

Emberly shrugged. "It wouldn't be a Captain Emberly Burnsfield production without just a little slight of hand."

"You women pirates are ridiculous. You probably can't stand to play nicely because your frail little egos would shatter under the pressure of losing."

"I will have you know," Emberly jabbed her finger into his face, "That my ego is anything but small and fragile. Some might say that its resilience is a bit of an issue, really."

"Point taken," the hostage resigned. "However, this whole time that I have been aboard your ship you haven't once used my name. Which sounds to me like the action of someone afraid of facing their hurt feelings."

"Hurt feelings?" Emberly scoffed. "I simply don't remember your name. And, as captain, I can call you whatever I please. It's a perk of the job."

"You don't remember my name?" He laughed. "That's a blatant lie."

Emberly tightened her lips into a line. It had been a lie, of course, but the man in front of her was so different from the boy she had once known, he might as well be a different person entirely.

"Remind me." Emberly raised her chin to look down her nose at him.

"You know my name."

Emberly stared blankly at him a few moments more.

He sighed, shoulders slumping. "Jakob."

"Ah, yes!" Her face lightened. "That does ring a bell."

Jakob started to say something more, to argue or protest or something equally as unimportant but Emberly was already walking toward the helm of the ship making a direct point to ignore him.

+

Emberly retreated to her cabin early that evening, her back cramping from being hunched over her desk for too long. Wax pooled underneath the candles that sat flickering from the corners of the desk, making the room glow orange and smell faintly of smoke, a contrast to the humid darkness that had now settled over the sea. Waves sloshed lazily against the ship, bringing Emberly peace in the chaos.

She poured over scrolls and papers, all of which documented tales of Calypso's Island and those unfortunate enough to have found it. It was an old and complicated tale that Emberly had heard her whole life. Calypso, the goddess cast down from Olympus and banished to an island in the middle of the sea, waited on the beach for ships to appear on the horizon. Legend said that whenever a crew found the island, she was there, willing and ready to grant their greatest wish.

Some sailed away, their desires granted, only to have a terrible tragedy overcome them on the journey home, sinking them to the bottom of the ocean. Some never even made it that far before death started calling their names. Though nobody had yet come home from Calypso's Island, Emberly was certain her crew could be the first. It would be her ship, the beautiful *Calamity* that would sail from one edge of the world to the next, which would succeed where all others had failed. It would be her ladies, drenched in seawater but still fighting, drunk as anyone had ever been but still having the true and unbridled courage needed to go forward. People had always disrespected and underestimated her and her crew. But they would stand for it no longer.

If they could find Calypso, all the power would be theirs and no one would ever doubt their endeavors again. They would be the richest pirates to ever sail the seas, wearing silk gowns on their adventures simply for the fact that they could afford them. They would fill washbasins to the brim with gold, the luxury pleasantly overwhelming.

Emberly looked back to the papers, taking mental notes of the tales and terrain, making certain her crew would be prepared when they faced the goddess on her island. The time soon approached when they would present their wish to her. They would beat Captain Gavin of the De la Rosa, leaving him to lose the gamble while she and her crew would be on their way to the nearest port to buy as many things as their ship could hold.

+

"Captain!" Amelia banged on the door. "Captain, it's urgent!"

Emberly shot up from her cot, still in her clothes from the day before and covered in a thin sheen of sweat from the stifling summer air. Aye, that was the life of a pirate. If you wanted a lovely smelling woman with good washing habits, you didn't find her on the sea.

Emberly swung the door open. Amelia stumbled forward a step as her hand was left with nothing to stop its momentum.

"What is it?" Emberly's voice was steady despite being just woken from sleep.

"There's a ship behind us, catching up fast," Amelia panted. "Gavin's ship."

"Oh, I don't think so." Emberly's face twisted into a snarl. "Tell the crew that I'm on my way. We'll outrun that scoundrel to the ends of the earth and back again."

"Aye, Captain." Amelia hurried back to the main deck, already shouting orders at the crew.

Emberly swung around, leaning over the desk and taking one last look at an upside-down illustration of Calypso's Island that she had left sprawled on her desk the night before. Then, stepping into the hallway and slamming the door behind her, she made her way to the main deck, her face set in a mask of stony determination as she stepped into the dark, early morning air, ready to fight her way through this and get to her rightful place: ahead of anyone who attempted to stop her.

+

Emberly stormed onto the main deck, meeting Amelia by the miz-zenmast and following her to the helm.

"You don't even need to be in the crow's nest to see him," Amelia said.

Emberly looked at the horizon off the back of the ship and swallowed, profanities flying from her mouth like poetry at what she saw.

Gavin's shiny Spanish ship was far too close for comfort and he was coming up on them far faster than the morning wind would have allowed the *Calamity*. Perhaps Gavin had gotten new sails?

She turned to look at Amelia, then beyond her. They were coming up to one of the more intense parts of their journey. She knew her crew could handle it but it would be a nail-biter, even without Gavin on their tail the whole time. They were nearing an island, one that was countless leagues in width, with a rocky arch in the middle. Going under the arch was a shortcut that would save them days of travel, the only alternative to going around the island entirely. But it was a risk. The arch was just taller than *Calamity* herself, with a massive wall of stone jutting out from the water just beyond the mouth of it, creating a dividing fork in the current. To the left of the split was open sea that would eventually lead a ship to many places, one of which was Calypso's Island. While the current to the right carried you through a day's journey of winding, treacherous cliff sides and jagged rocks that were perilous enough to tear your rig to shreds if you didn't sail through them just right. But if navigated safely, would lead directly to their goal. It would take a pirate of great and specific skill to pull it off.

"How did he catch up so fast?" Emberly turned once again to see Gavin's ship, now even closer than before.

"A magician must never reveal his tricks." Jakob replied loudly from the deck, still tied to the mainmast and looking miserable for it.

"Very funny, hostage!" Emberly shouted as she nodded to the helmswoman to relieve her from her post. The captain took up her rightful place at the wheel. If her women were getting through this maneuver, she was going to be the one at the helm. One jerk in the wrong direction and they were done for.

"My name is Jakob!" He called indignantly.

Emberly resigned her protest to a small groan. She shifted her hands, tilting the wheel minutely to the right, the sails catching the breeze just so. A horn blew far behind them, Gavin focusing more on making noise then on the carefully planned angles that would get them through the arch.

She spun the wheel a few inches to the left so *Calamity* sailed straight as they reached the mouth of the arch. Emberly started a count to five in her head.

"Emberly, are you sure you know what you're doing?" Jakob yelled.

"*Captain*—" Emberly started to roar, realizing that she lost her count a second too late. She shot a glance at the angle of the foremast with the inside of the arch and spun the wheel left, throwing her whole body into turning it as far as it would go.

The edge of *Calamity* just barely cleared the inner wall of the fork. It was so close that one could have touched it from well inside the rail of the ship. It wasn't until they were several moments past the obstacle before Emberly finally let out a breath. She whistled for the helmswoman to take back her post as the crew cheered and stomped their feet. Emberly took a dramatic bow and smiled at her loyal ladies before spinning on her heel and rushing to the back rail of the ship to watch Gavin's attempt, a wicked smile on her face.

The *De la Rosa* soared through the mouth of the arch, and Emberly watched as the helmsman turned the wheel a second too late. The ship started to tilt to the left, but the current had already grabbed it, tugging the blue and gold ship to the right, toward the perilous journey around the island. Emberly yelled with glee as the ship disappeared behind the rocks.

She could only imagine her second-in-command right now. Shauna must have been trying to suppress a beaming grin as she realized that Gavin's helmsman was going to fail the maneuver. Emberly hopped down the stairs onto the main deck of the ship, positively radiant with the air of victory. She sauntered up to Jakob.

"They failed?" Jakob asked with wide eyes.

Emberly nodded. "Looks like we don't even need to find Calypso to prove who the better pirate is."

"I don't understand what happened. Gavin knows how to handle that arch!" Disbelief stained his words. "They're going to be *days* behind."

"Then I suppose I should celebrate. He was too busy tooting his own horn, literally, to steer the ship himself. Besides, the damaged rudder probably didn't help."

"There's a special place in hell for women like you." Jakob shook his head and tugged against the uncomfortable ropes that still bound him.

"Oh, I hope so." Emberly looked to the clouds and sighed.

"You're twisted."

"Thanks for noticing." Emberly turned away to stand by the ship's rail. She gestured for Amelia to slash Jakob's bonds, then smiled at the golden water, which reflected the rich and rising sun. The world was coming into focus for a new day, the dawn casting long shadows along the *Calamity* and the water. The waves stirred with the morning tide, sending them smoothly on their way, this time without Gavin on their heels.

✦

The next afternoon, Emberly was lounging on the foredeck, drinking rum from a jug.

"Captain Emberly." A deep voice came from behind.

She smiled coldly. "Yes, Jakob?"

"Why'd you let them untie me?" He stood in front of her.

"Honestly? I hoped you would jump overboard and become lunch to an unlucky shark."

"You really wouldn't care if I jumped overboard right now?"

"Not at all," said Emberly. "Why should I? Because we once knew each other when we were young and stupid? Things change, Jakob. People change."

"Not you."

Emberly gave a sharp laugh, shaking her head and looking at the boy that she had once known, trying to recognize him by something other than his eyes. "Especially me."

"Your status may have changed." Jakob took a step toward her. Emberly took a step back, raising an eyebrow like a warning. "But you're still the Emberly I once knew. You still have a fire inside you. A fire that cannot be doused by the sea, only fed by it."

"I don't welcome or value your opinions," said Emberly.

"I was trying to say something nice!" Jakob flung out his arms in exasperation.

"Well, I'm not in search of validation, especially from you."

"What did I ever do to you?" Jakob's tone was genuinely perplexed.

Had he truly cared for her so little that he did not remember the promises he had broken?

"You never came back."

Jakob's eyes flashed with something she couldn't identify, just before she stormed away to her quarters.

"You can't just walk away after that!" called Jakob.

But that's exactly what Emberly did.

✦

Many days passed, sunsets and sunrises. The days were sweltering, turning their cheeks red and blistered when they stayed on the main deck too long. The nights were stifling while the dense air pulsed around them in the darkness. Most evenings were spent drinking and chanting about how rich they were going to be, fantasizing about how they would spend the gold. The Calamity crew boasted their lead on Gavin and thanked the stars for their never-failing luck.

The De la Rosa had not yet appeared in their sights again. Jakob's jaw was always clenched, eyes darting out at the sea as if he longed to be anywhere but aboard the *Calamity*. He had learned when to keep his mouth shut and not to argue. He settled for a dismissive blink and a sarcastic retort breathed into the wind. Emberly tried to ignore him, only speaking to him intentionally when she planned to say something rude, or in the early hours of the morning when she was not quite drunk enough to sleep. Jakob kept trying to breach the subject of their past, but Emberly wouldn't listen. She refused. Instead she let her anger fester, the constant wash of the waves *almost* loud enough to drown out her swirling thoughts.

✦

The morning of the day they were set to arrive at Calypso's Island, Emberly awoke to rain pattering against her window and a thin layer of condensation on the glass. When she peered outside, she found the sky coated so thickly with dark clouds that the water below them looked black. On the main deck, the crew wrestled with the rigging as they raised the sails to prepare for the worst.

"Emberly!" Jakob ran to her, his wet hair falling into his eyes. Emberly didn't bother to correct him with her title. "Emberly, it isn't too late to turn back, to call off the bet."

"We're so close!" Emberly argued over the roar of the waves. The rain made a loud hiss as it hit the ship. "My crew and I have made it through worse than this!"

"I'm sure you have but this is nothing to play with," Jakob pleaded. "Forget Calypso's Island. This was a bad idea."

"You just want me to call it off because you know that Gavin is days behind," said Emberly. "You're scared of losing."

"I would never be so childish! Especially not about something as serious as this!"

"We are not turning back," Emberly spat with finality. "Only a coward calls off a gamble."

"It would not be cowardly to save your crew," Jakob pushed. "It would be rational!"

"We are getting that wish, even if it is the end of us," Emberly said darkly.

"You would truly risk your life—and the lives of your crew—for gold?" Jakob grabbed Emberly by the arm when she turned to leave without comment. "You would look into the face of death for coins?"

"We all agreed to fight for this."

"Perhaps you were right," Jakob said. "Perhaps you *have* changed. And not for the best."

Emberly ripped her arm away from him. "We have sailed the sea for nearly a decade in search of a fraction of the treasure we're about to will into existence."

"Captain!" The helmswoman called.

"Coming!" Emberly shouted back. Jakob's eyes were wide, but he didn't say anything more. "If you'll excuse me I have a ship to commandeer. If you get scared you can hide below deck with the rats."

They stared at each other for a moment longer, the air between them seeming to spark with livid electricity. Then Emberly sprinted to the helm, shouting orders and helping her crew as the storm grew stronger. The smell of the ocean, like rotting fish and seaweed, filled her nose.

✦

The wood of the deck moaned in distress as the ship pressed back against the storm. Emberly was at the helm, soaked to the bone and shivering from cold and adrenalin. The women were shouting as they shoveled buckets of water back out to sea in a desperate attempt to keep the overwhelming waves that flooded the deck at bay. Lightning struck the horizon, turning everything purple for a millisecond, the light spider-webbed across the sky before plunging everything once again into darkness. Bellows of thunder filled every crevice, leaving nothing untouched or silent.

Jakob stood near Emberly. He braced himself on the railing against the onslaught of rain, wind, and the sharp sheets of water lashing across the deck. Waves grabbed at the ship, the sea craving to claim the *Calamity* for its own. But it would not sink that day. Not if Captain Emberly Burnsfield had anything to do with it. She tried to dig her heels into the deck of the ship, but found herself slipping re-gardless. Uncertainty flashed through her mind for the first time on this journey. At that moment, she let herself feel the pressure. Her grip on the wheel began to slip.

"Need help?" Jakob rushed over.

"No!" Emberly shouted on instinct. Another larger-than-life wave made the ship tilt sharply. The bottom of the *Calamity* slammed back into the water with a splash. Jakob took hold of the wheel and the pair double-teamed the helm. Water washed over the edge and swept several women off their feet as lightening etched itself across the sky, making everything bright for an instant. In that light, a mas-sive, jutting shape appeared a hundred meters ahead of them.

Calypso's Island. Emberly knew it from the countless illustra-tions that she had poured over on their journey. "That's it! The island is straight ahead!"

The women cheered, at least the ones that could hear their cap-tain over the deafening sounds of the storm. They forced their way through the storm until they were close enough to shore to lay anchor. Emberly abandoned the helm and sprinted to the front of the ship. The wet sails lowered around her. She leapt onto the railing while holding tight to a sopping rope as she gazed upon the beach. Her crew crowd-ed behind her.

"Emberly!" Jakob called. "Don't do this! Gavin warned—" But Emberly cut him off with a snap of her fingers. Two of her women rushed forward to muffle his protests.

Something about Calypso's Island was eerily calm, as if the storm were coming *from* the island instead of at it. Emberly looked down at the water and saw enormous, slithering things swimming un-derneath the surface. She shivered, a cold finger dragging down her spine as she averted her gaze. Clouds shifted allowing moonlight to trickle onto the sand. A wispy ghost of a woman appeared on the beach.

"Calypso?" Emberly's voice was swallowed up by the noise of the raging storm, but still the figure looked up. The clouds kept shift-ing, washing the moonlight away but the figure remained. She solidified into human form wearing a thin, white dress with her hair woven into a braid that fell to her waist. Emberly was taken aback by the goddess's beauty, her molten eyes and golden skin. "Calypso?" Emberly called again. Her crew whispered behind her in a fervent, wordless buzz.

"Have you pirates come in search of me?" Calypso's voice was crystal clear across the distance, as if she were speaking directly into Emberly's ears.

"Yes! We've traveled a great distance to find you on your island."

"Very well." Though the pirates were being drenched by the pouring rain and ripped apart from the howling wind, the goddess seemed to be unaffected by the storm. Her hair and dress were unbothered. "Tell me your wish and I shall grant it."

Emberly turned and met the eyes of each woman before her, grinning at them victoriously. Her crew was starting to stomp their feet in a rhythm. The water that was up to their ankles splashing with every slam of their boots. "Gold, gold, gold." They started to chant, and the roar of it filled Emberly's ears.

"Gold!" Emberly cheered with them, spinning back around to face the goddess. "Our wish is all of the gold we could ever dream!"

Calypso stared at Emberly for a moment, her face unreadable. "Gold?" The goddess asked in a small voice. "You have come all this way...for money?"

Jakob tried to interject.

"Yes!" Emberly said over Jakob. "We are the best pirates to sail the seas and now we wish to be the richest." Her crew cheered.

Calypso's fragile face saddened until it changed into something else. Something far worse. The goddess grew angry, her expression sharp, and her eyes narrowing. "Money is the root of all evil, greed the mother of all sin. How dare you come to my home and ask for gold?"

"We came all this way in search of treasure." Emberly envisioned the life she would have if Calypso would grant their wish. "You are a legend for being generous and granting the wishes of sailors. I find it doubtful that no pirate has wished for gold."

"I never said such a thing." Calypso's eyes became dark and shadowed. "But I did to them what I must now do to you. I can sense you, Emberly Burnsfield. You are used to winning and getting what you want. You have become corrupted by pride."

Emberly took a step back, her brow furrowed. She knew she was a little rough around the edges—she was a pirate, after all—but corrupt? "My crew and I are wholesome people."

"You sail blindly into danger, knowing full well what it might cost you. Yet in the face of consequence, you are not ready to pay the price."

"I am ready to do whatever it takes." Emberly met Calypso's wrathful eyes.

"Your arrogance will be your undoing." Calypso shook her head solemnly. Emberly's crew stirred behind her, their nervous banter hushed and urgent. "Your greed will drown with you all tonight."

"No," Emberly demanded. "Leave my crew out of this!"

Calypso smiled sadly. "I'm afraid I cannot. Your crew will become another of the countless, unfortunate tales of sailors who never made it home."

"Forget the wish, if you must." Emberly's stomach sank. "But let us sail free."

"Even the players who win every game must lose eventually." Calypso raised her hands up, the storm roaring with new life.

A current grabbed the *Calamity*, dragging them out to sea, away from the island. A chunk of the ship ripped away, the chain unraveling as the anchor stayed buried in the sand. The creatures that Emberly had seen around the shore circled their ship and filled the air with horrid screeches. Lighting struck the water all around. Violent waves crashed onto the deck and knocked the pirates off their feet, while their lungs filled with salty, stinging water. A bolt of lightning smashed through the *Calamity*, leaving a gaping hole in the side of the ship that was quickly filling with water. Emberly pleaded for the goddess to stop, as Calypso faded away, shaking her head sadly at the soaked captain. A barrel of gunpowder exploded, sending a wave of heat across the ship. A deckhand was set aflame in the blast and she screamed as she stumbled backward and over the railing, plummeting overboard. Emberly cursed, pushing back her tears. What had she gotten them into?

Jakob was rushing toward her. Emberly felt an unexpected pang of regret for the way she had treated him. She knew, deep down, he was the same boy that had befriended her in the prison cells of that dirty smuggler ship. They had been adolescents, just on the verge of becoming who they were supposed to be. Their lives had stretched before them then, and now they were coming to an end. This was the first time that Emberly had ever felt hopeless. There was fire and screaming all over the decks of the *Calamity*. Emberly didn't even try to fight against the tears as they poured down her face, mixing with the seawater and rain.

"This is what I was trying to tell you!" Jakob roared as he came up in front of her, spitting water out of his mouth and bracing his hands on Emberly's shoulders. "Gavin warned his men against greedy wishes!"

"I'm sorry." Emberly choked, the words unfamiliar in her mouth. "For everything!"

Jakob took a long look at her, his anger softening. "I'm sorry, too. For everything."

Emberly offered him a small, sad smile. An expression full of an unexpected forgiveness that could only have been realized in the midst of so much agony and regret and bleakness. She had spent her whole life chasing a horizon she would never reach. She had a crew that was like family and she could have had Jakob as well. She'd had it all and she hadn't known. And she had failed them in the worst of ways. All because she'd been so blinded by her thirst for money and status.

Amelia sprinted across the main deck toward a girl whose legs had been pinned by a flaming mast. A wave crashed over the ship and pulled Amelia to the ground, dragging her off the side of the ship through a gap where the railing had broken away.

"Amelia!" Emberly struggled toward her. She looked over the railing, but Amelia had already been pulled under the ship by the cruel current. Emberly screamed, the rage tearing from her throat like a monster breaking free of its cage.

There was a snap behind Emberly. She turned to see a mast falling. It crashed through the deck in a tragedy of splintering wood and spitting flames. Her beautiful *Calamity* was crumbling around her. Another wave came for the kill and swept Emberly overboard. She clutched the railing with all of her strength. Her feet pressed against the side of the ship as she scrambled for a footing she never got.

"Em!" Jakob yelled.

She hadn't been called that in years…not since they'd been close. The regret of everything she'd missed out on stabbed her heart once again. She choked back the pain as waves grabbed her boots. Jakob sprinted to her, grabbed her arms, and tried to pull her back on board. But it was useless.

They were too weak from the adrenalin, too slippery from the water, and the ship was sinking anyway. Emberly slid from Jakob's grasp until just their hands were holding. Their gazes locked and Emberly smiled at him, taking in the exact color of his eyes as they glittered with tears. Tears for her.

"Goodbye, Jakob." Emberly's voice drowned in the sounds of the tempest. She let go of his hands, falling like a stone.

"No!" Jakob screamed as Emberly splashed through the surface. A flaming piece of ship fell on top of her, slamming into her chest and blowing all the air from her lungs in a burst of bubbles and agony. The bodies of her crew and faithful companions floated past as endless regret filled her body. She tried to fight her way up through the waves but the current pulled her deeper into the blackness.

Emberly closed her eyes as the *Calamity* and its loyal crew finally met their match. She gave in to the tug of sleep as the darkness swallowed her. She released her final breath into the brash waves, and with it her last bit of pride.

So, the band of lady pirates that had once ruled the oceans without fear of demise finally drowned in their own kingdom, the sea. Their greed and their regret and the claws of the creatures of the deep tearing them apart as they sank toward the ocean floor.

The Men Tell of Mer-maids

The seventh day of September, year 1740

The men tell of the mer-maids. Beautiful sirens whose toxic songs have brought death to many sailors. I had not heard the stories before this sea voyage, yet the men seem genuinely terrified by the tales. Their frightened whispers have piqued my curiosity. They describe the sea-women as being more beautiful and dangerous than anything else that lurks in the ocean. More stealthy than a cat, faster than a Royal ship, and all with a single blue-grey fin instead of legs. It is said that they drag their victims down into the depths of the ocean, through the earth to the pits of Hell. How did these creatures, these Angels of Death, come to be?

It is only my first day aboard the Triumph on our journey from Boston to Brighton, England. From there, I will continue by carriage to London. The voyage is said to take about 7 weeks, so I have plenty of time to learn more from my crewmates, most of whom are experienced sailors.

The genesis of our journey could not have gone any better. Early this morning, we made it out of the bay and the wind has been on our side ever since. There hasn't been a single raincloud in sight.

I only hope that our journey will continue in peace.

— Caspian Durant

The tenth day of September, year 1740

I have been aboard this vessel for only a few days, but the crew seems to be growing fond of me. I have heard a rumor that the captain might offer me a job once we get to London. However I do not think I will take it. I am more of a scholar than a grunt worker.

I have kept my eyes on the sea whenever I get the chance. I hope to see the slightest sign of one of these mer-women, a flash of fin or a lock of hair, even the sound of a single high note from their mouths. The crew, though generally inclusive toward me, become very tense at my mention of these creatures. Only a couple of days ago, they were so forthcoming, but now are secretive about the topic. Perhaps they are afraid of some sort of attack by the mer-women now that we are on the open ocean.

I plan on befriending one sailor in particular, Davey Sawford. He seemed to know more than the rest about the mer-women. Perhaps I can convince him to tell me more of what I want to know.

In the meantime, I will stay alert.

— Caspian Durant

The seventeenth day of September, year 1740

It has been a week since I have last written. Davey is a tough old sailor, but he seems to be coming around to me. I spend as much time as possible by his side, listening to him talk about his wife and children back in England. He tells touching stories about his son James, who as a child, would get into all sorts of mischief with his friends. And he talks of his daughter, Illya, a curious tyke, who gathers flowers from the fields and brings them home to her mother, asking the name of each one. They remind of me of myself and Mercy when we were children. I have become quite fond of Davey, perhaps I will attempt to keep in touch with him after we get back to England.

Overall, he remains nervous about the topic that I really want to hear about. I do not understand why everyone on this ship is afraid of a legend. Until I can prove their existence for myself, they will remain a myth.

In the meantime, some of the crew has gotten sick with fever. Only two or three crewmembers are sick, and they are kept in isolation in an attempt to stop the spread of the disease. I am not a physician, but this illness is unlike anything I have ever heard of.

Luckily, Davey and I are so far unaffected. I will not let an illness slow down my progress toward learning more about these fantastic creatures!

— Caspian Durant

The twenty-second day of September, year 1740

It grows colder every day as more men get sick. This curious disease continues to baffle me. It starts with a soreness of the throat and eyes, followed by the swelling of the hands and feet, before settling into a hot fever that never seems to break.

I have kept up my companionship with Davey, and he has agreed to tell me more about the creatures tonight after the rest of the crew has gone to sleep. I do not know why, but he seems extremely skittish today. Perhaps it has something to do with what he plans to tell me.

The captain says that the wind is on our side and that we should reach Brighton in about five weeks. This means that I must continue to stay diligent in my search for the mer-maidens. I will write tomorrow about the things that Davey tells me.

— Caspian Durant

The twenty-third day of September, year 1740

Oh, the things that I have heard! Davey, my dearest companion on this ship, has told me the tale of the mer-maid! I do not know how this name was given. I only know the story of how these creatures supposedly came to be.

Davey told me of a time over twenty years ago when he was a crewmember on a ship called the *Endeavour*. A quarter of the way to Liverpool from Boston, a stowaway was discovered hiding among the lower decks. A woman named Mary-Elizabeth Hendstridge. She had been arrested and accused of Devil worship in the new world. Somehow, she escaped her execution. She was young, perhaps only seventeen or eighteen years old, but everyone knows that it is nothing but bad luck to have a woman on board. Especially a woman of sin and the Devil.

Davey told me how she did not fight, but only mumbled words to herself as the crew bound her feet, ankles and knees with rope. They left her hands unbound, knowing that she would drown at sea without the use of her legs. Before they threw her overboard, she began to sing

in a demonic language that nobody could understand. She sang a hypnotic, repetitive melody. Only Davey, the captain, and five other men
had the sense to cover their ears to protect themselves from the demon
song.

With one solid kick from the captain, the witch flew over the side
of the ship, still singing her deadly song. The men who hadn't covered
their ears went into a frenzy, all seeming to go mad at once. One after
the other they jumped overboard and swam to save the witch-woman,
every single man drowned in the ocean.

Throughout the rest of their journey, Davey would hear remnants
of the witch's song. On those occasions, sudden, violent storms appeared as if the skies themselves were trying to drown what remained
of the Endeavour's crew. Then the men started seeing giant fish fins
and hearing a woman in the water calling for help.

My only theory is that the witch became the first mer-maid.
Somehow, her demonic curse fused her legs together, a single long
fin. Although, the more I think about it, Mary-Elizabeth's curse may
have spread to cover the entirety of the ocean! Perhaps every woman
thrown into the sea is destined to be cursed in the same way. Gaining
a tail to haunt the men on the sea with their poisonous songs.

— Caspian Durant

The thirtieth day of September, year 1740

More and more men are becoming sick. It is nearly October and
the air gets colder every day. Only a few dozen men are able to work.
There is little time for rest though I still keep my eyes on the water
when I can. I still see no signs of mer-maids. I'm beginning to become
discouraged. My mind continually drifts back to the nights when Mercy and I would dance on the beach and wade into the ocean, kicking
the salty water at one another.

One night, a couple of years ago, Mercy so desperately wanted to
see the inside of our local pub. I dressed her in my younger brothers'
clothes and tied her hair up into a cap just to sneak her in for a pint of
beer. She looked ridiculous in oversized boots and my large winter
jacket covering her chest. I had to repeatedly bump her with my elbow
to remind her to speak with a deeper voice.

At the end of the night, she was found out and we were both
banned from the pub for life. Despite the trouble, we laughed, and
cherished the memory. I miss her now more than ever.

The only thought keeping me working now is Mercy. She would have scolded me for my laziness and continued to do my work for me until guilt and frustration would cause me to do it myself.

She is the reason I am going to London in the first place. Mercy always loved my taste for learning and adventure. When we were children, we would spend hours chasing squirrels in the forest and watching crabs skitter over the rocky beaches.

I remain hopeful that I will be able to see a mer-maid on this journey. For the time being, I will work, write, and watch the water.

— Caspian Durant

The first day of October, year 1740

The days grow shorter yet we work twice as hard.

Last night the first man to contract the strange disease died. In the hours preceding Ezekiel Miller's death, he went mad. As his fever spiked, he screamed and tore at his face with his fingers. It took three men to pin him down and tie his hands behind his back so they could not be used to harm himself.

He continued to holler into the night, thrashing and kicking his legs. He slammed his head repeatedly against the exterior wall of the ship. It was a horrific sight for us all. He was bleeding from his nose and from a rather nasty gash above his left ear. No one dared get near Ezekiel to try to calm him after he nearly bit off Joseph Williams' finger!

By morning, we thought he had calmed himself. We assumed he had experienced a manic episode caused by fear and seasickness. But when Davey went to check up on Ezekiel Miller, he was dead. Blood oozed from all his wounds and from the corners of his mouth.

Everyone who has the disease is afraid their fate will be the same as Ezekiel's. This ship is in chaos with ill men afraid of such a gruesome death. The few who are healthy are trying to remain calm and continue on, though our progress is slow. Some have proposed that we turn back to Boston, but we are too far into our journey. If we head back, we will die from lack of provisions and water. We must continue on to Brighton if any of us are to survive.

— Caspian Durant

The third day of October, year 1740

Two more men have died. Phineas Murphy and Jethro Baker. Though their deaths were different than the death of Ezekiel.

Jethro Baker, traumatized by what happened to Ezekiel, hanged himself from the figurehead—a representation of an angel with large feathery wings and a halo atop her long, wavy hair-on the bow of the ship. It took two men the better part of an hour to climb out there and cut him down. Since there was no way to catch it, his body was lost to the sea. I cannot help but wonder why he did not simply jump over-board or shoot himself. We have plenty of weaponry aboard. Why make the effort to climb on to the extended arm of the angel to hang himself? I suppose I will never receive an answer to this question.

For a while, Phineas appeared to be healing from the disease. His fever broke and he resumed working on deck yesterday. He claimed to be feeling "as well as an old sailor can". Suddenly, he became ex-tremely seasick, gagging and retching his lunch into the sea. Even after, he couldn't stop coughing. Blood foamed at the corners of his mouth. Crumpling to the ground in front of us, he choked on his own vomit and blood. We couldn't do anything but stare in horror as more and more blood pooled out of his mouth, staining the floorboards. He choked and vomited blood until he suffocated to death.

I cannot bear to write any more about the horrors that are sure to come upon this vessel. I am beginning to fear for our entire crew, and for myself. What will become of us? How have I gotten this far with-out contracting this strange and deadly ailment?

Worse yet, Davey claims to smell a storm brewing in the East. If this is true, we are sailing straight into it. At this point, there is no way to alter our course or we may lose our way and starve to death. I can only hope we will make it through this alive.

— Caspian Durant

The seventh day of October, year 1740

Three more men have died in horribly gruesome ways that I want to forget.

Storm clouds are visible in the distance, black against the endless blue sky. The waves have grown rough, though we are still miles away from the storm. I can tell that Davey is nervous about the storm. Perhaps it reminds him of the storm that hit all those years ago after the death of the witch-woman.

I have hardly thought about the mer-maids the past few days. I spend my time trying to help on deck as well as comforting the sick, neglecting my own observations. I am giving up hope of finding these creatures. If they existed, then certainly we should have seen one by now. If the legends are correct, they target ships full of men. Is the Triumph not considered "cruel enough" to be a worthy target? I do not know. As for now, I am preparing the ship for a storm unlike any we have seen before. If I do not write again, then presumably I will be dead. If this journal arrives safely to land, please reader, deliver this journal to Mercy James in Boston, Massachusetts.

In the case of my untimely demise, let these be my last words:

To Mercy,

My darling. We have been friends since we were children, despite our parents' wishes. We have laughed and cried, and then laughed some more during our time together. Throughout the good and the bad, I have loved you.

I first realized this when I was about twelve and you were ten. We were playing Indians in the forest when you fell and twisted your ankle. Unable to walk, I carried you into town and all the way back to your home. Horrified at my audacity, your father struck me across the face. But you defended me and kissed my bruising cheek in gratitude. I was a drunken mess of happiness all the way home. Collapsing into my bed and smiling up at the thatched roof, I silently wished that you would hurt your ankle once again, so I could relive the whole experience. Even if it meant getting struck by your father.

I realize now that it was a selfish desire. At the time, it was all I wanted. Growing up with you, I learned to push aside the boundaries in life. I could live how I wanted, with whomever I wanted. Society is a sea of prejudice and conformity and I did not want to live in that type of existence. I left to look for freedom from the single-minded society of my youth. I figured London would be a place of forward-thinking and progress. A place to live the way I want to live. It broke my heart that you refused to come with me, but I understand now. It is not my right to drag you away from everything you know. You love the city of Boston, and I have no right to take you from there. I am a selfish man. My hope is that you might forgive me one day.

With Love,
Caspian Durant

The twelfth day of October, year 1740

Somehow, the Triumph and most of the crew survived the storm. To my relief, this journal was unharmed after being stashed in a crate in the lowest deck.

The treacherous wind blew us off course and whipped freezing rain into our faces. Our navigator, Jimmy Wilson, proclaimed his compass to be broken, since it refused to point North. We sailed into the storm blind.

Though it was mid-day, the storm clouds and impenetrable fog gave the illusion of midnight. We were chilled to the bone, and rainwater weighed down our clothes. You could barely see five meters in any direction!

Within minutes, we were lost to the storm, the wind steering our ship. We did our best to keep our ship moving east, straight through the storm, only to be shaken about like a child playing with a ragdoll. There was no way to control this huge, wooden beast.

Massive waves crashed down into us. Wave after wave rocked the entire ship with violent force. I feared that I would never get the taste of salty seawater out of my mouth. We lost a couple of healthy men to the waves. They were dragged down, choking on the freezing water.

The sick among us stayed in the lower decks. Three died from sickness while we tried desperately to escape the storm. We lost five good men during that storm overall including our captain, Sir Harrison Clark. Davey stepped up to lead us all. After all, he is the most experienced and levelheaded among us.

During the storm, some of the crew, including Davey himself, claimed to hear humming. The sound of women singing a soft, lovely tune. I heard no such song, but Davey swears by it. He claims that it sounds just like the song that Mary-Elizabeth sang as she drowned so many years ago. I do not know whether to doubt my friend and call him mad, or to believe him. If he is right, I can continue my search for those deadly, mythological creatures. Everything about our predicament feels unnatural.

After the storm had passed, I climbed down into the lowest deck to locate my journal. When I retrieved it, I found something terrifying and wonderful. In a tiny crevice between two crates, I saw a crouched figure. I nearly cried out in fright but her face shocked me into silence. Mercy!

She had snuck onto the ship with the intent of surprising me once we arrived in England. She looks too thin and her long dark hair is matted with dirt and grease. I didn't know what to do. I cannot expose a stowaway hidden on our ship the whole time and expect everyone to be all right with it. Especially a woman.

I told her that I would try to bring her food periodically, but I could get in big trouble by simply knowing about her. She hasn't been caught so far, and I plan on protecting her for as long as I can. I will protect Mercy with my life.

— Caspian Durant

The sixteenth day of October, year 1740

We have only a couple more weeks on this ship before we reach Brighton.

More people have died of the disease. I try not to think of their families. Davey, as captain-proxy, has taken it upon himself to write out letters to each of these men's families. As for Mercy, she is still hidden safely in the lowest deck among the cargo. I brought her a little food and fresh water last night. When I asked her how she had managed to survive, she simply smiled and said "Men sleep pretty soundly. And sneaking has always come naturally to me." Then she glanced around the dark hold filled with large shipping crates. "How else would I have gotten onto this ship?"

When I started to get strange looks from the crew members who noticed me going into the lower decks, I knew that I couldn't do this alone. I decided to tell the man that I trust the most on this God-forsaken ship, Davey. He is respected by the rest of the crew and they will listen to him. I told him about Mercy hiding in the lower decks. Though he was acting in a calm manner, he still tensed his shoulders when I clarified that this stowaway was a woman. I didn't tell him that I know who she is. The last thing I need right now is Davey thinking that I hid her myself.

He promised to hide her presence as long as no harm would befall the crew or the cargo. Though he expressed his concern about the presence of a woman on the ship, I reassured him that she seemed harmless.

Some members of the crew are still convinced that there had been a woman singing in the middle of the storm. Mercy claimed that she had not sung during the storm, nor on this journey at all. I am concerned about the men. Could it possibly be mer-maids? Or is that just a silly superstition?

— Caspian Durant

The nineteenth day of October, year 1740

Two days ago, I found the Triumph in chaos. After I came out of the Captain's office, two men were dragging Mercy from the lower decks. Someone must have overheard our conversation. She was screaming and trying to tear her arms from the grip of the two men.

Anger took over as I punched the first man in the jaw with a sickening crack. I hardly noticed the pain in my fist as I lunged for the second man. Davey grabbed me and held me back. As the men dropped Mercy, she fell to the ground, gasping for breath.

"A stowaway, Cap'n," pronounced the second man. The first was still crumpled on the deck holding his broken jaw. A crowd of both sick and healthy men formed around us.

"What were you going to do to her?" I screamed at the second man. My vision tinted red around the edges. I bent to help her stand and she clung to me in fear. The crowd muttered in surprise and confusion.

Davey raised a hand, silencing the crowd. Then he turned to me. "Do you know this woman, sir?"

The fact that he didn't use my proper name and that he seemed to forget our previous conversation about Mercy sent a shiver up my spine. I stumbled for an answer.

"Yes." Was all I was able to muster. Davey stepped closer to the two of us. The crowds shifted for a better view. Why was Davey doing this? Had he not sworn to protect her?

"You knowingly brought a woman onto this ship?"

"No, sir," I said defensively. "I know her, yet I did not know that she was aboard this vessel. I thought I had left her behind in Boston." I assumed that accusing him would be useless. His actions seemed to indicate that he would deny any knowledge of Mercy's existence.

Davey nodded, and I hoped that he would keep his promise.

"Yet you did not seem very surprised to see her."

"I was, sir!" I was nearly begging Davey now. "Even if my face did not show it, my heart surely did." My voice faltered on the word 'heart'. Davey simply paced back and forth on the deck. The tension in the air was suffocating. The wind picked up and I shivered.

"Then what should we do with her?" he asked.

I felt Mercy's body tense next to mine. "What should we do?" I repeated dimly.

"Aye." Davey fixed me with a malevolent glare.

"I say we let her stay, since we shall arrive in Brighton in just a few days and—"

"No." His interruption was nearer to a growl than a word. Mercy's grip tightened on my jacket and I could tell she was shivering in her summer dress. "Women do not belong on ships."

"You cannot throw her overboard!" I shouted as some of the crew started to move toward us. I glanced at the sky to plead to God to save her life and to stop these men! I saw storm clouds gathering in the distance.

"As acting captain of this ship," Davey shouted over the crowd. "I sentence both of you to immediate death for illegal boarding, thievery, and lying!"

"Thievery!" Mercy suddenly pulled away from me and faced Davey. "I may have sneaked onto this boat and hidden for a few weeks, but never, in all of my days have I stolen a thing!" She jabbed a finger at Davey. "And as for lying? You know perfectly well that neither Caspian nor I have ever lied to you! Or to anybody for—" She was interrupted with a backhand to the face. I quickly pulled her back away from Davey.

"You little—" Now it was Davey's turn to be interrupted. A strange song played on the air. A sinful choir sung by a thousand angels with words not in any godly language. It was a soft sound, barely a whisper over the wind. Davey's face paled and he looked about to soil himself.

"The mer-maids," I whispered.

"No!" Davey shouted. "They're not real! I made it all up!" His face turned white.

Some of the crew looked around with uncertainty while others trembled in fear. Suddenly, half of the men in the crowd started moving toward us with limp jaws and blank eyes. The sick men shuffled toward us with red, swollen hands and feet. Instead of attacking Mercy and I, they ambled around us, leaving a five-foot radius in each direction. Some shoved past Davey, nearly knocking him over with surprising force. I noticed the man I had punched among them, his jaw was hanging at an odd angle but he no longer seemed to feel the pain.

One after the other they made it to the rail and formed a perfect row along the edge. They stood there staring, slack-jawed, out into the open ocean.

"Mr. Durant, I made the whole story up," Davey whispered. His eyes were pleading for me to believe him.

One man vaulted over the railing of the ship and dove into the ocean. The rest of the sick men stayed still. Forty-three remaining.

The singing got louder.

The remaining healthy crewmembers gasped and turned away their faces. I covered Mercy's eyes with my hand to prevent her from seeing the tragedy, though I could not tear my own eyes away.

"It is all a lie! The mer-maids do not exist!" Davey's face started changing color, from pale white to a bright red.

Two men vaulted over the railing of the ship and dove into the ocean. The rest of the sick men stayed still. Forty-one remaining.

The singing got louder.

"There was no song! There was no awful storm! There was no witch!" Davey's face was now the color of a ripe tomato and he began to yell over the haunting song.

Three men vaulted over the railing of the ship and dove into the ocean. The rest of the sick men stayed still. Thirty-eight remaining.

The singing got louder.

Davey pointed his finger furiously at Mercy. "She is the one doing this! She is the real witch! She will kill us all if given the chance!" He turned to me with sweat dripping from his brow despite the cold. "And you would help her." His voice was cold and accusatory.

Four men vaulted over the railing of the ship and dove into the ocean. The rest of the sick men stayed still. Thirty-four remaining.

The singing got louder.

I realized what was going on. Some dark magic had taken these men. Every time Davey lied, a man jumped to his death.

"She is the witch!" He pointed a shaking finger at a trembling Mercy.

All the remaining men vaulted over the railing of the ship and dove into the ocean.

The singing changed from a beautiful, foreign-sounding melody into a deafening screech like the sound of a pig when slaughtered.

✦

Most of the men rushed to the edge to see what had become of their crewmates and friends. I dragged Mercy away from the crowds and we crouched behind some crates of corn. We were crushed between the crates and the wall of the captain's quarters. I heard Davey shout for the crew to find the two of us but everyone was too preoccupied in their mania.

Thunder struck, and Mercy flinched at the sheer volume of the crack. I held onto my hat, expecting the wind and rain to come pelting down upon us. Through a crack between crates, I saw the crew whipped about by a sudden storm of wind and rain. From where we sat, Mercy and I were unaffected by the weather, though we had nothing covering our heads or blocking the wind. The temperature was pleasantly warm considering the autumnal season.

Chaos ensued. Men dashed about like headless chickens. Many attempted to block their ears from the horrific sound as if it were burrowing in through their ears and assaulting their brains. Several jumped off the ship in an attempt to end their suffering. All the while, Mercy and I were still unaffected.

I spotted Davey in the middle of the madness. Blood seeped from his ears while his eyes were wide and bloodshot. Pulling out a musket from somewhere, he frantically searched the scene around him, presumably looking for us. He spotted me peeking through the gap in the crates and marched toward where we were crouched. Mercy squeezed my arm and shrieked when a lead musket ball buried itself in the wall behind her. We were cornered.

I prayed to whatever deity would listen that we would be safe, make it through this alive, and arrive Brighton unscathed. Davey stomped toward us, his boots splashing in puddles of rainwater. Drenched in water, he raised the musket again and aimed right at us. Time slowed down as I watched him take aim and fire. The musket exploded and the lead buried itself in Mercy's left shoulder. Her grip on my arm faltered and she fell backward onto the deck. Blood pooled around her.

I looked up just in time to see Davey reloading and pointing his musket at me. I tried to shrink into the wall behind Mercy. But there was no shot. I looked up to see Davey cursing. Trying to shoot again, the musket just clicked. His eyes widened in realization as he realized his gunpowder was wet. There was no way he could shoot.

Davey threw his gun in a rage and started barreling toward us. I stood, ready to defend myself and Mercy who was lying unconscious in a small pool of her own blood. I grabbed the nearest object, a mallet, and rose to my feet to face my friend.

Before Davey could reach me, he froze. The shrieking stopped suddenly, leaving us in a confused silence. The only sound was the pattering of the slowing rain and the heavy breathing of the crewmembers. As fast as the shrieking and the rain had started, it stopped.

Among the silence, a new song began. It sounded as if it were coming from all around us. This song sounded like the first one, only darker. Instead of sounding light and pleasant, it seemed heavier. Though oddly beautiful, the demonic words sounded angry. The volume of it grew steadily louder and Davey looked around frantically. He seemed to have momentarily forgotten about us.

"No!" he shouted. The crew gathered around him with the same curiosity I felt.

"You cannot do this to me, witch!" That last word he shouted to the sky, spittle flying out from between his yellowed teeth.

Nobody else seemed affected like Davey. It was as if he were hearing something that no one else could hear.

Slowly, people started moving around the deck of the ship. Their eyes never left Davey, who continued writhing and screaming, everyone held onto something and tensed their bodies as if bracing for something. Then, I felt it too. A powerful influence washed through my body, telling me to grab Mercy and hold on for dear life.

Carefully, I hooked my arm around Mercy's waist and held her close to me. Then I braced myself against the wall, holding onto a wooden ladder rung with my free hand. As soon as everyone in the crew was safely secured in one way or another, the Triumph shook violently.

Wood screamed in protest at the shudder that reverberated throughout the ship. I was grateful that I was holding on. Otherwise, I would have been knocked to the ground by the force of it. In fact, Davey was knocked to the ground. He seemed to be the only one that wasn't prepared for a blow.

He was pleading now with the sky, screaming. "Mary-Elizabeth! My Mary! Please, darling, spare me!"

My Mary? He had known the witch-girl?

The ship shuddered again, rocking to the starboard side so suddenly that I nearly lost my footing. Davey slid across the still-wet deck until he crashed with a sickening crack against the railing of the ship. The ship leveled itself on the water with a splash. Waves as tall as the masts engulfed the ship. And still, Mercy and I had not a drop of water on us.

The ship rocked back the opposite direction. I braced my arm and strengthened my grip around Mercy's waist. Her shoulder was still bleeding, a few specks of blood stained the front of my shirt.

The ship's deck was nearly vertical as Davey flew from the starboard rail and tumbled over the edge of the portside rail.

The haunting music stopped. The ship returned to her usual upright position and the remaining members of the crew sagged to the deck in relief and fatigue.

I laid Mercy down gently before running to the railing of the ship. I was not the only one who wished to discover the fate of our acting-captain. I peered over the edge and gasped at the sight of roiling water and a knot of grey fins. I quickly realized what it was—the mer-maids.

All the stories I had heard of these creatures' unimaginable beauty were wrong. They were not beautiful sirens with long, wavy hair. In fact, they had no hair at all. They had one long grey flipper covered with sickly blue skin. Their sharp teeth glistened red with the blood of my friend.

Within moments, the bubbling mass of creatures had disappeared into the ocean. Only one of the bald, hideous creatures remained to stare at me with black pupil-less eyes.

Then I heard the softest voice in my head. "You defended her. Not like he did for me." Her voice was rough and deep as if it had not been used in a long time. Her lips did not move, but I knew it was her. I nodded once, and she bowed her head and dove into the ocean.

I must have fainted after my experience with Mary-Elizabeth Hendstridge. I awoke only today, after two days had passed. Members of the crew had patched up Mercy's wound and have treated her as if she were royalty since "the attack" (as the men are referring to it).

Our numbers are significantly smaller than before. Between the disease, the storm, and the attack, the Triumph's crew dwindled from eighty-six men to twenty-three men plus Mercy. There are barely enough people to help man the ship. Only days away from Brighton, we all are maintaining high hopes.

— Caspian Durant

The Twenty-Second Day of October, year 1740

With hard work, we will reach Brighton within the next forty-eight hours if the winds stay on our side. We are all exhausted and cannot wait for this all to be over.

I have taken over the responsibility of writing a personal letter to the families of each of the men who died during this voyage. I don't quite know what I will say to them. How am I supposed to explain the odd occurrences that happened aboard this ship within the last seven weeks?

What exactly did happen? I am not entirely sure. I assume that the mer-maids were created the way that Davey had claimed. That would explain their aggression toward him. I do wonder how there were so many of them. And what about the strange singing? Did the storm cause the ship to rock back and forth so dramatically? Was that due to the mer-maids? I do not know.

As for Davey, I do not think of him as mad. Obviously, I do not understand the extent of his relationship with Mary-Elizabeth. I suppose it does not matter now. I'm writing a letter to his wife and children. I do not plan on telling them the circumstances about his death. I plan on relaying only the good things like positive memories and the love he truly felt for his family. That is what he would have liked.

+

I have discarded my ambition of going to London to study. I plan on staying in the small port town of Brighton to further study these magnificent mer-maids. Though deadly, they seem perfectly capable of remorse as well as other human qualities. The further study of their telepathic abilities should keep me busy. Also, I believe that Mercy would be happier in Brighton. I plan on marrying her as soon as we reach England. This entire voyage has shown me that life is too short not to do what makes you happy, and Mercy makes me happy. We will stay in Brighton because she needs to live close to the sea. Ever since she was young she's loved the fresh air and vastness that the ocean brings. She would not want to live in a crowded, disease-ridden city.

+

This journal is now full. My research to this point as well as my recording of the events on the *Triumph* have filled this chapter of my life. From now on, I will be a researcher of all things strange and unnatural in the world with Mercy at my side. Wherever our findings take us, I am sure you shall find us there.

— Caspian Durant

EMMA PERRY

Swashbuckling

Marshalla had no qualms with boarding the pirate ship. Perhaps other ladies would have been frightened to be dragged from a sinking rowboat and surrounded by a couple dozen bloodthirsty buccaneers who lived to plunder, murder, and do as they pleased. Such ladies just needed to buck up their nerve a wee bit, Marshalla decided.

As she dashed water from her eyes and looked around at the calloused, dirty throng, Marshalla decided the real pain of setting foot on pirate ground was laying eyes on them. They were a rough bunch. Marshalla was as common as they came, but she took care of her plaid dress like it was the Queen of Scots' gown. These men didn't care for their clothing in the slightest. They hadn't even washed them! It instantly aroused Marshalla's indignation. Those were perfectly ordinary fabrics on their backs that deserved humanity, not to be tossed about and never given a good washing after all their toil for their masters. No, no, no. These men were *savages*.

"Not worth it," spluttered the man who'd pulled Marshalla from the water. He tossed the trunk onto the deck, where it amazingly didn't break. "Two jugs of rum says that's just their shoes."

"Well, we can wish, can't we?" Marshalla said as she shook out her skirt, trying to look at anything but their wardrobes. The men were taken aback to hear her Scottish accent.

"She speaks?" one gesticulated at Marshalla with his sword. "What woman speaks aboard a pirate ship?"

"Ya think I'll just—hey!" Marshalla exclaimed as a portly pirate captured her left wrist, probably trying to be aggressive. But he didn't rip her sleeve, so he couldn't mean that much harm. On Marshalla's entire dress, the sleeves were the most diligently tailored, tenderly cut and stitched with lace. Months of hard labor and saving had gone into Marshalla being able to afford that French lace, as Scotland, unfortunately, didn't specialize in such essentials. "Unhand me! These sleeves have already suffered the elements and don't need your filthy paws to finish the job."

The pirates around her chuckled.

"It's a Scot who thinks she knows style," one pirate laughed.

"She's judging our outfits," another ragged man said.

"And I certainly am!" Marshalla informed them. "You can't properly be devils if you don't dress like him, and I've heard he's always prompt with a smile and a clean suit. Wearing such ill-treated clothes will make your foes want to destroy you all the greater."

"She'd have us wear clothing to make our enemies swoon!" One man guffawed.

The men broke into uproarious laughter, but Marshalla couldn't see the joke. Wearing bedazzling clothing might so prove to be the key to winning a quick fight. But these criminals wouldn't even think to try it once. The laughter died down.

"Well, well, well, what do we have here?" A masculine voice said behind her. Marshalla's current view was painful enough that she wheeled herself around, desperate to see at least one garment that wasn't sewn with a hot needle and a burning thread. But in her turn Marshalla was not, never could've been and never would've been, ready for the beauty that stood before her.

Swashbuckling. That was the only word dignified enough to doff his merry hat and offer his sword to the solitary figure waiting there. The rest of the men were rough, unattractive, and sorry to the eyes. None of them stood as gracefully, and certainly none of them displayed such cleanliness. The personality was striking. Humor threaded itself through every fiber. First, the hat, offering a jungle of fresh parrot plumage stitched into place, brimming with jolly style. Then the shirt (oh, glorious day!) seemingly made from the first touch of the elements, the exuberant wind weaving the early snow into a cover that dove down the chest. The brilliant black breeches were kept from colliding with that heavenly sugar by a long silken sash, made from the most vibrant of all reds which sent Marshalla's heart bursting with a feverous excitement. It blew toward her, beckoning her to slide her hands along the godly material. The buckled boots were the sole style of her quaking soul. Even the cutlass he pointed at her vibrated perfection.

Marshalla had never understood the strength of love at first sight before. Now here it was, so pure and true. She had never before seen, nor anticipated ever again to see, such a handsome figure. This was her heart's only longing. The perfect swashbuckling figure.

Pity the human inside it was so dull. Marshalla didn't bother on his details. She could best describe him as dry sand.

"I see you've found your way onto my ship," the man wearing perfection said.

Marshalla could not respond. She was too busy looking at the shadows in the shirt, the creases in the breeches, and the heavenly light made from the silk's ripples. That was the best part she knew, the sash. It made the outfit, turning it from dull to exquisite, something of the extraordinary. How she yearned to own it. How she yearned to *wear it. All of it.*

The captain suddenly took notice of Marshalla's starstruck gaze. "And just what do you think you're staring at, wench? Heh, I suppose your local men lack such brawny chests."

Unfortunately but inevitably, the swan dive in his shirt's neckline exhibited at least half of the captain's chest, which was utterly hairy, distracting, and bothersome when called to attention. Had Marshalla been fortunate enough to be a tailor, she'd have kept the neckline much higher. But then, the greatness would perish alongside! No, it wasn't the shirt's fault, nor its inspired maker, if such a being existed. The man could not be blamed either; his unbecoming chest hair was beyond his control, and shaving it would only distract further. No. Fate of existence took the blame for this one. That was that.

"Well?" Impatiently, the pirate in glorious attire waited for an answer. He had his hands on his hips now, a very attractive stance for the clothes. Ruefully, Marshalla tore her eyes away, though it seemed that her eyes had grown golden threads to the outfit as she stared.

"Sorry," she responded in her thick Scottish dialect. "Uh, no, I dinnae care for your hairy chest. It's a bit of a drag on the shirt, to be honest. Maybe if you were to put another red sash underneath as an underthing, it might do the trick a wee bit better. There! That's an idea! I can actually do the tailor thing, now can't I?" Marshalla felt a surge of pride in her revelation.

Around her, the pirates stood speechless, the captain himself dumbfounded at her ingenious idea. With a problem like that, who could think of anything but such a quick, clever solution? Seconds passed, and the men still couldn't respond. Marshalla realized the pirates, contrary to their egos but true to their appearances, couldn't match the speed of a simple Scottish girl's tongue. Which meant, sadly, they hadn't actually heard her seraphic inspiration.

The stupefied silence was finally broken with a sniffle as Effie reminded them she was also aboard the ship. Effie was a real wee thing. Standing most a head under Marshalla, she accounted for little more than a pretty figure to distract the highland boys as it was their turn to kick the ball. Of noble birth, Effie kept good clothing and wore her dresses like a sweet woodland wisp. Though her dress was a bit bedraggled after all their seafaring, her usual care for her clothing appeased Marshalla.

"Oh, oh, please don't hurt us," Effie whimpered with that voice softer than baby silk.

"Now," the captain said, stepping unreasonably close to Effie, "this is a real pearl."

Marshalla bristled. She'd dealt out enough Scottish spunk to every cheerio chum come from England to feel confident around these brutes, but Effie was simple and scared.

Careful to protect her lace, Marshalla twisted her wrist free of the fat pirate and pushed herself in front of Effie, placing herself right up against the captain. Her cheeks burned as cool silk danced against her hand. Her fingers flirted back as its master stared down at her, unaware of his unfaithful belt.

"What—"

"—do I think I'm doing? Certainly none of your business to be sure, lout. If you haven't noticed already, you have two dames aboard your vessel and a head of clouded sea sand, so you can't even see the chest of gold and rum behind you. Do I need to speak slower for your marooned mental bits? You've…got…a treasure…matey. Savvy?"

Playing pirate with Dad must have done its work, because the man actually understood and turned to see the waterlogged chest. Marshalla's dress had also created its own ocean on the deck, due to her jump to save the chest. Her sopping dress and the royal robes of the pirate were the tragic love story Marshalla had always dreamed of.

The captain opened and sorted through the clinking contents of the chest, pulling out a bottle and a couple of coins. It was no surprise he liked the chest; there was enough gold and rum there to satisfy even a pirate's greed. "And where would two lovely ladies like you get a box like this?" His voice was too deep to match the casual glory of his garments, Marshalla judged.

"We found them adrift in a rowboat, sir," the same pig-like pirate said, explaining how the chest tipped over the side and 'the bigger girl' jumped over to save it. "Tried to keep it from sinking but hadn't the muscle. We pulled it out."

Marshalla began her defense. "Excuse yourself, luggers! I kept that trove from settling in the locker of Davy J—"

A pirate behind her clamped his hand over her mouth, and the men laughed. Marshalla elbowed him in the gut and yanked his hand away. Around her, the pirates cooed with surprise.

"You're a feisty one, I see." The captain neared her, the ripples in his shirt nearly buckling Marshalla's knees. Managing to stay upright, Marshalla realized with despair that the shirt and pants and everything that villain wore were just as unwilling slaves as Effie worried they'd become. While Marshalla couldn't save the clothes, she'd keep herself and Effie from the same fate. It was what the outfit wanted, she saw. They had allied together now, diehard friends forever.

"So then, missy, whatcha here for? Missing your *corsair* company?" A piece of spittle hit her nose. Marshalla didn't flinch.

"I don't care for your pirately presence none, neither. Effie has intentions in England, and we'll be there by the end of this here fortnight. You'll be kind enough to take us there, matey, and in return, I'll give you half that chest. And mark—" Marshalla tried to collect herself as the hat's feathers fluttered softly.

The pirate began speaking. "We'll take all the booty we please and leave nothing for whomever you deem worthy of such treasure. Hmmmm?" His hand reached for Effie's wrist, but Marshalla smacked it like he was a robber in her imaginary tailor shop.

"Hands off, rogue. That's not your girl nor shall she be." The captain angered at the thistle in front of his rose, but Marshalla wasn't done. "That's Effie right there, and she's untouched, and that's how she'll be staying for this voyage. I'll be acting as her personal guard, and you can call me Marshalla. Now, if you'd like to retain the rum in that chest and rid yourself of two unlucky dames such as ourselves, you'll be smartly pulling your rudder toward English soil. And if you hurry up with finding us a *private* dwelling for the voyage, I'll even throw in some coins as an extra reward."

"Listen here, *wench*. I'm the captain of this ship, and I'll be having my way. Savvy?" He turned away. "Take them to my—"

"Should I spell this out slowly for you? Haven't you heard or have you failed to read the writings of every seaman who ever hoisted the Jolly Roger and called himself a buccaneer? Girls...are...*unlucky* on a ship!"

He spun, his boots sanding smoothly but his sash whipping about unpoetically. "How so? I've had fifty—"

"—women on this ship without a predicament, plight, hurdle or hiccup, uncounting the men you've lost in battle due to distracted desires and sailors deserting to chase after the affairs of their heart? You're never vexed as ladies pull at the sails like they were sheets and turn rudders like stirring spoons? Or worse, never helped a lady use the privy on your privateer? Womenfolk are nothing but hassles aboard your skiff and better off than on."

This time, Marshalla quickened her tongue to blur the words together at a speed faster than the crew's stumbling brains could handle. The matters she'd mentioned were shallow and weak, but the crew murmured as they munched on Marshalla's mouthful. Incomprehension was key to persuasion.

"Well," the captain mused, "I suppose you're right. No one is to touch these girls, on penalty of the stocks. I'll have none of…anything she said. Not aboard this ship." He sneered and Marshalla was disgusted to see a gold tooth. It thoroughly mismatched the shirt and hurt the look in general, a clear cruelty to the grandeur he wore.

"Still, I can get a good profit out of you two. First your box, then there'll be a price on your heads when I get to Clew Bay. My comrades there won't be aboard a ship, so they won't mind at all. And you'll be back on your Irish soil." He touched Marshalla's chin then shoved them into the arms of two thugs behind them. "Chain them to the mast."

Marshalla's tongue kept busy while she watched the devil in angel's clothing enter his cabin. His sash waved sadly to her as it disappeared. Despite everything, Marshalla kept a little optimism.

If those incarcerated garbs could hold onto hope, so could she.

+

Night fell like a thin blue bedsheet over the ship. Effie lay on Marshalla's back, exhausted with her fears. She could only handle so many frights before wilting onto the tweed blanket like a rose on her grandfather's lapel.

Marshalla sat hunched forward, thoroughly uncomfortable. Her stockiness compared to Effie made it utterly hopeless to balance their weights as Marshalla had hoped, leaving her as Effie's human cushion. On any other evening, Marshalla would fiddle with her sleeves and skirt until she'd planned out every next stitch. She'd already tried using one of her short curly hairs as a thread to begin her next project, but without a lamp or needle it was useless. So rather, Marshalla stroked her fingers as her heart fluttered about the memory of the silk's magic against her hand. Such *avid amour* she'd never felt before. And swore she would never feel forevermore.

"Marshalla?" Effie whispered. "I never asked; are you all right?"

"I'm not the one getting married, Effie; I'm fine as long as that's a truth." Marshalla chuckled to try to hide her fear. When brought to mind, Clew Bay tended to induce a shiver. Pirate's bay, at its worst.

"I suppose this is easy for you," Effie hummed. "You've been on ships before. McGuffin's ship, God rest his soul, was frightening enough! Now we're surrounded by men who—who—"

"—can't even keep up with my pace. We'll be fine enough; you'll see. We'll get off this ship before the Bay, and the pirates will be left none the wiser. Now, stop whimpering and lean a little less against my spine. You're not exactly an oatcake, you know." Effie shuffled daintily. "I haven't ever been on a pirate ship neither, Effie. Going from a simple schooner to a pirate's plank is a bit of a whirl for me, too."

"But the men? You can handle them."

"Uhh…I'm not assuredly convinced. We're safe here, I think, but on that port they'll be a great number of burly—" Marshalla dragged herself to a stop at this point; Effie was weeping. "I told you, Effie, don't fret. We'll figure something out. If I can do it once, I can do it again," she lied.

Gullible little Effie believed her and snuggled back down, mumbling something about Marshalla getting it from her father.

Marshalla *pfffed*. Her father worked as a common sailor for their living. For two years, he'd been pressed into service on a pirate ship, which was where he'd learned all the pirate speak and think he'd taught Marshalla years ago. 'Twas hardly enough for Marshalla to get them out of their current plight, but she wasn't going to say so. Effie had only just fallen asleep, and Marshalla wouldn't wake her for anything less than the freedom of the captain's imprisoned clothing. Her head fell forward, thinking about the tricorn hat and its fulsome feathers. Her eyes began to overflow like a bucket drawn from a well.

"A piece of ham, miss? Can you…understand slow speech?" Marshalla looked up and saw the original brute who'd restrained her.

"About time you'd given us a bit of flavour! We've been about starving since you left us here. You can't properly treat us like pigs if you don't toss us a crust every now and then, now can you?"

His pockmarked face gaped at her, but he handed her the jerky anyway and sat, nearly crumpling the deck beneath him. "You fine, miss? Someone's plugged your eye drains if I see straight," he said just as she began another speech.

"Now don't you off and give one to Effie. She's fresh asleep and that's how she'll be staying till dawn—and my eyes are fine, I'll have you know. I'm just recollecting on some terrible tragedies aboard this chopped tree, the least of them being the painful splatters you've allowed to spill on that dispirited shirt. I'd cry more if I thought it'd wash that gravy off."

"I'm Biff," the man said when he'd decided he'd never understand a word she said.

"I'm Marshalla. That's Effie, but you can't rightly look at her. She's off and engaged to some British fellow and will be having no trouble from you." Marshalla's slower pace brought some comprehension to his eyes.

"No frets; I've got a sweetheart myself. Hope to make me way back before she gives up on me. So that's her dowry, then? In the chest."

"Sure right it is, and I'll be having none of you blighters touch no more than you already have. She's got what's she's got, and it won't suffer no fidgeting through. You off and tell your callous captain that."

"Too late there, miss. Are you off to your lover, too, then?"

"Lover! No, course not. I'll not be off and wed till I'm a haggard old maid and an old feller comes along and I'm too tired to resist him. Besides, my dowry ain't near as pretty as Effie's there."

"Well?"

"What?"

"Your dowry, of course. What is it?"

"Oh, well, I wasn't too thrilled about the dowry my mother had for me. She wanted me to be married off by now and still going by a frilly name. So, I took Dad's lot instead. I inherited his name and his yearning to become a tailor someday."

"Your dad's name's Marshalla?"

"Aye, right! My *dad* is a *Marshalla*! Nah, he's a Marshall by birth, and I'm technically a Maisie, but that's no name of mine. That's the calling cry of every Scottish maverick who thinks he wants some lovin' on Loch Lomond. No, I'm a good Marshalla, if ever there was one, which I suppose I'm the first." She wiped at her eyes. "Now don't you dare think I'm crying. Leftover liquid is all."

"From what? You can't really be upset about our clothes, are you?"

"I can and don't doubt it. You may have only one wardrobe, but that's no justification for keeping it muddy. A clean shirt'll do ya, you know. You pirates are merciless to such tormented clothing, but that's not the worst of it. Allowing that vile villain to wear such beautiful innocence is *appalling*."

"You mean the captain? Aye, that reminds me! I'm supposed to take you over to him." Biff slowly got to his overburdened feet. "Don't fret, and stop speaking so quickly; I can't understand a word. He only wants to ask you some questions."

Marshalla hitched her skirts up so speedily she forgot about Effie, who thumped on the deck in an unwelcome wake. "I have no intention to see that scoundrel till I save his apparel and make him walk the plank in his long johns! What—"

Biff rattled a key in her chains. "I can't understand you, but I don't think you need to fear. You can stay here, miss," he said to Effie who was whimpering like a chick at the mouth of a fox. "Captain only wants the bigger one, Maisie."

"*Marshalla*," Marshalla corrected. "But if you insist on calling us all by our real names, her name's actually Donalda."

"Maisie!" Effie exclaimed like Marshalla had shown her dressing room to Biff. Marshalla huffed and turned away, marching toward the captain's quarters so quickly Biff forgot to grab the key in his haste to catch up. She opened the door of the contemptible pirate commander.

"Well, what is it you want with me, *Captain?*" Marshalla demanded, determined to voice her frustration before the glory of his clothing overcame her. Her choice proved wise. Marshalla nearly fainted as he turned around. In the lamplight, the perfectly hued red, black, and white of his outfit made Marshalla wish to kiss and caress them. And yet, she could not while they were imprisoned by the captain. Somehow, their magic still worked: a dusty bottle of rum had never looked so good in a man's hand. The captain, of course, was still ugly.

"Aw, the little Irish girl. Give the fat one a little trouble, did you? I expected you minutes ago." He set the bottle on his table and motioned Biff away.

Marshalla began exercising her tongue, but the captain interrupted her, which was all well because Marshalla didn't know what she was saying.

"Marshalla. Interesting name, I'll admit. Didn't make the connection between you and your father till I remembered he said he'd had a kid with some Irish brat, but—"

Marshalla's tongue began to warm up. "First of all, we're Scottish. Not my father, no, he's the only good Brit that country ever made, and of that you can remind yourself every time you look in the mirror. Second, don't be insulting my parents. My mother is more of a bore than a brat, and that difference is great when questioning my father's taste in falling for her. Third, if you're the swine who pressed him, I'll be dealing this out to you." Marshalla stepped up to him, ready to slap, but the captain beat her to it. She turned away, her face smarting worse than the preacher's words on repentance day.

The captain continued, "Scottish, Irish. Really all the same, especially on Clew. No one there'll care where you came from. Tell me, whatever happened to your father? I'd like to kill him given the chance."

"Just try. He told us stories about your fight and how you begged him to spare you."

"Your father lied," he spat. "I let him go, but—"

"Then how'd you get that scar on your cheek?"

The captain swore and hurled the glass bottle against the side of his wall. Marshalla quieted, taking in the outfit. How long had it been subjected to this? It was young, the black in the pants and boots still inky, but all slightly wrinkled. Horror growing in her chest, Marshalla realized the captain had *slept* on it. A shudder hurried up her shoulders and nearly crippled her with hate.

Marshalla spied a pistol lying on the pirate's desk, begging Marshalla to pick it up and finish the rogue. But to do so would also kill the outfit. Though her hand twitched, she rejected the gun's offer. She loved the shirt too much.

"Where are you headed anyway? This trunk is the little one's dowry, isn't it? Question is, what are you doing here with her?"

"My father was off on a voyage, so I volunteered to guide her to England, her being unaccustomed to ships and all. Then our ship got under a wee bit of a storm, and we hit against the rocks. We haven't seen anyone else yet."

The captain scoffed. "You think the crew survived? With *you* in *their only* lifeboat?"

"I'm no airy optimist, but it's possible they're alive. But if they died, they'll be resting with Saint Peter now, which is better company than you can hope for. You and your burning ship will have eternity to argue with the devil, and he always wins down there, my preacher says."

The captain raised his palm. "Shall I hit you again? Perhaps you're just hoping a ship will *happen* along and save you now. I promise you, missy, there's not a single skiff from this here crew all the way to Clew Bay, so no rescue is—"

"SHIP AHOY! THERE'S A TRADER AT SOU'-SOU'-EAST!"

The captain shoved Marshalla to the side as he stormed outside. Marshalla recovered her balance and trailed him into the darkening night. No man minded as Marshalla approached the starboard side and peered into the gloom. A slight angle from their course, a couple lantern specks marked a ship out yonder, heading their way. Though the night had darkened to the blackness of a certain earl's waistcoat, the sliver of a silver moon beamed like a shining button, half fastened on said waistcoat. This little moon highlighted enough of the trader for Marshalla to recognize it by the thread-like gleam on the ropes and edges. It was a Scottish trader, one of the many identical ships her father worked for. The pirates merely saw their next prey.

As the men tripped and scurried around her, Marshalla hustled to Effie. "You ready Effie? We'll make our escape when they attack the trader. I'll know somebody aboard it, I'm sure; an old crewmate of my father probably. You used the key Biff left, right?"

Effie shook her head. "I was scared that he'd forgotten it, so I called him down and gave it back. I didn't want a pirate spotting me unchained!" Her pitch ascended as Marshalla nearly whacked her.

"Curse you, Effie! Now I've got to go track the bloke down. Stay right here and *don't* chain your other wrist while you're off losing your head!" Marshalla spun her skirts and hightailed back across the deck, muttering every curse word she knew at Effie. It seemed her swearing disguised her because no other mouthing-off man pulled her aside.

Biff was nervously sharpening his saber by the captain's quarters. Though he was built like a baby bull, Marshalla easily pulled him into the shadows. "Biff, I need that key. No time to argue, but me and Effie are getting off this ship and I need the key for that. Don't just stand there; we haven't got all day! Besides, you've got to give it to us because if Effie hadn't whimpered out, we'd both be free by now. It's not rightly yours, it's not."

"Wh-wh-wha—"

"Ah, just give it! You were pressed into this crew, aye? Well, I'll get you out. My dad was pressed here too, and now he's a free man again. You'll be back to your sweetheart in no time, and a better man for it. Say yes now, Biff."

Still stuttering like a babbling bairn, Biff took the key from his pocket. Marshalla clasped it and Biff's ear and hauled them both into the captain's quarters. "Now," she said, tossing him back the key, "let me get Effie's dowry, and we'll be on our way. Just as soon as that trader pulls up."

"That trader will be destroyed! We'll overrun it—"

"Not if you're distracted."

"How—"

"That's your part. Figure out the distraction quickly now! I've got to gather up this gold." Marshalla turned her back on Biff and decided she couldn't gather anything in this pigsty. Hands on hips, she mothered down on the disgusting room, tossing the hanging socks and long-johns into the basket and straightening the winter coats in the closet. When first purchased, they'd have preened more pompously than a peacock, but now dirt, rum and other unmentionables stained and scratched their surface. As she bustled about like a woman three times her size, Marshalla noticed the dowry. 'Twas disarrayed throughout the room: gold here in the bed and empty bottles there on the desk.

The cabin now shipshape, Marshalla attacked the bed and recovered the gold coins, extending her elbows as she explored down to the last piece. She left the rum for the pirates, deciding they'd use it better than Effie's fiancé. Clicking it shut, Marshalla hoisted the trunk and bustled out the door, offering encouraging words over her shoulder to the stagnant clothing. Biff had fled during her frenzy, stuttering something about unlocking Effie. *At least he's done it*, Marshalla thought as she viewed the moonlit scene before her.

"WHO'S THE FIEND WHO LET HER GO? WHO?" The captain roared, holding Effie's wrist high as she cowered like a child without her mother's concealing skirt. "We're off to battle and SOMEBODY thinks letting the girls go is a GOOD idea?"

Indeed, Marshalla realized, the trader was nearing. The pirates were pulling the old 'burning ship' facade, lighting old piles of rope so smoke billowed and fire licked like a mirage. The traders, being well-captained like any Scottish ship, were sailing to the rescue. In minutes they would be at the side, ready to offer their hands to the band of pirates who would kindly offer the pointy parts of their swords in response.

"I've got to distract them," Marshalla mused. "If they're busy when the ship comes…AYE!"

The captain released Effie as he realized his treasure was in the palms of a person other than himself. He might've started another tirade if Marshalla hadn't strode to the starboard, shoved the chest against a shipmate and drew his sword. The intoxicated pirate lost his sea-legs. As he tumbled over the side, Effie shrieked and rushed to the edge, bending over to catch the falling chest. Marshalla smiled, impressed as a tailor discovering decorative scissors to be useful. "You'll make a bride yet, Effie."

A heavy cutlass gleamed in the moonlight, pointing directly at Marshalla's face. "You think to fight me, Scot? You don't stand a chance."

It may have been dark, but Marshalla couldn't hide the warm blush in her cheeks as she realized this handsome poised figure was accepting her offer to fight. Trying to hide her uncontrollable emotions, Marshalla looked down at her thin sword. "Uh…"

The shining blade of reality swung at her, and she tripped back, her sword slipping free over the edge. Marshalla dove and joined Effie, so that both girls hung like laundry from the side, their kicking skirts probably appearing as if their owners had needed a bit of alone time with the sea. As she caught her sword, Marshalla noticed a dark rowboat beneath them, steered by a familiar mass of red whiskers.

"McGuffin!" The Scottish captain had *survived* and found the trader's ship like a breakfast muffin! He grinned, motioning for them to come down. Marshalla and Effie looked at each other and nodded—fretfully in Effie's case. The dowry lowered and Marshalla stood.

Flourishing her sword, Marshalla announced to the pirate captain that she had full intention of dueling him, and that he'd best pull his best stuff if he wanted to maintain his pride against a simple Scottish dame.

"Well then," he sneered, "en garde. I'll add some criss-crosses on your face to match that dress of yours." They stepped to the middle of the deck. This was a wee bit more that practice sticks with Pa. *Much* more.

Before Marshalla could properly ready herself for the exciting fight, the captain leapt, stabbing. Marshalla cursed and twisted to the side. She began a slice at his side but pulled away abruptly. Any cut to the captain was a kill to her true love! She gasped, aware now of her true conflict. The captain cut through her lace and Marshalla cried, then yelped as the tip of his sword sliced her cheek. Gasping and touching it, Marshalla began anew, thrusting furiously to gain forward momentum. This left her sword flung in the mast and Marshalla laying a regretful kick as she bought time to grab it. It destroyed her to dirty his pants.

Swash! Thunk. *Shing!*

In moments they were back at it, Marshalla's practical strokes rife with desperation to protect the captain's hostage, the captain's movements ornate and showy for his crew. He enjoyed the stretch.

Between ducking, swiping, and avoiding blemishing the innocence of the shirt, Marshalla prayed Effie had boarded the trader and the pirates were oblivious. Her arm was beginning to feel a feminine fatigue. It was time to draw this to a close. The captain was only getting started, tossing his sword hand to hand as Marshalla was distracted by his outfit. It was still, but she understood it like she'd raised its wool from its mother sheep. *Injure him on the hand. That won't stain me.*

So as the gold-hilted cutlass landed in his left hand, Marshalla darted forward and swiped at his right hand, trimming the first three fingers to the same length.

The captain roared. Blood stained his hand but thankfully not the shirt. He stormed forward as she fell back, blocking and blocking every life-threatening hack. His blade cut her palm and caught her hilt, throwing her sword into the air. Clasping her hand, Marshalla saw the sword point at her neck.

"Do...your...worst!" she spat.

The arc of the involuntary sword lurched and halted as the captain jerked backwards. Marshalla swiveled to see a plain-clad figure swoop in on a rope with a familiar whistle. Landing on the deck and picking up his daughter's fallen sword, the able-bodied sailor looked the startled pirate in the eye and said, "I think this dance is mine."

"Marshall."

"Kelly."

With a roar, the pirate captain attacked Marshalla's father, and the age-old dance began once more. Between the two men, thrusts and parries, slashes and sidesteps became an elegant ballet. Around the deck they spun, the common browns versus the swashbuckling sunset. Marshall hadn't lied: he was the better fighter.

Watching from her tippy toes, her core tighter than a corset, Marshalla watched the sword of her father as the men danced up the stern's stairs. It flashed up, always on the attack. Marshalla twiddled and gasped as she watched. "Oh, don't hurt him, Father," she whispered.

"Marshalla!" This was Biff telling her his feat. Between spasms in her sparring heart and organs, he told her how he had relocated a pile of burning rope to the mainmast. The remaining pirates would have to struggle to quench it. Many already lay in their injuries to varying degrees of liveliness. "Now, let's get a move on! Our ship awaits, and Marshall, your father, will be fine."

Hardly caring about anything he said, Marshalla only led him to the ship knowing they'd never let him aboard without her Scottish recommendation. The ship's weight shifted as Biff boarded the trader, and as the deck lifted, Marshalla's stomach sunk.

Marshall had led the fight, and by the end the captain was becoming desperate. His attacks were evermore lightning and skilled, but her father responded confidently, having practiced his swordplay regularly. Sparring on the bow, Captain Kelly made a beautiful, idiotic mistake and decided to spin for momentum. His sash was an angelic paintbrush stroke, and Marshalla nearly swooned for the first time in her life. But as the captain came around, Marshall struck the saber from his hand and caught it elegantly. The captain froze, faced by his own sword.

"Fine then," the pirate captain hissed. "Finish me off. My crew will kill you."

"Your crew is largely dead, Kelly. And I would kill you, except that these garments," Marshall's sword pointed at the white linen shirt, "are really *quite* extraordinary. When I become a tailor, I hope to have something like that in my closet, so I really couldn't harm a thread on your body."

Marshalla released her lungs. Her tongue was so busy describing her joy that she almost missed what the captain said next.

"Fortunately," Kelly replied, "I don't have the same limitation." Marshalla spotted a little blade slide into his pinched fingers.

She sprinted across the ship as Kelly's dagger bit into her father's shoulder. With a cry, he dropped the saber and fell backwards down the steps. Marshalla cushioned most of his impact and gently laid him down. "Here," she urged, ripping off her lace and pressing its white frill against the wound. He took it, wincing as the lace loyally lapped the blood away. Marshalla stood.

"Drop the sword," she demanded the devil.

He laughed. "I think not, wench. Your quick tongue won't save you this time." As if concerned his statement didn't punctuate his point, he stabbed his saber into the deck and leaned lackadaisically. The blade bruised his boot, filling Marshalla with so much fire that her digesting dinner disintegrated into dust.

"You think you can't be outwitted, do ya? Well, you missed two obvious damsels un-distressing themselves. You missed that honorable outfit betraying you. And even now you're missing what's creeping up behind you." She smirked at the empty air behind him.

As the concerned captain distracted himself with the view over his shoulder, Marshalla kicked his sword. Like a grandfather with a splintered staff, Captain Kelly lost his balance. He fumbled, dropping the sword. At first, they were both reaching for the weapon, but then

Marshalla slapped his flitched fingertips and he went with whining instead. After tossing the sword to her father, she took the pirate by the shoulder, relishing the shirt's proximity, and spoke.

"Didn't I tell you ladies are bad luck on a ship?"

Then she bloodied her knuckles across his face.

✦

In moments they'd left the pirate ship, leaving the halved crew to scramble at the burning sail. While the traders had scored a hefty point against the marauders, they knew better than gamble against short range cannons. As they had moved off, the pirate devil roared, attempting to pull out his pocket pistol and shoot one of the two Marshalls. But in that moment, the red silk sash had leapt up and barred his path, dancing in and out and thoroughly tangling itself to keep its favorite Scottish family from harm. Marshalla had collapsed in her father's arms, weeping bitterly. The ships sailed apart till the pirate craft was just a bobbing apple far away, yet the figure was always in her mind.

Biff leaned against the railing next to her, tilting the entire boat port. "You know," he said, "I don't think I've ever heard you so quiet as now."

Marshalla wiped her eyes stoically. "I'm fair puckled," she lied, not truly short of breath. "It happens to the best of us."

Biff scratched his chin. "Your father's certainly like you. You both look at that outfit like an angel or something—"

"Something better! Those garbs are more hea-heavenly than a-any of us!" Her voice was catching like a cloak snagging on tree limbs during a forest sprint. She slowed down to a walk. "They *saved* our *lives*." She closed her eyes.

"You know, Marshalla. I wouldn't give up on that outfit if I were you. I would even say you two were a perfect match."

At that prompting, an image sprung to mind that she'd been unconsciously working on all day. It was herself. She was wearing a pair of trousers, brilliantly black as the glorious boots. A hat on her curly hair, fluttering with feathers. Beneath the soft white shirt, she'd have the beautiful scarlet silk as an underthing. And to separate the shirt from the pants, a red plaid sash made from her dress.

Gasping, Marshalla hoisted her skirts and ran up the stairs to where her father and Effie stood, watching the ship like they were already planning the story for the next town Cèilidh. With a hug, Marshalla wished Effie a long-smoking English chimney. Her voice paused guiltily as she turned to her father. He looked her in the eye, but she held his gaze staunchly.

Marshall pulled out the tasseled hilt of the captured cutlass and offered it to his daughter. "Be back by breakfast," he said.

Her face beaming more exuberantly than ever before, Marshalla belted the sword, climbed atop the ship's guardrail and launched herself off into the tossing black waters. The waterlogged wool dress and heavy metal sword did not drag her down. The water was not cold as she swam with the energy of a gliding dolphin. The cuts on her face and hand did not sting in the salt, nor did her eyes, for they were glowing with the burning image of her glorious love, temporarily captive on the ship before her.

The vision of their swashbuckling union never once left her as she churned the ocean to reach her soulmate.

SARAH STANLEY

Sarah Stanley

Parrots and Politeness

"Er...sir? Excuse me?"

'Excuse me?' thought Captain Richards. *This is a pirate ship—no place for such niceties.*

Annoyed, he turned around, confronting the young man standing behind him. Neatly dressed, excellent posture, with well-trimmed blond hair—he didn't look like a pirate at all. The boy stood out against the dark wood of the pirate ship and the brilliant sky.

"If I could have a moment of your time—"

"You're a pirate, not a naval officer. Act like one," Richards snapped. "Pirates are more...disrespectful."

The young man nodded, straightening his stance. Then, thinking again, he forced himself to slouch. "Yes, sir. I'll attempt to be more disrespectful in the future, sir."

Richards turned away, shaking his head. He stared at the waves for a few moments, then realized the boy was still there. "What's the matter? Ship on fire?"

"Oh, no, sir," the young man said promptly. "If there was a fire, I'd have raised the alarm as outlined in the protocols."

Pirates have protocols? Richards thought.

"I have come on another matter. It's about the—"

Richards raised a hand, and the boy immediately stopped speaking. "What's your name?"

"Priv—er—Charles Bentley, sir."

"Bentley. Not exactly a pirate's name."

"Well, I can't exactly help that, can I?"

Richards raised an eyebrow.

"Just trying to be more disrespectful, sir."

Bentley waited anxiously. When Richards didn't reply, he cleared his throat. "There's a matter that requires your attention, sir, below deck."

"Tell someone else to sort it out. Move along, now."

Bentley didn't move, although he grimaced apologetically. "Sir, I—"

"You have my permission to be respectful for once. Obey orders—I have a feeling you're good with those."

Bentley obediently moved away, but he added, "I thought it's something you might like to look at personally, sir. It—er—*he*—belonged to the old captain."

"He?" Richards repeated.

"Yes, sir. We just found the captain's old parrot."

✦

Richards stared with disturbed fascination at the scraggly, bile-colored mess slumped on the perch. "Are you sure that isn't a feather duster?"

"His name is Percival, sir. And while I'm not sure anyone has checked, I can assure you with a reasonable amount of confidence he is not a feather duster." Bentley hesitated, then approached the disheveled pile and jabbed a finger at it. A dull, coal-colored beak snapped out of the feathers. Bentley flinched and withdrew. "It's most definitely a parrot, sir."

Richards nodded absently. He had already decided the thing would be better off with its old captain—fluttering through the Great Jungle in the Sky, or wherever parrots went to. "Dispose of it."

The young man looked horrified. "Kill the parrot, sir?"

"Have you never had experiences with killing? Not even in the…"

Bentley jerked his head, still looking shaken. "No, sir. Didn't have the stomach for it. That's why I left the army. Please don't kill Percival—I'm sure he's a nice bird—"

"I'm afraid I don't have experience in judging the personality of birds," Richards said dryly.

"But I've heard he's very smart. The old captain said he learned fifty-three phrases and could curse in fourteen languages."

"Oh?" Richard's interested piqued despite himself. "What languages?"

"Don't know, sir. They weren't words I knew."

Richards stroked his beard. The lump in front of him showed no signs of talking. "How do you make the thing speak?"

Bentley shrugged. "Hasn't spoken a word since the old captain passed away, sir."

"Well, then, I'll strike you a deal." Richards thought for a moment. "If you can get the parrot to speak within the week, I'll spare it. In the meantime, Percival will be in your charge."

Bentley's eyes widened. "Oh, *yes*, sir! Thank you, sir! I'll give him the utmost care. I've always wanted a pet."

Richards turned away, toward the ladder that led to the deck. "And I've always wanted a breathing feather duster."

⁺

"Come on, Percival. 'Pieces of eight.' Come on, you say it."

Richards paused at the door of his cabin. Bentley's voice was coming from the opposite room. Amused, he put his ear up to the door. *Three days and he hasn't given it up.*

"Percival, please, say something—preferably not a curse, but that's better than nothing. Oh, please, don't you get it? I'll give you this cracker if you say something."

Richards pushed open the door. Bentley flinched and looked up, flushing. Percival was sitting dejectedly on a table in front of him, appearing more depressed than Richards knew a bird could look.

"No luck, eh?" Richards said.

"Oh, no, sir. I don't know what's wrong. The old captain was— and I beg your pardon—a very crude man, and I'm treating Percival as kindly as I know how. I don't know why he isn't warming up to me, sir."

"Call the old captain whatever you like," Richards said. "He can't do anything about it."

Bentley shook his head. "I couldn't speak ill of the dead, sir. It'd be—well—"

"Disrespectful?" Richards said.

Bentley reddened. "I just couldn't, sir."

Richards tried to hide his smile. "Crude or not, he was fair, eh?"

Relieved at the change in subject, Bentley hastily nodded. "Oh, yes, sir. He paid us well."

"You've still got the wealth, I suppose?" Richards asked curiously. With any other man on the ship, it would be gone at the first port but not with a man such as him.

"Yes, sir," Bentley glanced nervously over Richards's shoulder. "Not with me, of course."

Richards heard footsteps retreating in the hall behind him, sounding distinctively disappointed. He stepped into the room and shut the door behind him. While Bentley didn't act like a pirate, he did act intelligently.

"In truth, though?" Richards lowered his voice. "Buried?"

"No, sir." Bentley studied Richards's face. "The captain didn't have any treasure left, if that's what you're wondering. And the parrot wouldn't know the location anyway."

Richards started. "How did you—"

"Parrots only mimic sounds, sir. They don't know the meaning of words."

Richards shook his head. Through his many years of experience, he managed to keep his face stoic. Bentley didn't seem like one to spy but he had to be sure. "I wasn't speaking of that. How..."

"Pirates are predictably dishonest, sir," Bentley said.

"And where did you bury the wealth, then, if not in the ground?"

"A bank, sir."

Richards stared at him. "A bank?"

"Dirt doesn't pay interest, sir."

Richards sighed. Something in his face must have spoken to Bentley, because the young man scrambled to his feet.

"I'm sorry about this, sir, I'll get back to my duties." Flustered, he stumbled over a chair as he tried to exit the room. Richards waved him down.

"Stay here, if you'd like. Be disrespectful. Go ahead and neglect your duties; you have my permission. Remember, tomorrow—"

"Tomorrow marks over half the week. I know, sir." Bentley's wide, distressed eyes latched onto Richards's, like somehow Richards would fix the problem. "I won't go back on our deal, sir. I'll get him to speak, just you see."

"Even if it's to curse?" Richards said.

"I'll be cursing myself, sir, if he doesn't speak soon."

Richards studied Bentley's innocent face. "Would you really?"

"No, sir," Bentley sighed.

✦

The next time Richards saw Bentley, he was scrubbing the deck of the ship with earnest, frantic energy. He hadn't taken the offer to neglect his duties, after all.

"Ho, Bentley!" he said. "You're an ill-fitted pirate."

The young man paused his scrubbing, then stood at attention. He read Richards's expression and quickly fell out of position. "Sir?"

"I told you to ignore your duties, and here you are, doing them," Richards said. "Insurrection, I'd say, besides not being pirate-like in the least."

Bentley shrugged. "I don't mind being unlike a pirate, sir. Work is satisfying. Besides, you're not exactly a normal pirate either..."

Richards stiffened, eyes narrowing. "Oh? How?"

Looking down, Bentley murmured, "You don't speak like a sailor, sir, even when you try. What were you before? A wealthy—"

"At the *moment*," Richards said, gritting his teeth, "I am a *pirate* and the captain of this ship and I will be a pirate to you. Understand?"

Bentley nodded. "Of course, sir."

Richards clapped him on the back. "Good lad, then."

"But not a good pirate, sir?"

"Of course not." Richards cleared his throat. "So, how goes the parrot—er—charming?"

Bentley's face fell. "Not well, sir. I've tried everything I can think of, sir. I played with him, sang to him, offered him treats..."

"Is that everything you thought of?" Richards said. "I suppose you told him bedtime stories and tucked him in, as well?"

Bentley winced. "Er—not exactly, sir, but..."

"But what?"

"Now that you mention it, I do tell him stories. I think he likes them. He tucks his head under his wing and stands on one foot when I talk."

Richards wearily held up a hand to his head. "You entertain my feather duster. Why not?"

"Oh, he's much more than feathers, sir," Bentley said eagerly. "He—"

"Bones, too, I'd suspect."

"Yes, sir, but he really is a noble bird. I know he isn't much to look at now, but he must have been majestic in his day."

"Oh, there's plenty to look at," Richards leaned against the mast of the ship. "Is any of it muscle, or is it all fat and feathers?"

"Some of the other crew members think he'd be good eating," Bentley said darkly. "They're all tired of Percival anyways. I can't figure out why. He's really sweet."

"With an impressive voice, coupled with early rising habits," Richards said. "No, I can't imagine why."

Bentley stiffened. "He's like a little rooster for our ship. He does his best, even if he—"

"Sounds like the screeches of a hoarse, dying cat?"

Bentley picked up the rag again and wrung it anxiously between his hands. "I know it's been a week, sir, but could you please extend my time? I think I'm making progress. This bird was very important to the old captain, sir."

"And I suppose he told it stories, too."

Bentley sighed. "Probably not, sir. He wasn't that kind of man."

"Why won't you let that poor, dejected animal rest in peace?"

Bentley shook his head. "I want to make him happy again, sir. I don't know how. I've tried everything I can think of."

"Yes, you've told me," Richards said. "Well, think of something outside of everything. You have until the end of the day. I'd tell you to neglect your duties, but…"

Bentley reluctantly placed down the rag. "Oh, I'll finish my duties, sir. I'll just get Percival to speak first."

+

Richards found himself considering Bentley's plea to extend the time. It kept the man occupied, after all, which meant Richards wasn't tripping over him and his endless questions.

I'll tell him now, he thought. *No sense in stressing the poor lad too much—he'd drop dead.*

With his mind made up, he descended below the deck. Raucous laughter spilled from the room. Richards paused, puzzled. Laughter itself wasn't rare, but that room was hardly ever used. Ill at ease, he pushed open the door. Noise burst and flowed out of the room like a tsunami of water. It seemed as if every man on the ship was there, crammed into the tiny space. They refused to budge as Richards pushed his way inside.

These men acted like pirates—yet Richards found himself missing Bentley's manners. Perhaps he *could* make a few changes. But that wouldn't be pirate-like.

"Oh, sir," a voice called. "Please stop them!"

Richards recognized it immediately. Even if it hadn't sounded more polished than the other pirates, Bentley was the only man on the ship that called him *sir*.

"Yes, lad?" Richards finally managed to push through the crowd to Bentley, who was holding Percival protectively on his arm.

"They're trying to kill him, sir," Bentley said. "They want to hang him like a criminal and make a big sport of it. I tried to tell them that was no respectable way to dispose of a bird, but—"

"The bird 'as to die," someone called. "The captain promised. 'E can't back out of a bargain like that. Why not 'ave a bit of fun?"

Richards hesitated, the words hovering on his lips. Looking weak in front his crew could end very badly. And he *had* made a bargain.

"The bird dies…respectably," he said.

Bentley nodded gratefully, but there was still pain in his eyes. Slowly, he held out the arm with Percival on it. "Do you want to do it, sir?"

Richards stared at the parrot, hesitating. He'd almost grown— well, fond wasn't the right word, but…*This is your fault, lad,* he thought, trying to muster up annoyance. He couldn't.

At a loss for what to do, he let Bentley tip Percival onto his arm. He felt the parrot's thin, sharp talons through his sleeve. Up close, he could make out the remains of a green sheen across the faded feathers with little shiny eyes peering out from them.

Around him, the pirates had gone quiet. Waiting.

"I'm sorry, lad," he murmured.

Bentley nodded, wet eyes glistening in the lantern light.

Richards started at Percival, wondering how this had become such a big matter. It was a *parrot.* But he could see the remnants of a noble bird.

Beloved to the captain, Bentley had said. A crude man.

A crude man.

Richards held out a finger and pointed it at the parrot. "Speak," he snapped. "And be quick about it, you mangy feather duster."

Percival relaxed on his arm.

"Pieces of eight," he croaked.

The room went silent. Bentley stared at Percival, then at Richards.

"It's a pirate's bird," Richards smirked. "I told you, pirates are disrespectful." He paused. "But not anymore. Let's have more respect around here. Get back to your duties, men, and give me a 'yes, sir' while you're at it!"

ARIANA HARRISON

Swallowed by the Tides

If you're reading this, you've either been taken by the Mertribe or you were dumb enough to steal from their archives. Either way, you've got this waterproof scroll in your hands. What are you going to do with it? Study it? Sell it on the black market? Display it like a prize?

Whatever you choose, be wary. The Mertribe are not a gracious people. They are warlike and cruel. Sure, there's the odd mermaid with a kind heart but they can't do anything for you. You're on your own. Who knows, if you deign to read this, I may be able to help.

My name is Quinn. Let me tell you a story.

✦

My twin brother Levi and I were poor fishermen, barely making ends meet. I enjoyed cooking, but after the move to the Aiscin docks had drained the last reserves of our money, I never had the ingredients to make anything more savory than bland oatmeal. Levi was a top-notch engineer, but couldn't afford the parts and metal he needed for his inventions. He often would try to make something out of the measly supplies he managed to scrape up from the trash heaps but they never lasted long.

On top of that, we were terrible fishermen. We scraped by, getting supplies on the cheapest discounts we could find, fishing from dawn to dusk, eating barely enough to sustain us.

Skies, we were a sorry sight.

One day, however, luck smiled upon us.

We were on our boat when a summer storm struck out of nowhere, throwing us to the sea and claiming our oars as a prize. When the clouds cleared up, we were stranded in the middle of the ocean with no way to get home. We were giving up hope when suddenly, a huge ship appeared on the horizon. We flagged them down with our shirts and were pulled aboard the Helical Downfall, a magnificent vessel run by pirates. You read that correctly. Pirates. The steampunk ship was run by none other than Captain Teresa, a pirate feared for her craftiness and able-bodied crew.

At that point, my brother and I were desperate for a different job. After Levi demonstrated his abilities by repairing one of the ship's broken engines, we convinced the skeptical captain to hire us instead of dropping us off on the nearest shore. That's how Levi became the ship's technician. As for me, I became the ship's cook after the previous one got sick of doing dishes and switched to night shift duty.

The first few days aboard the Helical Downfall were incredibly awkward. Levi and I kept to ourselves, doing our new jobs and avoiding interaction with everyone except the captain. Eventually Roan, the cannon master started talking to Levi and me, and introduced us to Rhea—a sweet young woman with the reflexes of a cat—and Kali, the captain's daughter. The five of us grew close quickly, laughing together and messing around in our free time. Soon enough, the crew fully accepted me and my brother. We were part of the family. Thus, a new life had begun.

+

A few months after Levi and I had joined the crew of the Helical Downfall, I was working in the kitchen, cleaning up after the morning meal. "Don't forget to take care of everything you used, Levi. I know you have a ship to take care of, but I'm not cleaning up after you."

"Quinn, the rocket boosters are due for a checkup!" Levi moaned, running a hand through his tousled brown hair. He turned to me with pleading eyes. "I need to take care of that. The captain also asked me to see if there would be a way to give this ship the ability to fly. She thinks it would be revolutionary in the sailing industry."

"Sorry," I shrugged, a grin tugging at the corners of my mouth. "Captain's orders are that every crew member cleans up after himself and that includes you."

"What are you two chattering about?"

I turned around and my heart skipped a beat, or five. Kali leaned against the doorframe, looking as gorgeous as ever. Little by little, I had slowly fallen in love with her in my time aboard the ship. Unfortunately, so had Levi.

"Captain Kali!" he teased, sweeping into a grandiose bow. "What are your orders today?"

Kali's sapphire eyes twinkled as she blew away a strand of curly black hair that had escaped from her ponytail. "For you to take care of your dishes."

"Not you too!" Levi groaned good-naturedly.

Kali giggled, picking up a dishrag and tossing it over to him.

"Is Levi whining about dishes again?" Rhea asked as she entered the room. "It would go faster if he didn't complain." She shot me a shy grin and shrugged.

"Ah, but stalling means I might be able to make Quinn do it for me!" Levi winked.

"I did it for you once, when you were too sick to even run through the daily checklist of ship maintenance —"

A tremor rumbled through the ship. Levi's dishes shattered as they tumbled to the ground, and everyone stumbled, struggling to stay upright. Rhea lost her balance and began to fall, but I caught her before gravity could claim her. When we had all regained our footing, we exchanged worried glances, and then ran topside.

I peered overboard into the churning water as dripping heads emerged from the ocean's depths. The merpeople.

"Crew of the Helical Downfall," a merman with indigo hair addressed us. "We know that one of you have stolen the Stormy Skies Artifact, which by birthright belongs to King Orauht of the Mertribe."

"We have stolen nothing!" Captain Teresa's hazel eyes flared with anger. "My crew is innocent!"

"It is not so!" cried a green-haired mermaid. "We found a ripped armband near the pedestal where the Artifact was kept when we discovered the theft last night. The armband was azurite-blue and decorated with metal gears, exactly like the ones your crew members wear!"

"That could have been anyone!" the captain sputtered, an incredulous expression on her face.

"Certainly not. No pirate who rides these waves dares to copy the symbols of Captain Teresa. They fear you too much to even consider it," replied the first merman. His cold blue eyes glimmered as if he enjoyed watching us flounder under the accusations he threw.

"Due to that evidence," the green-haired mermaid resumed. "We have deduced that the thief was one of your crew mates. You have three hours to locate the Stormy Skies Artifact. If you fail to return the Artifact, you will give us one of your most valuable crewmembers. If you refuse to cooperate, we will wage war on you and your descendants for three generations."

"Three hours? That's impossible! You can't expect us to agree to this insanity!" The wind whipped Captain Teresa's short strawberry-blonde hair around her face, making her look like a madwoman.

"We have set our terms. The clock is ticking," A turquoise-haired mermaid laughed maliciously as the merpeople sank back beneath the waves and left us.

"This is impossible!" Captain Teresa paced the deck. Tension was running high and tempers were short. We were dangerously close to an uncontrollable uproar. The crew murmured anxiously amongst themselves, desperately brainstorming for ideas.

"Mother, we have to at least try!" Kali pleaded. "We can't lose anyone!"

"Why do they want one of our 'most valuable' crew members?" Rhea asked.

Captain Teresa looked at the young assassin and sighed.

"Because they want to have another servant," she replied. "They know we have incredibly skilled people on this ship that they could use for their bloodthirsty goals. For example, if we couldn't find the Artifact and sent Levi down, they'd use his talents to make war machines and take revenge on us anyway. If we sent you, Rhea, you'd be forced to be a murderer again."

Rhea shuddered as she recalled the awful deeds she'd been forced to accomplish in earlier years. She'd been taken from her home and trained to be an assassin, forced to murder until she found the opportunity to escape. I winced in sympathy for her and knew instantly that if we couldn't find the Artifact, she couldn't be the one sent down. She was by far the most dangerous of the entire crew.

"We won't let you get taken," I whispered, trying to calm her down. "You won't have to take a life ever again. I promise."

"Th-thanks, Quinn." She glanced at me, blushed slightly, and turned away.

"We should poison the waters!" someone called from the midst of our crew. "The mermaids would die."

"No way, sandbrains!" a man behind me yelled. "We don't have enough poison to infect the entire ocean and there's no guarantee that it would even reach them. They could just swim away!"

"Then we kill them all. It'd take some effort, but we'd be free," a young, and relatively naïve, pirate suggested.

"They have the numbers advantage, as well as unknown powers. We wouldn't stand a chance. It's not worth the injuries and losses it would inflict," Kali gently reminded him.

"Then I say we get Levi to build a machine that contains them or kills them so we can escape!" the first pirate yelled.

"I can't build a war machine in less than three hours!" Levi protested. "The brainstorming, troubleshooting, and building would take weeks!"

"Wasn't Levi trying to add a contraption that enabled this ship to fly?" demanded a grizzled old seadog as he gave Levi a suspicious glare.

"Didn't you listen? He said it would take weeks," Rhea snapped.

All of the crewmembers started yelling over each other, creating a deafening cacophony of noise. Voices and varied accents overlapped chaotically, making my head spin.

"No one's building any war machines, poisoning any oceans, or killing anyone!" Teresa roared angrily over the shouting. "All of you shut your traps!"

Silence fell amongst the crew. A few people hung their heads in shame.

"What if we gave a few people the job of looking for the Artifact?" Levi piped up after a moment. "Captain, you could give them some authority for the search. If the group was small, they could easily get through the search before the three hours run out. If they succeed, no one will be lost to the Mertribe."

"Excellent idea," Captain said with an anxious smile. "Levi, choose two of your crewmates to be on your search team."

"Me?" Levi's eyes went wide. "I'm heading the search team?"

"Last I checked, there wasn't anyone else named Levi on this ship. Besides, you're thorough with the jobs I give you and you think outside the box. Those qualities are invaluable in times such as this."

"O-okay." Levi took a deep breath and turned to me. "Quinn?"

"You know I'll help you." I quirked an eyebrow.

He grinned nervously, then turned to the Captain's daughter. "Kali?"

"Sure," she nodded.

"That settles it, then," said the captain. "Crew of the Helical Downfall, I hereby give temporary authority to Levi, Quinn, and Kali as the Artifact Search Team. You will answer any questions they have with complete honesty, and if needs be, they have permission to search your belongings. Anyone who doesn't comply will be punished accordingly."

"What about you, Mother?" Kali asked. "Where will you be?"

"I'll be in my quarters researching better ways to deal with those infernal sea maggots," Captain Teresa grumbled. "There's got to be another way to compromise. In the meantime, everyone is required to return to their normal responsibilities—excluding the search team, of course. Get moving!"

Everyone jumped to do her bidding. Rhea tucked a stray piece of ruby-red hair behind her ear and gave me a tentative smile.

"Um, good luck with the search," she said shyly, then hurried away to accomplish her daily tasks.

I watched her go, then turned to my brother. "Where do we start?"

"Well, let's divide and conquer. Kali, can you take inventory of who's missing an armband?"

"Way ahead of you," she smirked, already heading below deck.

"Quinn, you and I will start talking to the crew members. Are you okay with that?"

"Sounds great! Let's get going."

We walked to the stern of the boat. Levi tapped on the shoulder of a tall, imposing man with warm, chocolate-colored skin. He turned and grinned when he saw us.

"Levi, Quinn! How goes the search?" His familiar Xerchan accent made me smile.

"We haven't found anything of interest yet, which is why we were hoping to talk to you first, Dreave." Levi adjusted the goggles he always wore on his brow. "You know everything that happens on this ship. We were hoping you could tell us who wasn't asleep in their hammock last night."

"Well, now, what makes you think I know that?" Dreave playfully raised an eyebrow and looked at us with mock skepticism.

I cut in before Levi could speak. "You like to play Ceoan Twilight Poker with some of the other crew members after the captain retires to her quarters for the night. It's typically the early hours of the morning when you finally quit your gambling and return to your hammock. It's okay if you don't want to cooperate but I wonder what

Captain Teresa would say if she knew of your late-night card-playing."

Dreave was silent for a moment. Then he burst into laughter. "You haggle for information with more skills than the merchants in the night markets! Okay, then, deal. I tell you who wasn't accounted for, and you keep quiet about my gambling."

"Fine by me!" Levi chuckled.

I smirked, proud of my quick victory.

"So, you two know that I'm a regular for the late-night card games," Dreave began. "Playing with me were Soames, Elden, and Renshaw. When I got back, the crewmembers missing were Alastair, Payton, Roan, and Elgar. Torp was missing too, but it turns out that he was only gone because Envi snuck a Damarian pepper into his dinner and he was topside trying to calm his upset stomach. That answer all your questions?"

"That's all we needed. Thanks, Dreave!" Levi gave him a little salute, and started walking away. I hurried to catch up with him.

"Who should we talk to first? Payton, Alastair, Elgar, or Roan?" I asked.

"I say we visit Elgar first. Do you know where he might be?"

"Isn't he typically on the quarterdeck at this time of day?" I frowned.

"You're right. Let's check there first."

Sure enough, when we reached the quarterdeck, Elgar was sitting on the floor, looking dizzy and disoriented.

"Elgar! We've got a few questions to ask you." said Levi.

Elgar moaned. "My 'ead 'urts," his words slurred together. "I shouldn'ta 'ad those drinks last night."

Levi and I exchanged glances.

"Did you sneak some of that Taasian whiskey again?" I asked.

"What's it matter to you?" He rubbed his temples. "It's not your 'eadache."

"Yes, but it's the whiskey that all of us profit from selling," Levi glared. "Quit sampling our goods."

"What are you going to do about it?" Elgar sneered.

"Well," Levi snarled. "I'm fairly certain Captain Teresa wouldn't like to hear about your whisky-related shenanigans."

"When did Teresa appoint you the first mate? You're just the bossy know-it-all technician," Elgar's words dripped with sarcasm.

"The technician who gave this ship rocket boosters, upgraded the cannons, and saved your hide last month," Levi shot back. "I could have let you die."

"What does that 'ave to do with anything?" the hungover pirate sputtered.

"You may remember a certain code among pirates." Levi allowed himself a little half-smirk. "If someone saves your life, you owe them a life debt and your respect. It's also highly advised that you listen to them when they give you a piece of advice or a direct order. How you're behaving currently is neither respectful or responsible."

"All right, fine! I'll quit stealing the whiskey if you quit nagging at me," Elgar griped. "Leave me alone."

Levi turned on his heel and stormed away. I followed close behind, easily keeping up.

"Shenanigans?" I snickered. "Never heard you use that one before."

"That's because I haven't used it before. It's a good word, though and uncommonly accurate when it comes to Elgar. Come on, let's visit Payton next."

"Did someone call my name?" The yell came from above us. We looked up to see Payton in the crow's nest, giggling madly. His curly red hair and beard rippled in the wind like brilliant ruby-colored flags. He started climbing down, then lost his grip and fell the rest of the way, landing at our feet. He jumped up, seemingly unbothered by the fact that he'd just fallen half of the distance from the crow's nest.

"Why, 'ello, you two," he hiccupped. "I thought you were twins. I didn't know you 'ad two other brothers. They even dress like you!"

Levi and I stared at him in confusion.

"Oh, wait," he snickered. "I'm seeing double. Sorry 'bout that."

Levi groaned as a realization dawned on him.

"You wouldn't happen to have been with Elgar when he was sneaking whiskey last night?" he sighed, pinching the bridge of his nose as if to ward off a migraine.

"Elgar?" Payton began to babble. "Oh, we drank some whiskey last night. It burns when you swallow it, but the burn goes away, and it's replaced by a warm glow, like there's a cozy campfire in your stomach." Payton's eyes crossed, and he fell to the deck, out like a light, and began to snore.

I exchanged a chagrined glance with my brother and sighed.

"I guess both Elgar and Payton have alibies even if they aren't the best ones." I stooped to pick up the drunken pirate.

After Levi and I had deposited Payton in his hammock, we began to look for Alastair. We found him in the cargo hold, securing some bags of gunpowder.

"Ah, hello." He brushed traces of dust off the sides of the bags. "What can I do for you?"

"We were wondering if you would be willing to answer some questions for us," Levi sounded so diplomatic. "Do you have a moment?"

"Just finished my duties. Go ahead and shoot."

"We heard from a reliable source that you were missing from your hammock last night. Do you have a reason for your absence?" Levi questioned.

"I do, actually." Alastair gave a sad half-smile. "I was trying to help Torp settle his stomach after he accidentally ate that pepper. You can ask him if you want further proof. I almost wish I was the thief, though," he confessed. "Then the hunt would end, and we wouldn't be in danger of losing a crewmate."

We all sighed in unison.

"Yeah, I wish we weren't in danger either," I whispered.

"Thank you for your time," Levi nodded. "Have a good day, Alastair."

Once we had left the cargo hold, I ran my hand through my hair in frustration. "One hour has already passed. We only have two more hours and one person left to interrogate before we're out of leads. Let's hope Roan knows something."

We started for the gun deck when we bumped into Kali. "Seven people are missing their armbands, but all of them say that they either got damaged or are being cleaned," she reported. "Everyone else showed me their armbands to prove they weren't lying."

"In that case, why don't we go interrogate Roan together?" Levi suggested.

"All right." Kali started walking away, my brother and I close behind.

When we reached the gun deck, Roan stood to greet us. With his muscular build and gray-streaked beard, he reminded me of a grizzly bear. The old cannon master stood tall and intimidating, but the smile lines around his chartreuse eyes hinted that he wasn't as mean as he looked.

"Any luck?" His deep voice and thick accent startled me for a moment. Our dwindling time had me on edge.

"Unfortunately, not much yet. So far, we've only discovered who hasn't stolen the artifact," said Levi. "Mind if we ask you a few questions?"

"Not at all," he smiled.

"Why were you out of your hammock last night?" Levi asked. "Dreave told us who wasn't there when he went to bed after his nightly gambling. You were among the men listed."

Roan froze for a fraction of a second. The hesitation passed so swiftly I almost didn't see it. His expression tensed, but not much.

"I vas here on ze gun deck, rearranging ze ammunition for ze cannons after Envi shifted zem around as a practical joke. I vould have done it earlier, in ze daylight hours, but I didn't discover the prank until I voke up to help Alastair vith Torp. Nothing out of ze ordinary. Envi is alvays causing problems." He waved his hand dismissively.

I felt a little uneasy but brushed it aside. "Thank you for your time, Roan. We'll be on our –"

"Wait." Kali held up her hand. "Where's your light source?"

We stared at her with confusion written all over our faces.

"Come again?" Roan asked.

"Your light source. You always keep a flameless torch of some kind in here at all times so that you can see what you're doing. You even fitted the torch sconce with a lock only you had a key to because you didn't want Envi to steal your light source as another one of her practical jokes. Where did you put it when you were done?" A guarded expression crossed her face.

Roan said nothing, alarm shining in his eyes, reminding me of a cornered animal.

"Quinn," Levi spoke slowly, keeping his gaze fixed on Roan. "I want you to go topside and look around where Torp was located last night. If the flameless torch isn't there, go check the water-entry deck. Kali and I will keep watch over Roan."

My eyes widened in horror as I realized that if the torch was where Levi suspected it might be, Roan could be our thief. I raced topside and checked the forecastle deck, where Torp had been trying to calm his upset stomach.

No torch.

Dread filled my heart as I dashed down below. The water-entry deck was a rarely-used deck in the very bottom of the ship, with a hatch that could open and let the crew of the Helical Downfall communicate with the creatures of the deep or go for a short dive. The culprit probably would have used it to get to the Artifact last night. It didn't take me long to find a flameless torch thrown haphazardly by a stack of crates, still glowing feebly. I picked it up with heightening horror. Why would Roan steal the Stormy Skies Artifact? Panic set in, choking me with its icy talons.

"I found it." As I reentered the gun deck, I clutched the torch so hard my knuckles were turning white. "It was in the water-entry deck."

The blood drained from Roan's face as he stared at the object in my hands. I could practically smell the guilt and terror radiating from him.

Levi whirled around to face Roan, his expression hardening. "Care to rethink your story, Roan?" Fury sparked in his eyes. Beside him, Kali said nothing. She just stared at the cannon master as her eyes glimmered with tears of anger and betrayal.

The weight of the stifling silence felt suffocating. At length, Roan exhaled slowly and pulled an unassuming brown leather pouch from his pocket. He opened it and emptied the contents into my hands.

There, resting in my fingers, was an intricate stone that seemed to be made from a combination of sea froth and storm clouds, with a streak of lightning through the center. It felt cold and heavy in my hands, and it emanated the faint smell of sea salt. It was set in a platinum ring, enabling the wielder to wear it if necessary.

The Stormy Skies Artifact.

"Before you say anything," Roan cut in as Kali opened her mouth to shout. "Let me explain. From ze beginning." He paused, gauging our reactions. When none of us spoke, he continued. "I became ze cannon master around ze same time zat Teresa joined our crew. Before King Orauht came to power and brought his var-lust with him, zings between ze pirates and ze Mertribe vere quite peaceful, if not a little distant. Ve vould even gather to ze vater entry deck and hold a semi-annual conference with zem to discuss how to avoid contention.

At one such conference, I saw ze most beautiful mermaid. She vas breathtaking, vith long amber hair and brown eyes...but ze details don't matter. Ze point is, after talking and meeting in secret, ve fell in love. I took a short break from sailing to live on land with her for a vhile and ve vere married. My vife stayed in human form so she could remain with me. Ve had a beautiful baby girl ve named Norah. Ve vere left in peace for a vhile, until Norah fell sick vith a deadly disease. I returned to ze crew of ze Helical Downfall to earn more money to pay for her treatments. My vife stayed on land to earn vhatever other money she could find vhile taking care of Norah. Eventually, ve earned enough to take her to a particularly skilled doctor but he could do nothing. He told us zat only an object of immense power could save her."

My eyes widened. I could sense the turn this story was about to take.

"So, ze last time ve vere in port, I stole a device zat allowed me to breathe undervater temporarily. My vife reassumed her mermaid form and ve took the Stormy Skies Artifact. I came back to ze ship and my vife vent back to Norah, but I kept ze Artifact to throw ze Mertribe off her trail." He lowered his head. "Ze plan vas for me to keep it for a vhile, then to give it back to my vife. She vould take it to Norah and our daughter vould be healed. I had no idea ze Mertribe vould realize ze theft so quickly."

I held my tongue with great difficulty. I wanted to scream at Roan for his foolishness. Yet I wanted to ask him about his daughter. I doubted anyone else on this ship knew Roan was married, let alone had a child.

"Why didn't you tell my mother?" Kali inquired in a wavering voice. "We might have been able to find a substitute or trade for an artifact. We could have saved your daughter without having to choose between the life of a little girl and the freedom of a crewmember. We could have helped you!" The anguish in her eyes made me itch to run over and comfort her but I forced myself to stay still. My attempts to help wouldn't accomplish anything besides taking precious time.

"I didn't zink," Roan admitted. "You know vhat it feels like to panic vhen a loved one is in danger."

Kali turned away, biting her lip.

"I think it's time to get Captain Teresa," said Levi.

I started for the Captain's quarters, dread hanging over me like a storm cloud.

✛

"I see." Teresa eyes flared with anger. "So, this whole nightmare has been the result of your stupidity. You did it out of love, which I admire and respect but it was still stupid."

"Yes, Captain." Roan cast his eyes toward the ground.

Teresa leaned back, the energy seemed to be draining out of her. "I can't let a child die, but I can't give any of my crew members to the Mertribe as a sacrifice. I could never force myself to do such a deed."

"Please," the shamed cannon master looked up for the first time since Teresa entered the room. "Don't make me vatch my daughter die. I'll do anything. I'd even sacrifice myself to ze Mertribe."

I looked between the Captain and Roan. Then my eyes fell on my brother and Kali. Her face was buried in his shoulder. His arms were wrapped around her as he spoke comforting things into her ear, trying to calm her even though he looked just as stricken. An idea forced its way into my mind. My heart throbbed from the slow shattering my plan would bring about but I knew it was necessary.

"I...have a solution." Four sets of eyes stared at me. I swallowed hard. "I'll go," I whispered. "I'll be the one who the Mertribe takes."

"Quinn, no!" Levi yelled, frenzied horror rising in his eyes. My throat closed up but I forced myself to keep talking.

"I can dress as Levi and he can dress as me. They'll be tricked and think that I'm more valuable than I actually am. Roan can save his daughter and be reunited with his family. Teresa won't have to choose anyone to sacrifice because I volunteer."

Teresa's face went white and Kali stared at me with a panicked expression. Roan appeared as though he didn't know whether to thank me or yell at me.

"Captain Teresa can join Levi and Kali in marriage before I leave. I'm aware of their secret engagement and that they love each other very much. I'd like to see my brother married before...before I'm gone." Every word punctured my heart like a bullet.

Kali emitted a strangled cry and Levi gaped at me.

"Quinn!" Teresa interjected. "I'm not letting you sacrifice your-self, there has to be another way—"

I shook my head. "This is the only way."

Teresa buried her face in her hands, all the fight leaving her.

"Let's hurry," I instructed. "We've got an hour to plan and hold a wedding. After that, we have thirty minutes to prepare for the return of the Mertribe."

✦

The next forty-five minutes were a blur. Time seemed to fast-forward through the preparation straight to the ceremony. None of the crew-mates questioned the abruptness of the marriage. Everyone needed a piece of joy before what was sure to be a tragedy.

Kali stepped lightly to where Levi stood by Captain Teresa. She wore her mother's wedding dress. It was slightly long on her but she looked gorgeous. Levi had speedily combed his hair and thrown on clean clothes. They both had several long, sky-blue ribbons tied to their wrists, trailing behind them. The loose ends of the ribbons were held by different pirates in the crew. I held the silky end of a ribbon tied around Levi's wrist.

It was silent as each ribbon-holder came up one by one and hand-ed their end of the ribbon to Teresa. When my turn eventually came, I walked up slowly, smiling remorsefully, knowing I'd never have a wedding of my own. I handed the ribbon to Teresa then strode back to my place, sending a fleeting smile to my brother and his bride-to-be as I passed.

Once Teresa held all the loose ends of the ribbons, she quickly and efficiently tied them into a knot, symbolizing their union. With their wrists bound together by ribbons, Kali and Levi laced hands and began to dance to inaudible music. Their feet tapped out a light rhythm on the deck as they whirled and spun together, the ribbons still in place. My eyes burned with tears but I smiled.

When they had completed the dance, they stood in front of Teresa once more. Teresa carefully removed the ribbons without cutting or breaking them, all while keeping the knot intact. She placed them on a slab of metal and took the oil-drenched torch Alastair offered. She lit it with the smallest spark from a lantern, waiting until it flared to life before setting it on top of the ribbons.

The smell of smoke tickled my nostrils as the ribbons burned. The ashes floated into the air, scattered by the wind, soaring up and away. Levi and Kali watched solemnly, their hands tightly intertwined. Once the majority of the ashes had been carried away by the gentle breeze, Levi leaned in and kissed Kali. I smiled through the heartache, knowing I was blessed to see my brother's marriage.

Just as the knot symbolized their union, the dance and the ribbon burning also held symbolical significance. The dance with bound wrists symbolized the life that Levi and Kali would lead together, side by side, in harmony. The burning signified how they would still be together, even in death. The scent of smoke lingered in the air as I furiously rubbed my eyes to expel the remaining tears.

There was no cheering as Kali and Levi pulled apart. Although the joy in the air was tangible, so was the suffocating tension and fear. The ceremony was over. I hugged my brother and his new wife, then looked to Teresa. She nodded, then stood to inform the crew of our plans while I quietly slipped away to change.

"Are you ready, Levi?" My brother awkwardly called me by his own name as I dressed in his clothes.

"Yes, Quinn." The reversal of names felt equally odd on my tongue.

There was a short silence.

"You're sacrificing so much," he said. "You've worked so hard to keep us alive, and now you're giving yourself to the Mertribe."

"Where are you going with this?" My brow furrowed in confusion.

"I know how you feel about Kali," Levi whispered. "I'm so sorry. When I found out that she loved me enough to agree to a secret engagement, I was only thinking of myself, and now…I feel terrible. I am so, so sorry."

I looked directly at him and placed my hands on his shoulders firmly. "Do you love her, Levi?" I demanded. "Do you love her?"

"W-with every fiber in my body," he stammered.

"Then that's enough." With a sad smile, I loosened my grip. "She deserves someone who will treasure her forever. Treat her like a queen. Live a life filled with joy. That will be enough."

His eyes filled with tears and we embraced.

"I'm going to miss you so much," he sobbed, hugging me tightly.

"Even if it's not in this life," I reassured him through tears of my own. "I will see you again. Remember that, brother."

We parted, furiously wiping our eyes.

"Skies watch over you, Quinn," Levi murmured.

"You as well, Levi." We embraced one last time, then he walked slowly away. I watched him leave, then turned to look out across the open water. The sky had become overcast with ominous gray clouds, and the breeze had picked up, occasionally strong enough to throw some cool sea spray into my face. I licked the salty taste from my lips and looked behind me to see the entire crew standing behind me in a ring like a legion of guardians. The sight was comforting, even if I knew it wouldn't make a difference.

Two more minutes until I faced my fate. I took a deep breath, trying to calm my galloping pulse. My skin felt clammy and dread settled over the Helical Downfall like a thick blanket. I glanced at Captain Teresa and nodded to her. She nodded back, pain in her eyes. I tried to give her a reassuring smile, but she turned away sadly. We stood in complete, stifling silence as our three hours officially ran out.

For a moment, all was still.

Three pillars of frothing seawater exploded upward out of the ocean. They each carried a Mertribe warrior dressed in ceremonial blue-tinted armor. The warriors towered above us for a moment before they jumped from their pillars onto the deck of the Helical Downfall, morphing to their human forms as they leapt.

"You offer up the technician Levi?" A warrior with brilliant orange hair nodding at me. "Wise choice. We accept. Come – "

"WAIT!" Rhea broke away from the ring of crewmembers and dashed toward me. She threw her arms around my neck and kissed me. I froze, cold shock flowing through my veins as furious heat rushed to my face. My arms encircled her waist as astonished gasps rippled around us.

"I love you." She sobbed, anguish written all over her sweet face. "I couldn't let you leave without telling you." She allowed herself to be pulled back into the safety of the crew by an astounded Alastair.

"R-Rhea," I whispered, my aching heart pounding furiously in my chest.

"Are you quite finished with that pointless display of affection?" A purple-haired warrior stifled a bored yawn.

"It appears so," stated the first guard, his lip curled in disgust. The third warrior, a young merman with icy blue hair, stayed silent, looking between Rhea and me, something akin to pity on his face.

"Say goodbye, human," the purple-haired merman sneered. "You'll never see them again."

I opened my mouth to say one final farewell, but before I could utter a word, the Mertribe warriors grabbed me roughly by the arms and hauled me overboard. The goodbye that had been forming on my lips transformed into a shocked cry as I fell with them. The last thing I heard were the anguished screams of Rhea and my brother as I plunged into the icy depths of the deep, dark sea.

✛

There you have it. The story of how I came to this wretched place.

Barely a day after I was taken, the Mertribe discovered my discrepancy. They took me back to the Helical Downfall in the dead of the night, claiming I was not valuable enough and demanding Captain Teresa trade me for the real Levi.

For as long as I live, I will never forget what she said.

"Quinn has a heart bigger than the entire sea," she had scolded. "He sacrificed himself to save a little girl he never met and to ensure the freedom of our crew. That alone makes him easily the most valuable crew member I have ever had the blessing to know."

Her words didn't save me from the depths of the ocean, but holding on to them was one of the few things that has saved me from insanity.

Instead of being a technician, I became the Mertribe scribe. It was quite a boring job, but I was grateful I couldn't be used as a weapon to inflict revenge on my former crewmates.

The blue-haired warrior took pity on me and would deliver letters from the crew as long as I promised to destroy the evidence. I always received a letter from Levi until the day he retired from being a pirate technician to live on land as an inventor. The last thing I heard from him was that he and Kali were expecting twins. I hope he and his family are living peacefully.

Roan wrote me one letter of gratitude before he left the crew to live with his wife and daughter. I pray his daughter is healthy again. Rhea wrote a few letters before kindly explaining that she could not continue because of the emotional pain. I wish her only the best and happiest life. Captain Teresa and the rest of the crew wrote me frequently, giving me random tidbits of news and sharing stories. They all found their own happiness eventually.

As for me, I will remain swallowed by the tides, continuing to serve as the Mertribe scribe until my soul ascends to the eternal blue sky.

Good luck, reader. I pray you escape.

Svenishta

The wind blew my blonde hair into my face as I stood in my father's beached fishing boat, eyes fixed on the point on the horizon where I used to watch the sunrise. "Svenishta," father had called it: the Everything and Nothing.

When I was a child, he told me stories of nymphs and dragons that swam there, of pirates who sank at its border, and of fishermen who found it and loved it so much that they stayed there forever.

"But can real people sail there, Dad?" I had asked him.

"Of course! Where else would we get these stories?" he'd answered, caressing my hair as he held me in his lap. "I'm sure you'll see it one day, Jeannie."

And that was my dream. I spent most moments staring out at the ocean, thinking about what it would be like to sail past the horizon and end up in that magical place. When I was a child, it had seemed natural that once I was a grown up, I'd be able to explore everything.

I gazed out at the blue waves crashing against each other and turning white, as if they were fighting to grasp the gray clouds in the sky and pull them down. "Come on, Jeannie," I said under my breath. I thought of all the things I wanted to know were true. I thought of Svenishta, and how badly I wanted to see the creatures and places my Dad had told me about—to sail like him with all his knowledge of the sea.

I tried to force the lump out of my throat with a sigh. "Not anymore, Jeannie," I said through clenched teeth. I jumped off the boat and walked back up the beach to the house.

Home was the only building on our island. It was a lonely little cottage perched on a hill surrounded by flowerless bushes that hadn't seen real sunlight in ten years. The stone walls were damp from the relentless rainstorms, the thatched roof leaked and smelled like mildew, and the floor creaked.

I forced the wooden door open with a *crack* and made it inside just as the first plump drops of a storm fell on my neck.

"I'm home," I sighed to myself, taking off Dad's old coat and my galoshes. I glanced at the chair near the fireplace where my father used to sit, smoking his pipe. On the floor was a tin bucket to catch the rain from the leaky roof.

I turned on a light and the radio to chase away the silence. The radiator hummed in the background. I lit the stove in the corner and banged a pan down onto the flame, punctuating the sound of heavy rain outside.

I took a small, dusty potato from the bowl on the table behind me, sliced it with my dad's pocketknife, and plopped the pieces down on the sizzling metal. I gave myself permission to use a little bit of salt and pepper and watched the potatoes cook, smelling their scent mingled with the smell of wet dirt and ocean as my mind wandered over distant memories of sunshine.

As night fell, the darkness and fatigue I'd come to know since my parents' deaths fell over me. It was like a blanket pretending to comfort me while smothering me instead. The storm intensified as I ate, making the lights flicker and interrupting the man on the radio with static.

"I want to leave," I said to no one. "I want to take Dad's fishing boat and sail to Svenishta."

I stood, flicked off the radio, and tried to ignore the sound of the waves and rain. I left my plate on the table and went to my bedroom.

I got into bed without changing out of my dress. "Goodnight," I called. Dad told me once that good spirits could hear children. I wasn't a child, but I felt like one. "A useless kid," I said to myself, laying down. "Still Little Jeannie, who talks to spirits and believes she can sail to Svenishta, but isn't brave enough to do it."

I closed my eyes.

✦

After being alone for a year, I'd become paranoid about noises in the house. Sounds that had been familiar when my parents were alive turned into startling cannon blasts. I worried about people being there that didn't belong. Not only that, but I worried about going mad, and hearing people and things that weren't there at all. I was afraid of human intruders, but I was terrified of supernatural ones, so when I suddenly heard footsteps in the hall, I felt like my stomach had jolted upward and knocked my heart into my throat.

I cautiously looked into the darkness, and my eyes met the face of a boy standing in my doorway, serenely playing the violin. I sat up, head spinning.

My voice was caught in the back of my mouth, and I had to force it out in a strangled, almost savage yell. "Who are you?"

The boy opened his eyes and glanced sideways at me. He straightened up and dropped his violin, which disappeared into smoke. He was tall and about my age.

"Ah, good," he said, "I was waiting for you to wake up."

He stepped toward my bed. I leapt *out* of my bed and backed up against the wall. "What are you doing in here? I don't know you, I—" I pressed myself closer against the wall as he easily vaulted over my bed.

"Don't come any closer," I said.

"Don't be afraid." He held out his hand. His face was soft and concerned. "I thought you would be pleased to see someone, after all this time."

"I don't know who you are—"

"My name is Canlagh. I'm here to help you find your soul."

"I've got one of those already, thanks." I sidled past the window and around my bed to the door. I gripped the doorknob, inching into the hall, my shoulders tense.

"The one you've got is struggling to survive. You need a replacement."

The boy jumped up onto my windowsill and summoned his violin to his hand. "Take some time to think it over, but keep in mind, time is something you're a bit short on at the moment."

I stared at the boy. He'd closed his eyes again and was playing another song, a sort of happy jig that didn't fit the mood at all. I closed my eyes and turned away from him, hand on my forehead. My dad had never told me about any creature called Canlagh. He looked like some kind of spirit, like the ones who would challenge you and then steal your eyes or lure you to your death in the ocean. Some of the stories said that if you ignored them, they'd leave you alone, but he was still playing that stupid song! I whirled around.

"How do I know you're not some sort of—some sort of demon? How do I know you aren't after my blood? Maybe you wish to possess me or make me go crazy? I don't know if you're really there, after all—I *could* be crazy! I'm distraught, I'm over-tired, I've been prone to delusions in the past, and I don't know if I—"

"Slow down, Jeannie, and I'll answer your questions," he said. "First off, the only devilish things about me are my looks and rapier wit. And my mother, I suppose, but I'm really more like my father. If you're looking for demons you'd have better luck under your bed or in the fireplace or in the kitchen sink. Anything else?"

I was speechless for a moment. He hadn't even opened his eyes. "How do you know my name?" I said, slowly.

"Now, that's a more reasonable question. To answer: I read it."

"Well, that's not a very reasonable answer. Where did you read it?"

"In the Devil's book."

I huffed in surprise. "You—"

"I'm only joking! Sorry, that was uncalled for." He sighed and sat up, propping his violin on his knee. "It's carved on your bed." He pointed at my bedstead with his bow, where I'd written "JEANNIE" with a rock when I was seven. "Any other questions?"

"You said I need to find a new soul."

"Yes."

"What exactly do you mean by that?"

"Just what I said. A journey. A quest, if you like."

"Hah, well. It seems this quest has already ground to a halt. We're on an island. There's only the beach, the house, and some rocks and grass." My heart was beating quickly, but my apprehension had subsided enough for me to speak calmly.

"And a boat."

A flash of lightning illuminated the room. The ground rumbled. "Hah! I'm not sailing in this weather! That's suicide!"

"It's suicide to stay here, Jeannie." Canlagh stood and took a few steps toward me. I backed into the hallway and looked at the front door. What on Earth was he talking about? I was fine where I was.

"It's raining hard…" I said.

"I can't make you do anything, Jeannie, but you can make yourself. You're running out of time quicker than you think."

"You're scaring me." My mind was at war with itself. I knew I wanted to leave this sad and lonely place that was killing me. But this place, this island, these feelings…they were the only things I knew. Leaving meant changing.

"You have to do what you've only dreamed of. Something only a child would think is possible."

Water was lapping up under the front door. I ran into the kitchen and yelped—the bucket by the fireplace was overflowing. I pulled the front door open and the wind almost knocked me over.

The sea had risen up to our garden. Leaves floated in two inches of water. The rest of the island down to the dock couldn't be seen. The only thing signifying there might have been a dock was my father's fishing boat pitching around in the distance.

"My boat!" I shouted. "How could this happen?" I turned around to where Canlagh now stood, with tears streaming down my face. "What did you do?"

"What did *I* do? I can't control the sea! Now I suggest we get going before your beloved ocean drowns your house with you in it."

"Wait—"

"I told you we didn't have much time. We need to get to the boat now."

"The boat—how will we get to the—"

"It'll be all right." An excited grin crossed onto his face. Once again, his violin vanished into smoke. "Collect anything you might need."

I ran off to find a sack. I returned to the front door a minute later having filled it with potatoes, a needle and thread, and some extra clothes. At the last minute, I snatched my father's pipe from the fireplace mantle. I put on my father's coat, shoved on my galoshes, made sure I had my pocketknife, and stepped into the garden.

"Well?" I asked. I looked left at Canlagh, wondering if he expected me to swim all that way dressed like I was.

"Let's get a move on," he replied, offering me his hand. Cautiously I took it. I was almost surprised that it was solid and warm. Lightning struck once again in the distance, and I jumped. Canlagh started walking forward, but I stayed rooted to the spot. When Canlagh got as far as my arm would let him, he squeezed my hand and I found myself being propelled forward by my legs.

The water came up around my boots. Canlagh kept walking. My steps became stiffer as I braced myself against the drop off that I could see coming. Canlagh started going faster and I prepared to hold my breath.

"Don't be afraid, Jeannie," Canlagh shouted over the pounding storm, "I've got you."

We leapt off the hill, but instead of the cold shock of water I was expecting, I felt something come up under my feet. It almost threw me off balance and I gasped as I looked down through the clear water at the beach a few feet below me.

At the next flash of lightning we broke into an unsteady run, sloshing over the surface of the sea to where the fishing boat jumped around in the waves. The sea, though unexplainably solid, was still stormy and fluctuating up and down. It was like walking during an earthquake. I almost tripped a few times, and water splashed up around my knees and into my face. Gasping and wet, I clambered into the boat and collapsed onto the sagging wooden bench. My wet dress clung to my knees under my heavy coat.

My mind was racing. My heart was beating wildly. There was that ecstatic pressure in my throat and jaw that comes when you want to shout but feel you shouldn't. I put my head in my hands and started laughing in spite of everything.

"That was terrifying!" I yelled.

"That was the first step," yelled Canlagh. "Now, the second step is sailing to the end of the world."

I threw my bag below deck, dumped the water out of my galoshes, and went to the stern. "Sailing to the end of the world," I repeated. "Svenishta." With the next bolt of lightning, I turned the key. Miraculously, the motor started immediately, and as soon as I put my hand on the tiller to steer, there was a strange halt in the storm. The wind died down. The thunder and lightning stopped. It was still raining, but the drops were finer.

I took a deep breath of cold air and turned my head to take a last look at my house—the only thing left above water. It looked haunted now. The hairs on my arms and neck raised as I thought about my house being beaten to driftwood and washing up on the mainland.

"You should go to bed below deck," Canlagh said. He was sitting precariously on the side of the boat.

I was staring past the front of the boat, at the dark horizon. My heart was pounding at the thought of perhaps seeing the sun rise—maybe in a couple of days.

"Jeannie?"

"Are you ever afraid that if you fall asleep you'll wake up and realize that what you thought was real was a dream, and you're really just..." the rest of my sentence got lost in a thought. I was sailing to Svenishta. What was Svenishta? It was a fairyland at the end of the world. A myth. A dream. I was chasing down a bit of mist that flit farther away the closer you got. For some reason that didn't worry me.

"Are you all right, Jeannie?"

"Just fine."

Canlagh stood and walked over to me. He put his hand over mine on the tiller. "Do you want to get some rest? I can watch the boat."

I shook my head. My hand was gripping the tiller so tightly that my knuckles were white.

Canlagh resumed his place at the side of the boat. "You know, usually, a human would collapse after running across the ocean during a storm. They're not used to that much magic."

"Hm?" I used to wish that I would wake up from a nice dream and it would be true—that a beautiful movie star would come for dinner. That there were fairies in my mother's rose bushes.

"I asked you if you were a good witch or a bad witch."

"Hm." Later, I wished that the war was over, and that Dad would come home.

Canlagh started playing his violin again, and my mind drifted away.

✦

My stomach rumbled. I stood up and looked at the gray sky, wondering what time it was. I hadn't realized until now that I'd forgotten to bring a watch. It was morning, still overcast, but it wasn't storming anymore.

I walked forward and checked that we were still sailing east.

"Back to reality, are we?" Canlagh called.

"I'm not so sure," I responded, turning my stiff neck to glance at him.

"Well, dreams are more fun anyway."

"*Is* this a dream?"

"Heavens, no. All this work just to realize you'd been asleep the whole time?"

"Then for Pete's sake what are you talking about?" I said, exasperated.

"It's nicer if you believe it's a dream. It's easier to do things you wouldn't normally do."

"And what exactly am I *doing?* What next?"

"You'll know when we get there. You're worrying too much."

"I'm *worrying* too much? Isn't this a little bit important? My soul and all that?" I threw my hands up in the air.

"Of course it's important. That's why you shouldn't worry."

I threw my hands in the air and groaned. I stomped down the couple of steps into the cabin. I needed breakfast.

I found the contents of my sack strewn across the floor. "Great. Easter egg hunt time." I got down on my hands and knees and crawled around, picking up the stray potatoes. I turned on the cookstove. As I stirred the potatoes I thought about my dad. We'd taken a lot of trips together on this boat when I was young. I used to pretend I saw mermaids in the distance and point them out excitedly to him.

"Look, Daddy! Mermaids!"

"You're right, Pumpkin! A whole school of them off the port side."

"Daddy?"

"Yes?"

"Are they really real?"

Dad would look off into the distance and say, "Well, I'll tell you what I do know about mermaids and fairies and things. Believing in them makes the world seem a whole lot nicer, doesn't it?"

"Yes," I agreed, laying my head on his chest.

But when the war started, I wasn't so sure anymore if all those things existed. If Svenishta was real, why hadn't any of the magical beings there stopped the torpedo that sunk my dad's ship?

The boat rocked dangerously and I stumbled forward. Stupidly, I thrust my hand out to catch myself and I hit the stove. I pulled my hand back, swore under my breath, and turned the stove off. I ran back up to the deck.

"What was that?" I said.

"It could be a number of things," answered Canlagh. "Angry nymphs, a dragon, a witch..."

The boat jerked so violently that I fell and rolled to where Canlagh sat. He wasn't even phased. I looked to the starboard side of the boat just in time to see a giant orange pillar shoot out of the ocean, drenching me and the deck as water sloshed down the stairs.

"Definitely a dragon." said Canlagh. He stood up and put his hands into his pockets.

I looked at him incredulously through my wet hair.

Canlagh smiled and looked back at the giant snake-like monster that was now towering over my swaying fishing boat, its giant mouth open and dripping salty water and hot air. It only moved to blink its eyes.

"What does it want?" I whispered, arms out defensively.

"Why don't you ask? He seems like a reasonable fellow."

I turned back to the monster. I stared at his white teeth. My mouth wouldn't open.

Canlagh came up behind me and patted me on the shoulder. "What can we do for you?" he shouted to the beast.

A rumbling noise so deep and loud spilled from the dragon that covering my ears wasn't enough to muffle it. It wasn't for a few seconds that I realized he was speaking.

...fisher's daughter sails so far on troubled waters with a Tschalla Aatmach as a guide...

"We seek safe passage to Svenishta."

My name is Mizu Kasai, the dragon's mouth didn't move as he spoke, *I guard the gate to Mithyavayi. The human girl cannot go farther without proper authorization.*

I started at the name Mithyavayi. That's what my father's stories had called the spirit world. Was I dead? What did he mean, "proper authorization?"

"She's seeking her Aishling."

The human girl cannot go farther without proper authorization.

"What does he mean?" I whispered to Canlagh.

"You need a token. *'An object pure to prove the heart, an oath of strength to prove the soul'* and whatnot."

"I don't have a token."

"Check your sack."

"My sack—but what does a token look like?"

"You'll know it when you see it."

My heart sank into my stomach as I walked on shaky legs to the cabin. I'd come so far, and now a dragon had thrown a monkey wrench into the works. A dragon—ha! A dragon and an infuriating fiddle-playing ghost-boy. "Mithyavayi," I muttered.

I dumped out the contents of my bag onto a shelf. I rolled the potatoes into a corner and looked at what was left. I shook my head at the needle and thread, the extra socks—nothing notable there. I picked up my father's pipe and rubbed my thumb on the wood. This, at least, meant something.

I weighed it in my hand and heard something rattle. I furrowed my eyebrows and shook it harder. What could've gotten stuck in Dad's pipe?

I looked into the bowl. My eyes widened at something bright and bronze glinting back at me. I turned it out onto my hand. It was some kind of coin, the size of my thumbnail and embossed with a Chinese dragon coiled around a tiny crescent moon. I'd never seen it before in my life.

I ran back on deck, holding the coin so tightly that it bit into my fingers. I clutched my father's pipe in my other hand.

"Is this a token?" I showed it to Canlagh.

"Ask the dragon, not me."

I looked up at the towering dragon. "Um," I cleared my throat. "Is this okay?" I held my hand palm-up above my head for the dragon to see.

The dragon brought its head down to my level, and I skittered backward so I wouldn't get smashed by his massive jaw. Steam poured out of his mouth as he spoke:

"With these possessions you may cross the portal to your sacred goal."

The dragon opened his mouth, exposing teeth as white as a cloud. Steam escaped from within his deep throat into the air. I held my breath, waiting for whatever came next. I felt a sudden cold wind as the dragon sucked in, and I closed my eyes against a hot gust of steam.

+

The sun was brighter than I remembered. The sky, splotched with a few white clouds, was an unnatural blue, warm and cool at the same time. The dragon was gone, as was the token. My shoulders relaxed, and I looked around. We were bobbing in place in the middle of a grouping of small, grassy, mound-shaped islands. A larger island covered in thick trees was half-visible a little farther off behind a thin mist. And the sunlight...

Tears welled in my eyes. I dropped to my knees and covered my face, feeling the light on my shoulders.

"Am I...dead?"

"That's a difficult question for more than one reason." Canlagh pointed toward the largest island. "That's Svenishta. 'The Everything and Nothing.'"

"And that's where I'll find my soul?"

"That's where you'll find your soul."

"And..." I didn't want to say what else I had in my head. But if this was the spirit world, then...wouldn't Dad be here too? "Canlagh...have you ever seen any humans—human spirits—in Mithyavayi?"

Canlagh's face fell. "Jeannie...don't get your hopes up about anything like that. That's not what you're here for, and besides, living humans don't usually see the Chidi. Not unless they have the right kind of soul."

I didn't reply. I didn't want to keep talking about something that I didn't know the outcome of. But another part of my mind wouldn't stop talking. *You're about to get a new kind of soul.*

+

"You'll need to take your boots off, too."

I paused in the middle of taking off my coat, not sure I'd heard him right. "What?"

"We'll have to walk from here. The boat's too big."

I figured walking on water this time would be easier, or at least less strange in the calmer, shallower water, but I didn't understand why I needed to take my boots off. I was deciding whether I wanted to protest.

Canlagh patted my shoulder. "Stop worrying about things before they happen. Go on," he signaled for me to take my shoes off. "No galoshes in the spirit world."

I sighed and held the skirt of my dress in my right hand as I awkwardly tugged off my boots with my left. Canlagh helped me out of the boat and into—or rather *onto* the water. It was warm and came up to my ankles like I was simply standing up in a shallow bath.

"I'll race you there."

"Are you joking? I can't walk on water by myself—"

"I'm not joking. And you're going to lose."

Canlagh dropped my hand and began running toward the island. I screamed, but to my surprise, instead of sinking, I only lost my balance a little. I scowled, and then my scowl turned into a challenging grin, and I took off after Canlagh.

+

Soon the water became mud and the mud turned into dewy green grass. Canlagh slowed, and I caught up with him. We didn't stop running, but my legs didn't ache like I was overexerting myself. Instead they felt sleepy, like they weren't a part of me. I breathed slowly, like I was dreaming. The sudden feeling of cold stone under my bare feet was the only thing that told me this was real.

I was in a circular clearing completely paved with mosaic tiles. It was completely silent, like walking into a vacuum. It was so quiet that I reached up to my ears to check if I'd gone deaf.

"Go over there to that big square stone in the middle," Canlagh said. His voice sounded far away.

I walked across the mosaic tiles to the big red stone Canlagh had indicated. I looked back to ask him what came next, but he was gone. I stared at the open sky framed by jungle trees. The only thing running through my head was *I'm here...I'm here...I'm finished!* "I'm here," I whispered. It sounded so wonderful in my mouth that I said it again, louder. "I'm here!" I clapped my hand over my mouth as the words echoed and the ground began to vibrate.

Something bright blue rose up from the cracks between tiles. It was like a diamond-shaped flame, pulsing and flickering like it was alive. It got higher and higher until it was level with my eyes, and then flew straight at my face. The force knocked me onto my back, and all I could see for a time was white light.

Then a picture came into my mind. It was the night before my dad left. He and I were sitting in half-darkness. He was smoking his pipe, staring straight ahead. I was tired from crying, and just stared at the fire in the fireplace thinking about tomorrow.

Dad started humming. It was his favorite song. He sung it while he worked, while he cooked, while he read...

It was a happy song about pressing forward and having hope—a fast song that you were supposed to sing loudly. He hummed it slowly and quietly and it sounded weak, like he wasn't sure hope was worth anything anymore.

Dad halted his singing and took his pipe out of his mouth. "You've got to keep going Jeannie. Whatever happens, it'll be the right thing." He put his pipe back in his mouth, and continued staring forward.

The white light whooshed out of my vision, and my ears popped. The sound of my dad's voice echoed in my ears, and a gust of sadness swooped over me. I felt like I was late. My father had talked about Svenishta—a place I knew he loved with all his soul—and now I was here, and couldn't see him. It wasn't fair. It wasn't a good ending.

"Jeannie."

I sat up, looking for Canlagh. He was nowhere in sight.

A hand came down on my shoulder. I reached up to check whether it was real and felt rough fingers and human warmth. I looked, and sure enough it was there. It was connected to an arm, which was connected to a shoulder, which was connected to Dad.

HEATHER DRABANT

Windsong Pass

If I'd known they'd kick me off my own ship, I would have turned it around sooner. A mosquito whines in my ear as I drag myself out of the sand and to my feet. My ship becomes a dot on the horizon, with no more than a backward glance, I'm sure. I glare into the sun and turn from the water, the heat slowing everything down. It was a muggy and miserable day before the mutiny, but after that blasted storm almost blew us to bits, I should have expected this. No one wants a captain who shows a lack of storm judgment.

My boots crunch in the gravel as I enter a small seaside town that smells of rotting fish and moldy docks. The chatter of people washes over me—as does a wave of annoyance.

"Good day, sir!" A chipper man with a round face and a bright jacket greets me as I pass, making to shake my hand.

"Nothing good about it, mate. You'll want to keep moving." I push past him, toward the tavern with a chipped gold sign. Wiping the sweat from my brow, I pass through the swinging doors, inhaling deeply. Ah, yes, stale booze and smoke.

A man plays the piano to my left, the uneven keys making awful noises and mixing with the laughter and clank of dishes. I claim a bar stool, slap some coins on the counter with a rattle, and grunt out an order.

The bartender eyes me with interest. "What brings you around here? I don't recognize you and I never forget a face, I'll tell you that much my friend. Say, did you happen to know a Martha? I swear you look like this one bloke I knew and—"

I grip the front of his shirt in a quick movement. "I suggest you find someone else to annoy before I lose my patience." My smile is void of mirth as his eyes bulge, and he nods his heavily blemished face. I release him, smooth out his collar, and give him a firm thump on the shoulders. "Better be getting that order then."

He swallows thickly, stammering, "Yes. Of course."

As I settle back into my seat, someone whistles and a voice comes from my right. "Wow. And here I was thinking maybe you'd leave the poor man be."

I turn with a retort ready to fly, when my eyes land on a tall woman leaning on the counter as if she owned the place, picking at her nails with a knife. Her eyes lock into mine, embers of coal sparking with life, deep and rich as they come. The candles on the tables wash over her like she's meant to wear the flames, smoothing over dark skin and scars. A flash of white teeth in the dark. "I'd be flattered if you stopped."

I straighten my posture to meet hers. "Did you have something to say?" My voice is full of nonchalance as my drink arrives in shaking hands.

She studies my movements. "Only that I don't think you're as tough as you think you are..." She pushes away from the counter. "...and that I know who you are, Alcoy."

My skin bristles, and I stand with a rattle of weapons latched to my belt. "You know nothing about me, darling," I growl.

She laughs, a surprising, sharp, and clear sound that silences the room. "I'm sure you believe that." She saunters out of the room before I can react.

This stranger. Who does she think she is? The tavern stays quiet. "What are you idiots gawking at?" I sneer.

They turn with haste, resuming their card games and drunken conversations. I slam down my drink and cross the room. Bursting from the doors and onto the quiet street, I scan the road for her, cursing as I turn in a circle. She couldn't have moved that fast, yet she's gone.

"I can help you," her voice says from behind me. I jerk around in surprise. She's apparated out of the shadows. She smirks, stepping forward into the light. "I'm sure you've heard of the massive bounty the governor has listed." She moves around me in a calculating circle.

I search my memory for the knowledge. "Ah, yes. For the monster." I match her smirk. "Not interesting enough for me."

She's made her way around me now, and I move to face her. You don't want your back to someone like this.

She chuckles. "Yes, maybe it wasn't. But, if I'm not mistaken, you are in a much more binding situation than you were mere hours ago."

"What would you know about my state of hardship?" I glare.

There's that tinkling laugh again. "I already told you. I know who you are."

"Okay, so say I need some good luck. Why would you help me? What's in it for you?" I lean back on the rail to the tavern.

She swallows. "There are many people interested in this job."

A slow smile spreads across my face. "Ah, I see. You can't do it alone."

"I never said that," she sneers. "Wipe the smug look off your face, or I will."

I straighten. "Oh, I'd love to see you try, darling."

She takes a deep breath. "You need a ship and a crew. I need to kill this monster before anyone else reaches it, and it'll go faster with two of us." She steps closer, and my shoulders tense. "What do you say we help each other out? Split the bounty?"

I click my tongue. I don't want to admit she's right. I could use the money desperately but I have no way to claim it without a ship. Repulsion ripples up my spine as I jab my hand toward her. "50-50."

"70-30," she scoffs. "I have the ship and crew."

My teeth grind. "Very well,"

She grips my hand with a satisfied nod. I pull her toward me with a jerk, close enough to see the dark freckles across her nose. "Don't cross me or you'll regret it, I promise that."

She doesn't flinch, only narrows those startling eyes. "You should keep that in mind for yourself," she warns and yanks her hand out of mine.

As I fix the collar of my jacket with a flick, I notice a man admiring his blade from the other side of the street, his eyes locked onto me and the woman. Everything about him screams fight as he pushes away from the wall and moves toward us. I sigh and reach for my sword, a clean sound of steel sliding through its sheath. "They never learn."

More mercenaries emerge from the shadows of alleyways and saloons. The woman turns in a flash of steel, hurling the intricate knife at a man who'd drawn a brass pistol from his jacket with bad judgment. The knife meets its mark with a gurgle.

I charge at the man creeping up on my left, our blades catching in a cross until I push back, causing him to lose his balance. He comes again, blindly flailing at me like an amateur. Dust stirs as I side step him and slice my blade up his back, kicking him into the gravel as another one comes at me with nothing but fists. I make a move at him, but he's fast, faster than me. He hooks an arm around my neck, arching me back to his height. He bends my wrist, and my sword clatters from my hand. The fingers on my free hand strain for the knife tucked into the top of my boot as I choke on sweat and lack of air. My fingers curl around the hilt, but another knife, the handle design proclaiming the woman as its owner, has already found its place buried deep in his eye.

I push the screaming man off, searching through the fray for the woman. Fellow pirates who perhaps had once been friends have come from everywhere, but through the crowd, I see her scaling a massive brute like a tree and bringing him to the gravel in a ruthless twist. I deflect a poorly thought out attack, disarming a raggedly bearded man with a simple flourish of my blade and kicking his knee in, made easy by his poor stance. I move through the pairs of fighting pirates, pausing to stab another idiot in the kidneys.

Someone tackles me from behind, and I use the momentum against him, throwing him over my shoulders and staking him to the ground, pulling my sword free as I move toward my new business partner.

"How are you fairing?" I shout over the noise and duck as a man flies over my head like a limp doll.

She kicks away from her opponent, the girl falling to the street with her throat staining the rocks. "I'm fairing," she says with labored breath.

A slight man jumps from the roof behind her and I yank her out of the way, the man finding my blade instead. I push him off with my boot, grimacing at the gore.

The woman's sharp eyes track the fighting. "This is our opening."

I look back at her. "Aye."

She jerks her chin toward the dock. "Let's go."

She takes off down the path, and with a curse, I duck after her.

All this for money. When the governor put out the bounty, I'm sure he didn't expect to have to deal with a brawl in the middle of his town, but hey, that's what you earn when you hire pirates. I cut through the side trails leading to the shore, pushing off the rough bark of a palm. The sun casts strange shadows along the sand and grass, long, stretched-out shapes spilling across the ground. I jump down the bank onto the sand, my boots twisting in the loose footing as I run. Her shadow dances along the dock.

"Hey!" I shout, my hands cupping my mouth. "Which one's yours?"

"We'll have to row out," she calls from the dock without slowing her pace and keeps running to what I assume is the dingy she came to shore in.

I vault onto the rotting wood and thump down the planks after her. As we're rowing out to her ship, I curse my situation: a captain, forced to hitchhike. Unacceptable. Once on deck, I speak my mind. "I don't find it fair that you know my name and I not yours."

She plods up the stairs to the wheel, laughing with contempt. I follow her, eyeing her stance at the wheel; not bad. She keeps her gaze ahead as she speaks. "Does this bother you?" A snort. "I hope you didn't think I'd let you sail my ship."

My hands grip the rail, the sun beginning to sink. "If you don't get us killed, who can complain?" My mind strays to where my ship could be at this moment. Who is her captain now?

"Sidney."

My eyes jump to the woman.

"My name is Sidney. But you call me Captain Carver. Got it?"

I grin. "It's a pleasure."

One of her crew rushes up the stairs to us. "Captain, if you'd give us a heading? Aye?"

She checks her distance from the shore with a keen eye. "We merely needed to make some space. We'll head for the next port until Alcoy and I can land on a lead."

The man rushes off to relay the orders. He's wiry, his skin sun-damaged beyond repair, gaunt face with a long, scraggly braid flicking down his back as he moves.

"Your second?" I ask.

She nods curtly.

I scoff, remembering the way my own second had only this morning put a pistol to my head. "Watch your back."

She cuts another look my way. "You know nothing of him. I trust Finn with my life."

I cross my arms, turning to face her at last with a shake of my head. Let her believe it. Not my problem. "Now about that heading…"

+

This was not the correct choice of conversation. We've been arguing for what must be hours and are not any closer to figuring out where the blasted sea monster is. I throw my hands up in surrender. "All right, all right!"

Carver huffs from her side of the table where we'd escaped to her quarters to use the map. Her fingers inch toward the blade beside her.

I slam my palm down. "If you throw one more knife at me, you're on your own, woman. Jesus!"

She flicks her unruly hair off her shoulder, moving her hand back to smooth down the map. "Fine. Then listen. We can't pass through here, it's invested with sirens and you know it."

My fingers rake through my hair to keep them from strangling her. "Yes, of course, but as I stated many times before, we can use the candles."

"We don't even know if the blasted beast is over there!"

I yank one of her knives from the table. "But it could be. Maybe that's why no one else has found it yet."

She mouths something to herself, maybe a prayer. "It's not worth the risk," she says at last. The lantern casts dramatic shadows across her face, making her golden-brown eyes flare. "Sirens have been known to feed on men for weeks, Alcoy."

I rub my face with both hands. "If you weren't prepared to take some risks then why did you take on this job?"

She crosses her arms, but says nothing.

"And call me James." If I hear her address me as Alcoy one more time, I'll break something. Captain Alcoy had a crew and a ship.

She leans over the map again, her forehead creased in thought. Her shoulders tense under her ragged shirt and vest, tucked into the belt full of knives resting on her hips. She sighs in defeat. "If we must pass through Windsong then we'll have to stop at the port. We'll need more wax."

I grin. "There's a girl."

Her eyes dart to me in a sudden glare and her hands clench. "Don't call me girl, Alcoy."

My muscles tense but I lean in to meet her over the map. "Don't call me Alcoy."

We listen to each other's breathing over the bump of waves on the hull until a soft rapping comes from the door.

"Enter," Carver barks.

We both lean back in unison. She folds her arms and crosses her ankles atop the table, the picture of ease. Finn announces our approach to harbor, and he's gone again. The silence stretches on. My elbows press into the table as I survey the primitive pictures depicting the sirens. Lines drawn in red ink.

"Why not call you Alcoy?" she says at last. "I heard you were a proud man, proud of title and name."

"That was before my first mate set a gun to my head and told me to beat it, backed by the entire crew." The memory flashes into my mind. "Captain Alcoy no longer exists."

She breathes deeply. "You white men and your titles." My gaze snags on the exposed part of her neck, a familiar circle of damaged skin curving around it. Her eyes simmer. "You're complaining of hardships to the wrong person, mate. You'll find no sympathy here."

A clock ticks on the wall. The smell of musty velvet and salty sea air wraps around us in a haze as we size one another up. She gingerly removes her boots from the table, standing and moving to the door. "If anything is missing when I return, I'll strand you at this port." She whirls from the room.

"Nothing new," I say to the flame of the lantern.

✛

The small trading port is washed in a veil of orange as the day ends. We see no more than three others out by the docks—none of them hostile, if we're lucky. I rest a hand on the pommel of my sword, eyeing Carver from the corner of my vision. "We'll want to make this snappy."

Annoyance ripples across her features. A smirk settles across my face. "No stopping to browse fineries or the like. I know how you women can be."

She balls her fists but does not break stride. "I can assure you, Alcoy, that will not be an issue." She forges ahead. "Pick up your pace. Wouldn't want to see you tempted by any pleasures of the flesh. I know how you men can be."

I stare at her back as she pushes into the supply store. The night air brushes over my face with the lingering taste of winter. Thoughts of Maria rush at me with such a startling pain my lungs struggle to work. A light dragged from this world too soon, undeserving of the fate she was thrown. Would she have been as quick witted as Carver? Would she have been kind like our mother, brave like our father? These questions will never leave me. What would my sister have become?

I take a steady breath and smooth the straggly hair from my face as I push through the still-swinging door and into the cluttered store, where the prominent smell of leather and dust assaults my senses.

Carver is already speaking with the clerk. "I'm aware of the risks, buddy, now take the money and hand it over."

The man in question has defeat all over his potholed face and pushes the cubes of wax over the counter. "Yer digging yer own grave, lass."

He counts the gold, and Carver takes the purchase, turning to me. "Oh, glad you could make it. Time to go." She brushes past me and is out the door before I can turn on my heel.

I go to follow, realizing too late the hanging basket in my path. It jingles with fishhooks as my head connects with it. I reach to steady it, muttering obscenities. Once free, I jog after her, shaking stars from my eyes. "So, someone advised against our little trip, eh?"

She swings the bag of wax at her side like it could be a weapon. "Yes, of course," she scoffs. "I even advised against it. I still do."

I adjust my collar. "That's neither here nor there. It's the best route and you know it."

I can almost hear her teeth grinding. She turns on the spot, clutching the bag. "You have two choices," she says, holding up two fingers. "You can either shut your gab or stop being an insufferable ass."

My eyebrows rise.

"I'll use this," she warns, shaking the wax. "Don't think I won't." She marches up the ramp and onto her ship.

"Well damn," I say to myself, boarding The Golondrina. "No need to be violent."

Once back onboard, she shows me to a small room near her quarters for the night. It has a sad looking cot rumpled in one corner and a chipped washbasin by the door. I push on the cot, the springs complaining loudly, and laugh.

"Be grateful I didn't put you with the crew." She rolls her eyes, closing the door behind her like a prison grate. Dust plumes into the air as I sit on the cot, the only source of light a candle left flickering on the floor. I watch the flame dance, trying not to think of Maria and thinking of nothing else. It's her face that sticks to my minds-eye as I snuff out the candle with damp fingertips and let the sea lull me to a fitful sleep.

+

The morning wind bites as I stand near Captain Carver. The world is silent save for the sounds of the waves and men working. If the monster isn't in Windsong Pass, I can't begin to suspect where it could be. But that's a problem for after we've followed this lead, which is nothing but a gut feeling from experience—

"You screamed last night."

My attention snaps to Carver.

She keeps her eyes on the horizon as she speaks. "Such pain filled your screams, as if all you loved was being cleaved from you."

The railing cuts into my hands. "You'd do better not to comment."

She doesn't heed my warning. "I know because I once shared those screams with everyone on this ship." When she looks at me, a small glance in my direction, her eyes hold unexpected warmth. "This is not a place you should be ashamed of your pain, James."

Her words knock me back a step. This woman, this stranger, has surprised my judgment.

No words come to me as the sea wind kisses my face.

"We've all known that type of suffering here," she says.

I believe her. I've heard stories of the slavers and the raids that make even me shift uncomfortably in my clothes. Before I can even begin to come up with a response, she moves away. "We should tend to our weapons," she calls over her shoulder.

The crew's tension rises as we sail along, the well-worn fear wafting off them. Sirens, the bloody, haggard enchantresses of the sea, ready to rip us apart all the way to the bone. No man should willingly sail into those waters. But none here have sought to leave. Not a single one stayed at the port. How has she managed this kind of loyalty?

Carver sharpens her knives in a hypnotizing pattern, the sunlight glinting off the blade. The scars along her neck draw my attention again as she focuses on her task.

"How old were you?" I ask, working on my own blade.

Her motions pause for a beat, barely enough to notice. "When?" Her neutral tone is full of careful steel.

I scan her posture, sure I'd find matching scars on wrists and ankles. "You know what I'm asking."

Her eyes meet mine, always so startling. "Your question has no answer. There was not a sudden shift of freedom to chains, James." She buries the deadly knife inches from my face into the door to her quarters. One of her men glances but says nothing as I watch the handle vibrate. "I was born in them." She yanks the dagger out of the wood.

Anger flares in my chest. How many stories match hers? Countless, endless.

Her eyes spark. "Keep the pity off your face or I'll cut it out of your eyes."

"No, you won't." I laugh around my empathy. "You need me, remember, Sid?"

She moves to her next knife. "You can live without eyes. So don't push me. And don't call me Sid."

A laugh chokes out of me. "Now who's being picky about titles, hmmm?"

She glares, but a smile plays at the corner of her mouth.

"I watched my family be massacred when I was young." The words float out of me, a soft acknowledgment of her suspicions.

Our stares meet again with unspoken understanding. It was supposed to be a straightforward voyage to my father's new command post. Simple. Easy. Until the pirates arrived. I watched my little sister be gored like a fish, my parents cut down and tossed to the sea. That was the day my heart turned black. She watches my face, is maybe about to say something.

But Finn shouts from the wheel. "Looks like bad news, Captain."

Carver rushes to the helm and pulls out her telescope, cursing. I follow suit. I'd noticed the pickup in wind but had hoped against a storm system. I try to shake away those bloody images that follow me like ghosts. "Can Golondina handle it?" I ask.

She stares out at the dark clouds forming ahead of us. Ocean stretches on in both directions, nowhere to seek shelter, leagues from Windsong Pass.

"Carver?" I press.

She collapses her telescope, turns on her heel, and marches to the wheel. "She can make it."

Finn lets the wheel spin and she catches it deftly, barking orders I would have given. The ship gains speed as the sail catches the storming wind, and rain spits at us as Golondina bursts into the system. Wind rips at my jacket, rain claws at my eyes as I grip the railing in front of the wheel. We should be able to pass through, I repeat to myself, my skin going clammy trying to find grip. My boots slip on the sodden wood. I squint over my shoulder at Carver, her teeth gritted and arms shaking with strain. But she's holding it. The salt water burns my eyes, my hair plastered to my face like seaweed as The Golondina barrels through the choppy waves. Images from the storm that cost me my ship and the loyalty of my crew force their way to the front of my mind. How had a storm snuck up on me twice in one week?

I hear a shout, someone crying out, someone's screaming *man overboard*. I dash down the stairs, and the sea pitches me off my feet as I stumble toward the rail, pushing through people and sloughing off my jacket and sword before propelling myself off the deck and into the biting waves.

The cold shocks my system as I swim toward the struggling figure. My eyes burn as I grab his shirt in a vice grip, dragging us back to the surface. "I've got you!" My words are lost to the storm as I cough around them, swimming with my free arm back toward the ship, which is making slow progress to my benefit.

"Throw a rope down!" I holler up to the shadows of faces at the rail. My head sinks below the thrashing waters, my fist still locked onto the boy as I work to gasp in another breath above water. A rope ladder slaps down in front of me at last, and I hook a boot onto it, my free arm straining as I position the boy onto my back. "Hold onto me!"

He's shaking but conscious as his hands lock round my neck and I strain to pull us up. Shivers race along my skin as I collapse back onto the deck, lungs straining to keep up. Hands pat my shoulders, but there is no time to celebrate. We aren't out of the storm yet.

I force myself to my feet and brace on the slick rail, pushing away and back toward quarterdeck where Carver still grits her teeth. Her hands are bloody, and I lunge for the wheel as I sense us tip and sway, with a creak and a groan. My hands burn as we both muscle the ship back into place.

✦

Hours later, when we're in the clear, Finn takes over to sail the smooth waters. I spit the salt from my mouth, my hair hanging in clumps as I sink onto the planks next to Carver, utterly soaked.

"Well, Carver, that wasn't so bad, eh?"

She cuts a glare at me, but smirks. "I wouldn't relax just yet." She heaves herself to her feet, offering me a hand. "And call me Sidney."

Her hands, strong, slender and rough with sea life, pull me up. "Sidney it is."

She inclines her head. "I saw what you did, for Milo. He's one of our youngest and—" she doesn't need to finish for me to understand.

"I may not be the most morally inclined person but I'm not about to let someone drown."

She breaks the look, her attention on the horizon. "We're nearing Windsong Pass. I hope you're right about this, James."

I trace her profile with my gaze, her hair pushed back in the wind. "Me too."

Her mouth forms a line of contemplation. "You asked me why I'm risking so much for this bounty. It's simple: the kind of money that is being rewarded can provide freedom to many. To the ones I left behind in chains."

Her reason makes mine look pale and weak. She wishes to liberate people. I wish to regain my place on the waves for no one's benefit but my own. But is that all? There must be more. But these are questions that will have to wait.

The sun is high by the time we reach the pass, the mouth of it narrow enough to cause even more nerves. "We'll fit." Carver... Sidney says at the wheel once again.

I nod in agreement while tying my hair back. Once the crew weighs anchor, I jump down from the quarterdeck, pushing off from the railing and landing soundly, gaining the crew's attention. "Okay. I've dealt with Sirens before so you'll want to listen to me." I assume Sidney gave a sign of allowance, because they all turn their focus to me.

The bag of candle wax thuds as I swing it onto a barrel. "This is going to be an important barrier between you and Davy Jones' locker, 'ight?" They all bob their heads with unease. I open the cinched burlap and explain the process of using small amounts of wax to plug their ears. "Is everything clear?"

Murmurs ripple through the crew.

I narrow my eyes, the boards creaking with each step forward. "I said, is everything clear?" My voice rises.

"Aye!" they chorus.

I sketch a bow. "Much better. Let's begin."

✦

Mist curls over the glassy water's surface as I push myself out of the rowboat with a splash. The wax earplugs are working so far but the sirens will be the true test. The water is shallow here but still passes my knees. It promises to be a hassle when the fight breaks. Not ideal, but we're here now and this is what we have. I tap Sidney on the shoulder and gesture to her weapons. She nods, pulling her twin swords free. The comforting weight of my own sword rests in my palm as we trudge through the lukewarm water. A shadow passes over us. I eye a looming boulder that jets out overhead. It's unsettling not being able to hear. The silence is stifling.

It happens fast. One minute, I'm counting the men and women following us, and the next, Finn is sucked under the surface like a doll.

My boots push into the sand as I slog toward where he went under. A flash of mangled scales catches my vision to the left. My heartbeat thunders in my ears as I dive after it, catching the fin of its tail and pulling, pulling, until it turns, its face stretched and covered in scales, its sharp teeth locked around Finn's neck as it seethes at me. I plunge my steel into its tail and lunge for Finn as it howls, sending bubbles to the surface. My sword pulls free and I drag Finn away as blood fills the water. He bursts to the surface, gasping.

I scan the water for Sidney. The sirens came out of nowhere, dozens of them, mouths wide open and singing, though I hear nothing but my own blood racing through my body, my heart pounding in my chest. The men are faring well, but where is Sidney? I shove Finn toward a boulder, hoping he makes it to safety, and turn to look for her. My eyes snag on movement near me and—

The injured siren lunges out of the water, knocking me back under with painful strength. Her sharp nails dig into my neck as I struggle, my sword knocked from my hand. My nails claw at her as my lungs scream, her snake-like eyes filling with malice as I yank on her gnarled hair.

I throw my strength into flipping us. I gasp in a gulp of air before splashing back under the surface and drive my knife into her heart. Her body shudders, and I push away, swiping my sword out of the silt and blood.

I've lost my earplugs. I scan the water with frantic eyes but—

Calm washes over me, the sound of beautiful, pure singing. There is no danger, it says. You may rest. My sword arm lowers as a cry sticks in my throat at what's before me. They're not ugly. They're beautiful. The fight drains from me as I take a staggering step toward my family. They lay along the rocks, laughing. They beckon me, my father's crisp uniform un-bloodied, my mother's throat un-blemished, her pearls resting around her neck un-broken. And Maria, dark curls bouncing as she calls to me. "James!"

Maria's voice is wrong but she smiles at me. She reaches for my hand, our fingers touch. "James!" The shout sounds far away then something slams into my chest.

Sidney. She shakes me by my shirt. Her wax is gone too, but how—there's no time for questions. I shove Sidney out of the way, skewering a siren on my sword as she lunges for us.

"We need to shove through or we're goners!" Sidney yells over the screaming men and alluring songs that pull at my mind.

My head bobs too many times in acknowledgment, my vision swimming. I lock onto the cave entrance, a gaping hole of shadows a good twenty yards away. We charge for it, a roar ripping through me as we do, my sword finding siren after siren, blood splattering across my face and running into my mouth, bitter and toxic. Illusions pull at me but I ignore them. I did not skewer my sister. I did not slice my mother's throat.

A claw rakes down the side of my face in a searing slash before its owner is cut down. I look away from the bodies floating face down in the water, being ripped apart as we pass, sirens wearing faces of loved ones. Sidney shows nothing but determination as we slaughter the sirens. What does she see? What faces haunt her?

We stumble to the mouth of the cave, the opening much larger now. A trail of gore and severed limbs behind us, we look at each other in the new silence. Bloody water drips from her features.

"Let's finish this." I hold out my hand.

She grips it, her hand slick with blood and salt. "God willing."

We plunge into the darkness.

Two sensations strike me immediately: the smell and the looming weight of being watched. We have long since released the other's grip but I can still feel the callousness of her small, deadly hand pressed in mine. Jagged rocks jump out from the darkness as we move through the cave, water to midcalf. A shiver ripples over me and I grip the hilt of my sword tighter to keep it from dragging in the salty brine.

"What do we know about this monster?" Sidney says, almost to herself.

"It's big," I offer.

Her glare reaches me even through the darkness. "Do we know any weaknesses? Strategies?"

I think back to the sunken ships. "I remember a surviving sailor mentioning to stay away from the tail." Another fact leaps to the front of my mind, the warning dying in my throat as a thousand eyes blink into existence a few feet in front of us. "It also has camouflage skills," I whisper unhelpfully late.

Sidney makes a sound of indignation. Her knives sing through their sheaths as she frees them. The beast stays still as if it hasn't seen us yet. My hand switches, restless to fight. The beast screeches a glass-shattering sound, all those yellow eyes locking onto us.

"I'll take left!" I yell over the vibrating cave walls, diving to one side of the monster.

Sidney swears colorfully as the beast takes a chunk out of the ground we stand on, spitting out a shower of dirt and rock. My eyes try to adjust to the darkness, the shape of the monster undefined. Its tail slices through the water, lashing out at every sound we make on either side of it. I run for its back. Its cries rattle the rocks above us as my blade drives into its spine.

My hands burn as I'm thrown, my sword coming with me as I tumble through the silt. I cough on seawater. "Don't touch it!" I yell to Sidney who, from the sounds of it, is fighting with its tail.

"Too late!" she yells.

My hands blister from whatever coats the blasted beast. I scramble back as its maw snaps for me, missing by inches and tearing out a chunk of rock. My sword rips through three of the bloodshot, yellow, orbs as it's pulled back. It bellows, teeth snapping as I dodge another strike, the chaotic echoes of battle bouncing around my head. Its breath smells of decaying bodies and seaweed.

"Sidney!" I duck under its long neck and try not to touch its scaled body.

"It's not a tail!" She yells from the other side of the cave. "It's another head. Oh, shi—"

My legs work hard to run to her "Sid!"

"I'm fine!" She grits out a scream.

I see a fuzzy outline of her slicing through its scales and landing back into the water. The monster's main head catches up with me faster than I react. Its many teeth sink into my leg, fiery pain racing through my body. A roar tears out of me as I slice at its head, trying to force it to release my leg, my skin shredding from the bone as it yanks me through the water.

"James!" Sidney is in battle with the other head. "Hang on. I'm coming!"

I drive my sword into it again, dragging the cut down to its mouth and causing it to release me at last. I fall from its grip, my leg in agony as I hit the watery ground. A scream strains through my teeth as I stand, the salt eating at the wound.

Sidney. Where's Sidney? I hobble as fast as I can. The monster still screams as it moves after me.

"Take that you stupid bastard!" Her blade slices through the second neck, the head falling with a splash, with putrid blood spilling out around us. The monster's remaining head bellows at the loss, snapping toward us and missing, barely.

Sidney grips my arm. "Can you fight?"

My breathing shallows at the blinding pain. "Of course." I heave my sword tip out of the water. "Never better."

Sidney levels her knives. "Then we move now."

We charge for the thrashing monster, Sidney flipping onto its back. I duck a blow, teeth snapping behind me as I slide under its neck, slicing my blade across its throat and springing back to my feet on the other side.

Still not deep enough. My leg buckles from the maneuver but I dodge another strike. "Sidney?"

"I'm a little busy!" she yells back.

"We need to do it at the same time!" The cave shakes around me from the monster's movements. "On three, we sever its head!"

Its teeth miss me by inches.

"One!" I duck under its snapping head, running toward the middle. "Two!" I angle my sword.

"Three!" Sidney yells with me as we both cut through the neck from top to bottom.

The skin tears with a rip. The bone splinters, releasing the head. I step back as it falls—as powerful as a tree crashing into the watery cave floor—sending a wave of mucky water up to my knees. Sidney jumps from its back, as that too collapses. She stumbles from the shaking corpse and into me. I curse as her weight makes my leg give out, slipping with a splash and cushioning her fall. She hisses with pain, pushing back from me with bloodied arms.

"We did it." She laughs with disbelief, her hands still bracing herself on my chest. I can almost make out her face in the dim cave, her eyes alight with victory; a ringlet clings to her damp cheek.

"We did it," I echo. My vision blurs but I reach out shaking fingers to lift the ringlet out of her face. My fingertips brush along her cheekbone as she goes still at the touch. I'm sure it's my imagination when she leans into it—surely a side effect of losing so much blood. All pain shoves its way to the forefront of my mind and a cry bites its way out against my will.

She scrambles off of me, releasing a pent-up breath. "You need medical attention." She slings one of my arms over her shoulders, hoisting me up.

"I'm fine."

She snorts. "Don't give me that, James. Lean on me."

And I do, as we make our way back to sunlight. We both squint into the orange, evening sun. I swallow another cry as the water rises past my mangled leg. Siren corpses float around us, dissolving into sea foam. Human bodies float, too.

A swell of relief washes over us as we spot some of our crewmates tending to wounds on a rocky beach that hugs a jagged edge of the pass.

Finn beams at us as we limp over. A bloodied bandage covers his neck. "It's over then?"

Sidney smiles, glancing at me. "Yes, my friend. It's over."

But as I look at her, at the crew, at the setting sun casting the ship in a silhouette, I feel as though it's the beginning.

MERLIN BLANCHARD

Maskmaker

The flooded loading dock buzzed with motion and emotion as the feet of the Farlander sailors splashed in the ankle-deep water. They rushed between raised platforms and massive Runeships, struggling to haul large wooden crates before high tide rendered the dock unusable.

Serin was silent as he followed his father through the hectic loading dock, eyes briefly skimming over the sailors. He regretted the motion, which had elicited a faint *discomfort*, his emotion expressed in the Coil as the texture of rough fabric. The sailor's faces, however well covered by the cloths, were still too exposed for decency.

The young man's gaze fell back the flooded ground as old memories of his studies resurfaced. The Runeships only set sail when high tide covered the docks, to ensure the water was deep enough for them. Then, the dock was abandoned until the water uncovered it.

Closing his eyes and forcing a deep breath, Serin focused on the dense *resolution* extending from his father. The familiar feeling was a guide amidst chaos of the Coil, which, at the moment, swarmed with the unrestrained emotions of the Farlander sailors.

The young man pushed his own stone-like *resolution* into the Coil, hurrying after his father, steps splashing in water. The older man stopped to wait for Serin, his dense *resolution* softened to a warm *concern*.

Gaze sweeping over his father's ivory mask, with its pristine glint and intricate designs, Serin's own manufactured *resolution* succumbed to *worry*. His certainty of returning to the island was fading with every step.

His father gave a nod, putting an arm around his son's shoulder.

"Remember yourself," the older man whispered, bringing Serin into a hug. The Coil brimmed with soft threads of *compassion*, more comforting than the hug itself.

"Be true," his father spoke, voice shaky as soft threads of blue *sadness* stained the *compassion.* "Be true."

Serin felt the density of *resolve* bubble in his own chest, and let it bleed into the Coil, hugging tighter.

"I promise."

The hug lingered for several moments. Serin's father was the first to release, letting his hands go to his son's shoulders. The Maskmaker focused on his son's eyes for several brief moments, then wandered to look past the young man.

Serin glanced over his shoulder, following his father's gaze.

"Up there," the older man said, letting go as he nodded towards the broad ramp leading into the Runeship. "Be safe."

His words were neutral and quiet, but the dichotomy of the *joyful* and *sad* threads within the Coil colored them with more accuracy and brilliance than any tone could hope to accomplish.

Serin simply nodded, blinking back tears as he turned away, gait slow and firm despite the water.

He paused as he set his foot on the metal ramp, and forced a breath, holding onto the threads of his father's emotions. The young man didn't want to leave. Not yet.

But, after that moment of hesitation, Serin summoned the fullness of his own *resolution*, and walked up the ramp.

With each step, he drew closer into the ship. With each step, an old life ended, and a new one began.

✢

"Work hard, or we'll throw you into the ocean. Got it?"

Serin gave a nod to the old sailor who stood before him. The large man leaned against several wooden crates, his face covered by the strips of cloth required of Farlanders to wear while in port.

Sludgy *grogginess* and the dull thud of *grumpiness* permeated the Coil, surrounding the man in a tight ball as if he'd just woken up from a nap.

The old sailor grunted, waving for Serin to follow him through the labyrinth of boxes and sailors filling the hold.

"You'll address me as Runemaster, no matter what the crew calls me."

The Runemaster's voice was crisp and sharp, despite the *exhaustion* that wove through his emotions. This gave the young man pause. He'd been warned about the dishonesty of the Farlanders, but he hadn't expected to encounter it so soon.

"You'll do as you're told," the old man continued, eyes looking everywhere but at the young man. Sparks of *irritation* began to manifest, "Obey the Captain's rules, and keep doing your work."

They stopped at the far end of the hold, in front of a pair of metal doors. They glowed a slight blue, the light radiating out of the runes marking the doorway. The Runemaster paused in front of the door, eying Serin.

"Never wake me. Ever."

The *grogginess* dissipated, the sludge transforming into the multiplying sparks of *irritation*.

"I don't care what's going on. If I'm napping, you'll leave me alone."

With an abrupt turn, the old man opened the door. It struck the wall with a slam, making Serin have to quickly step through to avoid being hit.

"Nobody's going to wear these wrappings once we leave, so you'll have to get used to seeing faces without them."

Serin felt *irritation* simmer, falling into a rough *discomfort*.

"I don't know what else you Kevans do, but I don't want to hear about any of your island rituals, or other stuff."

Nodding, the young man let the light of *understanding* flood the Coil.

"I will keep this in my heart."

The Runemaster paused and glanced back at Serin. His eyes seemed to crinkle in time with the brief flash of *puzzlement* that passed through the Coil. A blink interrupted the pause, and the old man shook his head.

"Fine. We'll stop by your bunk later. One of your mask-person friends convinced the Captain to give you a room alone, but that's the *only* privilege you'll get. Otherwise, you're getting treated like the rest of the crew."

Serin nodded, letting a small puff of *gratitude* fill the Coil.

Several awkward moments of stagnation passed before the young man remembered why the Runemaster didn't respond to the emotion.

By then, though, it was too late to rectify his mistake. Serin jogged after the retreating form of the old man, sheepish *embarrassment* snaking through his gratitude.

Blue crystals lined the barren metal walls, doing little to alleviate the darkness that lingered in the passage.

"Why isn't the light brighter?" His calm voice echoed slightly.

A small grunt sounded, followed by sparks of *irritation* filling the Coil.

"Captain seems to think proper hall lights aren't needed."

Serin took a breath, unsure how to respond. "What about lanterns?"

"The oil to keep 'em going is too expensive."

"Is there a way—?"

"Boy, if I had a penny for every member of the crew I've argued with about this, I'd finally be able to retire. Quit talking about it."

Serin fell silent, looking down. Out of habit, he let the beginnings of his raw *hurt* and flickering *anger* enter the Coil, keeping them faint. After a moment, he let the faint emotions fill the entire space, trying to detect any change in the Runemaster's emotions.

The hot sparks of the Runemaster's *irritation* still showered down without any regard to Serin's own emotions.

After that moment, the young man withdrew the fullness of his emotions, holding in a sigh as he stared at the back of the old man's dirty white shirt.

Adjusting was going to be harder than he'd thought

⊹

"This is the engine room," the Runemaster said, his voice rising as he pushed the door open. Bright light streamed into the hallway while a continuous humming mixed with intense burning heat. "You'll only come here with another member of my team."

The old man entered the room, and Serin followed quickly after, bowing his head.

This room was much larger and brighter than the hallways, lit with both blue crystals and oil lamps that hung on the walls. Copper piping ran around the room in an odd tangle of twists and turns, each pipe lined with glowing blue runes.

In the middle, there was a large contraption linked to several massive crystals.

"Boy, that over there—"

"You were supposed to be here four hours ago!"

The angry voice that cut off the Runemaster belonged to a woman. She swiftly approached, ducking under one of the pipes and carried a large, dense book in hand.

Serin's gaze snapped down when he realized her face was uncovered.

Unable to suppress the heat of his *shame* and *embarrassment* from filling the Coil, the young man closed his eyes, trying to shove the image of her soft, contorted features out of his mind. The flames of her *anger* beat inside the Coil.

"I told you before, Ivelys, I had to pick up the new assistant."

A pause. Serin felt the woman's eyes flash over him with a sharp burst of *frustration* stoking the *anger*.

"It doesn't take four hours to pick up one person. I know you were napping again, Eand."

"My title is Runemaster," the old man growled, his *irritation* finally sparking into flames of *anger*.

"And mine is Second-Runist," Ivelys retorted, the Coil becoming almost as hot as the room, filled with the flames of both her and the Runemaster's *anger*, "You call me by my title, I'll call you by yours."

There was another pause which let the flaming *anger* simmer, but only slightly.

"Train the boy," the Runemaster responded through gritted teeth, "I've got things to do."

Ivelys let out a scoff. "Right. Like sleeping."

Serin brought his gaze up from the floor to watch as the Runemaster whirled around, striding out of the room. The door slammed shut behind him, shaking the metal wall surrounding it. Serin's gaze fell back down as he heard the woman let out a sigh, her *anger* fading into sparks of *irritation*.

"Always does this..." she muttered, then whirled on Serin. "You, what's your name?"

Serin's gaze flashed up to her neck, forcing himself not to look Ivelys in the face.

"S-Serin."

"Why won't you look me in the eye?"

Gaze dropping back down to the ground, the young decided that staring at footwear was more comfortable than staring at a neck, and took a breath.

"You...your f-face isn't covered."

Serin had to splutter out the word 'face'. He wasn't used to speaking so candidly of such private things.

There was a pause as the Coil filled with jolts of *confusion*, slowly morphing into frozen *outrage*.

"You won't look at my face because it *isn't covered*?"

Shrinking back, Serin closed his eyes, daring a quick nod.

The woman didn't respond. Gritting his teeth, Serin waited, each moment an eternity he felt her *outrage* slowly intertwine with threads of fiery *anger* and *disbelief*. When the flaming emotions came to a searing culmination, Serin flinched as he heard the sound of a step.

Then, in the space of barely a breath, the emotions fell, quenched as flaming *annoyance* replaced them, followed by a loud sigh.

"At least he's not like the others…"

Serin opened his eyes to see Ivelys turning on her heel, and marching towards the engine. Ducking under several inconveniently placed pipes, the young man followed, glancing over the unfamiliar runes inscribed on them.

It wasn't much of a surprise that he didn't recognize them. From what little he understood, Farlander runes had vast differences from the runes of his people. Their runes tended to be more functional and compact in their design compared to the runes of his people, though theirs seemed to use more energy to function.

"Do you know what this is?" Ivelys asked loudly as she crouched next to the engine, interrupting Serin's thoughts.

"Yes."

"Do you know how it works?"

"No."

There was a pause as the woman stared at the engine, then released a sigh through clenched teeth. Her right hand went behind her back, and withdrew an elongated tool with a crystal head. The body looked similar to the runescribers Serin had used in his father's workshop, but the head was too broad to effectively write anything.

The young man held back a yelp of surprise as she stabbed the tool into the runes, working it back and forth in the etched lines. With practiced efficiency, she tore it back out again, almost flinging the globules of black sludge that now coated it across the room.

"These are 'dregs'. It's a waste that builds up as the energy from those large crystals pass through the pipes. We have to maintain these every day, or the runes block up, and the Runeship stops working. Understand?"

Serin nodded, reaching for the tool, eyes cast down so he didn't look at Ivelys' face.

The woman pulled the tool away.

"I don't think you do. What would happen to the ship if the runes stopped?"

Ivelys' fluid *concern* filled the Coil, strained by the strands of *anger* and *irritation* lingering from her encounter with the Runemaster.

"Um...it would sink."

The woman let out a laugh, *concern* solidifying into *derision*. "It wouldn't *sink*. First, the waves would topple the ship faster than a kid knocks over a cup on the edge of a table. Then, everyone aboard would sink to the bottom of the ocean and drown, or try to swim and get every bone in their body broken by the waves, *then* drown. Or, better yet, an aberration finds us before the ship gets beaten down, and then it tears the whole ship apart to get its breakfast. The lucky ones get torn to bits by its claws."

Serin was silent as he stared at the engine, letting the import of the woman's words wash over him. He closed his eyes, letting powerful *recognition* and *understanding* flood into the Coil.

"You're doing an important job," Ivelys continued, slamming her tool, still caked with sludge, onto the rim of a nearby bucket, dislodging the gunk. "And if you skimp out, everyone dies."

The woman crouched, offering the tool to Serin again.

"Any questions?"

The young man paused, letting the lingering threads of *irritation* rolling off of Ivelys simmer.

Questions...

Slowly, Serin reached out to grasp the tool, and quietly asked, "What are the aberrations like?"

The Coil flared with Ivelys' *irritation*, but the emotion twisted into a stagnant *satisfaction*. When the woman finally responded, her voice was slow and measured.

"You don't want to know."

Standing abruptly as the Coil filled with her flaming *anger* and *dislike*, Ivelys ducked under a pipe, walking to the door. "Do all the runes in the room, then you'll be done for the day."

"I have to have a—"

The door slammed shut before Serin could finish, and he was left alone.

Looking at the tool, he nodded to himself, using *resolution* to overpower his *anxiety*. He would just do what he was told.

The emptiness of the Coil left a quiet in his mind, a silence which only broken by a slight rustling, like a wispy breeze skimming over sand. Serin shook his head, and forced himself to jab the tool into the runes etched into the engine. His silken *disgust* at having to disrespect the runes filled the blank space left in the Coil.

Today, he would suffer through committing disrespect. The voices returned when he was idle, and he couldn't afford them twisting his thoughts. Not today.

This time, he would be master.

As Serin dug the dregs out of the lines, the blue runes seemed to glow a little brighter.

+

Serin glanced up from his work as the door slammed open, hearkening the return of the Runemaster. The young man's gaze dropped to the ground as he realized the man's face was uncovered.

"Where's Ivelys?"

The young man let his resurfacing *anxiety* seep into the Coil as he continued to wrench out sludge from a pipe running into the ceiling. "She left, Runemaster."

The Runemaster let out a loud sigh, rubbing his face through the wrap as his *suspicion* became a flood of sparking *irritation*, which then ignited into *anger*.

"I told 'er to teach you..." he muttered, closing his eyes, speech becoming too quiet to hear across the room. His *anger*, however, flared brighter and brighter.

The tool jerked loose in Serin's hand, sending a bit of the sludge flying onto the floor. Depositing the remaining stuff into a bucket next to him, the young man scooped up the free bit with the filthy head of his tool. If he waited too long before cleaning the dregs up, they would begin to eat through the floor, and Serin wasn't keen on leaving spots like that during his first job.

"Wait. She left you to do dreg duty *alone*?"

Serin looked up at the Runemaster, primed to give a response to help alleviate the man's flaring *anger*, but the man stormed over, ripping the tool from the young man's grasp, and stabbing it into the bucket.

"You missed the dinner bell," the old man said. He placed a large hand on Serin's shoulder, his raging *anger* softened only by thick threads of *concern*, which worked to contain the flames in some part. "But we might be able to get you something to eat if we move fast. Follow me, maskboy."

Serin paused, but quickly stood, letting slight taste of his *displeasure* with the epithet filled the Coil. It still felt more natural to send them to float free in that space, even if the others couldn't feel his emotions,

It was all the young man could do to keep up and keep from getting lost, between the confusing turn and the old man's long strides. The Runemaster strode down the passageways almost at random, going the full length of some, and even taking extra round-about turns at others.

Finally, though, Serin was given time to catch his breath as the old man pounded on a large wooden door.

"Open up, Valt!"

Silence followed for several moments before the sound of shuffling footsteps echoed through the door. A sliding click met the young man's ears as the door opened a crack, letting out slivers of light, and revealing the face of a man. He had greasy black hair tied back into a short ponytail. Serin looked down before he could see the man's face— assuming it was uncovered—but he could feel the slick *displeasure* that entered the Coil.

"Eand, I've told you before: I don't serve anything to anyone after dinner, so quit pounding on my door."

The Runemaster stepped forward, wedging his foot in the door. A faint glimmer of his *satisfaction* shone in the Coil, slipping around the man's *displeasure*.

"Valt, I've got a new recruit here who hasn't gotten any food—"

"How stupid do you think I am? This is the third time this month you've tried that. Now pull that foot out of the door. You're not getting anything else until breakfast."

"He's—"

"I'll report you to the captain if you don't *get out*."

Serin felt the Runemaster's *anger* flare up again, burning out that glimmer of *satisfaction*. The young man tensed himself, waiting for another shouting match.

However, the Runemaster slowly removed his foot, letting the door slam shut and lock again.

A sigh came from the Runemaster.

"Guess it was worth a shot," he mumbled, resting a hand against the door. He looked up, turning to Serin. "Let's get you to your room."

Serin tried to keep his *puzzlement* from the Coil as he looked at the man.

"Why are you so worried about me needing food?"

The old man's *concern* overrode the rest of his residual emotions. "Aren't you hungry?"

"I rarely eat this late."

The man shook his head. "Well, on this ship we do. You'll get used to it."

He pushed himself up from the door. "Come on, we're wasting time best spent sleeping."

The Runemaster lumbered down the hallway, suppressing a yawn with his hand, Serin following close after.

+

Over the next few days, as he attempted to learn the many duties he was assigned, Serin found few opportunities to enter the Runeship's mess hall. However, Serin was grateful for this. It meant he could eat his food alone. Or, at least, mostly alone. Sometimes Ivelys would remain nearby to instruct him or ask questions. When it came time to eat, he would have to go hide in the corner for privacy.

From what he'd gathered, it appeared that the crew regularly ate in the same large room, watching each other devour food with uncovered faces.

The practice sounded obscene, and Serin was happy to avoid it for as long as possible. But, for the discomfort he avoided, things aboard the ship were not growing easier.

Serin's attempts at figuring out how to express emotions without the Coil were becoming less and less successful. The young man rarely was able to look others in the eye, and that, paired with the challenge of keeping the Coil active amidst the combination of unbridled and unrestrained emotions, created a continual emotional exhaustion.

The Coil helped him to understand what the crew was feeling, but, ever present in Serin's mind was the coming of the day when the energy of the crystal in his mask would be utterly spent.

The crystal powered the runes on his mask allowing access to the Coil, and without more crystals, Serin estimated losing access to the Coil within two weeks.

Serin had spent several weeks attempting to find was to procure replacement for the crystal inside his mask on the ship, as bringing any of his people's crystals off of Keva was forbidden. Asking Runemaster Eand and Ivelys about it individually, though, only resulted in similar answers about the strict control of the crystals to ensure the ship was always able to maintain its schedule. There were barely enough to spare in case of an emergency, so his chances to receive one, at best, were slim.

Serin found himself turning off the runes on the inside of his mask at the end of each day to preserve as much energy as he could.

Without the Coil, though, the young man found a hole opened in the back of his mind. It was dark and cold, filled with whispering rustlings. In the times he was free to deactivate his connection to the Coil, Serin filled the void in his mind by studying the Farlander runes around him, delving into their formation and practical uses to fill the void.

But at night, when he sat by his bedside, Serin found that other things tried to fill the emptiness.

Voices, similar to the ones he'd heard back in his homeland, whispered quiet words of darkness, hate, and deceit, as if to try to convince him of the futility of his life, his position, and his efforts.

They spoke heresies, babbling of the return of the Lady of Mists, an old legend of his people, mumbling that she would arise from the deep, would come for him and his people.

Serin tried to ignore the voices. During these times, he kept the Coil on longer, and lingered around the other crewmembers.

No matter how exhausted he was by nightfall, though, the voices whispered in his mind. Their quiet mutterings would keep him up for hours, their inane words a poisonous honey. When young man could endure no more, he would pull on his mask, activating the Coil, focusing on his own fearful emotions to drive out the voices. This was only a temporary remedy, for it failed when the crystal finally ran out.

✢

Serin worked some sludge out of a close grouping of runes inscribed into the copper pipe, careful not to glance towards Ivelys, who was reading through the same dense book she'd had when the young man had first come on.

Serin was guessing from the recent lack of yelling that she and the Runemaster had settled some kind of unsteady truce.

Dropping the dregs into the bucket, the young man found himself dissatisfied with the ways the sailors dealt with problems. If these people wore Kevan masks, the conflict would have been resolved long ago, and maybe never would have occurred in the first place.

Serin reached out to let some of his *frustration* into the Coil. Instead, he found it absent.

Reaching up to touch the runes on the chin of the mask, he let out an unconscious sigh. Immediate *displeasure* bubbled up within the young man at that dispelling of air. He was picking up Farlander habits.

"What's wrong?"

Ivelys' voice startled the young man, who called out as he dropped the tool and stumbled back from the pipe, right into an overhanging pipe.

Rubbing the back of his head, Serin brought his gaze up to the woman's bare neck, but, after an awkward moment, shifted his view so he was staring at the wall past her shoulder.

"I forgot to do something," the young man responded, brushing the runes on the inside of his mask. Sometimes when the runes ran low on power, they turned off without warning, and just had to be turned on again.

Several seconds passed without the return of the Coil, and *worry* blanketed over his *displeasure*.

Why weren't the runes activating?

"It isn't anything important, is it?"

Stooping down to grab the tool with one hand, ignoring the soreness on his head, Serin used his other hand to repeatedly brush the runes. Each motion, however, refused to coax back the comforting hum of energy against his skin.

"I…"

Serin stood numbly, staring at the ground. The last respite was gone, his primary defense against the voices.

Silence followed. The young man could feel Ivelys' gaze boring into his forehead.

The Coil *was* important. It was almost as important as wearing his mask. But how could he make a Farlander understand that?

"It was."

A sigh came from the woman. "You don't need to go fix it right now, do you?"

"I…am unable to, now."

In the ensuing silence, Serin reflexively grasped for the Coil as he searched for emotions to help him understand how to talk to Ivelys. The emptiness of the air reflected the emptiness of the void in the back of his mind. A gnarled knot of tense *dread* formed in the young man's stomach, as his longing for the Coil grew stronger.

"Well, what is it?"

Serin's gaze flicked up, almost to Ivelys' face. Stories had said that Farlanders showed all their emotions on their face, and he wanted to know what she was feeling. Needed to know what she was feeling.

The temptation to look, only briefly, pressed against his thoughts.

"I...I don't think you would be able to understand."

Jabbing his tool back into the runes, the young man pushed himself to dive back into the work. He needed to fill the void somehow, some way.

"No. Put that down, and look at me for once."

The weight of the woman's tone slammed into Serin. He paused, gripping the tool tighter as he closed his eyes and took a breath. He'd been told to obey.

Lowering the tool, the young man sat on the ground across from Ivelys, not looking at her.

"It's just my face. It's not *that* ugly, is it?"

Serin slowly opened his eyes, staring past her at the wall behind.

"It wouldn't be respectful," he choked out, closing his eyes again and lowering his head.

The silence that followed drew on a little too long.

"My people believe looking upon an uncovered face is an impure act," Serin stumbled again, his voice growing quieter, "Especially the faces of those who are not family."

"Why?"

Forcing a breath, Serin whispered, "Your face is sacred."

The shock of laughter that burst from Ivelys sent the young man's stomach plummeting. He stood quickly, barely avoiding hitting his head on the pipe again, and returned to his work, head still down.

"Whoa, wait! Sit back down. That's not what I wanted to talk about—"

"I do not wish to be mocked," Serin said, trying to effuse his voice with angry emotion like the Farlanders did. The attempt sounded wrong, like a plant stem attempting to mimic a tree trunk.

"I'm sorry," Ivelys responded, the sounds of her standing accompanying the thud of the book closing. "I didn't mean to offend you. I just didn't expect that answer."

Serin was silent, but slowly looked up. "Then what did you wish to speak about?"

"Give me a moment. I'll cover my face so you can look at me."

Serin scrubbed the rune with his tool as he waited, *doubt* roiling in his stomach. Farlanders liked to use deception to make fun of those around them. Was this one such time?

"Done."

Looking over carefully, Serin saw that Ivelys had indeed covered her face with a makeshift wrap made from her long jacket and several kerchiefs. Since it had to be tied in several different spots to keep both areas around her eyes covered, it looked odd but worked sufficiently. A few small patches of skin were left bare around the eyes

However, he was forced to take a breath as he met her eyes. They were a startling blue, bright and piercing.

"So," said Ivelys' muffled voice as she sat back down, putting a hand up to keep the jacket from falling down her face. "What were you saying about forgetting something?"

Serin looked at her, and took a breath. "Why are you asking now?"

The skin around her eyes crinkled. "I'm tired of reading this book. Now, talk."

The young man reached for the Coil out of instinct in an attempt to read Ivelys' emotions. The knot in his stomach tightened as it met the emptiness. "What do you already know?"

"Besides what you've told me? Nothing."

Serin glanced down, closing his eyes for a moment. Slowly sitting, he then looked up at the woman.

"The masks my people wear are special, sacred things—"

"You obviously haven't lost your own mask."

Serin felt annoyance burst up within him. "No, I haven't. I lost something else."

"Then why are you telling me about the mask?"

The young man stopped, staring at the woman as his *annoyance* began to spark. "Do you wish to hear this, or not?"

"I asked to, didn't I?"

"Then listen, please."

As Serin spoke, he instinctively tried to push his emotions into the Coil, and each time the sense of emptiness created more sparking *frustration* and *anxiety*. He took a breath, setting his palms on his thighs and beginning his explanation again.

"Our masks are sacred. Inscribed on each is a series of runes, which allow us to connect to the Coil. My own mask has used all its power, and I no longer have access to the Coil."

"What is that? The Coil?"

"The Coil is allows my people to feel the emotions those around them."

There was a pause as woman's eyes narrowed, suddenly seeming to bore into his soul. "You can *feel* the emotions of others?"

Serin nodded, noting that Ivelys' tone had changed. It now seemed a bit more forceful than before, but he was unsure what to make of it.

"*Everyone's* emotions?"

The young man nodded again. "Of course. It allows us to connect with those—"

"I never gave you permission to do that," Ivelys said abruptly, cutting Serin off. Her eyes were aflame. "Pull off your mask."

"But why—" Serin began, before he was cut off.

"You can't invade people's minds like that! Pull it off, or I'll pull it off for you."

Ivelys' shouts echoed in the room as surged towards Serin, the jacket over her face slipping down to reveal a large portion of it. The young man's gaze snapped back down as he stumbled backwards, crying, "It doesn't work anymore!"

He fell, catching himself with his forearms, eyes closing to prevent an accidental glimpse of the woman's face.

"Stay out of my mind, got it?"

Serin could feel the presence of the woman looming over him. He quickly nodded, slowly pushing himself back up, and opening his eyes.

"Good."

Ivelys whipped around, striding back to her corner as she tore the jacket off her face, tossing it to the ground. Serin, eyes downcast, grabbed his tool and returned to cleaning the runes, *shame* bubbling within him like steaming water.

Taking a shuddering breath, the young man forced himself to hold in the emotions.

They'll never accept you, never; they'll keep you from being anything, everything—

With the voices continually whispering in his mind, Serin finished cleaning the runes on the pipe. Then, without speaking another word to the woman, he left for his bunk.

The Runemaster was right. He probably did need to try to sleep more.

+

"Mask-boy, get up!"

Serin jolted from his sleep, blinking groggily in the darkness of his room. Was it morning already?

His door shook from the force of the pounding. Strapping on his mask, the young man stumbled towards the door, and opened it.

Runemaster Eand stood outside, carrying a small lamp and wearing a cloth face-wrap.

"You have five minutes to get ready," he said, his voice sounding muffled and strained, "I need you up on deck."

Serin simply nodded. After finishing his morning preparations, he tried to shake off the exhaustion.

Coming, coming, it's coming to get you—

The change in the tenor of the voices made Serin stumble. Something was wrong.

He began to stride to the door, but the floor flew out from under him. As the young man fell to the hard ground, he let out a cry of surprise

The room was still rocking slightly as Serin pushed himself up, holding his left arm, which felt bruised from the impact. He stumbled again towards the door, pulling it open to reveal the Runemaster bracing himself in the doorway.

The ship had almost stilled, so the Runemaster grabbed Serin's arm, and began to tow him down the hallway.

"We need to get to the deck," he said without looking at the young man, "They're going to need support up there."

"What's going on?" Serin asked as his stomach grew more uneasy with each step. He'd avoided seasickness for most of the trip, but now the pains associated with it were eminent.

"Aberration attack," the Runemaster responded, pulling them down another corridor, "Most of the others are tied up keeping the engine and shields running, and I need someone to help me maintain the runes holding the deck together."

"But I'm the least experienced," the young man protested, a flurry of *doubt* inflaming within his chest. His eyes glanced over the lights. They seemed to be dimmer than before.

"And that's why you're coming with me. We need all hands working, and you'd just make a mess of things in the engine room."

"But won't the deck be dangerous—"

"Of course it will be!"

Serin fell silent, looking down. The anger in the Runemaster's voice was apparent, even despite the young man's inexperience with tones and body language.

They stopped in the middle of the hallway, and the Runemaster got in close to Serin's face. The young man could smell his breath from beneath the face-wrap.

"This whole void-cursed ship is dangerous, boy," Runemaster Eand said vehemently. His eyes displayed the fire of *determination*, lacing his every action. "Your only options are to sit in your room and cower, or to help me keep the entire ship from being smashed to bits by the waves."

The Runemaster strode away.

"If Raile's messengers have come to claim our souls tonight," he yelled, "We may as well be taken fighting."

Silken *confusion* fluttered within Serin at the mention of 'Raile'. He knew it was the name of the red moon, the sister of the larger white moon, Leira, but what messengers could a moon have?

But that wasn't important right now. Discarding the thought, Serin took a deep breath as the density of *resolve* took over, following the Runemaster through the rocking ship. Somehow, the man's gait was continually sure, despite the unsteady ground.

The voices continued to whisper in Serin's mind.

You shouldn't have come at all, the powerful waters make this ship rock so violently this aberration was sent for you—to eat you, kill you, take you—

The voices cut off as violent winds and rain seethed through the hallway, physically forcing Serin back. The Runemaster pushed him forward, shouting, "Get to the top and pull out your 'scriber!"

Nodding eagerly, not trusting his voice to be loud enough over the wind, Serin grabbed the railing that ran up the open stairwell as the rain pelted his bare skin. As he set foot on deck, the young man felt a punch stall him as light of *fascination* and the creeping coldness of *horror* overtook him.

Thick mists covered the waters, and a dark shape, impossibly massive, loomed above the Runeship. The sight was slightly obscured by a thin wave of shimmering blue, which blocked both part of the pouring rain, and large portions of the torrential waves, which slammed against the sides and front of the Runeship. But, with each hit, the blue shimmer seemed to become a little darker. The shield was weakening.

Sailors dashed about the ship, readying weapons, preparing and fixing various parts of the ship Serin was unfamiliar with. It was chaos.

And, somehow, he could once again feel their racing *fear*.

The voices returned, louder, as the intense emotions filled Serin's mind.

Give up give up give up give up, let it take you—

Crying out, Serin fell to his knees, only to be seized at the shoulders and forced to stand.

"Go reinforce the runes! You Kevans can do that, right?"

The strong voice of the Runemaster now held a firmness of *re-solve* that bolstered Serin, dulling the edge of the *terror* which whipped through the Coil.

Nodding, even as he stumbled along the rocking deck, Serin fell to his knees next to a series of runes etched into the ground.

Ripping his runescriber out of his pocket, he jammed it into the symbols, scooping out the filth. When runes glowed brighter, he moved to the next set, rune after rune, pushing his rain-drenched hair out of his eyes even as the voices called in his mind.

Let it take you take you, it'll devour you and them—

Serin brought his focus to the rain, trying to ignore the voices screaming in his mind.

If it doesn't take you they'll die and you will too and everything will—

The tool slipped from Serin's hand, sliding across the deck. As he scrabbled toward it, the voices rose into a cacophony, and, in a moment of pure instinct, he tore off his mask, holding it in front of him.

In that moment, the voices and emotions were gone. There was only Serin, and his mask.

The floor flew out from under the young man, and he hit against the railing. Scrambling to stand again, the young man glanced up at the aberration. The dark ever-morphing skin was barely visible through the rain, but it created an ugly symmetry with the yellow-inflamed eyes that made Serin's stomach lurch. Each massive hand rose and fell with lethargic slowness, but the motions created waves that hurtled towards the side of the Runeship, each hit only barely absorbed by the blue shield surrounding the boat.

Serin's grip tightened on the ivory mask. The creature's eyes seemed focused on him.

Struggling to stand, the young man stared up at the monster, the harsh rain beating against his unprotected face.

It was going to kill them, and there was no way to stop it.

He looked down at his mask.

The voices had told him this aberration was coming.

Were they somehow connected to it?

Serin felt a pain in his gut.

The voices only spoke when he had his mask on.

This mask on.

Looking at his final reminder of home, Serin scanned the intricate designs in the ivory. He had made it himself, with direction from his father, paying careful attention to the way the designs framed the eyes, and contrasted against dark hair.

This was his masterpiece.

But he had to do *something*.

Without a second thought, Serin slammed the mask against his knee, splintering it in half, and tossed the pieces into the waves beyond.

He whirled around, and slipped, slamming into the deck.

A deep moan shook the air.

Serin seized the nearby railing, dragging himself up, daring a glance at the monster. Its head tossed about, suddenly confused and lost. Its arms moved quickly, aimlessly, and its yellow eyes were now dark.

No longer battered by gargantuan waves, the Runeship was able to turn away from the aberration and escape.

A loud cry of victory was let up on the deck.

Serin collapsed onto the metal rail, drawing in a deep, shuddering breath.

It was gone. His mask was gone.

Letting out a sob, Serin fell back down onto the floor of the deck, covering his face as he drifted into unconsciousness.

+

It took a week for Serin to recover, a week spent in bed, and marked by the lingering wish that he could sleep as much as the Runemaster could. For that week, unconsciousness was preferable to reality

But, not long after that week, he returned to his duties of cleaning the runes, and taking the Runemaster's place when the old man decided to take an impromptu nap. He began to cover his face in one of the Farlander wraps, finally coming to understand why they hated the cloths so much.

Several weeks after donning the face wrap, the Runeship finally arrived at their destination: the port of Ithris.

+

Serin was gathering his possessions from his small room when the Runemaster entered.

"So, this is the end of your voyage?"

Serin nodded as he glanced up at the man, blinking in surprise as he realized that the Runemaster was wearing one of the facewraps. A wet *sadness* bubbled up within the young man, but he pushed it back down.

Repressing emotions was something he had been taught never to do, but, with no Coil and few outlets, there was little else he could do.

"Yes. This is the end."

The Runemaster paused, then nodded. "There's a free spot on the ship for you, if you wanted. Ivelys is leaving, and need a few more recruits besides."

Serin paused, glancing down at his pack. He shook his head. "I'm afraid I can't accept. I have other obligations."

Letting out a sigh, the old man nodded. "Thought you'd say that. Well, if this is it, then I've got something for you."

The Runemaster began to rummage around in a large pocket.

"I seem to remember being told that you used to be a maskmaker—"

"An apprentice."

Serin grimaced. Interrupting was not one of the better Farlander traits to pick up, though, without the Coil, it was understandable.

"Same thing," the old man said, waving his free hand dismissively. "I figured that losing your mask during the storm wasn't good, so I asked around and found this. Thought you could use it to make a new one."

The Runemaster proffered a large block of wood.

Serin reverently took it, and began to inspect the grain. His mind spun with the sudden world of possibilities that block represented. He would need to find a tool to carve it, materials to keep it in good condition, and way to set a new crystal, and a plethora of other things, but...

Yes. He could use it to make a new one.

"Thank you," Serin said quietly. He slowly set the block down in his pack, then looked the Runemaster in the eye. In a quick motion the young man moved to the old man and embraced him.

The Runemaster returned the hug with an awkward back pat.

"You're-you're welcome," the Runemaster responded, his voice taking a higher pitch, which Serin took to denote uncertainty.

Serin released the man, and, after the brief pause, he returned to placing the last few items in his bag. Slinging it over his shoulder, the Serin nodded another thanks to the old man. He paused again as he exited the room.

Taking a deep breath, the young man nodded to himself, and began following the maze of dimly lit passageways.

Somehow, despite the troubles, this ship felt like his home now. The feeling of *loss*, while not quite as poignant as when he'd left Keva, still held strong.

He found the ship's exit amidst the confusing metal corridors, and took his first steps down the gangway.

Before him, bright buildings rose to majestic heights, and people with uncovered faces roamed about in an ever-shifting crowd.

Amidst it all, there was a stark outlier: a solemn man wearing an ivory mask waiting on the dockside.

Dense *resolution* rose in Serin's chest as he strode down the creaking gangway towards the Kevan ambassador and left the weathered Runeship behind.

ALLIE STAFFIERY

The Princess of the Sea

Based on the true story of Princess Alwilda of Scandinavia

The captain marched down the stairs, his heavy footsteps echoing around the hull. Wyn did not flinch like the other imprisoned girls. She was more powerful than any man—she had proven it time and time again. She clenched her jaw and stood, feet firmly planted. Her arms folded behind her back.

"You must be the infamous Captain Wyn." Laiken, the rival ship's captain, addressed her though she couldn't see him.

She moved to the front of her cell, where moonlight from the porthole shone down. Yet, he stayed back, unseen. "You hide from me in the shadows, like a coward, so that is what you must be."

"Brazen woman, are you unfamiliar with whom you speak?" The man tightened his fists, trying desperately to maintain the same composure shown by his adversary. She was beginning to annoy him greatly, however. Surely, it was evident in his voice.

"You have yet to reveal yourself to me." Wyn glanced around the dark cells which held her silent crew. If she squinted, she could make out a few of her girls by the moonglow streaming through the portholes. Most were too dark to identify.

The young captain stepped into the same pale light as Wyn, the gold adornments on his crimson suit glittering. Wyn raised an eyebrow. Blonde hair, green, piercing eyes—*he must be of the north*—and a suit of red and white. She fiddled with her thumbs behind her back, racking her brain for where those colors hailed.

"Do you not recognize me, *Princess*?" Laiken sneered, his pink lips curling up in disgust.

Wyn's bored facade cracked as her interest bloomed. Until this moment, no one had recognized her. He must have some connection to her family.

"Who are you?" She snapped then stopped herself. She ought not have let him under her skin.

Laiken smirked, having received the reaction intended. Now he held the upper hand. The possibilities were endless.

"That is no way to speak to your captain." He clicked his tongue at her in a mocking way. "It does not become you, *Elowyn*."

Wyn struggled to wipe her face clean of any and all emotion. Eventually, she would kill him. "You still have not disclosed your name."

"Ah, it would seem as though you are correct." He raised an eyebrow and tapped his chin with a long, bony finger. Wyn's gaze zeroed in on the captain's jaw, strong and defined. She internally shrugged. *At least it will be a pretty mantle ornament.*

"Come, dress yourself in something more becoming and join me for dinner. I will reveal myself to you, and in turn, you shall tell me how it is you came to be in my cells, Elowyn." He grinned slyly. Turning on his heels, he began the trek back to the deck.

"And what if I refuse?" Wyn longed for her sword.

"I will sail us all back to Verona and have your father, the king, hang your beloved crew for treachery." Laiken glowered in the darkness. A girl in the cell nearest him suddenly threw herself against the bars and growled, her arms scratched the air, desperate to attack. He stepped back, laughing a little before leaning toward the girl, remaining just out of her reach. "Or perhaps, I ought to throw them overboard now?"

"As you wish, Captain. But you will do so to me first. I brought them to this, it is only fair that I die before they do." Wyn paced back and forth in her cell, unaware of the captain's gaze.

"No. I don't think so. That will take all the fun out of it." Laiken summoned something dark in him to force the words out. In reality, he would *never* be able to force himself to murder these females, dangerous pirates or not. They were merely girls. Some young enough to still live under the care of their mothers. "I think I shall tie you to the mast and force you to watch."

"You *monster!*" From the corner of Wyn's cell, Marchie jumped to her feet and reached to her hip, where her sword should have been.

Laiken's heartbeat quickened. He had no doubt that if these women had kept their weapons, he and the majority of his crew would be dead right now. Elowyn was as alluring and beautiful as the sea itself, but all the while she remained just as dangerous and lethal.

"Marchie!" Wyn threw her arm out, successfully blocking the movements of her furious first mate. They stared intently into each other's eyes until Marchie finally surrendered.

"My apologies, ma'am. I didn't mean to disrespect you." Marchie lowered her head, but spoke loud enough for the other girls to hear. Marchie knew just as well as Wyn that you could not run a successful crew if the first mate challenged the captain's will publicly. Wyn was in charge and that was how it ought to be.

"I will meet with you, Captain, and I *shall* know your name." Wyn announced into the darkness, unsure if the mysterious young man was even still there.

"He is not here anymore, ma'am." Lexa, the girl who'd tried to attack their captor, informed her beloved captain.

Laiken nodded to himself, a smirk on his face, before closing the hatch. He had barely heard her, but it was enough. He ordered his first mate, Ulmar, to select a gown from his chambers and deliver it to Elowyn. Basking in the ethereal white moonlight that shone down on the deck, he nearly glowed in contentment. Those wenches had been in captivity for nearly a week now, and *finally* they were beginning to show promise.

"Wynnie, you can not seriously consider this man's offer! All for his name?" Marchie whispered fiercely. She and Wyn moved to the back of the cell and huddled close together so the other girls wouldn't hear their conversing.

"Don't worry, Marchie. I have a plan set in place. Have you forgotten I still have this?" Wyn whispered, pulling a small glass bottle from her bosom. The brownish-yellow liquid still seemed to glow in the dimness of the cell. Marchie's eyes widened. Wyn quickly stuffed the jar back down and pressed her finger to her lips. "Before you scold me, of course I kept it. One does not simply dispose of something this *powerful* because they do not currently have a use for it." Wyn leaned forward, nearly cheek to cheek with her first mate. "And I plan to use it today, but do not ask any more of me."

"Captain Wyn?" A shaky male voice broke the near-silence.

Wyn released a tremulous breath and turned slowly, walking steadily to the cell door.

"And you are?" She sassed in the same bored tone she'd used on the captain before.

"My name is Archimal Ulmar a-and Captain Laiken sent me." The older man forced himself to the cell door. He held some sort of fabric in his hands which shook violently as he approached. "He says to give you this."

"Thank you." Wyn offered a wicked smile. The gray-haired man was terrified of her and she was determined to play that to her advantage.

"I-I'll be o-outside… Just call me when you're changed and I'll release you." The man scurried away.

+

Wyn changed out of her normal 'menacing pirate' attire and into the black-violet and lace gown Ulmar had brought. Marchie even braided her hair in intricate plaits to make her look more royal. And malicious. Had the girls not known it was their captain walking down the corridor between the cells, they would have been inclined to believe she was a sorceress of the deep sea.

Per crew superstitions, Wyn's hands were bound behind her back, and she was led in by three soldiers. When she reached the deck, every available crew member stood with a gun in his hand, guarding either side of the pathway to Captain Laiken's chambers. Wyn, although fully aware that at any moment they could execute her, continued to smile. For all the crew knew, she was some witch powerful enough to keep the monsters of the sea at bay so a *crew* of *women* could roam it.

Ulmar quickly unlocked the door to the captain's quarters and ushered Wyn inside. The room was small, lit only by the three windows at the very back. There was a hammock in the corner and a wall of weapons. She noticed her silver rapier hanging atop them all.

"I have collected them from every pirate I have thwarted successfully." Laiken raised an eyebrow, his glance shifting from the enchanting pirate-girl to the wall of swords.

Wyn's attention flew to the blonde captain. Her heart pounded with indignancy as she subtlety tugged against the ropes binding her. "You have my sword and have yet to defeat me." Her voice remained eerily calm, though her eyes sparkled with ferocity.

"I am prepared for your unconditional surrender." Laiken grinned, amused with the beautiful girl who only hours before he was willing to kill. He pulled his legs off the table and stood, gesturing for her to sit across from him.

"Tell your men to release me." Wyn stuck her chin in the air, a powerful threat in her voice.

"How have they kept you captive?" Laiken's amused grin faltered as his curiosity piqued. Wyn glared at Ulmar over her shoulder before spinning around and showing the captain her bound hands. His first mate would have ran out the door, if Laiken's demand for the princess to be freed had not stopped him.

With shaky hands, Ulmar released Elowyn from her confines, then exited the room, slamming the wooden door shut behind him. Wyn turned around with a devious smile on her lips and faced the blonde boy. Laiken gulped, taking in everything he could now see of the pirate-girl.

"Please, sit, Princess Elowyn." He smiled lightly at her and gestured to the chair across from him.

Wyn bit her lip. Was this not the *fiend* who held her girls captive and only hours before threatened to end all their lives? Who currently had her sword hung in his chambers as a token of victory over a battle not yet won? Nevertheless, if things were to go as she had planned, she would have to pretend.

And, oh, was she a good actress.

Wyn took a seat at the wooden table across from Laiken.

"I have lived up to my end of the bargain, now you shall live up to yours." *Or not live at all.* Wyn pushed the thought to the back of her mind.

"Only in part," Laiken pointed out.

Wyn rolled her sea-blue eyes.

He sighed and raised his hands. "As you wish, then. My name is Laiken."

"Ulmar previously disclosed that information to me." Wyn sighed.

"What else could you want to know?"

"How it is that you know my true name and status." Wyn leaned forward and twirled a loose curl of her black hair around her pale finger, pretending to be oblivious. Laiken smiled, half in amusement and half in frustration. She was nothing like any other woman he had ever met before.

"Your father betrothed us before you disappeared." Laiken reclined in the wooden chair, resisting the temptation to rest his feet on the table. "I am Prince Laiken of Alredar."

Of course her father had sent him to find her.

Wyn overplayed her pretend shock with wide eyes and a gasp of disbelief. "Are you really?" This would be the only time she hoped to appear as gullible and dimwitted as the other girls he had surely courted.

"Now tell me, Elowyn of Verona, what are you doing out on the seas, disguised as a pirate?"

"If you have spoken to my *father*," Wyn forced that dreaded word out, "you would know that I was never one to settle. I am as free as the wind and endless as the sea. I will admit, I never wanted to marry you."

"Am I so repulsive?" Laiken chuckled, glancing around the room. He was determined to look anywhere but at the princess before him. Something about her both intrigued and scared him.

"I was never shown your portrait. For all I knew, you were some pruny old man with a fat belly and little hair. But that's besides the point, I had already decided the sea was my calling. Marchie—pardon me, Lady Marchessa—and I commandeered one of my father's navy ships. We picked up every able-bodied woman at our every stop, most of whom were daughters of sailors or fishermen who already knew the workings of a ship. Somehow, we managed to remain low and hide from my father and the people he sent to find me. But one day, Marchie and I decided we would not hide." Wyn continued, staring off at the water outside the window. "I killed a man for the first time that day, after he tried to hurt me."

"With a sword?" Laiken leaned forward, elbows on the table.

"With my sword, yes. I cut off his head." Wyn clenched her jaw, willing the unwelcome memories away. She had a plan and she did not need distractions throwing her off-topic.

"I meant to say, did the man hurt you with his sword?" said Laiken.

"No. He attempted to steal my virtue." Wyn's eyes blackened and her face paled. Her knuckles whitened as she gripped the arms of the wooden chair, still staring out of the windows into the watery depths of the ocean.

In that moment, Laiken was sure she was the sea-witch his crew members believed her to be. She had a storm raging within her deep blue eyes and waves crashing within her soul.

"Wyn..." Laiken's calm facade vanished and his hands shook slightly.

"Do *not* feel pity for me!" Wyn screamed, pushing back her chair, standing, and letting her true anger shine through. "I killed him—ended his life as he tried to with mine. And from then on, any man who tried to harm my girls reached the same fate. I will not allow your pity. You were not the one to save me. *I saved myself.*"

Laiken retreated, unsure of how to handle the sea witch. She was no average woman whom he could comfort with a flirtatious smile and simple embrace. She would kill him if he moved within a yard of her.

The plan... Remember the plan. Wyn picked her chair up and sat in it once more. She may have spent the last three years becoming the sea's most feared pirate, but that did not mean she had forgotten her manners.

"Perhaps some wine?" Laiken's heart beat wildly, half in amazement and half in fear.

"Yes, I suppose that will do." Wyn breathed, a plot to fulfill her plan blooming. "May I fetch the glasses?"

"As you wish. They are in the cupboard to your left." Laiken moved to the bureau where he kept the ale. However, they seemed to acquire new bottles daily, and he could not remember where he left the wine.

"Thank you." Wyn smiled to herself. She found the glasses and reached for the jar in her corset. She glanced at the blonde prince to make sure he wasn't looking but the sight of him pulled at her heart. Though his threats said one thing, the man had not harmed her nor her girls. He was crouched down on his knees, head deep inside the cabinet, rooting around piles of bottles.

But she would *not* go back.

Clenching her jaw and biting her cheek, Wyn poured a decent amount of the liquid on her finger and rubbed it around the rim of the glass. For good measure, she rubbed some on her lips. The witch who gifted her the poison enchanted it so no matter what, the poison would not affect Wyn.

"There it is!" Laiken snatched the bottle and crawled back out. Wyn's eyes widened, and she quickly closed the jar, stuffing it—and her emotions—down and out of sight. She grabbed the cups and quickly slid into her seat. "The finest wine in Alredar!"

"Sounds delightful." Wyn smiled lightly, trying to hide any traces of her panic.

"What shall we drink to?" Laiken popped the cork off the bottle and poured a relatively even amount in both glasses. He motioned with his hand for her to choose which she wanted. Wyn immediately pushed the poisoned glass toward the prince.

"To the sea." Wyn reminded herself that this *must* be done. Innocents were lost to war all the time, this was nothing new.

"To the sea." Laiken sipped from his glass.

Wyn slowly raised the cup to her lips and drank, all the while keeping her eyes on the prince. He smiled leaning back in his chair as he emptied his glass.

"Now, finish your tale." He demanded.

Wyn bit her lip to keep from shouting. *Why was the poison not working?*

"I would rather not." Her eyes flitted around the room. "Is there not something else we could do?"

"I merely promised you my name." Laiken's voice beginning to slur. He blinked a few times, trying to clear the fog that had surrounded his vision. It was nothing intense, only as if he had just woken from a deep slumber and could not shake the sleep off. The wine must be *very* strong or perhaps during his search for Princess Elowyn he'd lost his tolerability for the beverage.

Wyn sighed. "Where was I then?"

"Beheading." Laiken tilted his glass to one side as if pointing to the moment where she left off. He took a deep breath as Elowyn began her story, suddenly feeling incredibly winded.

"Afterward, we realized pirating is not as bad as it had seemed when I was the one being robbed. So we continued, and now we are here." Wyn slowed her voice so she did not sound as nervous as she was. The poison was taking effect!

The Prince's eyes suddenly widened, and his mouth fell open as if he could not suck in any air. He stood from the table, hands on his throat, desperately trying to breathe. Wyn stood as well, externally panicking.

"My Prince! What is wrong?" She rushed to him and rested her hands on his shoulders. His bright green eyes searched her deep blue ones, and he furiously pointed to his throat. All at once, his eyes rolled back into his head and he collapsed on the ground. Wyn tucked the fly-away strands of her hair behind her ear. Laiken's body convulsed on the wooden planks of the floor and his green eyes rolled around wildly in their sockets.

"Prince Laiken?" Wyn heard a voice from outside the cabin.

"Don't...do...this..." Laiken struggled to speak to the princess. He grabbed her arm and made her look into his panic-stricken eyes.

"I cannot go back to my father. I'm sorry." She peeled his hand off her arm. "I will not be tied down. I cannot." In that moment, the prince's quaking body ceased its movements.

Wyn had succeeded. Her first act as a free pirate was to retrieve her sword. Just as she unsheathed it, Ulmar and a few other crew members burst into the room. When their eyes landed on the deceased prince and Wyn holding her sword, they instantly dispersed to retrieve their swords. Wyn smirked, grabbing an armful of weapons and walking calmly out of the captain's quarters.

She encountered a sailor on her journey into the hull, but before he could make a sound, she had her blade in his chest. He gasped, wide-eyed like Laiken, but she only grinned. Removing her blade, she rested a hand on her shoulder and carelessly pushed him into the churning waters.

Wyn marched into the hull of the ship. "Captain!" Lexa announced, rushing to the bars of her cage. "What's happening up there?"

"The prince is dead and now we must fight." Wyn grinned wildly. Her girls were the best fighters the sea had ever seen. She would show her father. She would not go back and this was just the message to send. She removed a pin from her hair and quickly picked the lock. Once free, she handed each girl a sword and instructed them to wait at the entrance in case of 'company.'

"You did it, Wynnie." Marchie whispered in awe as her beloved captain freed her last. Wyn swung the door of the cage open and handed her first mate a sword.

"I told you I would."

"Captain! We have movement!" Lexa shouted.

"Are you with me?" Wyn asked her first mate.

Marchie smiled. "To the death, ma'am."

NATHAN SCHAFFER

Treasured

Edwin walked hand in hand with his love down the soft, white sand beach.

"I wish you no longer had to venture to sea. It's so vast." Marian sighed.

"Not as vast as my love for you. I shall always return. The merchant's life is a lonely one, but the thought of you, my love, will keep me strong."

She blushed. "I know only one thing stronger than your love for me." She looked up at his perfect hazel eyes. "My love for you."

Edwin rolled the legs of his trousers to his knee. He ran into the waves with Marian chasing after him. The cool water splashed around his ankles. A shimmer caught his attention. Half buried in the sand was an emerald necklace, surrounded by sapphires.

"Edwin?" Marian approached his side. "Is everything all right?"

"Look." The gem dangled from his hand by its golden chain.

"Oh Edwin," she gasped. "It's beautiful."

"As are you." Edwin slipped it around her neck. It glimmered against her tan skin.

She placed her hand around it, allowing it to slide over her palm.

Screams from the pier caught their attention. He locked eyes with Marian. "Stay here and wait for my return or go home." He turned and sprinted through the sand toward his docked ship.

144 · BAND OF MISFITS

As he approached the wharf, he heard shouts amidst the clatter of swords. Edwin's fellow crewmen, along with others from town, struggled to fend off the pirates. Edwin recognized the one standing in the middle of the mayhem as Cursed Captain Carter. An evil grin showed through his thick, unkempt peppered beard. He held a body upright by the collar to gain easy access to hidden pockets.

Cursed Captain Carter? I thought he was a myth. Edwin gazed in horror at the bodies of his shipmates strewn upon the sun-worn wood. He spotted his friend, Captain Daniel O'Neil, pierced by his own sword. Anger and sadness welled inside Edwin, blinding his fear.

He stepped over the lifeless cabin boy and picked up the pistol that lay by his side. The round hadn't yet been fired. He took aim at the pirate captain and pulled back the trigger. The gun erupted with a bang and the bullet clipped the captain's plume in two. The captain turned.

"Oh dear," Captain Carter dropped the body and removed his hat. "Look at how you've ruined my feather, boy." His scarred face scrunched into an awful grin as he approached Edwin. The captain's fancy clothes were tattered and dirty, his breath smelled of whisky and rot. "Now what is a boy like you doing here at a time like this?" The Captain ruffled Edwin's hair. Edwin flinched and shrank away. "Tut. Tut. You shouldn't play with guns. Someone could have been injured if you knew how to aim."

"Edwin!" Marian called out, drawing the pirate's attention.

"And look at this. A beautiful maiden comes to save you. How lovely." He passed Edwin and approached Marian. "Such a pretty little lass." He caressed her soft cheek with his rough hand while he played with the end of her hair in the other. "What a stunning necklace." Looking into her green eyes, he grasped the pendent and yanked it from her neck. "At last." He tucked it into the pocket of his red velvet cloak. He grabbed Marian by the wrist and she gasped in pain.

"No!" Edwin lurched forward, punching at the Captain's head. The captain ducked and landed a solid fist against Edwin's jaw. Edwin stumbled back and fell to the ground. Marian jumped on the Captains back and wrapped her arms around his throat. He easily threw her to the ground then drew his cutlass.

"Cap'n, sir, the ship's been loaded and is ready to shove off," his first mate shouted.

The captain snarled and delivered a solid kick to Edwin's ribs before joining his filthy crew aboard the *Maiden of the Seas.*

Edwin watched through tears as the ship pulled away from the dock. He propped himself up on his elbow and turned to look at Marian. "Are you in pain Marian?" he asked between labored breaths.

"Not much," she said through tears of her own.

"I asked you to stay away."

"I know but I'd much rather be dead than see you lying here with the rest of these bodies." She wept, and he embraced her. "That awful man hurt you."

"Thank heaven he took the necklace instead of you."

"That was my necklace, you fool." The couple started at the new voice. They turned and saw a short, hunched old lady with pale skin and dark greenish hair. Her cloak was full of holes and she walked with a driftwood cane.

"I beg your pardon," Edwin tried to compose himself.

She snarled, showing her yellowed teeth. Her black eyes seemed to stare into Edwin's soul. "You stole my necklace from the beach. I watched you grab it from the water."

"That was yours, madam?" Edwin asked.

"Yes, it was, and you took it."

"I am dreadfully sorry. I didn't realize it belonged to anyone."

"It's too late for sorry now. It was important to me and you let that pirate steal it from you before knowing whose it was."

"We didn't let that pirate do anything," Marian replied, slightly alarmed by the old lady's accusation.

"Nonetheless, it's gone. Now I must take something special from you." She pointed at Edwin with her cane, then scurried over to Marian. "For stealing my things and losing my treasure, she must now tend to my every pleasure."

"Absolutely not," Edwin protested.

"Oh, but she doesn't have a choice." The old lady waived her stick in the air and chanted "When I touch you, skin to skin, you shall grow a mermaid fin, and because you lost what belongs to me, you'll serve with unwavering loyalty." She reached out and grabbed Marian by the hand. Marian's legs fused together and grew shiny, silver scales. A large fin fanned out where her feet had been.

Edwin scrambled away in fear. "Marian!"

Her eyes were glazed over, and she gave no reply. The old lady picked Marian up with surprising strength and dropped her off the edge of the dock into the water. "Now, my dear. Go to the Isles of Death and wait for me there." Marian dove under the surface of the water and was gone. "And as for you—" she pointed at Edwin and shuffled toward him. He scooted away from her and lifted his arms in defense. "If you ever want to see your love returned, you must find my necklace and bring it to me in the Isles of Death."

"How will I be able to do that? I'm only the lowly deckhand of a now dead crew."

"Take this." She pulled a sword with a spectacular hilt from beneath her cloak.

"I'm no swordsman."

She laid the sword on the ground and waved her cane over it. "Any creature, great or small who raises their hand to harm you at all, will be dead at your feet before they've had time their task to complete." She paused for a moment or two. "Any captain, who falls on their ship to the blade in your hand, will pass on their crew, obedient on sea or on land."

"Wield this sword and you will not fail." She held the hilt out to him.

He grasped it. "What if the sword gets stolen?" He gazed at the rapier. "A piece like this will be a target of theft for sure."

"You need not worry. If another person tries to take the sword, death will be their only reward." The old lady lifted her cloak above her head and it crashed over her like a wave, then she was gone.

+

One week after the massacre on the pier, Edwin stood at the docks of a coastal town to the north. He searched for a ship that would take him onboard but was turned away each time. He sat on a bench, defeated. Taking Captain O'Neil's hat from his head he brushed his long blonde hair from his brow and looked to the horizon just as *The Jackrabbit* glided into the bay.

When it let down anchor and planked on the dock, he wandered over to admire its beautiful structure. His leather boots creaked as he climbed up the plank and on board. Though the ship was small, it was well kept with a good crew and solid masts. Deck hands roamed the vessel, moving barrels and crates from the haul.

Edwin approached the captain's quarters and tapped on the ornate door. An older man with expensive clothes and a clean-shaven face opened the door. He adjusted his monocle and asked in a gruff voice, "Who are you, chap, and what do you want?"

"I'm looking for the captain of this ship," Edwin replied

"That would be me."

"I was wondering if I might have a job aboard your fine vessel."

"You want a job?"

"Yes, I'm well skilled."

He sighed and rolled his eyes. "Well, I'm not in need of anyone."

"Please sir. I'm looking for something very important that pirates took from me. I'll work for free."

"Free you say? Fine, you can scrub the deck. I'm not sure what you're thinking though. We won't be stopping any pirates. I avoid them as much as possible. You don't become as wealthy as I am by being pirated." He breathed on his monocle and wiped it off.

"Thank you, sir." Edwin let the slightest sign of a smile show through.

"Call me Captain or I might change my mind. Now I really must get back to my paperwork."

"Yes, Captain." Edwin turned and fluffed the collar of his blouse trying to wick away some of the heat of the day. He approached a young man who was scrubbing the deck. "Excuse me?" The man turned around. "Do you know where I might find another bucket and sponge?"

"Aye." He pointed to a crate beside some coils of rigging.

After gathering the supplies and filling a bucket with water he began to clean the deck. He'd been working hard for half an hour or so when a voice came from behind him.

"Who are you?"

Edwin turned about and saw a well-dressed man with greying hair. "I'm the captain's new hire."

"Are ya now?" The man squinted at Edwin, then grinned and let out a throaty laugh. "Well, welcome aboard lad. How are you this fine day?"

Edwin was surprised by his friendly manner. "I am very well, thank you."

"My name is Mason Smith, first mate of this here fine ship, and what might yer name be?"

"Edwin Hughes, sir."

"Well, Edwin, *The Jackrabbit* is a fine ship, isn't she?"

"Yes sir, but the captain…"

"Ah, aye, Captain Crenshaw can be a bit cold." He gave a sigh. "But he hasn't steered us wrong yet. Just do as he says and be sure not to cross him when he's drunk and you'll do fine." He gave a wink and patted Edwin on the shoulder. "As you were, Mr. Hughes." First mate Smith walked away greeting other crewmen as he went.

+

The next morning, ship and crew set off before the sun had burned the fog off the water. The deckhands went about their duties with high spirits.

Captain Crenshaw came from his quarters. "All right, men. We should arrive at the next port in two weeks' time. There looks to be smooth sailing ahead. I expect every one of you asleep by the time the sun sets and awake by the time it rises." He scanned the crowd. "First mate Smith will oversee the crew until this evening. I'll be in my quarters. Do not disturb me." His eyes met with Edwin's. "New boy, you can see to the polishing of the cannons. Everyone else, go about your regular duties."

There were eight strong cannons, set to fire twelve-pound cannon balls. The weapons gleamed already but Edwin set to work polishing every inch of them. He'd almost finished the third cannon when Mr. Smith came and stopped him.

"It's ridiculous to re-polish those guns lad. They were polished not a week ago." He reassigned him to sails and rigging after learning about his previous experience

Edwin worked well past noon and was winding the halyards in the rigging when someone hollered his name. He looked down to see a red-faced Captain Crenshaw.

"What are you doing in the rigging, lad? I told you to polish the cannons." His words were slurred.

"Mr. Smith asked me to tend the riggings, Captain Sir."

"Well, I'm telling you to get down here."

"Aye, Captain." Edwin climbed down swiftly.

Captain Crenshaw swayed and took a few uneasy steps toward Edwin. "I told you to do something and I expect it to be done." He leaned much too close, his breath smelling of wine.

Edwin took a step back and gave a little bow of respect "Yes, sir, but you put Mr. Smith in charge of the crew and he—"

"I told you to call me Captain, boy!" he barked. "I realize what I said, but I'm the captain." He swayed and grabbed the side railing of the ship to steady himself.

"Yes, Captain." Edwin felt the whole crew watching.

"Don't give me that tone!"

Smith approached. "He always gets excitable when he's been on the bottle. You'll get used to it."

"Shut your trap, Smith or I'll have you thrown in the brig!" Crenshaw shouted.

Smith gave a mock curtsy and the crew laughed.

"Stop laughing! All of you or I'll, I'll..." The Captain muttered then switched his attention back to Edwin. "Now polish those cannons till I can see my face in them or *you'll* be in the brig."

"Yes, Captain but the sun will be setting soon and I'll..."

"Stop trying to get out of it boy!" There was a fire behind his eyes. "Is that fancy hat of yours making you feel powerful?" He grabbed Captain O'Neal's hat from atop Edwin's head and dashed it to the ground, stomping on it several times. "Get to work!"

Edwin gazed upon the smashed hat then back at the fuming captain. "Captain, that hat was—"

"Don't care about the hat!" He let out a grunt. "I'll have your head for your insolence!" Captain Crenshaw drew his blade from its scabbard and lunged. Edwin drew his sword and it seemed to parry the captain's blows on its own before running straight through the captain's heart. The captain's eyes widened. Blood reddened his white blouse and dripped from the corner of his mouth. Edwin watched in horror. He had never killed a man before. The body of Captain Crenshaw slipped from the smooth blade and slumped on the deck in a puddle of his own blood.

"I...I didn't mean...how...?" Edwin stammered, staring at the blade in his hands, not sure what had just happened. He knew he would be hanged or imprisoned for such a crime.

"What's wrong, Captain? He was mutinous. You did what had to be done." Mr. Smith said.

"What?" Edwin gasped, confused.

"Captain Hughes, we can clean up this mess. You seem unwell."

"Captain? No, I...killed the captain." It became more real when Edwin said it out loud, and he choked back tears of disgust.

"Are ya feeling well? I suggest you take a nice rest in your quarters, sir." Mr. Smith guided Edwin toward what had been Captain Crenshaw's quarters just five minutes ago. "Darby and Lars, clean up that insubordinate." Two crewmen nodded and walked over to the body of Captain Crenshaw, unceremoniously throwing him overboard.

"That's no way to bury your captain at sea," Edwin protested.

"No, sir, it isn't. If ye were to die, we'd do it respectful like." Mr. Smith led him through the ornate doors and sat him in the immaculate captain's chair. "I'll give you some time to get yer wits about ye, Captain, sir." Mr. Smith left.

Edwin sat, stunned, unsure of what just happened. A portrait of Captain Crenshaw hung on the opposite wall. Gold leafing surrounded every border of the room. A large safe sat locked tight in the corner. After glancing around the beautiful space several times, Edwin stared at the portrait with remorse. "I killed that man, and nobody remembers or cares."

The old woman's chant entered his mind.

"Any creature, great or small who raises their hand to harm you at all, will be dead at your feet before they've had time for their task to complete. Any captain that falls on their ship to the blade in your hand will pass on their crew, obedient on sea or on land."

"It's your fault." he shouted. "Your cursed sword plunged itself into the man!" He sobbed against the ornate wooden desk, heaving with the tears. Something told him that this wasn't the last person to die if he ever wanted to see Marian again.

After a while he heard a knock at the door. "Come in." He wiped the tears from his eyes.

Smith entered. "I have yer hat, Captain Hughes, sir. You left it on the deck."

"Thank you, Smith." He got up and took the plumed hat, reshaping it with his hands. "Gather the crew, Mr. Smith. I need to talk with them."

"Aye Captain." He turned and exited through the door.

Placing the hat upon his head, Edwin glanced into the mirror that hung near the door. Captain Hughes took a deep breath and sighed. He pulled on the purple overcoat that hung on the captain's shining silver coat rack. This was all part of getting Marian back, he reminded himself. He took a breath and pushed both doors open at once walking out onto the deck. His crew stood waiting and watching.

"Thank you for gathering." Silence. "I must apologize, I'm fairly new to the position of captain." He scanned the crowd searching for words to say. "I will do my best to guide this great crew to the best of my abilities." Another pause. "Thank you, goodnight." He swiftly turned back to his quarters.

As he opened the doors, Mr. Smith called out," Three cheers for Captain Hughes!" The whole crew shouted "Hurrah! Hurrah! Hurrah!" Edwin turned and gave a half smile and bowed before closing the door behind him.

Edwin lay awake for hours thinking about how the sword seemed to take control of him. He felt bewitched or cursed. He wished that he could just leave but he needed this crew to track down the necklace and to find his love.

✢

Three weeks into their journey, Edwin had settled into his role of captain and had learned how to run a tight ship, with the help of first mate, Mason Smith.

Following the guidance of an old sailor claiming to have been a member of Captain Carter's crew, Captain Hughes stood at the bow of his ship, the cool salty breeze dancing in the plume of his hat. He stared at the silhouette of a ship on the horizon. "Mr. Smith?"

Mr. Smith came trotting up to his side. "Yes Captain?"

"Do you see that ship in the distance?"

"Aye, Captain." Smith nodded.

"All righty, crew! Do you see that vessel starboard and ahead a little way?" Edwin kept his eyes on the ship.

The crew replied. "Aye."

"Steer toward that ship…"

"Aye, sir!" They replied and began moving around the deck.

"Do ya think that could be the ship that took the cursed jewelry?" Mason asked.

"We can only hope." Edwin clenched his jaw.

"I understand captain." He looked out over the calm sea at the ship. "I've hoped that every ship that we've passed was the right one. Losing yer one love is like losing yer soul."

"Quite right, Mr. Smith." Edwin said, saddened by the thought of Marian cursed and alone in the deep sea. "Please, go entertain the crew. I like them to enjoy their work. You seem to be able to make them cheerful."

"With pleasure, sir."

An ominous feeling saturated the air as they approached the ship. Debris floated in the water and the large masts were snapped in two. Holes were scattered across the haul like flies on a rotting carcass. The grand ship was tilted at an angle, beached on a large sandbar. The breeze carried the scent of putrefying flesh. The bodies of pirates drifted in the tide. Edwin studied the side of the massive vessel and read the tarnished name, *Maiden of the Seas*, sprawled in white paint across the wood.

"Lower a dingy!" Edwin commanded, nervous that they were too late.

"Dingy away!" one of his crew replied.

Captain Hughes lowered himself into the small boat along with Mr. Smith and several other faithful crewmembers. They cautiously rowed around flotsam and bodies. As they pulled up next to the skeleton of the once frightful ship, Captain Hughes caught hold of the broken boards and lifted himself up to the deck. Captain Carter's crew lay strewn across bloodstained boards.

"Search the entire ship. Loot the pockets of every fallen man. Find what you can," Edwin said after being joined by his men. Walking in separate directions, they searched the bodies for treasure, trying to avoid breathing in the stench.

Edwin scanned the lifeless crewmen, unable to find the captain of the dreadful bunch. He walked to the hatchway and climbed below deck, well lit by sunlight through the holes. More dead men, but no captain.

Edwin looked for the hatch to the lower deck and found it, pinned under a rather large pirate. He rolled the man from atop the door where he had fallen and pried it open. It creaked with age. The dark blue water that flooded the lowest deck reflected filtered sunlight up at him. He descended the rugged ladder into the waist deep brine. His boots sunk into the layer of sand that had drifted in from the sandbar. The water chilled him to the core.

He spotted Cursed Captain Carter speared on a large splintered beam, his mouth agape and eyes glassy. His legs drifted back and forth with the soft movement of the sea. Carter may have been a man feared in life but he was a coward in death. The only carcass in the belly of the vessel. He wasn't trying to save his crew, he was hiding.

Edwin trudged through the water toward the spineless man. "What is a captain like you doing down here at a time like this?" He reached into the pocket of the tattered cloak. It was empty. Edwin's heart sank.

Mr. Smith called from above. "Captain, she's been cleaned to the bone."

Edwin looked at the awful remains of the dreaded Cursed Captain Carter one last time, then retreated back up the ladder.

✝

Edwin knelt in front of a large pile of gold and jewels, running his hand through it. Grabbing hold of a shining goblet, he looked at his reflection. His face scrunched with anger and he let out a roar as he threw the thing across the room. It bounced off the wall and rolled to a stop at the feet of his first mate.

"Sir, we've spotted another ship. It looks to be pirates." Smith bent to retrieve the golden chalice gleaming in the candlelight.

Edwin looked up from his squatting position on the floor. "I suppose that we best get ready for another boarding." His jaw tightened and he kicked the pile of gold coins, causing metal disks to burst in all direction. Then, he stormed up the ladder to the top deck.

Taking a deep breath of cool sea air, Edwin looked at the stars that appeared as the sun's last glow was consumed by the vast ocean. Readjusting his hat, he faced his second ship that trailed behind. "Let the lads know we're ready for a boarding," he hollered. A man in the crow's nest waved his arms and signaled to the other watchmen about the plan.

Edwin moved to the bow and looked over the sea. They were fast approaching their mark. Before long, *The Jackrabbit* pulled up alongside the slow-moving vessel. His second ship, *The Ruby,* hemmed it in on its other side. Now his crew simply waited for an order. "Like always, loot the ship, lads, but leave the captain for me!"

Planks were dropped, and crewmen spilled over both sides of the sleeping ship. The poor watchman who had fallen asleep at his post, woke with a start at the sound of hundreds of boots hitting the deck. He sounded the alarm, but too late.

Battle ensued. Pirates of the defending crew climbed, sword in hand, from their sleeping quarters. Shouts of pain were heard. Steel against steel and the bang of black powder muffled the outcries. Before long the other crew knelt on the ground, hands behind their heads. Half of their men lay dead, while only eleven of Edwin's crew were lost.

The crews of Edwin's two ships stood silently in a circle, pointing their blades and fire arms inward. The captain of the defeated ship knelt in the center with his hands raised over his bowed head. The circle parted, and Captain Hughes stepped in front of the cowering man.

Captain Hughes' glare softened as he read the terror on the man's face. *No pirate deserves mercy.* He repeated to himself as his face hardened. Drawing his sword from its scabbard, he lifted the blade and beheaded the man in one smooth swing of his arm. The headless body fell forward to the deck. Edwin shuddered and turned. The survivors of the crew that once were his enemy now stood mixed with his crew awaiting his command. "Put the loot in *The Jackrabbit.*"

Captain Hughes ordered a team of men to set barrels of powder with a long fuse in the haul. As the two ships pulled away, the empty Brigantine was engulfed in a ball of flames. Edwin watched it slip under the surface of the peaceful sea.

"The necklace was not in the loot, sir," Mr. Smith said.

Edwin's face saddened. "How many men must be killed before we find it?" Edwin turned to look out over his crew of Caribbean pirates, French Royal Navy, Chinese merchants, English fishermen, and Jamaican sailors.

"Well, sir, if I may be so bold, you did say to stop every ship." Smith looked over the crew as well.

"And?"

"Is it necessary, Captain?"

"Yes, it is, Mr. Smith. We don't know the whereabouts of the Cursed Jewel. It may be anywhere and I don't want to miss it."

"But all this to save one person?"

"Most of those we kill are pirates, Mr. Smith. Since pirates plague the seas, it is not a great loss. And that *one* we're saving is the woman I love."

"Aye, sir." He looked at the ground. "You used to leave most of killing to the crew but now you do it with little remorse."

Edwin didn't reply.

"In the past, you have only killed in self-defense. Tonight, ye killed a man who hadn't attacked you first."

Edwin showed no reaction, though guilt crept into his heart.

"Well, it be gettin' late, sir. I think I'll have the crew turn in." Smith turned and left the Captain alone with his thoughts.

✦

"Are ya sure, Captain, sir?" asked Smith.

"We need to go into port either way." Captain Hughes stroked his now bearded face as he sat behind his desk.

"But, sir, Looters Holding is a pirate town." Fear spread across Smith's face.

"Good. We can rid the world of more pirates and gain our supplies for free."

"Ya want to loot Looters Holding?" He began to pace. "That's insane, Captain."

"I have faith in our crew."

"Yes, sir." He nodded. "I'll tell the men to sail toward...Looters Holding, then." He cleared his throat and left the room.

Captain Hugh's three ships full of crewmen sailed into port at Looters Holding a few days later.

"Take what we need men and don't be afraid to rid the world of the cretins!"

The crew cheered and ran ashore, swords held high. Chaos began. Shouts and screams from every building were heard as people banded together to fend off Captain Hugh's crew. Edwin pulled his now tattered, purple velvet cloak over his shoulders and stepped ashore. A chain spilled from the pocket of a dead man at his feet. Edwin hoisted the dead man up by his collar in order to reach the pockets. A smile spread over Edwin's face in the hopes that the necklace would be found. When he uncovered a simple pocket watch, he let out a deep sarcastic laugh.

A gunshot ripped through the white plume of his hat and made him shudder. He raised his gaze to a young man no older than nineteen standing in a shadow of a building. Edwin dropped the body and moved closer. He stopped within five feet of the boy when he heard the shout of a girl.

"Phillip, no!" the boy startled but didn't take his eyes off Edwin.

Edwin glanced up and saw a fair young maiden standing confidently with the cursed necklace around her neck. He gasped and walked toward her but was halted by the words of the boy.

"You...You're Horrible Hughes...I...I've heard of you."

Edwin was taken aback. His own experience from three years ago came flooding back to him. He shook his head and looked around at the carnage. The burning buildings and fallen bodies were an echo of his past. He rubbed his bearded face and felt his tattered cloak brush against his legs. He looked at the girl with the necklace. "Where did you get that neckpiece?"

She shuddered "I...I..."

"Where?" Edwin raised his voice. His hand reached for his sword. "Don't approach me, boy, or you will die."

"I found it in the pocket of a drunken man" Phillip lowered his dagger.

Edwin reached out his hand. "Give it to me." Her eyes teared up. "It's a cursed thing." His face was pleading. His free arm reached for the sword again. "Stop, boy. I do not wish for you to die this day. I mean no harm to either of you. Just give me the necklace and I will be on my way."

"Give it to him," said Phillip.

The maiden pulled it from around her neck. She laid it in Edwin's hand then stepped away in fear. Edwin gave a small bow and turned away.

"If it is a cursed thing, why do you wish to have it so badly?" the girl called after him.

Edwin paused mid-stride and, without looking, replied. "Because, it's the only reason I'm a pirate." He faced the couple now, standing side by side. "My love was taken from me and this necklace is the only way to save her." The infamous pirate captain stood vulnerable before the two, young lovers.

"Captain, sir, the ships are loaded and we're ready to shove off." Smith shouted.

Edwin climbed aboard *The Jackrabbit* while the couple stood and watched.

+

"We sail for the Isles of Death tonight!" Edwin strode into his office to search his map.

"Ye found it, sir?" Mason watched with excitement.

"Aye, indeed I have. Gather the crew. I wish to speak with them."

"Aye, Captain." Mason excitedly left to collect the crewmen. Captain Hughes looked into the mirror as he had done a hundred times and pushed aside both doors at once to meet his waiting crew.

"All right, men! I've been in search of one thing through all of our looting. I finally found it!" The crew cheered for their captain's success. "Tonight, we set sail for the Isles of Death for a matter personal to me." He scanned the crew. "I know that you can handle it. We are the best of the best." Another cheer filled the air, and he smiled as he waited for it to die down. "Tonight, we will celebrate. Feel free to partake of our bounty of booze and fine fruits. Play instruments and make merriment, for this is a joyous time." More cheers of excitement. "I will be in my quarters until further notice. You will be answering to Mr. Smith until I reemerge." He gave his first mate a solid pat on the shoulder, then retreated to his office.

"Three cheers for Captain Hughes!" cried Smith.

The crew replied. "Hurrah! Hurrah! Hurrah!"

The night passed swiftly and dawn awoke the hungover crew. The sea was smooth, but before long clouds shrouded the peaceful sunlight. Wind and rain pounded against the three vessels and they struggled to stay on course. Several times the shout of, *"Man over board!"* could be heard. Some of those men where lost to the waves forever.

Lightning struck the tallest mast of the third ship, *The Northerly*, causing it to catch fire. Before long, the ship lost control and drifted away from the others. Together *The Ruby* and *The Jackrabbit* struggled through the raging storm through the day and night.

In the morning, the seas had calmed. They stayed on course toward their destination.

"Captain, our crew took a beating and *The Northerly* is nowhere in sight." Smith looked grave.

"Send the *Ruby* to look for them. We need only one ship for the rest of our journey."

On its own, the *Jackrabbit* set full sail and cut through the water at great speeds. Soon the ship approached a mass of jagged ridges and cliffs emerging from the ocean. Several ships were wrecked upon the massive outcropping, so they slowly made their way between the obstacles.

As the ship emerged from the shadows Edwin spotted the Isles On the horizon. The crew cheered loudly, but something felt wrong. Even though the sea's surface was smooth as glass and not a breeze could be felt the ship heaved unevenly. It rocked, paused, then rocked again.

He looked over the side of the ship just as a giant creature with sword-like teeth and deep green scales burst forth from the depths. Its spindly, clawed arms reached out and madly grabbed for flesh. One of Edwin's men was dragged into the mouth of the beast. Raising his head, Edwin saw the claws of the monster coming straight for him but they stopped short wrapping around Smith instead. He had thrown his body in front of the captain. Their eyes locked, wide with fear.

"Run!" Smith shouted as he was dragged across the deck and into the mouth of the beast.

Edwin cried out and drew his sword. He leapt from the deck and plunged his blade deep into the beast's slimy black eye. The beast shrieked and flung him off with its pointed claws. It writhed then slid back into the dark depths of the sea.

Though he would have liked to have taken a moment to mourn the loss of his friend, Edwin's thoughts turned to Marian. He ordered the crew to press onward to the Isles of Death. He approached the sandy beach of the mysterious island in a small dingy. He stepped ashore. Alone.

"So, you finally made it. Took you long enough." The little sea hag appeared a few yards away.

"I've brought your putrid necklace." Edwin grabbed it from his pocket and threw it into the sand at her feet. She scrambled to pick it up. "Where is Marian?"

The hag cackled. "I quite like the help she is to me, so mine, of course, she still will be."

"What?" Anger arose inside Edwin. "I've searched the sea for that necklace with the promise of my love's return."

"I lied, fool! What's mine is mine. I'll never give her up."

Edwin stood dumbfounded. How could this wretch not keep her end of the deal after he had lost so many friends and traveled so far. Her greed had no end. He wished to strike her dead. Knowing that his skill could never match her magic, he formed a plan.

"Is your mind made up?" Edwin asked.

"Yes. Now be gone, filth."

Edwin dropped his shoulders in defeat. "I suppose you can keep the girl. I'm sure I will find love again. And now that I have three hauls of treasure, I'm sure I can find happiness." Edwin turned to go.

"Three hauls. Full?" The hag hobbled forward. "Give me the treasure. You wouldn't have any riches if it weren't for me. Therefore, it's mine"

Edwin faced her. "I don't believe I will."

"You will if you want to see your love returned."

He knew not to trust her bargains again.

"I have learned about true power. The girl is no longer my heart's desire. I thank you for the lesson. Now that you have your cheap necklace, I'm no longer bound to you."

"Wrong! It is mine!" she sputtered. "You will unload your ships on my shore and leave with nothing. That is how it always happens." Her wrinkled face contorted in rage.

"The treasure is rightfully mine. I will not let you take it. Consider it compensation for my time and your new slave."

The sea hag let out a scream that split the air. "Then you will die!" She lunged at him, staff raised. Edwin's silver blade flashed forward and pierced her heart.

"But…but how?" she sputtered.

"Any creature, great or small who raises their hand to harm you at all, will be dead at your feet before they've had time for their task to complete."

Surprise swept over her face before it went blank with death. She turned to ash and the blade crumbled in Edwin's hand. He stepped back from the remains of the witch and began searching for Marian.

"Edwin!" He turned in time to see Marian emerging from the waves in a bright light. They ran toward one another across the golden sand.

"Marian!" He embraced her, bursting with emotion. "Oh, I missed you, Marian." He studied her face.

"And I missed you." She ran her hand over his bearded cheeks. "Oh, Edwin, you've changed." She scanned his sun beaten features.

"Yes, I have, and I may never be the same." A twang of sadness overpowered his joyous feelings of reunion. "But my love for you will never change." He caressed her face and gave a sincere smile.

"I have changed too. It was so awful. I hope you will still accept me." She looked out toward sea. Edwin wondered what her life had been for the past two years.

"Of course, my love," he reassured her. "Soon, we will share tales of our journeys apart but for now it's just you and me on a soft sand beach at sunset." Beneath the pink clouds of sunset, Edwin's lips touched Marian's and they fell into a full embrace.

Mary Celeste's Secret

The New York harbor of 1872 was bustling with the November crowd, yet the docks were quiet as Captain Briggs admired his new ship, *The Mary Celeste*. He brushed the wood, roughened by the many waters it had sailed. He breathed the pungent air of the vast sea that lay before him and checked again the wizened list in his pocket with folds upon folds in the paper, making the list of crew members a bit hard to read though he knew a few from before.

"Captain Briggs?"

He turned and looked at young Albert, his first mate and right hand man. "Yes?"

"Rumors encircle this ship something foul. You sure you want her still? You could resell her for a pretty coin."

Captain Briggs looked at his first mate in curiosity. "I've never known you to be the superstitious type, Albert."

"Most of the rumors had to do with the death or bankruptcy of the captain. There's even a rumor that it was so cursed, they couldn't sell it till they changed the name." Albert's blue eyes stayed down, worried of the scorn and chastisement he might receive.

Captain Briggs smiled, placing a reassuring hand on his shoulder. "Albert, I'm glad you're worried about me but I don't believe in rumors."

Albert nodded before scampering off again. Captain Briggs' shook his head and looked back at the ship. *She'll keep my secret.* He patted the side of the ship before lumbering off to make sure everyone was ready to set sail.

+

Captain Briggs gripped the helm, a smile smothering any other emotions his face may have belied. The ship was already a day away from New York Harbor, which was now a speck in the distance to them. The weather had been nasty for a few days before they left but it had cleared up just in time. The skies were lovely. The sun glittered like a doubloon in the sky. He smiled down at his hearty crew, his first mate Albert looking over the charts on a table to his right. The sea stretched before them like a blue blanket for a child to play on. Captain Briggs looked to his left where the dark mahogany chest sat like a sleeping dragon. For a second his smile faded. Did he dare embark on this particular adventure?

Too late. He'd already agreed and he'd stick to his word. He let the smile come back onto his face, only it was less of the carefree smile of before and more of the grim smile of a man running off hope. The twinkle in his eye, only a reflection of what lay in the sea.

He heard the men starting to get rather raucous and told Albert to take the helm while he settled it. He walked down to the deck and looked at everyone who had immediately lined up on either side for their captain. That's when he found the source of the commotion. Seven men, including his first mate Albert, had signed up for the voyage. Yet there were seven men on deck and Albert was still at the helm. He looked at each and every face, scanning them one by one. A height gap of a couple inches forced him to look down at a boy. His hat, pulled low, cast shadows about his face, hiding his big brown eyes.

"I don't recall hiring you, lad. You're a stowaway." Captain Briggs growled.

"I promise, I'll work hard." The young man sounded like he had gravel in his throat.

"How can you work hard?" Captain Briggs swatted the boy's hat off his head. "You're a lass."

Her curly brown locks fell to her shoulders. Her soft, feminine features scowled and her brown eyes turned stone cold. "That I'm a girl means nothing. I was clever enough to fool you for a day."

The whole crew tensed. No one talked like that to the captain. Captain Briggs glared at her, his face so close he knew she could smell his breath. "As long as you are on this ship, I will not tolerate such outlandish behavior. Shape up or you will take a long walk into the ocean, lassy."

"My name is Ann." Her eyes flashed in defiance.

He straightened his back and headed for the helm. "Everyone, get to work."

+

The crew seemed restless, giving Ann a wide path anytime she walked by. They acted as if her bad luck and foul temper were a plague they feared catching. Except Albert, who was not superstitious. Each day Ann did as much work as the rest of the crew, if not more. She deserved the same respect as the other crewmembers. Albert scowled as he measured each place on the map. Something wasn't adding up—the map's course wasn't the same as their current course. He would have to bring this up with the captain very carefully.

+

Ann's bucket of water sloshed and her mop made a nasty splat sound as she scrubbed the floor. While she was below the deck, something started to bother her.

The cargo. There was so much of it and it all seemed to slosh. She shuddered with memories of the drunkard who had helped raise her. He always came home shaking a bottle of whiskey and yelling.

She knew the cargo at the bow end of the ship was their food supply, but the other—the sloshing cargo—was their cargo to sell. She shook her head continuing to swab the floor instead of getting herself into trouble by snooping.

Yet the urge continued to pull at her as she cleaned around the many barrels and crates. She finally decided to do just *a little* snooping. Maybe it was wine? She leaned over and sniffed at the barrels then recoiled. Unwelcome memories of her childhood flooded her mind like a rain of gunfire. This was straight, ripe alcohol. She looked around at the dozens of barrels. This had to be illegal. This much straight alcohol was a fire hazard. A few misplaced sparks and the whole ship would be eaten alive by fire.

She finished mopping around the barrels and decided getting out of there was the best thing for her. She heard a clink from one particular barrel over in the corner. Glass? Or crystal, maybe? This barrel was different than the others. It was petite and made from cherry wood with a substantial dent in its side. She would have to investigate later.

+

Captain Briggs looked into the face of the new winds as they sailed. Albert, still at his side, kept recalculating. And Briggs knew why.

At last Albert got the courage to ask him. "Captain, I don't mean to be disrespectful, but we're headed straight for the Azores Archipelago. How are we going to reach the Strait of Gibraltar in time?"

"Aye, you are correct, Albert, but why don't we keep that between you and me and simply raise your pay?" Captain Briggs smiled, tossing him a small bag of coins. Sure enough, the lad opened his mouth only to shut it again, pocketed the money, and walked onto the deck to help the crew. Captain Briggs stroked the wheel of the ship. *Just a bit longer, my sweet. Keep my secret just a bit longer.*

He went down to his cabin later that night. His kind-eyed wife Sarah was there, holding their baby daughter Sophia. He kissed them both on the cheek with a soft smile reserved only for them. They ate dinner, and Sarah fell asleep later in his desk chair with Sophia resting against her. He chuckled, pulling up a different chair so he could observe the markings Albert had made on the chart. He headed for the helm to relieve the poor lad of his duty. Albert had been right, of course. They were on route for the Azores Archipelago.

When Briggs reached the helm, Albert was staring out into the glory of the night, the stars and moon shining on everything like a silver cloak around the world. Captain Briggs took the wheel and Albert stepped aside with tired eyes.

"Thank you, sir. May I ask what we're searching for in the Azores Archipelago?"

"I'm sorry, Albert, but you'll find out with everyone else when we reach land." Captain Briggs smiled.

Albert left. Though this had happened many times before, Albert always found out before everyone else anyway. He would do his own searching for clues.

+

Ann walked slowly down the stairs to the cargo hold, humming a sea shanty her mama had always sung to her. She was finally living her dream, to sail on the open sea. She stopped mid-way through the cho-rus when she heard someone jostling the barrels. She grabbed the mop, unsure what she'd do with it, but sure she'd do something crazy if it came to it. Suddenly, Albert popped out from amongst the barrels. Ann instinctually knocked him flat to the ground with the mop.

"Oh my goodness! Sorry, Albert!" She apologized, helping him to stand. She'd learned the names of the crew by impersonating them on the first day—except him. She'd learned his name was Albert from word of mouth only. He shook his head, some of his golden hair fall-ing out of his skimpy ponytail and into his eyes. He smiled even though she could tell he still had the wind knocked out of him.

Ann glanced at the barrel he'd opened. Inside were three vials and an empty breadbox. She tilted her head. "The captain's?"

Albert nodded. "Not sure what for—he won't tell even *me*."

She helped him close the barrel again and they parted ways pre-tending nothing had happened.

+

Ann slung the mop bucket over her shoulder. It was now empty, and her mop was moderately dry. As she walked, she didn't even look up. She was used to the men clearing a path for her. She was as cursed as a witch when it came to this ship. If it wouldn't have destroyed their boat, she didn't doubt some of them would have burned her at a stake to be rid of her.

She bumped into something and fell flat on her back. She looked up. Since when had there been a mast there? Only there was no mast—it was Albert. She blushed lightly as he helped her to her feet and collected her runaway bucket and fallen mop.

"Sorry. I didn't see you there. I wasn't looking where I was go-ing." *For the second time.*

Albert smiled good-naturedly. "Quite all right."

She simply looked down, still too embarrassed to speak. He qui-etly began walking again, and she found herself following him before she even realized what she was doing.

"Why do you treat me normally?" The question tumbled out of her mouth before she could stop herself, and she wished instantly that she wasn't so impulsive.

"Because you're just another crew member on this ship. I am not superstitious. I base my opinions on experience and fact not on ru-mors."

Just another crewmember? Why did that bother her?

"And Ann?" Albert said. "Maybe you and I could get a bite to eat when we reach Italy?"

Ann nodded smiling softly. "I would like that."

Albert nodded happily and went to the helm.

The next few days blundered by, stormy and frightful, before clearing up again. The crew seemed fine but soon became on edge as the shores of the Azores Archipelago came into view. The crew began to murmur and, at last, Captain Briggs came clean.

"We're here to gather cargo and continue on to Genoa, Italy." That was all he would say. But most of the crew was content enough with that. Albert and Ann were the only ones still suspicious.

When they reached port and tied down their ship, Captain Briggs kissed his wife and daughter farewell and left them onboard. He led the majority of the crew down to the nearest bar, lugging the petite cherry wood barrel under his arm. He plunked the barrel next to where he sat with four members of his crew. Albert, Andrew, Volkert, and Gotlieb joined him at the table. He was about to tell them their purpose there, when Ann plopped herself down in the empty chair next to Albert.

"I believe I asked you to stay on the ship." Captain Briggs glared.

"Well, I'm here. So, why don't you speak up and tell us your plan?" Something about the captain bugged her. She struggled to not lash out at him every chance she got.

Captain Briggs growled. Normally he wasn't so ill tempered, but she was getting on his nerves. "Fine, but you better obey me in the future or else we'll strand you in Italy."

She nodded, waiting for him to speak again. He sighed and opened the barrel, laying out the items on the table.

"To collect our cargo, we need to collect some other items first. A lock of a mermaid's hair, the dew from a spider whose back looks like a man's face, and gold from the caves. All are located here in the Azores Archipelago."

Ann raised an eyebrow but didn't complain. The crew all nodded, being used to their captain's often obscure requests. They'd never been caught or injured in all their years of service to him. So why not follow him now? Captain Briggs packed away the items in the barrel and then ordered whiskey all around.

+

They headed out into the sweltering summer heat, hiking up the trails into the shady jungle laced with danger and lush with wildlife. Animal calls bounced around them. Ann smacked at the leaves and other growth that got in the way as she walked.

"Keep your eye out for spiders, men!" Captain Briggs bellowed.

Ann peered around every green thing she could find, but the spider they sought was nowhere to be found. "Where are we heading?" she asked.

"Mermaid Falls. On the way, we are supposed to find the spider and beyond the falls is the cave in which we will secure a piece of gold." Captain Briggs explained.

Ann scowled, putting her hair up into a ponytail with a piece of spare string. Then she marched on, scouring every leaf and flower for a spider with a man's face. She'd found more than her fair share of spiders but none fit the description from the captain's list.

She felt something crawling up her arm and pulled back her hand to swat at it.

"Don't move!" Albert hissed. He came up behind her. She didn't even breathe, feeling it creep slowly along her arm. Albert gently took the glass vial and scooped the spider inside.

"We got it!" He grinned.

Ann relaxed, looking in the vial at the furry, gray spider. Sure enough, centered on the spider's back was a marking that resembled the face of a curmudgeonly old man. Albert smiled then tucked the vial in with the other containers, and closed the barrel. Captain Briggs picked it up, with seemingly no trouble, and they continued on.

The slope became steeper. They panted as they trudged on. Albert helped Ann over the last bit up to the fall when she saw them, her jaw nearly dropped. It was beautiful—like pure, iridescent light tumbling over polished river stones, the pool so deep and vivid blue that she couldn't see the bottom. They sat by the edge of the pool, shakily, worried any minute a mermaid would shoot from the water and yank them in.

"Come on, lads. Sing! You have to sing. I'll be right 'ere to grab ye back out."

Ann wrinkled her nose at the captain's weird accent thinking how odd it was but shrugged it off. She knew mermaids only liked men so she began to climb behind the waterfall to a cavern. While descending, she found a silky river leading away from the falls and the pool. Ann looked back. She despised the cowardly captain for shoving his men forward so eagerly like bait, human lures for the human fish. Ann untied her hair and sighed. Sitting on the stone riverbank, she kept glancing over to the falls, knowing there was nothing she could do.

The water in front of her began to bubble and boil. She scrambled to her feet, stepping back to watch the crowd of froth zip downstream. Ann followed quickly after them, catching glimpses of the mermaids underneath. She ran faster and faster until she burst through the waterfall gracelessly and soaking wet.

"They're coming!" she shouted just as one of the mermaids grabbed Albert and plunged back into the pool.

Ann yanked off her boots and dove into the water. She gave no thought to the danger of entering a river full of mermaids—even when her lungs began to burn for air. When she reached Albert's captor, she grabbed the mermaid's hair violently. The mermaid shrieked, clawing at Ann, trying to free herself, in return, dropping Albert who tried to swim to the surface. Ann pulled and pulled, not releasing the thick, tangled mane until she knew Albert had escaped.

Once he was safe, Ann released her hold and swam away. Her lungs throbbed with a need for oxygen. She could see the sunlight as the surface of the water grew near. Desperate to take a breath, she kicked her legs harder. The tips of her fingers touched the air. Then a clawed hand grabbed her foot, and pulled her back down.

Ann thrashed and kicked and finally nailed the mermaid in the face, a cloud of blood spurting from the mermaid's nose. Ann swam for the surface as the mermaid's shriek echoed beneath the deep.

Arms wrapped around Ann and dragged her out of the water. She gasped for air, vomiting up what felt like gallons of water until her stomach cramped from emptiness.

"Breathe, Ann, breathe! I'm so sorry!" a voice said above her.

She tried to stand. Albert wrapped his arm around her shoulders, helping to steady her. A meaty hand grasped her wrist and untwisted something that had wrapped around her. A lock of golden mermaid hair.

"We got it, lads!" Captain Briggs said. "Now we can move on to the gold!"

The others cheered while Ann still trembled. Albert, still helping to hold her up, stayed silent—watching the beloved captain he'd known for so many years fall to gold lust. Whatever they were searching for, he valued it far above the lives of his own crew.

+

They continued into the yawning cave behind the waterfall, finding nothing.

"Here, let me carry you." Albert offered.

"I'm fine." Ann laughed, though she continued to stumble on occasion.

The crew began to grumble.

"I can't see a blasted thing!" the captain snarled.

They had been walking for at least an hour since finding the mermaids, and not a speck of gold had been spotted. Albert calmly took a few lanterns from his bag of supplies. Volkert lit them with a match from his pocket. Andrew took one and the captain took the other. The golden glow of the lamps showed the winding paths before them.

"It has to be 'round 'ere somewhere. The bloody map doesn't ever say which way to turn 'ere though!" Captain Briggs was slipping from a composed American merchant captain to a filthy pirate, even in his speech. They came to a split in the tunnels. "Alrigh' lads; we're splitting up—three per group down each pathway. Watch yer step."

He motioned for Albert and Ann to come with him while Andrew, Volkert and Gotlieb headed down the other path. The paths darkened and deepened but still no sign of gold. Captain Briggs continued his incessant muttering and tugging at his beard. Ann prepared herself for the worst. He seemed to be slipping into madness over this one little thing he needed to trade for the cargo. What kind of cargo was it anyway? He hadn't ever said.

A dizzy spell hit Ann and she skidded forward, landing on her knees and hands, scraping them badly. She couldn't believe the lack of oxygen from her fight with the mermaid was still affecting her. Albert helped her up, looking at the scrapes. Without asking, he scooped her up in his arms to carry her. She didn't refuse, though it hurt her pride to be handled like a little lady.

"What are we looking for?"

"Nothing to concern yerself with, lass, especially since yer a stowaway," Captain Briggs muttered.

"Then tell me, at least," Albert said.

Captain Briggs halted and turned to him. "You, my most loyal first mate, who has followed me blind to hell and back—you are questioning me?" His voice was low and cold.

Albert nodded. "I'm sorry, Captain, but I am."

The captain glared at him. "Fine, but if I tell you, you can't tell another blasted soul on this crew. Either of you." He looked at Ann sharply. Captain Briggs turned back to the path, still walking as he spoke. "Remember when I went to the tavern? The day before we left? Back when the weather hadn't cleared up?"

"Yes, I remember," said Albert.

"Well, I went to see an old friend of mine. He'd just visited Genoa, Italy. So I spoke with him. Old Gull told me all about a man who was searching for something that had been buried in myth on this very island. Back in Portugal, there was a queen. Each day she brought bread to the poor. The king's right hand man told him she was wasting their money, so he went to her and noticed she had something in her apron. She said they were roses for the Catholic Covenant. The king didn't believe her, since it was winter, but she revealed snow-covered roses. She left without another word and when she reached the people it had turned back to bread."

"And...?" Albert asked.

"Shut your trap! I'm not finished," Captain Briggs grumbled. "So, this man was fascinated with this legend. He came to Portugal and found out how she did it from the diary of a maid in the castle. Not only that, but he found out the roses weren't roses at all, but roses made of ice and snow. There were three things that, when used in an incantation, would turn bread into these roses. This man wants these roses. He's willing to pay two thousand dollars to each crewmember. That's why I brought Sarah and Sophie. We can finally move to Italy, as she's always wanted."

Albert's jaw dropped. *Two thousand dollars?* That was more than they'd ever been paid.

"Now you know. So help me find this blasted piece of gold!" Captain Briggs growled.

They continued on in their search for gold—not a single piece to be found—only more darkness and more slithering things in the dark. Captain Briggs at last put down his barrel and they took a break.

They were all right until a breath of wind made the lantern go dark. Albert set Ann down and searched for something in his pockets. When he found it, he struck it on the ground. It was another match. And when it lit, it illuminated a gold piece the size of his palm right beyond his shoe. He picked it up in wonder. Captain Briggs stared at him before taking the lantern and using Albert's match to rekindle the wick. In the darkness, they heard scraping along the stone. They all turned to see an enormous shadow rear its head. A snake. The gold piece still in Albert's hand, they realized, was a scale.

"Run!" Albert shouted, smacking the snake as it came close.

Captain Briggs grasped the barrel and dropped the lantern. They ran as fast as their legs could carry them. The huge snake hissed violently after them and nipped at their heels. They sprinted blindly into the darkness, running into walls and skidding on the sparsely pebbled ground. They ended up more scraped and bruised than anything they would have imagined as the snake followed after them. They heard the snake's hissing echoing savagely off the cave walls and felt the ground shake under the serpent's massive body. When they reached the split in the tunnels, they saw lamplight, illuminating Gots, Volkert and Andrew who were standing in the way. They continued to run, and finally made it out of the cave.

Ann looked around, her eyes widening. "Where's Albert?"

+

The snake writhed and bit at him. Albert threw a rock at its head, stunning it for a moment before it came back enraged. The golden snake's body coiled around Albert's legs, causing him to fall. He barely caught himself, but the serpent only wound around him and slid up his body, curling tighter and tighter like a coffin, suffocating him.

He tried to reach the knife in his pocket, but his hand was pinned just above it. His fingers could brush the handle but couldn't grab it. He tried to stretch farther, but the snake only squeezed harder. Albert began to lose feeling in his legs first, then the feeling climbed up through him. His heart pounded violently in his chest, adrenaline blurring his vision into a jigsaw puzzle of splotchy color. He tried wrenching his wrist from the snake's grasp, but it only writhed more—constricting harder until a burst of pain flooded his chest as he heard his ribs splinter like twigs.

Albert gasped in pain. Then, slowly, he began to relax, leaving the knife where it was, the pain coursed through him. He felt every second slip before his eyes. He found no reason to reach for the dagger just centimeters from his grasp. He'd sacrificed himself for his captain and the crew. The crew. Ann, with her sweet and fiery face. Ann with her gentle hand that had smacked him with a broom and then helped him back up. She'd saved him from the mermaid and he had intended to save her from this monster. He felt the life slowly drain from his body.

A hand that wasn't his own yanked his knife from his pocket and drove it into the snake. Albert gasped for air, his blurry vision turning to black as he closed his eyes and simply breathed, even with all the pain it brought him. When Albert opened his eyes, he saw his dagger on the floor with spatters of blood and a trickle of crimson coming from the serpent's head. His vision slowly cleared to see Ann's hands specked with the same blood.

She looked at him. "Albert?"

"I'm all right." He smiled softly. She'd saved him again. He reached over, clutched a scale, and ripped it off the snake.

Ann helped Albert bandage his ribs to keep them from being broken further, and Captain Briggs gave him some whiskey to help with the pain. Albert downed a swig and shook his head.

"Vile snake…" he muttered.

"Aye, it was very nasty indeed." Captain Briggs nodded.

Gots' worried eyes scanned their surroundings as if the snake would lunge again any second.

"It's very dead, Gots," Albert assured him, taking another dose of whiskey.

Gots nodded, but still he glanced around nervously, influencing Andrew and Volkert to do the same.

"What's next, Captain?" Albert asked.

"We head to the market for bread."

The other three looked at him like he'd lost his mind, while Albert and Ann nodded and followed back down the dusty path they'd climbed.

꙰

When they reached the marketplace, it was a little past high noon and fairly crowded. The air was cool as evening approached but still bright enough to be out. Captain Briggs purchased two prime loaves of bread. They took the barrel and loaves and lugged them to a secluded hub on the outskirts of town. As they stepped inside, the sun was beginning to set and cast its colors like foreign jewels upon the land.

Captain Briggs set out the items they had collected on a lanky table in the corner of a room occupied only by an old man sleeping and the owner cleaning dishes. He approached the owner and asked if he could leave them in private for a time, paying him with a small sack of coins. The owner woke the old man and they left the room together as the captain pulled out a piece of crinkled paper with scribbled hand writing.

Take the mermaid hair and drape it over the loaves.

He did so simply.

Take the spider and scrape the dew off its back. Distribute it onto each loaf.

Albert handed over the barely-alive arachnid, and Captain Briggs, using a pair of tweezers, pushed a drop of moisture off its back onto each loaf.

Now take the gold and put shavings on each loaf.

Captain Briggs took a knife from Gots and carefully shaved off pieces of the scale for each loaf before handing it back to him.

Now, speak these words: Mermaid Hair, Spider Dew, and Slithering Gold, bring back the Alchemy of Old.

Captain Briggs took hands with each of the men till they encircled the table. He told them the chant, and they chanted it softly once, twice, and a fearful third time beginning to wonder if it would work.

The table began to glow snakeskin gold as the bread absorbed the ingredients in the order they'd been presented. The glow then changed to a bright, elegant blue like the feather of a bird, and the loaves began to melt and change before their eyes. They frosted over and melted into pools, reforming their very shape into that of roses with stems of icy glass, leaves of frost, and petals of snow.

When the light finally stopped, two bouquets of ice roses lay on the table. Captain Briggs carefully picked them up and put them in the barrel before marching out of the shop. The rest of the crew followed him in a bit of a daze. Onward to Genoa, Italy.

Back on the ship, they gently placed the roses in a chest and set sail with ease. But Albert was still restless. He stood at the helm, making sure they were headed in the correct direction.

Ann came onto the deck and looked at him smiling. "We're alive."

"Yes, we are. I'm alive thanks to you."

"Well, that was pretty heroic to try and kill a python all by yourself." Her eyes sparkled at him. Her fingers ran themselves over the helm until they brushed over his. Albert's heart collided with his ribcage as she let her hand rest on his.

"What's this for?" he chuckled, trying not to let on how nervous he was.

"For being alive, for being brave, for not treating me like I'm some sort of witch just because I'm a girl who likes to sail," Ann spoke quietly.

"Of course." He smiled softly at her.

Her face came closer causing Albert's heart to skip like the wing beat of a fledgling robin.

She smiled up at him. "You're not going to do it, are you?"

"What?" he asked, completely lost.

Ann rolled her eyes and grabbed his shirt, yanking him forward into a surprisingly delicate kiss. His heart fluttered before he gingerly kissed her back.

She pulled back gently.

"Talk to you later, Albert," she whispered with a smile before she vanished beneath the deck and headed back to her post.

Captain Briggs came and took over the helm just as the first drop of rain slipped out of the clouds.

✦

It wasn't long before the wind picked up. The crew pulled and tugged at the ropes. Where had this bizarre weather blown in from? Captain Briggs looked into the wind, sure that the horizon would clear and make way for them.

"Captain! We're a man short." Arian yelled over the tumultuous wind, his German accent cutting clean through the storm.

"What?" Briggs shouted back.

"The men. We only have six men!" Arian reported.

Captain Briggs looked out over crew, trying to count them as they scrambled about like bees to keep the ship afloat. Arian was wrong—the situation was far worse. They only had five men, including Arian, for a boat that required a crew of at least seven

"Get to work then. Make up for the slack!" Captain Briggs commanded,

Rain pelted the deck like gunfire. Captain Briggs stayed at the helm, clutching it like it was the only thing keeping him from spilling into the ocean. He glanced at the kegs on deck and thought about the swords and pistols below. Was this punishment for his dishonesty? All these years as a pirate were just about to pay off. He'd been begging for this moment, and now he worried the storm was about to wash it all away.

Never. He was not going to let that happen. Yet he couldn't help but wonder where the storm was taking his crew. He wanted to stop for them, but in this storm it would be impossible. The waves continued to crash onto the boat. He watched as, before his very eyes, his crewmembers began to vanish with each wave. Five, four, three, two.

Only Albert and Ann were left. They clung to each other, sensing they couldn't escape. Something was terribly wrong about this whole trip—this whole ship. There was no escape. They were all going to die.

Captain Briggs watched as a giant wave came toward them. Surely, this was his punishment. He'd taken the roses that were meant to help the people and had angered the powers that be with his actions.

The wave crashed upon them, sweeping away Ann and Albert in their final embrace.

Before he could react, his wife came onto deck with Sophie.

"No!" he shouted in anguish. He watched their terrified faces as they were lifted from the ship by the waves and swallowed by the sea.

His crew, his wife, his daughter. All gone. Everything he loved and cared about. He stood alone as the storm raged around him. Slowly, he walked out onto the deck and accepted his fate. A strangled cry came from deep within as the captain sank to his knees and waited for the sea to take him.

✦

December fourth, Eighteen seventy-two.

A man on-board a Canadian Brigantine wrote in his journal just as he heard shouting from above. He climbed up to see what was the matter. A seaworthy vessel had come up alongside them, creaking and groaning, but it seemed devoid of any life.

A few of the crewmembers went aboard. The man went along with them. The ship was sound. There were food rations still in abundant supply. They found cargo and belongings, all in place. Strange...no bodies, no signs of a struggle.

They came upon a black chest that none of them could open.

"What should we do with this?" a crewmate asked.

"Put it with the rest!" the man ordered.

He eyed the unusual chest. Maybe, one day, he'd find out what lay inside.

Just Causes Are Subjective

For the entire world, one thing is constant: water is a symbol of peace and calm. Free, open, and vast, a chance to begin again. The ocean is purity.

Now that I'm here, though, so close to water, so close to freedom, I try to look past the horizon, the glimmering sparkles of freedom and purpose. I don't see any such thing. I just see a lot of water and the same places and people I saw back east.

For several years I saved all the money I made to get here. And now, I can officially see that it was pointless. I walk through the streets and continue my life as it was before, taking odd jobs so I have something to eat. The crowded streets of this harbor town are foreign to me. It's uncanny, to see the same streets yet not recognize them. I crowbar my thoughts away from my surroundings and focus on walking. Maybe the water is better up close. I land my feet at the end of the wooden docks. The water is foggy and dirty. I've seen cleaner rivers.

"Hey, kid!"

I turn to see a salesman type. I would normally ignore him but he's standing in front of a ship.

"Kid, do I have an opportunity for you."

"I'm not planning on buying anything," I turn to go back into town.

The man lands his hand on my shoulder. "Hey, hey, hey. I'm not planning on selling anything, kid. How would you like to make some easy money?"

I groan. "How much?"

"Flexible, depending on how well you do."

I stare him down. This sounds like an obvious scam.

"Fine. I get it, kid. You don't trust me. Well, I have to go get my cargo. And once you see how profitable my cargo is, you'll want to get a cut."

+

I don't know why I am waiting for that jerk. I literally have nothing else to do and being on a ship is better than begging for jobs. So, I suppose that's my best guess. I stop spacing out for a moment, noticing a few men walking toward the ship. I hear the clanking of chains. The captain wasn't joking about his trade being valuable. He has slaves in tow.

"Kid, you rethinking whether or not to stay on for a trip to the Caribbean?"

I nod. He has money.

The man at the front of the slave train stops a fair distance away from me. He's wrapped in dirty, brown and white rags across his torso. The man covers up the rags with a brown coat. The man's scruffy beard makes his face look large and his hat allows him to cast a large shadow over me. The shadow of the hat covers his face.

"I'm Argyle," says my new boss. "I expect you to call me Captain Argyle."

I nod once again. "Yes, Captain Argyle!"

The man walks up to me. Only now do I realize he's a full head taller than I am. He pats me on the shoulder then he, and several sailors, pull the slaves onto the ship. I follow the last slave on board.

I've never been on a ship before. I try to take in the sights and sounds and experience some sort of wonderment. The ship is massive, triple my height not counting the sail or what is under the water. And that's nothing compared to how long the ship is, over 25 times as long as me laying down.

"Hey, kid, were you even listening?"

I look behind me.

"I said to clean the lower decks." Capitan Argyle shoves a mop into my hands.

I roll my eyes and follow orders as the ship leaves the port behind.

✦

The main deck looks pretty clean, but the lower deck is just...disgusting. The sailors have buckets of foul smelling junk, which I hope is rotting food. A few of these buckets are spilled over. I try not to look at what's in them and lazily plop the mop near the closest pool of filth. Argyle shuts the hatch leading to the upper deck, cutting me off from the light.

I resign to my fate. Another average odd job. The crash of a barrel hitting the floor jerks me toward its direction. In the dark, I almost miss it—a leg disappearing behind a pile of crates. I take a deep breath and hold my mop in their direction. "All right. Come out. I saw you."

Silence.

I strain my eyes to see in the dark. Whoever it is doesn't come out. I know full well whoever this is may kill me, but I take a few cautious steps. As I turn the corner, a slave girl hugging her knees comes into view. We exchange long, hard glares.

"Don't tell anyone you saw me, please. They throw escaped slaves off the side of the boat."

My mind conjures up images of Argyle. I'm on his ship with his men, not to mention he is a foot taller than me. I take the slave girl by the upper arm. "Sorry, but I could get killed."

She drops the act quickly and slaps away my hand, then tackles me to the floor. She presses her arm into my neck. "Sorry, but I *will* be killed once they see shark fins in the water!"

I brace for impact but then slowly open my eyes, realizing she's not going to punch me. Gulping, I tap on her forearm. "Fine, I won't tell them. Please, don't hurt me!"

The slave girl backs off. "Thank you." She sits on one of the crates. "I was never going to hurt you. I'm sorry. I'm a bit jumpy."

"Oh my god, you scared the hell out of me!" I pick up my mop and go back to scrubbing the impossible to clean floorboards. "Wait, you speak English?"

The slave girl stares at me. "A lot of slaves know English. Well, at least slaves owned by people who speak English." She chuckles to herself. "I would love to see a slave owner who doesn't speak to their slaves - do this and do that."

"Tell me about it."

The slave girl's expression drops. She throws daggers with her eyes, waiting for me to justify what I said.

I think through my response several times. I give up. "What? We have the same lot in life."

"No. We don't."

"What do you mean? We both work for relatively nothing."

"You work for *relatively* nothing. I work *for* nothing." The slave girl pulls the mop out of my hands. "If we both went to a farm, and I was injured, I could be shot in the head or made to be a birthing machine. You would get medical treatment or just be fired."

I swallow hard. "Okay, I see your point but I can't do anything to really help with that."

The slave girl takes me by the shoulders. "You can help us, plain and simple."

"Help you, how?"

"Help me escape."

I back away. "I have to get back to work. I can't help you escape."

"Why not?" She breaks my mop on her knee. "You're not just a grunt on a ship. You have the opportunity to help."

I look around. Now that I'm used to the dark, I'm able to see the entire room. On all the walls I notice iron latches that open windows for cannons, yet no cannons are set up anywhere. The room is filled with crates, some only waist high while a handful of them are tall enough to be scraping the ceiling. I spin around trying to think. I look to the slave girl trying to figure out if I could help her. And if I should. I just met her but I find her familiar. I only barely remember what Capitan Argyle looks like apart from being tall and scary. She seems more real, somehow.

Finally, I nod. "I'll help." It makes me sick to my stomach with fear but I'll try.

+

I follow the slave girl to the opposite wall of the ship. With the occasional beam of light from a hole in the deck to give us light, I scan the room over and over again. Storage crates and piles of barrels surround us. I can't stop glancing at the hatch to the upper deck. My heart is pounding out of my chest. If even one person comes down…

The slave girl stops at a door. "This is where all the other slaves are being kept."

I want to protest, tell her that I never agreed to help the other slaves. But instead, my hands move on their own, gliding across beams of solid air as they are forced toward the lock on the door. I dig through my pockets and find my lock-picking tools. I tap lightly, traveling from tumbler to tumbler, trying to find where these suckers would click. One by one, they lock into place. I turn the lock slowly, until the door opens. "There we go."

The slave girl falls silent.

My heart leaps and I pull open the door. A few slaves fall out. They were packed in tight. "I can't believe they put them here like this."

"I slipped away while the crew was stuffing us in. I've been stuffed into enough transports to know what it's like. It's as uncomfortable as it looks." She shakes one of the slaves and whispers. "Everyone, you're free!"

A hushed murmur passes through the group.

+

Finally, I can see why the slave girl got so offended when I insisted we were similar. I run from crate to crate, busting them open one by one. I find a box of five guns and some ammo. I toss the guns and ammo to the slaves. I keep searching until I finally find what I'm looking for.

Cannons. Long thin ones. I pile them near the hatch. Running back to the crates, I start to push the taller ones into position to make a small hallway around the entrance to the hatch. The slaves help me push the crates. I take a rifle from one of the slaves. The ammo is in a small cart made of wax or tough animal skin. I bite the cart open and stuff a bullet into the gun alongside some gunpowder.

Opening the hatch, I see a few sailors nearby. My heart stops as when the old, metal latches creak. To my luck, the closest sailor doesn't notice. He's facing away from me, completely oblivious to the fact that I've let out all the slaves. We could wait until we're in town to make our break. No, then the authorities will surround the boat. We must do this now, or never. My heart feels like it's being squeezed, as I squeeze the trigger.

The bullet hits the back of his neck. I duck back down quickly. I steel myself as the clamor of boots above my head grows louder and louder.

"Get your guns ready!" I jump over the pile of prepared cannons.

The sailors cautiously come down, slowly walking toward us, swearing as they bump into the crates and each other.

"Fire!" the slave girl yells.

We fire into the sailors, killing the ones in front, blowing their heads off, and forcing them to trudge over the corpses of their allies. I fire as fast as I can. Finally, the wall of the dead gets close.

"Light the fuses!" the girl yells.

We all take a few steps back as the cannons go off, pushing the sailors back, killing, dismembering, and disabling all of the sailors below deck.

A few more sailors come in and this time they sprint over the cannons, guns in hand.

I dash behind the crates. I try to press my back against the crates to cut off the path to us but I only manage to bump into a slave. He shifts me to the side as he holds his gun close to his chest. He smiles as the sailors rush out the killing corridor.

"Now! Now! Now!"

The slaves rush the sailors from the sides and wrestle them to the ground, stealing their guns.

I'm awestruck by the ingenuity of the slaves. I would have never thought to use the moment before the sailors spotted us to our advantage. I count the sailors again, just as I had in that short moment before Captain Argyle forced me down here. That should be the last of them, apart from the captain. I poke my head out of the hatch to see where he is.

"Big mistake!" The captain grabs me and throws me across the deck. My back smashes against the wall of the stern. "Kid, you've just cost me my entire life." Capitan Argyle casts his shadow over me, pointing a handgun at my forehead. "Now, I have to ask. Why? Did you think I was going to snuff you out of payment? Were you really so mad that I made you sweep and mop? I don't get it."

"Take a wild guess, you disgusting waste of a human being."

Captain Argyle's face contorts, like he stepped in a pile of manure. "You think what I'm doing is wrong?"

I nod.

"Really brave, I must admit, kid. But, I have to pose this counter argument. I'm doing what I need to survive. A sailor now days only makes profit by going to the new world. Nothing makes more money than the slave trade. Just causes are subjective. I have my own reasons."

I see the slave girl aiming her rifle.

I smile. "Go to hell and take your subjective bull with you. Just causes are *not* subjective. There is evil in the world. Taking freedom away from people is evil. You can try to justify it if you don't give enough of a damn. But it's never okay."

"This isn't opinion, debate, or a subjective idea. This is cold as lead fact."

The captain's head splatters across the wall just above me.

The slave girl helps me to my feet. "Nice speech for someone who didn't care ten minutes ago."

I blush and nod.

"By the way, I'm Anna, or at least that's the name you people can actually pronounce."

"Nice to meet you, Anna. I'll go and find a few people who know how to sail a ship like this."

"Heading home?" she asks.

"Only to take you back," I say. "I want to do this for the rest of my life."

Anna grunts, confused.

"Freeing slaves."

"Count me in," she says. "No way I'm going to let this happen anymore."

I look to the horizon. "Actually, what if we head to the Caribbean? It'll be easier to hit slaver ships there."

"Like we're pirates?"

I smile at Anna. "Pirates fighting for a just cause."

As the day ends, I see the purple and orange hues of the sky. Looking behind us, I can see the sunlight on the water. The shimmer of freedom, a chance to begin again, the faint glimmer of peace in the distance.

Cwwnty Carlisle

EMILY CARLISLE

Bloodtides

A thick, frayed coil of rope was rapidly looped around my waist, nearly squeezing the breath out of me. Weathered hands worked on a complicated knot, securing me to the mast. The wind howled through the sky, whipping a flutter of thrilling excitement into my chest and thrusting the breath out of my lungs in a burst of euphoria. The rolling waves, aggravated by the oncoming storm, reached new heights, like they were trying to give the hull a high-five.

I stood, open to the angry gray sky around me, as thunder tumbled in the distance. Icy drops of rain began to fall, chilling me. I tapped the rope around my waist and glanced back. One hand held sturdy to the railing, while the other set to work with tying my hair out of my face. "Is it secure, Ray?" I shouted over the ocean.

"Yes, Lady Mercer!" came the frail cry of the worn, older man behind me.

I watched as Ray uncoiled a long length of bungee cord, seamlessly tied to the rope around my waist.

I glanced down, smiling at the sea-tossed ship below us. Huge waves lapped at its decks, sending it rocking back and forth like it was little more than a dinghy. Its soaked sails were whipping in the wind as people struggled to maintain control.

Ah, privateers. Their brains were soft, their ships pampered. I'd grown accustomed to their ships being off-limits. Only a fool would make a direct attack on the aristocrats. I supposed that had all changed when the nobility threw the first punch.

The image of our ships falling in flames was seared into my mind. Every time I closed my eyes I could see it, hear the desperate screams, the splintering of wood, the screechings of failing metal. I remember the sound that no one speaks of. The sound of hundreds of people realizing their time in this life was up.

It was time to fight back.

And, boy, this was going to be easy.

My smile grew wider as the royal crew below began to stir in realization. Sea ships had no defense against threats from above. The storm had given us the perfect cover until we reached them. Now, it was too late.

A heavy hand came to a rest on my shoulder. I glanced over at my father. "I'll need my sword, Captain," I said.

Father placed a smaller piece of wood and metal into my hand instead. "No, Kendra, take this. It will suit you much better."

I held the device, examining it. Father adjusted my grip, sinking my fingers into the leather grooves. One finger was poised over the trigger, the barrel pointed up toward the sky. He pulled a small lever, producing a tiny click.

"It's a gun," came his voice beside me. "A flintlock."

The device fit comfortably in my hand. Shouts of alarm filtered up from the ship below, and my heart began to pound with anticipation. Exactly how much damage could this gun inflict? I leveled it at the privateer ship.

"Why a gun when I've been skilled in the sword for years?" I asked. The device felt strange in my hand, unbalanced.

My father's voice was tinged with pleasure. "A better weapon, to kill a bigger beast." He held my hand steady, the grip cold and slick with rain.

I fired the flintlock, the recoil sending vibrations up my arm. I took a step back with shock, the sound still echoing in my ears. My skin buzzed. "It's excellent."

My father left my side to smoothly shift into stance as Captain Edmund Mercer of *The Plague*. He held the air of nobility, regal and commanding. The polished hilt of his longsword stuck out against his black overcoat, which flapped in a dark trail behind him as the winds roared. I felt a beam of pride when I noticed that the dark leather handle of his own flintlock made an appearance as well, his hand perched on his belt nearby. The captain and I—we had the best weapons. His steely eyes focused on the scattered mass of his crew before him.

As if with a single, unspoken thought, all motion on the airship stopped. Burly men discontinued managing the sails, while a skinny lookout slid down from the crow's nest to stand at attention. A few men came forward, likely from steering the fins in the back control room.

All eyes were on the captain.

I stepped down from the edge of the ship, tucking my gun into my waistband.

"Today is a big day, men."

Father's proclamation was met with shouts of glee. Just one chance to play justice, one chance to avenge the fallen. It had been a gnawing itch in the back of everyone's minds since the rest of our fleet had been shot down. Friends, brothers, families, had been on those ships.

These men were entitled to revenge.

Captain Mercer stepped down from the main-deck, standing amongst his men. "Let us fight for our lost ones with tact and skill. We were lucky today; the skies have granted us a chance. A chance to fight back!"

The crew roared, the commotion filling my ears. My stomach fluttered in excitement as a slight smile crossed my lips. I fidgeted, ice-cold streams of water trailing down my neck, eager to jump off the ship and *win* this.

That was the thing about looking down on your enemies, I suppose. A side-effect to having complete control.

Confidence.

Looking back, I can see where I went wrong. Where we *all* went wrong.

Thunder cracked, a sharp whip, and the captain shouted over the noise. "An unsuspecting ship full of palace rats...all *alone*."

Uproarious laughter.

The grin slowly faded off my father's face, to be replaced by an image of pure determination. He turned toward Stick, the pilot standing beside him. I could barely make out the captain's voice through the wind. "Stall *The Plague*. Drop the anchors."

In response, Stick and five other men darted toward the small engine room, the door slamming shut behind them.

A persistent groaning permeated through the crashing waves and rain, like protesting metal that was pushed beyond its limits. The enormous fins on both sides of the ship were curved like great bronze dragon wings. Slowly, they tilted back, their spindly structures blocking the wind and rain. Little sheets of tin and steel slid off the fins with the exertion, bit by bit exposing the bronze skeletons beneath. Metal flew through the air, a panel of steel wedging itself into the wood beside me.

My heart leaped into my throat as I leaned over the airship's edge, the roiling ocean below me. The barest mists of foam sprinkled my brow.

It was refreshing, being so close to the heavens. I closed my eyes, breathing in the crisp, cleansing air. We were put in the skies for a reason, after all. Our purpose was to explore, to sail, and now, to fight. We had this ship, the ship had a crew, the crew had my father, and my father—well, he had me.

I was vital, and everyone knew it.

I leaned closer to the edge of the ship to enjoy the hyperactive thrum that vibrated my core and shook a smile onto my face. It had been awhile since I'd last stepped foot on dry land. I could hardly remember the people there. The boring, ordinary people that were missing that spark that I clung to so tightly.

Excitement, adventure. Were any of them truly alive without it?

The sounds of our crew and the storm dulled, and I distantly heard the stretch and tug of pulleys as I moved forward. The cool breeze propelled me with invisible wings of mist and cloud. The ocean was a living thing, a writhing force of nature that was never satisfied, always hungry. It could speak to you in a language that only the most experienced knew.

Right there, in that moment, I could feel its voice deep in my chest with an understanding like I'd never known before.

"Lady Mercer! You'll fall!"

My eyes snapped open. It was Ray, that stubborn old mule. My breathing hitched, while my heart nearly exploded at my dangerous position. Rough hands ripped me backward and reminded me of the man's usefulness. I landed on the deck with a wet thud, the breath stolen from me. My eyes were glued to the sky, the frigid rain coating my face.

I blinked the water out of my eyes, slowly getting to my feet.

Had I really been about to go overboard?

At a safe distance away from the ledge, I took in my surroundings once again. Ray hovered around me, suddenly the perfect caretaker. I had to get started. I had to *jump*. The sheer urge to do just that set me aflame.

As an answer to my pleas, I heard the Captain's voice through the commotion, shouting for the first twelve jumpers to get harnessed to the pulleys. We were attached to the privateer ship with a razor-sharp anchor that had just been dropped. The enemy crew would be terrified at this point.

I heaved a soft laugh. *Finally.*

Ray untied the safety rope around my waist and replaced it with a leather harness. It dug firmly into my spine. I could hardly breathe without feeling the secure pressure against my ribcage.

I rested a careful hand on the handle of my gun as the eleven other men were quickly tethered to the ship. We were well-trained. These were our lives. The men beside me were just as eager as I was. This is what we loved most. To *jump.*

With a word from the captain, we took our places near the edges of our ship, the wind roaring fiercely. Really, could we have asked for a better storm?

The last thing I heard before I jumped was my own laughter.

A split second of pure bliss. A split second that made my life worth living.

I bobbed in the air, the tension of the cord strapped to my back releasing in bursts, the privateer deck nearing fast.

I waited for the perfect moment, then ripped off my harness, landing on the deck with a roll. I rose from a crouch with my gun drawn, legs shakily adjusting to the tossing sea. Already, men were dropping from the sky around me, swords flashing. Big sneering men, meant to distract. They would cover me, while I made for the good stuff.

The treasures, the wealth. I got them every time.

The poor men on this ship never stood a chance.

The path to below deck was practically cleared as I sprinted down the steps. I kept my feet light, nearly soundless, although I doubted anyone worthy of a fight was near. All the tough ones would be above.

The first room I came across was empty. Just wooden walls and flooring, damp and musty, and no lighting.

The next room I came across was…well, it was empty too.

As was the next.

And the one after that. Just, vacant.

I clenched my gun. Already, my infamous temper was wearing thin. I bit my lip, painfully aware of the striking sounds of battle from above. Metal on metal, thuds, shouts. How many of those fallen men were my father's? Each sound made for a handful of sand sifting from one end of the hourglass, down to the next.

I quickly approached the next door. If these were all empty—

The shadows moved.

I jumped back from the door handle, finger poised over trigger. I couldn't focus because the shadows were everywhere. A rippling, squirming mass, like liquid darkness. It *steamed*, a horrific hissing filling the air around me. My skin crawled, a whimper stuck in the back of my throat.

Then, the shadows coalesced into a man.

I held back a yelp as he rushed toward me, movements fluid and lithe. His skin seemed to shimmer, ethereal like the night sky. The shadows seemed to cling to him in bursts of static. An ink black blade was pressed against my neck.

I fired my gun.

The sound splintered through the eerily quiet air as I struggled for breath, swallowing away the sting against my neck. The man crumpled like a doll, soundless, light as a feather.

I could only watch as that same hissing sound imbued the room again. The man *sank*, deflated like a torn waterskin. Tiny grains of jet black dust sifted through the hole I'd blown through his chest.

Smoke hovered lazily above the body of that *thing*.

It wasn't dust. It was ash.

Robotically, I tore my gaze away from the man and threw open the door before me.

Don't think. Just do.

I could hear my own breathing as I stepped into the room.

This one was filled to the brim with books.

Books. Why books?

The walls were painted in breathtaking, exquisite murals from floor to ceiling. I saw nothing but red, swirling clouds and a shifting sea that seemed to move with your eyes. An airship. A lightning strike. An ocean-tossed vessel, filled with an ongoing battle.

Eyes wide, I wove through the books, touching the walls.

Engraved on the side of the airship, was *The Plague*.

I gasped.

"They're beautiful, aren't they?" A low, gravelly voice.

I whirled around.

A man bound in chains, slouched against the wall opposite of me. A robe clung to his body with sweat and grime, the hood pulled low over his head.

"Who are you?" I demanded.

"I should be entitled to the same question," he said. I couldn't see any sort of movement. No rising and falling of the chest for breath, no ringing of chains. "This is my ship. Who are *you*?"

I couldn't find the correct words. What was I supposed to say? Something told me I should have shot this man by now. I could have been in and out of the room, faster than a blink.

But I held back.

The chains clanged as he gestured toward the murals. "I painted them myself."

I couldn't resist bringing my gaze back to the paintings, and I was shocked to find the ocean ship empty of the battle that had been occurring only moments before. I squinted. Odd.

"Red," I murmured. "You like red?"

The airship swayed in the virtual air. "I...I truly do. I truly crave it."

The hairs on the back of my neck stood on end. I carefully shifted my finger over the trigger of my gun. "The guards," I began, "Your crew. Up above. They fell easily. You're alone now, and I have the rights to your cargo."

A soft chuckle, or something like it. It sounded more like a knife scraping against rock. "Is that truly so?"

"These paintings are stunning," I heard myself say. I was so enraptured. Rapid blinking tore me away from their spell, and I turned toward the odd man again. This nonsense had to stop. I had to *focus*.

"It's blood," he whispered, rocking in his chains.

I frowned. "Blood? What are you talking about?" In that moment, I understood. He was a madman, maybe a former member of the crew. He'd been locked up to keep out his disturbed ramblings. It all made sense now. I shook my head and raised my gun to his hooded gaze. "You know, your guards didn't do a very good job keeping me out, did they?"

He laughed.

I felt something cool pressed against my temple. I felt numb. My gun. It was digging into the sensitive flesh beside my eye, my finger still on the trigger. "I... I... "

"Truly foolish child." The man's voice was a low rumble, poignant and scornful. "Keep you out? You. You're the last one left. I'm so glad you've come. Truly. I've been waiting for someone so truly ignorant and malleable to fall so low as to find *me*. You're the last one, and the first. For, you see, I can truly use you."

Chills scraped up and down my back and I shivered, trying desperately to move. I couldn't. I *couldn't*.

The gun jammed into my skull, and I cried out.

"Unchain me, or I'll shoot."

Seaworthy

Elka looked back toward the Tisana Harbor as it faded into the mist. She fingered the dagger her father had given her, tracing the Shorken design etched into the handle from the shark's head down to the seahorse tail. Both the design and the weapon were beautiful, yet deadly.

Taking a deep breath, she turned back to face the bustling ship— *her* bustling ship. A stiff breeze filled the sails and tugged at her cat-like ears.

This crew belonged to her now. With only minimal help from Aldrew, she was off to prove herself and lead them to good fortune.

It was an intimidating, yet thrilling, prospect being the sole leader. Perhaps that was why her father had given her the dagger. She needed to remember being a captain held dangerous responsibilities. If she didn't use her position correctly, horrible things would happen. Zarbin had proved that on his own solo voyage, only four years ago.

Elka's fur bristled at the thought as she shook it off. She wouldn't repeat his mistakes and bring her father shame. Aldrew glanced at her across the ship, one of his dark ears lifted questioningly. She smiled, assuring him all was well.

The first day at sea went by quickly. Elka visited with the other two women on board. Anna, a brown-haired human served as the ship's doctor, and Mikkia, a fellow kattian with tortoiseshell patterned

fur, would be the ship's cook. It was rare to have more than one woman aboard. Elka found it a pleasant change from past voyages. Her
father must have hired them to keep her company.

She also met with the apprentices and their mentors, going over
duties and training schedules. Syan, a black furred kattian youth, was
on his naming voyage—the coming-of-age ceremony boys performed
at 16 to earn their last name. The younger boys looked up to him with
the same hero-worship they gave their mentors. Working alongside
Aldrew and the other mentors inspired Elka. They worked hard for
everything they got, and they trusted her to lead them true so their
hard work would pay off.

Clouds obscured the moon when Elka stepped out of her cabin
that night. She bit her lip.

*This can't be happening right now. I need to know our location
so we can head to the tropics in the morning—*

She moved toward the bow, trying to ignore the nervous flip-
flopping feeling in her stomach. The sky looked no clearer from this
vantage point. A breeze rustled the pages of her logbook and she held
it tighter in the crook of her left arm. She set her sextant and map on a
crate with an audible huff. She glared up at the sky, as if she could
clear it with her gaze. Her ears flicked upward. Someone was approaching.

"Too cloudy?" The sailor on watch came beside her. She noticed
a small, monkey-like creature curled up on his shoulder. A fronkey?
She couldn't see much besides the furry brown back and tail, the
scaled underbelly and webbed feet were concealed. How would a poor
sailor get a fronkey?

"Yeah." Elka glanced at him. "I need to make sure we're staying
on course, but with this sky…"

He nodded. "At least the sea is calm."

They fell into an awkward silence. Elka's cheeks grew warm
with embarrassment as she struggled to find something to say.
"What's your name again? I don't think we've been properly introduced."

"Edge, Edge Truman." He smiled. His eyes met hers for a second
but then moved back to look over the ocean.

Elka caught a glimpse of those eyes, they were full of sadness
and strength. His black hair stirred in the breeze. Her cheeks blazed
hotter when she realized she was staring with her ears pricked forward
in interest. She hurriedly looked away and lowered her ears.

*Seriously? What are you doing? You barely know him! Besides,
he's probably just lonely.*

Glancing back at the sky, she noticed the clouds had moved. Not enough to matter, unfortunately.

"I love the night watch," Edge said. "It's much more peaceful than any other time."

"Really? I think it would be lonely and creepy. Staying out all night in the dark, cold air."

He shrugged. "It gives me time to think on my own."

Elka liked that answer. "I guess it would be nice every once and awhile. But doesn't it get tedious? Don't you run out of thing to think about during all that time?"

"You'd be surprised." He took a deep breath. "There's a lot to think over. I ponder my future, set goals, remember the past."

"I guess you're right."

He looked back at her. "Have you ever wondered about your future?"

She hesitated. "I don't know." She hadn't, really. She had followed the plans laid out by her parents, wanting to not fail them like her brother Zarbin. Maybe that was part of the reason why she was so afraid to fail on this voyage—because Zarbin had failed, even with her father there to help him. "I guess I haven't, really." She looked over at him slyly. "I mean, *besides* wondering about the weather."

Edge laughed, and she joined him, glancing back at the sky. The clouds had thickened instead of clearing away.

"Well, I'm not going to get anything more done tonight. I had better get some sleep." She reluctantly gathered her supplies. "But thank you, Edge. You helped me feel at peace."

He nodded. "Goodnight, Captain Elka."

She hurried back to her cabin, trying not to think about the heat in her cheeks.

+

During the next two weeks Elka started developing a habit to visit with Edge when he was on the night watch. She considered him a friend after talking with him so often. They mostly talked about his favorite places to visit on voyages. He also told her the story about rescuing his fronkey from a breeder who was planning to put her down. Edge showed her the tiny baby the fronkey had.

Eventually, they reached a small port city but it had little trade to offer. Elka gave the sailors a day's leave of absence. She, along with Aldrew's help, bought some trifles to trade down south. The rest of the day they spent calculating trading prospects in each scheduled ports on the chart.

The sailors returned from their personal excursions near sundown. Edge had his head down, a frown hardening his features.

"Edge, what's wrong?" Elka came beside him.

"I'm fine."

"You don't look fine."

"Then stop looking." Edge turned away.

"No." Elka planted her hands on her hips, glaring at his back. "You're a part of my crew and I won't be dismissed. What happened?"

Edge growled in frustration. "You have no right to pry into my private affairs, *Captain.*"

His fronkey chittered at her from his shoulders, as if agreeing with him. While it was truly none of her business, his tone made her fur itch.

"Well, sorry for caring then." Elka huffed.

He sighed, glancing at her for a moment but left without another word, heading for his quarters.

She stalked away.

The conversation followed her all day, nagging at the back of her mind. Had she pushed too far? She didn't want to ruin their new friendship.

A knock came on her cabin door that night.

She opened the door. Edge was standing there, examining the woolen hat in his hand. *It must be time for his watch.*

"I want to apologize for my harshness earlier." He looked up at her. "I was in a bad mood but that doesn't excuse me taking it out on you when you only wanted to help."

"I'm sorry too." She reached out and touched his arm gently. The touch sent a wave of unanticipated exhilaration through her. "I shouldn't have pried."

He smiled. "Thank you."

The bell rang for second night watch, causing them both to look up.

"Well, goodnight." He said, putting on the hat. "I'm sorry, again."

"That's okay. Goodnight." She closed the door, lingering behind it for a moment. It was good to know they were still friends, even if part of her wanted to be more than that.

As the weeks passed, Elka found herself spending more and more of her time talking with Edge. The other crewmembers started to comment on how much time they were spending together. A few of the unmarried men said Edge had a sweet spot for her, but she didn't believe them. She spent time with him because she felt comfortable around him. He always respected her, even if he didn't always agree with her opinions. Even if a nagging part of her wanted him to view her romantically, she didn't think it would happen.

Finally, they arrived in Mezero. Elka smiled at the bustling port, ears set forward with excitement. It was invigorating, seeing the progress they had made on their voyage.

Aldrew leaned on the railing beside her, grinning. "You found your confidence." His blue eyes twinkled in their familiar way.

She laughed, ears lowering modestly. "I had a few role models to help me find it."

"Your father would be proud."

She nodded, bumping shoulders with her grey-furred mentor and relaxed a bit.

"Captain," one of the men yelled. "Someone wants to come on board."

She turned, glancing at Aldrew with confusion. Down below, a well-dressed kattian gentleman and his human servant stood on the dock.

"Why are you here, sir?" Elka raised her voice so he could hear her clearly.

"I'm looking for a sailor by the name of Edge Truman." He called up to her. "I've been told that he had been hired to work on this ship. Is that so?"

"It is. Come and wait while my crew finishes stowing the rigging." Elka lowered the ramp for him.

He climbed up, fumbling with his cane for a few steps before tucking it under one arm. It took him much longer than she had expected. He stopped halfway up for a few moments as if to catch his breath.

When he reached the deck, she held out a hand in greeting. "I'm Captain Elka."

"Flicker Altinez." He shook her hand. "Pleased to make your acquaintance."

Edge climbed down from the rigging. His face drained of color when he saw Altinez.

"Ah, there you are my boy!" The aging kattian smirked, tail flicking in a self-satisfied way. He tilted his head, talking conversationally to Elka, but loud enough for those around them to hear. "Edge, here, owes me a very steep sum."

Elka felt a weight settle on her heart. Altinez had to be lying. Elka tensed, hoping it wasn't true.

Edge looked down, ashamed. "The money isn't due for another six weeks, Flicker."

"Do you think I don't remember that?" Flicker's smile turned into a scowl. His long, black-tipped ears went back threateningly. "I might not be young anymore, but I haven't lost my faculties, *boy*. I was informed that you were coming this way and decided to pay you a visit. Surely you weren't hoping to worm out of our deal."

"Never," Edge said vehemently. "I gave you my word and I plan to keep it."

"I hope you keep that sentiment. Thank you for your time, Captain." Flicker pointed at Edge. "I expect my payment promptly on the agreed date, do you hear me? I won't wait a second longer."

Edge glared at him. "You'll get it, Flicker."

The kattian gave a curt nod. He turned and climbed back down to the dock, his human servant lagging behind.

Elka whirled to glower at Edge.

"Listen—"

He opened his mouth to answer but she growled to cut him off, her hands clenched into fists.

"I *trusted* you!" She was trembling. She grabbed the front of his tunic, glaring at him. "My older brother Zarbin stained my father's reputation in Nirra-Tok. Because he indebted himself through his reckless gambling, he got an entire shipment confiscated. He killed five men while trying to escape. Where did you get these debts?"

His eyes were filled with tears. "When I was eleven, my parents were sick, my younger brothers were starving, and I was the only one to provide for them. I tried to get a job, I tried begging, but I had no time! I was taking care of my family around the clock. I searched frantically for someone to help me, I even went to the moneylenders! Only Flicker allowed me to contract with him."

Edge paused for a shaky breath. "He saved my life and, ultimately, saved my family's lives. Even though my mother died a month later and my father's mind never recovered from the sickness, my brothers got the food, care, and the education they needed. I may pay this debt with my life, but I do not regret the decision I made."

Elka leaned into him to steady herself. His arms wrapped around her, holding her gently. Thoughts swarmed her, disjointed but urgent. She couldn't figure out what to say, so she just hugged him back, closing her eyes for a moment to block out the world.

"This is what you were thinking about that day you snapped at me. Wasn't it?"

He nodded.

"Why didn't you say something?"

"I didn't want to burden you with my worries," Edge said softly. "I didn't want anyone else dragged into this mess. It is my responsibility."

"How can I help?"

He recoiled, alarm in his face. "No, you can't. Didn't you hear me? I need to deal with this myself."

She raised an eyebrow at him.

The next six weeks passed far too quickly. She tried gifting him a few expensive items but Edge refused them. Fortunately, trading had been successful, and they made a fair profit. Useful commodities had been acquired for their return voyage as well.

Edge entrusted his ledgers into her care during the sixth week. His handwriting was small and angular. His spelling was faulty but his figures were neat and well checked. According to his ledgers, he had enough to pay the remaining debt. He didn't have much more than that, though.

✦

Elka woke after having the most wonderful dream in which she and Edge were getting married. She couldn't fall back to sleep because she kept thinking about it so she climbed out of bed. Was it foolish that she was enthralled? He *was* human—

But did that really matter? His blood was as red as any Kattian man. Plus, he had morality and grit. She knew he was an honest worker and that he would protect her.

What would she do about her father's business, though? She couldn't just abandon it—she was the heir. Marrying Edge would make it difficult to go on all the voyages. Plus, the bias against humans would probably stain her father's reputation *again*.

She pulled on her coat. Perhaps a walk would help clear her head. The cool night air was damp with thick fog. Shadows and mist combined to create an environment of mystery and intrigue, making the night seem even darker than usual. Aldrew and the boy, Syan, were keeping watch near the bow, looking out off the starboard side.

She leaned against the port railing. The blank wall of fog was lightened by a single lantern hanging from the mast. A low *creak* alerted her to something unusual in the night. She whirled.

Aldrew and Syan heard it too. They peered into the mist, looking for the source of the noise. Aldrew waved her off, signaling that he and the dark-furred youth would deal with what had made the noise.

Elka relaxed a bit. She watched them move to aft, and fade out of sight. It was unsettling, seeing them disappear. She waited anxiously, ears pricked for the slightest sound that would indicate what was happening.

A dull thud followed by a yell of surprise reached her ears. Grabbing for her dagger, she realized it was missing. She opened her mouth, planning to yell for help.

"Don't you dare," a low voice threatened while a dark shape stalked into view. "Scream, and one of your crewmen dies."

Two others followed behind, hulking shapes emerging from the darkness.

The first kattian looked familiar, his long ears lowered threateningly. Aldrew was slumped unconsciously against him, a knife being held at his exposed throat.

"Where is Edge?" The kattian demanded.

She looked closer. A rough-spun sleeveless tunic revealed thin, but incredibly muscular arms. The tan-grey fur was tousled with a pirate's uncaring manner, but the black tipped ears were unmistakable.

Flicker Altinez had gone to great lengths to disguise himself.

"He's in his cabin," she answered, sounding as unshaken as she could muster.

Flicker's tail flicked at one of the big thugs. "You, go get him."

"No," Elka intervened. "I'll get him."

Flicker made her swear to only bring Edge, then let her go.

Running into the hold of the ship, she quickly found Edge's hammock and shook him awake. "Altinez is here."

He stood quickly, alarm on his face. "He's here? How?"

"Pirates. I think he's their leader." She waved away any other questions. "He's holding Aldrew and Syan hostage."

They ran to the main deck as quickly as possible.

Flicker was waiting.

Edge stepped forward confidently. "I have enough to pay you."

Flicker sheathed the knife, holding his now free hand toward Edge. "Let's see it then."

Edge handed over the piece of paper listing all his valuables. Flicker looked it over.

"You miscalculated." He tucked the paper into his belt, eyes hard.

Edge hesitated a second. "I have something else." Edge coaxed his fronkey and her baby out of hiding. She hissed softly in displeasure. The lantern light didn't catch the pattern of her fur, but it reflected off her fangs.

Flicker raised an eyebrow. "An exotic pet? How quaint."

Edge glanced at Elka, his jaw tightening. "A priceless pets. Fronkeys have a venom sought by many medical professionals."

"Venom?" Flicker looked unimpressed. "You're lying. Everyone knows fronkeys aren't venomous. I can't accept it as payment. You are short of the full amount." Flicker Altinez unsheathed his knife once more.

Edge hung his head, hope draining from his eyes. "Then, I give myself as your slave, fulfilling our bargain."

Edge turned, walking slowly to the door.

Flicker nodded at Elka. "Go with him, make sure he doesn't kill himself."

One of his thugs laughed darkly.

Elka stiffened, ruffled by the command. This was her ship; he had no right to give her orders. But he had Aldrew and Syan captive. Syan looked terrified. She turned sharply and stalked past Edge into the hold of her ship, tail flicking in anger.

Edge followed.

"How *dare* he." Elka hissed. "I can't let you just surrender yourself to that *filth!*"

"I don't need your permission." Edge's voice was gentle and sad. "I gave him my word. I choose these consequences."

"You were a child." Elka shook her head. "You didn't have a choice!"

"I chose this. I knew enough to make this decision." Edge took one of her hands. "I knew I would not steal, and I knew that I would be an honest man no matter the consequences."

She could feel his hand shaking.

"But *Flicker Altinez* isn't an honest man."

Edge laughed nervously. "True." He paused, looking at her with a strange expression on his face.

"There is one thing I have to tell you." He pulled her closer. "I told myself that I would never marry until I knew my debt was paid. And, honestly, I never thought I would find a woman who could capture my heart, until I met you."

Elka froze. What was he saying?

He leaned in and kissed her.

Her ears went back in surprise. Emotions swam through her, crashing against her consciousness like waves against the rocks. She felt her cheeks grow warm. She pulled him closer.

He pulled away first. "I'm sorry—"

She shushed him. "Get your things. Flicker's waiting." *Not that I'm going to let him take you away now.*

She ran to her cabin and grabbed her pistol and sword, stuffing her father's dagger into its sheath at her belt. If Flicker thought he could hold her crew hostage and hurt Edge, he was wrong. She was ready to fight. As an afterthought, she grabbed two other pistols.

She returned to Edge who was stuffing all his meager belongings into a sack.

"Here." Elka handed him a gun. "Even if you insist on going through with this, I want you armed."

He accepted it dubiously. "He'll take it from me—"

"Keep it anyway."

After he collected the final items, she led the way back to the deck. Flicker still held the knife to Aldrew's throat; his thug still had Syan constrained in a painful looking way.

"Good. Glungar, take his bag."

The second thug, the one not holding Syan captive, moved forward. He reached for Edge's bag.

Elka shot the thug in the chest. He fell to the ground with a whimper.

She whipped out the second pistol, aiming it at Flicker's head. Aldrew was still slumped unconsciously in the pirate's grasp, Flicker's knife moved dangerously close to his jugular. "Drop my first mate." She demanded. "No more of this."

Syan gave a strangled cry, and she caught a glimpse of his captor choking the boy with his beefy arms.

A pronounced click informed her that Edge had drawn and readied his pistol.

Altinez hissed, lips curling into a grimace. "Do you think you can beat me?" The knifepoint pricked Aldrew's collarbone, drawing blood.

"Justice demands I be paid, girl." Altinez continued. "Or are you like your elder brother, trying to evade debtor collectors?"

Elka yowled, taking a step forward. The knife pressed closer to Aldrew's neck.

"Leave her alone, Flicker," Edge said.

"Tell her to back off." Altinez's eyes flicked to the gun in Edge's hands, his grip on the knife slackening slightly. "You were willing enough to pay the full price before she intervened. She has no right to meddle in my affairs."

"And yet you meddle in mine by capturing and harming two of my crew with the intent of taking another!" Elka's eyes blazed with fury. "How can you claim to be seeking retribution while trying to force Edge to pay an unjust price for his debt?"

Altinez cursed. "Enough of this. I demand satisfaction!"

"I will not barter with a *pirate!*" Elka yelled.

The thug holding Syan glanced at Flicker, shifting uneasily. He dropped the boy and scrambled back the way he had come. Edge let him run. They heard him yelling at an unseen crew, begging to leave. Altinez cursed again, ears lowering. His eyes filled with sudden fear and hot rage.

"Traitors!" He bellowed. "Cowards! Come back and fight you minnow-headed lumps!"

He glanced between Edge and Elka, taking a step backward.

Edge moved slightly. Flicker stiffened, arm jerking the knife dangerously close to Aldrew's unprotected neck.

"Steady there, Flicker." Edge spoke with a calm, soothing tone. "We don't want anyone else getting hurt."

Flicker forced a laugh. "Don't try to suggest you aren't going to kill me. I know the laws dealing with piracy."

"Well then, I guess the question is whether you want to die in the ocean, right here on the deck, or on land." Edge lowered his pistol. "Which is it?"

Altinez hesitated. He glanced over his shoulder at the hidden depths of the sea.

He lowered his knife in resignation. "Land." He voice broke over the word. "I would rather die in Mezero." The look in his eyes said that he was really hoping for a way out.

Some of the crew had come topside to see the commotion, and they helped tie Altinez up. Mikkia checked on both Aldrew and Syan as Altinez was led into the hold.

Edge gave Elka a mysterious look. She lowered her eyes and tucked her pistol into her belt, feeling self-conscious. Would he agree with her actions? As he placed a hand on her shoulder, her brown eyes found his.

"Thank you." The emotions in his eyes were more complex than the simple words.

Elka hugged him, allowing herself to relax.

"There is one problem with this situation," Edge said after a moment. "I still owe the debt."

Elka tried to suppress a laugh. It wasn't funny; she knew he felt guilty for the part he had played in Flicker's capture. "Maybe he has a wife. If nothing else, you could give it as a gift to the Mezeroan government."

Edge nodded thoughtfully. "That is a possibility."

She kissed him softly on the cheek. "It can wait." But one thing couldn't. She pulled back and looked into his eyes. "Were you serious, when you said I'd captured your heart?"

+

Four weeks later, after a quick stop in Mezero to hand over Flicker Altinez and pay Edge's debt to Flicker's wife, they were back in the home waters of Tisana. Elka's family celebrated their return. Then, after a few short weeks of preparation and council, Edge and Elka's were married.

Not many attended, but their family and friends approved of their match. There was a simple ceremony, held on a cliff top overlooking the sea. It was a beautiful clear day.

Elka's father pulled her aside afterward. "I'm proud of you." He hugged her tightly.

"My tigerlily, you have done well. You are seaworthy."

Jacob Willden

JACOB PAUL WILLDEN

Sailor for Thought

V incent walked across the main deck, disgusted by the stagnant air. Peering around the collecting crowd of crewmembers, he spotted Captain Bolivar looking over the restless crew.

With his usual serious voice, Bolivar boomed, "We've miscalculated our bearings and have ended up in the middle of the doldrums." The windless region of ocean around the equator. "This will delay us a couple of weeks, however, I ask that you continue your duties as usual. That is all."

The crew stirred as they went toward different decks and back to work. Vincent noticed First Mate Sorrel walking closer to Bolivar with a raised eyebrow.

"We're completely at the mercy of weak currents," Sorrel said quietly.

Bolivar adjusted his blue hat and coat.

"If it wasn't for this, we'd have gotten through the doldrums in three days instead of four weeks."

"We have plenty of supplies. We'll be fine," said Bolivar.

"Yet again, we've ended up in the wrong place. There are only three major currents to carry us out of this mess," said Sorrel. "After that, nothing for months!"

Bolivar walked down the stairs to his cabin silently. On cue, Vincent began his way back below deck to continue his cargo work.

With no wind to catch the sails in the doldrums, the next few days passed sluggishly. The same flat line of an ocean surrounding them with no islands or storms. The bell swayed back and forth, creating steady, quiet clangs. The cook made the same meals. When crewmembers finished their work, some sulked in the lower decks away from the moist heat.

In the cargo hold, Vincent pulled at his thinning hair. He debated where to place each box and how they should be stacked. He stepped around the cargo pile, glancing over it at different angles. "I have no time for this, but I also don't want to put anything in the wrong place."

He turned around and spotted a piece of faded parchment on a desk. It was most likely a map, with the slightest grey impressions of a landmass in the center. After a minute, he returned with quill and ink. Tearing the parchment from the wall and placing it on one of the boxes, he began to draw a diagram to represent the deck along with some squares for the cargo. Despite the visualization, he still couldn't fit the boxes. He scribbled everything out and tried again in the one corner left untouched. Nope. The other side of the parchment. No luck.

The foreman came down and scolded him for using a parchment covered in the purser's important financial information. "Stop daydreaming and work."

Vincent wished to tell the foreman that he wasn't daydreaming. In fact, he was working the best he could. But he didn't want to offend him. Granted, he wasn't as bothered by the foreman as he had been when he first started working here. He was getting used to his tone. Still, it was always best to stay quiet.

The foreman departed and Vincent picked up a crate. Moving it to where he thought it should go. "What must I do to get the job done on time? Do it haphazardly?"

"What're you up to, Vincent?"

The voice startled him enough that he dropped the crate. The wood for the lid strained and some rice spilled out of the gaps.

"Arabelle, please don't do that."

Arabelle crossed her arms. "You've been working on that set of crates for an hour now. Don't you have other work to do?"

"You're not the first one to say that." Vincent began picking up the rice grains.

Arabelle leaned in close. "Then I'll be the first to tell you that Frank, the Younger shipman, and Valerie, the armorer, are dating in secret."

"Isn't that their personal business?"

Arabelle shrugged shamelessly. Vincent gave an exasperated sigh. He finished picking up the rice grains and found that Arabelle was running off again.

The workload wasn't terribly heavy that day. He performed the usual swabbing, equipment checking, typing ropes, and arranging cargo as the need arose. Moving cargo always required moving multiple crates to find the one in need, and it necessitated regular rearrangement of the cargo.

Later, under orders from the foreman, Vincent met with Arabelle to start some paint work on the main deck.

The chipping paint on the railing was curled. As their first job together on this voyage, Vincent and Arabelle scraped it off one bit at a time. Handkerchiefs shielded the back of their necks from the sun. Arabelle worked down the railing quickly, until she reached the end of her area. Vincent was less than halfway through his part, but he glanced up occasionally, hoping she would wait. Arabelle began to scrape beyond her quota, until she ran into him. Vincent dropped his scraper on the deck.

"Careful, Arabelle." He stooped to pick up the scraper.

"Why have you been so fussy lately?" asked Arabelle. "You used to be the most productive worker on the seaboard, at least when you were a dockhand."

Efficient, maybe, but probably not productive. Then the last part of what Arabelle said sunk in. Vincent's eyes widened, and he noticed Arabelle's eyes doing the same. He knew she was thinking back like he was.

✦

A strong, healthy breeze hit the tides by the dock. The waves had returned a small boat back from sea that was now floundering toward the dock. The sky turned slightly orange while the sun approached the horizon. When the boat reached the dockside, a man threw a rope from the boat into Arabelle's hands. She tied the rope around the piling. Vincent held it in place.

"How's your son been doing with the apprenticeship?" asked Arabelle.

"Marvelously," said the man. "Mr. Benson has said only great things about him. How about little Irene? Has her loose tooth fallen out yet?"

Arabelle smiled. "Just two days ago. She's still a biter though."

They began carrying boxes down the gangway. "Handle the boxes with care," said the man. Vincent and Arabelle nodded, showing that they understood.

Vincent exhaled as he set the last box down. He looked at a village in the distance, knowing his wife was cooking that amazing chicken she promised.

Walking through the village, Vincent and Arabelle chatted with each other. Lanterns adorned each house and corner they passed. They spotted a mother calling for her children to get out of the mud and into the house for supper. Reaching an intersection, they went in separate directions toward their homes. Vincent waved until Arabelle was out of sight.

He strolled along the dirt path, his eye spotting light from his cottage that stood out against the early evening darkness. He wiped his feet on the mat in front and the door opened. The warmth and scent of chicken from inside greeted him first, followed by his youngest son, Chandler, and finally his wife.

"Was the weather treating you all right today, dear? How's Arabelle doing with her husband? Does the chicken smell weird to you?" The questions came all at once, but Vincent didn't mind.

✦

The two gave wistful sighs. "Do you miss the village too?" asked Vincent. Arabelle nodded. Just then, they heard some ruckus from the other side of the deck. A rope maker was positioned a few feet away from a clerk, and they were staring each other down like men before a duel. Some onlookers were encouraging them to start a fight. Sure enough, a brawl started, and Vincent looked away in disgust.

"Are we the only ones here with any dignity?"

"Wouldn't be surprised," said Arabelle.

They both turned around again when they spotted the first-mate running onto the deck.

Sorrel scrambled through the crowd of onlookers to separate the two fighting men. "You two will be sleeping in quarters on opposite sides of the ship tonight."

"It's strange, but I hadn't felt this homesick until we started working together," said Vincent.

Arabelle thought for a moment. "The feeling is mutual." The two gave each other concerned looks before continuing their work silently.

Later that day, Vincent was searching through the stacks of the junk, looking for a rope. A seaweed smell caught his attention. He noticed the source, a middle-aged gunner, also looking through the supplies. Vincent had talked with him a couple of times, but had never noticed this particular scent. He asked the gunner what he was looking for.

"Looking for some oars. Arabelle told me they were around here," said the gunner.

"There are few things on this ship that Arabelle doesn't know about," said Vincent. "Pardon me for asking, but why do you smell like seaweed, at least more than usual?"

"I was assigned to clean the barnacles off the starboard side of the boat. Usually it's Arabelle's job but I did it this time in exchange for finding the location of the oars. It was more than worth it."

Vincent began to search the clutter even more frantically. After finally finding the rope, he walked up the stairs to the middle deck or the one below the main deck. Off to one side, sitting on a footstool and against the wall, Arabelle had an exhilarated expression. "Wait until you hear about this. Someone supposedly smuggled poison on board, but I just found out—"

"There are other things that matter besides uncovering obscure secrets," scolded Vincent.

"Yeah, like spending hours arranging a couple of boxes?" Arabelle snapped.

Vincent fought the urge to throw the nearest crate at her. He didn't notice the gunner passing by him until the man was next to Arabelle.

The gunner carried a bundle of oars, handling them like kindling. "Thanks again, Arabelle," he said. "As my son always says…"

The rest of the gunner's words went unheard while Vincent fought the ensuing images of Chandler. He noticed a similar look on Arabelle's face. Vincent decided to return to work immediately, hoping to take his mind off those images. Walking down the steps, he saw a gaping pile of cargo ahead.

+

The gunner brought the oars to the main deck in the evening some other crewmembers followed him to the side of the deck. Soon, there were three small rowboats in the water, tied in front of the ship. The crewmates in the boats started to row. "Watch us get out in half the time," said the gunner confidently.

Sorrel was watching the sea through a telescope until he heard the gunner's remark. Gazing over the front of the ship, he clamored for the people in the boats to get back on board and to bring the oars with them so they wouldn't be lost. Begrudgingly, they complied and placed the oars in a pile. "What's the meaning of this?" demanded Sorrel.

"Thought we might speed us up. There's hardly been any wind in days," said the gunner.

"This vessel is much too large to be rowed. We need your skills on our ship, not in front of it."

The gunner scoffed. "There's nothing for me to shoot, not even a gull. We should try to row it for a little while longer. Maybe it'll make a bigger difference than you think."

Sorrel walked over to the pile of oars and hoisted them up in his arms. Promptly, he threw them overboard. Some of the crewmembers began to protest.

"Are you mental?" one exclaimed.

"You need to stay up here. That's an order. We've already missed one of the currents thanks to the likes of you." That last part silenced the crew.

✦

Vincent joined the expanding crowd of crewmates on the main deck to hear the crew's local minstrel, who was about to continue an ongoing tale that he'd been adding bits to for days now.

Vincent was near Arabelle, and he expected they would continue their previous conversation, but then the minstrel cleared his throat.

"When we left off, our pirate friend and his ancient parents were struggling in the fishing business." Vincent and Arabelle shifted uncomfortably. "His children were applying for university." Vincent's foot oddly twitched and Arabelle winced. "And his younger sister was apparently being betrothed to a cat." Vincent got up and walked to the edge of the deck, while Arabelle went in the opposite direction.

It wasn't long before the sun met the ocean again. Vincent was carrying a large wood plank when the foreman reminded him about putting a second layer of paint on main deck railing. He gently laid the plank next to several others before heading up the stairs. Once on deck, he saw Arabelle was painting the railing already. Her eyes narrowed as soon as she spotted him. "About time."

Vincent tried to explain himself. "I'm sorry, Arabelle. I had an extra job and—"

"That'll do. Just pick up the paintbrush."

He did so stiffly. The two finished the second coat and began the third on the spots where the paint was sufficiently dry. While he was stooping down to dip the brush in the tin again, he noticed Arabelle's expression soften.

"I noticed you were flinching earlier," she said. "It was during the minstrel's story. Was it because of—"

"The pirate's family? Yes," said Vincent.

"Me too, but I wasn't so bothered by the story yesterday," said Arabelle.

"I couldn't make it that day."

They continued their painting quietly. Vincent could hear the small waves below, pushing the ship tediously forward. Being near the edge of the deck, the rocking back and forth was somewhat noticeable, moving them up and down slightly.

"I don't want this to hurt our friendship. We've worked together for so long," said Arabelle.

Vincent nodded his head in agreement. With the brush going from side to side at a regular pace, the job became rhythmic. He spread the white paint parallel to the grain of the wood slowly and regularly.

Finally finishing the job, Vincent and Arabelle said their goodnights, while Vincent set out to return the tins of paint. He trudged across the deck until a carpenter came into view, stopping right in front of him.

"One of my workers is still getting over a fever. I need a replacement to pull out some boards on the spar deck tomorrow. Know anyone who could help? It would only take half an hour," said the carpenter.

Vincent thought about his schedule for the next day. He had plenty of free time, as long as fixing the mast didn't take an hour longer than expected. "I could do it."

The carpenter looked at him skeptically. "Anyone you can work with?"

"I can work with Arabelle."

"Fair enough. See you in the morning." The carpenter left.

Vincent started on his way again, but not before Arabelle passed by and gave him an approving smile.

Later, Vincent was tying the ropes to the sails in their proper places, a task that was second nature and required no reconsideration. If only other tasks were as simple and quick as this. At that point, an idea came. He finished the tying the ropes and ran back to his lookout area, grabbing his telescope.

Just one or two scans over the horizon should be plenty. He tested his theory and it seemed accurate, he saw only a clear sea.

Why would I need to do extra scans if I already know how things are?

There must be other ways to increase the efficiency.

"Hey, Vincent, did you see that rock formation over there?" asked a fellow worker. Vincent checked again and was surprised to see the formation.

"How did I miss that?" He was left at a loss.

"Overlooked it, huh?" said the other worker. "If I were to skim the horizon that fast, I wouldn't have seen anything either."

The cargo seemed as frustrating to arrange as ever, while the gear was even harder to maintain. It was time to try something different. Putting the smaller boxes in first was a disaster. The resulting mess caused the carpenter to roll his eyes as he walked past.

When did this relentless inefficiency start? Then he remembered.

＋

Despite his wife's concern, the chicken was delicious. His son talked about the pay from his apprenticeship, and all the things that he could buy with it. Vincent's youngest son talked about catching a lizard with a friend. A banging from the front door interrupted them. Vincent answered.

"You need to come back to the harbor right now," said Arabelle.

Unsure of what to expect, he followed her. Arriving at the dock, they saw the ship they unloaded earlier was now on fire. The flames reached toward the sky, as if they were in agony themselves. Earlier, Vincent had the job of checking to make sure everything was off the boat, but he overlooked one small bag of gunpowder.

The next day, Vincent triple checked the boats that they unloaded, and he was still anxious.

＋

Anyone on the upper two decks could hear Bolivar's yell of frustration in his cabin. "We missed another current?"

"Maybe you should spend more time on navigation than on maintaining the crew," suggested Sorrel, although he didn't seem to share his captain's frustration.

There was no doubt that the crew was becoming more restless. The next day, Bolivar made another announcement. "All the crew will stay on their respective decks during working hours."

The crew shuddered anxiously. Those working on the main deck didn't appreciate having to sweat excessively in the sun during breaks. A couple of the crew had to be treated from heat exhaustion, which required the captain to loosen the rule somewhat.

Vincent didn't mind the rule, but it may have helped that he was struggling to keep up more than ever before. Looking at his schedule, he scratched the bald spot on his head. Perhaps appeasing the foreman would allow him to be given more time to compensate.

Vincent couldn't see the foreman being so generous though.

+

Vincent was preparing his hammock for the evening when he heard a familiar yell from two decks up. "Arabelle, you've gone too far!"

Scaling the stairs, and peeking over the main deck, Vincent saw Arabelle standing outside the door of the captain's cabin. Bolivar stood in front of her, speaking louder than Vincent had ever heard him. "It's bad enough you've been distracting the crew, but digging around in the classified papers in my cabin?"

"I'm sorry, Sir. I was curious," said Arabelle.

"That's no excuse!" snapped Bolivar. "Extra jobs for you until I can trust you again."

Vincent felt an emptiness in his chest, the kind of feeling that usually happens after hearing a boisterous argument. The foreman caused him to feel that same emotion quite often. He watched Bolivar storm off. Vincent made eye contact with Arabelle while he gripped the cold, hard handrail.

"I'm sorry, Arabelle," he said.

Arabelle remained silent and walked off, leaving Vincent on the vacant deck.

+

The final current was approaching. The helmsman waited patiently. Bolivar stood at the front of the ship to watch for the current. He had lifted the rule on staying on deck, but he knew some were still resentful. "We have a small window to grab it. Don't turn until I say so," he commanded. The boat continued to slog forward. "Ready, now!" The ship didn't budge. Bolivar turned around. The helmsman was trying to turn the helm, but three sets of hands were preventing him. All belonged to crewmates, one of which was Sorrel.

"What are you doing?" said Bolivar.

"You remember when we were headed for Peru, and we ended up in Argentina when you made a slight miscalculation when navigating?" Sorrel gripped the helm tightly.

"That was years ago," said Bolivar.

Other crewmembers came to see what was happening, and some began to support Sorrel. "The first of many mistakes. It's time for you to listen to us!"

Vincent heard most of the ruckus from the down below, but couldn't make the words out. The noise stopped, and Vincent took a quick glance at a schedule on the wall, listing the jobs of all the crewmembers on that deck. He continued his swabbing duties until Arabelle came up to him.

"The man who was supposed to paint the main deck faked his sickness. Remember how we had to cover for him the other day?"

"That's fantastic," said Vincent. He was distracted, trying to get the work done. "Care to help me out, if you're not too busy?"

"I have things to do," she said quickly.

Vincent looked at the schedule again, noticing that Arabelle still had several jobs left. "Ah, like helping with repairs on the hull, right?"

Arabelle shunned the question. Vincent had little trouble guessing why.

"Are you avoiding work?" asked Vincent.

Arabelle remained silent.

"We can't afford you doing that," he said critically.

"So?"

"Arabelle, consider the consequences of your actions for once. Why can't you stay out of trouble?"

She left the room.

Resigned, Vincent went back to work, listening to the struggle continue again above him.

Sorrel was being restrained by some crewmembers.

"This mutiny ends right now. Back down," said Bolivar.

Hopelessly overpowered, Sorrel reluctantly conceded to Bolivar's order and stopped struggling. He was then taken below deck to the prisoner's quarters.

The second-mate joined Bolivar. "I'm glad that's over," he said with a chuckle.

Bolivar sighed. "I expect it will be the first of many mutinies, now that we've missed the last current we'll see for months."

The second-mate's smile disappeared. "Do we have sufficient supplies?"

"I believe so, but I doubt our assurance will appease the crew." Bolivar went back into his cabin, sat at his desk, and pulled at his hair. He heard a knock at the door. Opening it, he saw Arabelle. "Look, if you want me to lift your punishment—"

"I'm not here for that. I have something important to tell you. Something that could get us out of the doldrums *today*," she said.

"Go on," said Bolivar, with a surprised look.

"If we could steer sharper, we would be able to get back into the current, right?"

Bolivar nodded.

"What if we added more than one rudder to the ship?"

For a moment, Bolivar remained silent. "A crazy thought, but why don't you try it."

Arabelle thanked him and sprinted out of the cabin and down to the deck where Vincent was moving cargo.

"Vincent, I need one of those large planks. Captain's orders," said Arabelle.

Vincent could tell she was serious, so he began to look through the piles of supplies. Yesterday, everything had been in order. Who moved everything around? He searched frantically. *I need to find them for Arabelle. Where are they? Where are they?*

Arabelle put her hand on his shoulder. "Slow down and think about it carefully."

Vincent looked her in the eye. She seemed serious, but she gave him a reassuring smile. Vincent carefully considered the crates, looking through them until he grabbed a large plank from the pile. He carried it up the stairs to the highest deck at the back of the boat where Bolivar was waiting. Arabelle followed with some rope. Once they reached the top, one end of the rope was thrown overboard, leaving it to dangle a few feet above sea level. "I'll climb down, and you hold the rope," said Arabelle to Vincent.

Vincent nodded as Arabelle slowly made her way down the rope with one hand while holding the plank in the other.

"Are you sure you can handle holding that?" asked Bolivar. He moved his eyes between Arabelle and the apparent location of the current every few seconds.

"I'm stronger than I look," she said.

The crew began to gather around Bolivar, watching the action below.

"Vincent being helpful. That's a first," muttered one of crew-mates.

Some of the crew cast a couple of derisive looks to Bolivar or Arabelle, probably thinking they were going after a lost cause. Ara-belle lowered the plank into the water, turned at the same angle as the rudder.

"Turn the plank as the rudder turns," instructed Bolivar. He looked at the helmsman, who appeared ready. "Turn 30 degrees port!"

The helm was turned accordingly, and Arabelle twisted the plank in sync. The ship tilted slightly to the right, throwing off Vincent's balance somewhat, but he held the rope firmly. Over the next little while, as ship-mates went back to their duties, Vincent's hands turned red and swollen, but Arabelle was still holding the plank. Then, an unexpected sensation caught Vincent's hair. It was strong, steady wind.

It wasn't long before others noticed. Cheers echoed throughout the ship. "Our sails know the sweet taste of the wind again," said Bol-ivar triumphantly.

Arabelle climbed up the rope to the deck and lowered the plank. "My arms are so sore." She stretched her arms gratefully. "I can't wait to tell my daughter about that experience."

"Not homesick anymore?" asked Vincent.

Arabelle shook her head.

"Me neither."

"My husband wouldn't want me worrying about him anyway," said Arabelle. "He told me to focus on doing my best."

Bolivar approached them from behind, catching them by surprise. "Amazing work, you two. You've done a real service to this crew." He paused. "Well, back to work!"

Later that same day, Vincent pondered the organization problem. *There must be a better way.* He examined the bright yellow hill of boxes, each container rimmed with rusted nails. Wait a minute, what if the heavier boxes were arranged on the bottom? He decided to test that theory. He organized them into place, and then adjusted them as necessary. Success, in record time. Vincent gave a relieved sigh.

The foreman came down, expecting the boxes to be scrambled as usual. He was surprised to see a perfect stack of cargo with Vincent wearing a satisfied smile instead of a worried expression.

"Keep it up, Vincent," he said. "And don't forget to clean the deck."

+

Vincent admired the sparkling ocean while he walked down the gangway and into the village. Arabelle was right ahead of him, going to see her husband and daughter. Vincent spotted his wife and youngest son. He ran and embraced them both.

"You were gone so long," said his wife.

"We were stuck in the doldrums for a few weeks," said Vincent.

"I hope you did something useful while you were waiting," said his wife lightheartedly.

"He became the most efficient worker on the ship." Arabelle walked over with her family.

Vincent smiled. What a pleasant thought.

Kaleah Gordon

KALEAH JACKSON

Songs of the Sea

Water rushed past Seabreeze's face as she shot forward, moving faster than the current around her. She shut her eyes, leaving her perception of the world to just the liquid on her skin. Even with her eyes closed, she could feel the vastness of the ocean around her.

With a smile, she changed directions, kicking her webbed feet until she was heading straight up. Pushing even harder, she gained speed. Eyes now opened, she watched the approaching surface, the water around her growing lighter. Seconds later she burst forth, launching nearly ten feet into the air before twisting and flipping back until she faced the water again. Time seemed to still, the wind catching her hair and pulling it along its course. Then she hit the surface, piercing back down into the ocean's depths.

This time she didn't immediately swim off again, instead she let herself drift. In the depths she could see the coral encrusted rocks and schools of colorful fish swimming through their underwater home. The reef was a truly beautiful place, a rainbow of life.

Suddenly she felt a vibration. It rippled through the water, but she felt it even more prominently in her mind. _The sisters call._

She kicked, propelling herself toward the dark shadow that filled the water to the east. As she once again broke the surface of the water, the dark shadow rose up in front of her. An island, it's surface dotted with sparse undergrowth and trees, yet still an emerald enchantress in the expanse of open water.

As she neared the beach, Seabreeze pushed herself up onto a rock, looking out over the waves. Her sisters were appearing as well, curiously peeking out of the water. More were gathering on the beach, their stark white hair and purple tinted skin standing out starkly from the dark rocks. Most were far older than her, centuries older. She was merely nearing a hundred.

The vibrations from before hit her even stronger, a lilting song that penetrated every fiber of her being. Her throat hummed as she joined in, adding her voice to the tune. It rose and fell, joyful and inviting. The Song of Welcome. That could only mean one thing.

Seabreeze smiled as she hummed, twisting to look away from the island toward the vast open waters. Her sisters would only have begun the song if... *there*. She pushed herself to her feet, moving higher up on the rock. Her sisters followed suit, looking to see what was approaching over the sea.

A ship, Seabreeze thought giddily, staring at it as it came closer. The sails were large and white, a flag flying at the top of the highest mast. It was a majestic ship, a true compliment coming from her as she had seen many in her life—though not as many as she would have hoped. Intricate carvings adorned the railings, some spiraling down farther along the ship's side. On the prow resided a wooden woman, her arms crossed against her chest and her head bowed. Large looping symbols had been painted right behind the woman, the metallic paint flashing when the sun caught it just right. Seabreeze had never managed to learn the human language. Some of her elder sisters had, pouring over pilfered books they had obtained from previous visitors to the island.

As the ship grew closer, the Song of Welcome grew in volume, a unified chorus of voices that filled Seabreeze with excitement. She noticed webbed hands gripping just below the waterline of the ship. Bubbles rushed toward the surface as her sister's legs churned, guiding the boat safely to the shore.

Just as the ship began to run aground, they left it and swam to shore, walking gracefully out of the water. Seabreeze leapt off her rock and joined them, the water flowing off her skin and short dress, causing her to glisten.

The vibrations intensified, calling to the sailors on the ship, beckoning for them to come down. And come they did, throwing down rope ladders and dropping into a foot of water at the bottom. Seabreeze danced up to one of them, kicking up water with her step.

The man closest to her cocked his head, which gave her a good look at his eyes. He seemed to be struggling to focus, a glossy look covering irises that were a brilliant shade of blue. He didn't speak; neither did his fellows. They stood in a cluster just off shore, not comprehending what was going on around them.

Suddenly the tone of the song changed, filling out with new harmonies. A figure approached from down the beach and they all turned to watch her arrive. Seabreeze ran up to the gathering of her sisters, standing respectfully to the side as they split apart. Queen Risingtide smiled to them as she passed, moving until her bare feet touched the edge of the water. Her hair was longer than the rest, ending far below her waist. She wore a headdress of pearls, others adorning her neck, wrists, and ankles.

"Welcome, weary travelers." Her voice stayed in tune with her sisters' song. Her voice both rose above and melded with the tune at the same time. "My sisters and I are pleased you are here. Which of you may I address as captain?" Seabreeze's eyes left the Queen as she watched one of the sailors come forward. He wore a striking blue suit with golden trim and appeared pleased at the Queen's attention, though not much emotion escaped those washed out eyes.

"It is I, your humble servant," he bowed. The Queen smiled knowingly, pearly teeth glittering. Then her eyes caught on something over the captain's shoulder. Some of the men near the back were shaking their heads, appearing confused and distracted. The Queen pursed her lips, the song shifting again. Seabreeze and a few of her fellows moved toward the men, each selecting one to focus on. She found one of average height, his sailor's coat nicely buttoned, though his light hair was messy and windblown. Approaching him, she increased her song, letting the vibrations fill her.

Even as he began to see her clearly, she touched his arms, letting her humming pass through her into him. It took longer than she would have liked for his eyes to cloud over again, his concern turning to a pleasant smile. *I should be better at this by now. I need more practice.* As her song filled the man, she began to feel his mind, the songs that had been sung in his life—his hopes and his love of the open sea.

She released him, stepping back. It was not yet time for connection. That song was to be sung later. It was the way of things, how her sister's had performed since the beginning. She returned to the gathering of her sisters. More had arrived, eyes hungry as they peered at the men. As Seabreeze's bare feet once again touched dry sand, the captain accepted the Queen's invitation. Risingtide laced her arm through the captain's and drew him up the beach. The rest of her sisters encircled the sailors, prompting them to follow in a dazed stupor.

Seabreeze grinned widely, clasping her hands in front of her as she walked. She wanted to dance, to sweep across the sand. It had just been *so long* since a ship had come to the island. She had begun to feel tainted, weak. That all seemed to fly away from her now as she gazed at the men. She felt a thrill surging through her, making her heart pound with excitement. Her hunger would be sated soon. She would feel young again!

When her feet hit grass instead of sand, she hesitated, looking up toward their destination. It rose at the peak of the island, a castle with crystalline walls. The sun was already setting on the far side of it, its powerful light refracting and causing the entire building to glow.

Seabreeze turned, beckoning the men onward. Their jaws dropped when they saw the magnificent structure. The walls were perfectly smooth, no cracks or seals of separate pieces. The castle's creation had happened long ago, before Seabreeze had been born. Her elder sisters had been there though, all those centuries before. They told a story of beauty and power, of sisters in the past charming the earth with their song. The rocks had been so moved by their passion, they had grown—straight from the earth—a castle in which her sisters could work.

Seabreeze wished she could speak to those sisters, the ones who had sung, but all who remembered such ancient songs had passed on. They had departed in the era of drought. There had been over a hundred years where no sailor touched their shores. Those who were older had drifted away, their moving songs lost with them. Seabreeze could feel that same pull on her soul; the same unearthly aching that drew her toward another place. She straightened her shoulders, glancing at the men. *The ache will be gone soon enough.*

Some of her sisters were already waiting at the castle. They pulled open the massive doors as the group approached. The Queen led the way, still holding onto the captain, who was practically drooling as he looked around. The group moved down to the end of the front hallway to another set of massive double doors. As with the walls, the doors were crystalline. Sisters rushed forward to push them open, allowing the Queen to continue without stopping.

They followed after her, herding the men into the room with sharp smiles. The natural light was dissipating, the sun finally drifting below the far horizon. Instead, spots of light glowed within the room, flames brought by men at the end of wax. What peculiar inventions the humans came up with. They seemed to fear the dark, not embrace it.

When all of her sisters had been gathered, the Queen walked to a rising in the floor near the front. She turned to face them, splaying her hands to the side.

"It is time." Risingtide shut her eyes and lowered her head. Immediately the Song of Welcome ceased, the echo of vibrations drifting for a few moments longer. Then another tune began, a deep enveloping sound that made Seabreeze's heart leap.

The Song of Passion.

She joined in enthusiastically, adding her voice to the flood. The passion was slower, more twisting and enthralling than the Song of Welcome. In answer to their song, the men came forward from where they had hesitated at the door. They came as if led by an invisible hand, gathering amongst her sisters in the large ballroom.

"The connection begins." Queen Risingtide held out her hand and the captain of the sailors came forward, walking up to stand in front of her. As she laid her hand on the man's shoulder, she began to change. The song became more turbulent, with drastic ups and downs. Seabreeze watched, holding her breath as the Queen shifted. Her hair became as black as night, her skin growing pale, her torso thinning, her hips widening. The webbing on her hands and feet disappeared, the gills on her neck melded into her skin. The transformation took mere seconds, leaving a beautiful woman, a *human* woman, standing where the Queen once was.

The captain's eyes opened wide, then he smiled, clasping the Queen by the hand. The rest of her sister's took it as a signal, turning on the men, a hungry light in their eyes. The more vivacious sisters immediately launched forward, latching onto men. As the connections were made, more and more shifted, taking on faces of human beauty and majesty.

Seabreeze stepped forward, spotting a man. He was tall with a firm jaw and mischievous brown eyes. She reached her hand toward him. Just before she made contact with his shoulder, her sister Coral suddenly shoved her out of the way, grabbing the man instead.

"This one's mine," she hissed. "You're not strong enough to charm him anyway. Go find another."

Seabreeze rolled her eyes. Coral was always picky with her men; best not push her on it. Even as she watched, Coral began to change. She grew taller, her hair turning to a light blond then curling into perfect rings. She laughed at something the man said, then clasped his hand in hers as she led him across the room.

Seabreeze turned back toward the main group. As she tried to find another man, she found that most had already been taken. After some searching and much pushing around, she found one waiting near the edge of the room, his arms glued to his sides as his dazed eyes swept the scene before him. Strangely, it was the same sailor she had nearly connected with earlier in the day.

She moved slowly toward him, attuning even closer to the Song of Passion. The tune was no longer a simple melody, but a tempest of twisting tones and pitches—each of her sisters adding their own lines to the song as they lured in the men. As she neared the sailor, she reached forward and found her hand shaking. *Am I really that nervous?* Her hand continued to shake. *I've never been good at this. What if I mess this up? What if this doesn't work?* The worries had always been there. She had expressed them to her elder sisters many times. They always laughed at her, telling her to give in to her nature, that her instincts and the songs would guide her.

Lowering her hand for a brief moment, Seabreeze focused on the Song of Passion. She let it fill her, feeling the vibrations move throughout her body. The Passion was the oldest song they knew, the one closest to the old days of magic. It was the song that released her sister's magic, allowing the connection to be made. Feeling its strength, Seabreeze reached forward and grabbed the man's arm, pulling herself closer to him. Then she opened up her mind.

As her song filled his soul, his returned something to her as well. Her instincts kicked in, her subconscious mind searching his, discovering his secrets. It pulled out something else as well, something vital to the connection. Her mind latched onto his and she could feel herself begin to change. Consuming men's minds was not enough to sustain Seabreeze or her sisters; they required something else, more potent and lasting. They needed men's souls, their love and their passion. Only then could her sister's continue on. That is why they changed, why they shifted their faces.

They had to become what each man saw as the most beautiful.

Seabreeze released the man, stumbling back slightly as she looked down at her hands. Her skin was tan, the hands rough and calloused. *What is this?* Feeling her head, she found that her hair fell just below her chin, a mat of rough mousy brown strands. Grimacing she left the man, moving to a mirror along the wall. As her eyes fell on it's surface, she gasped, grabbing her face. She was so *plain*. A small chin and a nose that turned down in an unpleasant way, thick eyebrows that furrowed over dull eyes. She had a small scar that stretched along the edge of her jawbone, its discoloration standing out starkly against her brown skin. *Something must have gone wrong.* Seabreeze hugged herself. *I messed it all up; I knew I would!*

She felt his presence before she could even hear his footsteps—an extra side effect of the connection. Turning she faced the sailor, who she now knew was named Thomas. She expected him to appear disgusted, to turn away from her plain face and follow one of her other more beautiful sister's in the room. But what she saw instead was awe.

"What?" she asked.

He took another step forward, eyes wide, hand gripping the bottom of his coat. "Lena?" he asked softly. "Is that really you?"

Seabreeze felt her jaw drop. She trembled, backing up into the mirror. *By all the songs in the sea,* it had happened to her. She had heard others tell of it happening to them, but she had never suspected—never even guessed—that it would ever in a million years happen to her.

"I'm... I'm your wife," she whispered.

Thomas laughed out loud, rushing forward and pulling her into a firm embrace. He spun her around, grinning broadly. "It's been so long! I can't believe you're here! It's a miracle."

When her feet finally touched the ground again, she pushed back away from him, looking at his face. "How can you love me?" She nervously glanced at the others around her. She didn't think any of them had noticed. "How can you care for me when I am so plain?"

Thomas chuckled, cupping her chin in his hand. "I don't know what you're talking about. I'm looking at the most beautiful woman I have ever seen in my life. How could I ask for more?"

Seabreeze met his eyes, staring into their depths. They seemed strangely clear for one under the spell of her song. He stared at her like she was the rising sun, the brightest light in the sky. She felt herself tremble. She knew that look, she had seen it before on the other men she had charmed. She couldn't even remember their names. Yet at the same time, Thomas' gaze was different, deeper.

She forced herself to look away, her eyes falling on Coral. It was always a little disconcerting to see her sisters in other forms. They always appeared so... human. The connection also led them to act differently, as evidenced by Coral playfully curling a strand of her hair around her finger as she sung a response to her connected sailor. The locks seemed to shimmer in the candlelight.

How much have I been affected by the connection? Seabreeze wondered. Feeling a hand on her arm, she turned away from Coral to look at Thomas. As she met his eyes, she felt her cheek twitch. *I have been changed,* she realized. Her thrill of feeding on his soul had fled, replaced by only an aching feeling of remorse. She winced, staring down at the ground.

Thomas looked at her, his eyebrows lowering. "Are you all right?" He rubbed his thumb across her wrist. She looked down at his hand, unable to meet his eyes. Those passionate eyes. "I'm fine."

"You seem upset. Is there anything I can do to help?"

Seabreeze pulled her hand out of his, backing up slightly. He cocked his head, the concern on his face growing. "Lena, what's wrong—"

"I'm not Lena!" Seabreeze shouted. As soon as the words left her she immediately clamped her hands over her mouth. Her head pounded as she watched Thomas nervously. He seemed taken aback, but instead of looking angry, he just looked more worried.

"What's going on?" He stepped forward and grabbed her shoulders. This time she didn't pull away, instead she forced herself to remain still. Everything seemed to go quiet as she met his eyes again. It took her a second to realize that the Song of Passion had ended. Then, gradually, one voice at a time slowly joining in, another song began. It was a dark, ominous tune that made her stomach twist. The beats were solid, like the thump of the drums she had once heard on an arriving ship. She felt her heart match the beats, jerking in her chest. She inhaled sharply.

It was the Song of the Kill.

One of her sisters—Swiftcurrent—immediately acted, grabbing her sailor's head and pulling it toward her own. Then she kissed him, holding him close. The man shut his eyes, thoroughly enjoying the embrace. That is, until he started smoking. Thin tendrils began to drift up from his skin, the flesh going grey. His eyes snapped open. He tried to jerk away, but Swiftcurrent's hold was too fierce and he was weakening. Seabreeze heard his muffled screams. None of her other sisters paid attention. Normally, she wouldn't have either.

Glancing back at Thomas, she found him watching the man with concern. "I think he's in pain."

Seabreeze raised a fist to her mouth. Some things were getting through the spell. Not as much as they should have, but he was at least noticing that something was off. When she looked around again, she found multiple sisters staring at her. She realized that she had never joined the song, and they felt it.

She nervously began to sing, the vibrations quiet and low. Thomas sagged ever so slightly when the vibrations washed over him. He put a hand to his head, looking dizzy. He appeared to be preparing to say something, but stopped when he looked at Seabreeze again. She was hugging herself, glancing this way and that as more of her sisters latched on, sucking the lives out of the other men. More muffled screams.

"What are you afraid of?" He gently laid a hand on her shoulder. "I'm here for you, whatever it is."

"No." She pulled back.

His grip hardened. "You don't need to be fearful. You're safe with me."

I'm not the one in trouble, Seabreeze thought. She shifted her weight, the crystalline floor under her bare feet felt cold. The vibrations in her throat grew even quieter as Thomas leaned forward, his hands going to cup her face. *No,* she thought. Wasn't he the one who was supposed to be weakened by the song? Her limbs felt like seaweed being pulled by the current. His gentle guiding hands forced her to look at his face as he closed his eyes, moving in for a kiss. Could she do it? Could she drain the soul out of this man? Was she strong enough to take his life force and feed off of it to live a further year? Another scream echoed behind her. The pain always overcame the spell. No matter how thick the fog was over their minds, the men could feel it when their souls ripped apart. Could she listen to Thomas' screams?

She dropped to the ground, ripping free of his hands. When he stumbled back, shocked, she scrambled to her feet, moving to stand a few steps away. His expression was one of confusion. He raised a hand toward her and she immediately turned away. The Song of the Kill was barely a whisper within her. What she saw made her heart clench as it never had before. Nearly three fourths of the men were dead, her sisters seeming to glow as they stood over them with triumphant smiles.

What has changed in me? Why can I no longer follow in their paths? Her eyes found the Queen. She was walking through the crowd, congratulating her sisters. She had already reverted to her natural form, her skin almost seeming to sparkle as she came up to Seabreeze. Risingtide looked over Seabreeze's shoulder and her eyes found Thomas. Her brows lowered.

"Sister?" She folded her arms. "Why have you not joined the feast?"

"This human has been troublesome," Seabreeze said quickly. "I'll need another night."

The Queen nodded, eyes narrowing as she looked at Thomas again. "As you wish. You can use a room upstairs if you need."

"Thank you, sister." Seabreeze backed up and bowed. The Queen gave her one more glance before walking away. Seabreeze let out an unsteady breath as she left. It wasn't uncommon to give some sailors another night to let the spells sink in, but she still felt like something was off. She turned back to Thomas.

"Lena," he started.

She hushed him and grabbed his arm, dragging him out of the ballroom. He followed in curious silence as she brought him up a set of stairs to a hallway lined with a series of smaller rooms. At the last one she opened the door and pushed him inside. The room was nearly empty except for a thick rug on the floor. Looking back through her memory, Seabreeze could remember the ship her sisters had gotten it from. The fabric was of a deep maroon and seemed to absorb most of the light that was given off by the sparse candles hung from hooks on the walls.

Seabreeze let go of Thomas's hand and moved to the far side of the room. He followed after her, his eyes sparkling in the darkness.

"I'm glad we're alone now," he said. "It's been so long, there's so much I want to know, so much I want to tell you."

"Can you not sense that something is off?" Seabreeze asked. She sidestepped as Thomas moved closer, keeping herself at the far end of the carpet from him.

"Lena," he said with a half-laugh, "I don't know what you're talking about."

"This is not right, you have to know that!" She pushed him away, though it went against every fiber of her being. She could feel the emptiness inside of her, the hunger that sought for nourishment. It wanted to consume. But she fought it, holding it back from its prey.

It would be so simple, a part of her mind whispered. *One kiss, and you will feel so much better. Why protect a man who is already lost?* It was an inborn instinct within her, the very fibers of her nature. Yet still she denied it. Something had been sparked within her when Thomas had first spoken his wife's name. She clenched her fists at her sides.

Thomas stopped in the middle of the rug. "Have I done something wrong?" He suddenly looked at the ground abashed. "I was gone too long, wasn't I?" he said quietly. "You felt I left you behind, that I no longer cared for you." He looked up, eyes damp. "Lena, you couldn't be farther from the truth!"

"I need to break the spell," Seabreeze whispered with realization. No words could draw him from it. *No words.* She stopped singing, letting her vibrations die away. Pursing her lips, she watched Thomas.

He straightened ever so slightly, but his eyes remained clouded. "It's not enough."

"Lena," Thomas walked toward her again. "You have to believe me, I have never loved you more. Just let me show you."

"No," Seabreeze said quickly, holding up her hands. "You'll only get hurt." She paused, mind working. *Get hurt.* Suddenly she lashed out, her fist connecting with his jawline. His head snapped back and he stumbled to the side. When he recovered somewhat from the strike, he looked at her with wide eyes.

"Ow!" Seabreeze cradled her fist. She had seen men pick fights before when they first arrived on the island but she had never realized how much it *hurt* to be the one hitting. "That better have worked."

She glanced at Thomas. He was no longer looking at her. His eyes roved over the crystalline walls and floor and he ran his hand through the thick carpet. Mouth moving wordlessly, he returned his gaze to Seabreeze.

"Where am I?" he asked. Standing up, he ran to her, grabbing her shoulders. "Lena, where are we? How are we here?"

She let out a sigh of relief, but it caught in her throat. What had she just done? She trembled in Thomas' grip as the implications of her actions hit her. She had released a man from the spell. Hundreds of years of rules and traditions had been broken by one simple act. It had all happened so fast. Her sisters had sometimes teased her of being weak. Was she proving it now? Was her refusal to kill Thomas merely because she was afraid?

Maybe I am weak. Seabreeze flinched as her bruised fist bumped against her leg. *Maybe my connection has brought me more humanity.* "Thomas?"

"What is it?" It was obvious he had noticed her nervousness, his features a mix of worry and curiosity.

"I'm not Lena."

He raised an eyebrow, a smirk touching the corner of his mouth. "What are you talking about? Of course you are."

"No, you don't understand. I'm not Lena, I've merely shifted to take on her appearance."

"Shifted? You aren't making any sense."

Seabreeze shook her head. Taking a deep breath, she pushed away from Thomas, then held out her hands. Closing her eyes, she looked within herself and found the connection. Then she severed it. Thomas gasped. She opened her eyes just as he was stumbling backward, staring at her with his mouth opened wide.

"What are you?" he asked. "What have you done with my wife?"

"Nothing." She raised her hands in a calming gesture. "My form came from your memories of her. She was not harmed at all. She isn't even here."

Thomas ran a hand through his hair, eyes wildly flitting about. Everything must have seemed so strange to him. She raised a finger to her lips, thinking. What to do now? She had revealed the truth to him, released him from the spell, but what to do from there? The answer came in the form of a knock at the door. Seabreeze paled, looking between the door and the alert Thomas. He had frozen at the sound, eyes piercing into her, the question in his face clear.

"Who is it?" Seabreeze put her ear against the door.

"It's me." Seabreeze's knees grew wobbly. It was the Queen. "I was just checking to see if you are all right."

"All right?" Seabreeze whispered to herself. *What is she talking about? The song,* she realized. Her sisters could feel it when one of them wasn't joining in, and the Queen was the most attuned of all. *I'm so foolish,* she groaned. *I didn't even think.* Her eyes found Thomas. "Plug your ears." She mouthed the words, hoping he'd understand.

"Why?"

"Just do it."

Thankfully he complied, slipping over to the side and plugging his ears. As he did so, Seabreeze began once again The Song of Passion, then she pulled open the door a crack, facing the Queen.

"Sister." She resisted the urge to glance over at Thomas. "Do you need something?"

"I was worried for you," Risingtide replied. "You ceased singing."

"My apologies for worrying you, sister," Seabreeze said, making sure to emphasize the song in her voice. "I was distracted for a mere moment, nothing more." She looked at the ground, poking her foot against the side of the door. "You know I have never been the most capable."

The Queen smiled kindly, touching Seabreeze's cheek. "My dear, there is no harm in weakness. That is why we practice. You are doing fine. Like a seabird learning to fly, some things take time."

"Thank you. I'd better get back."

"Oh, yes. I'll leave you be. Fare thee well, sister."

Seabreeze nodded then watched as the Queen gracefully left. At the end of the hall, the Queen glanced back once more and Seabreeze's stomach dropped. It was a look of suspicion. As soon as the Queen was out of sight, Seabreeze quickly shut the door then rushed over to Thomas. He stood with hands lowered, his eyes glassy.

"No, no, no!" Seabreeze cried. "Why couldn't you just listen to me?" She paused. "I guess you actually were listening, just to the wrong thing." She shook her head. *Let's try this again.* This time she slapped him and though her hand stung, she found it much better than using the fist. She risked cutting off her music for a moment and Thomas came to once again.

"Wha...what just happened?"

"You unplugged your ears," Seabreeze hissed.

"I wanted to listen to the conversation."

"Well my song put you back under a spell. Now if you don't want my sisters to notice I've stopped singing again, you're going to need to follow every one of my commands."

Realization dawned on his face and he took a step back, pointing at her. "I know what you are. You're a siren! Aren't you? This entire place is filled with sirens!"

She slapped a hand over his mouth, fear making her brash. "Yes, that is what you sailors call us. Now listen to me. If you want to get out of this alive, we need to move *now*. And this time," she looked at him pointedly, "keep your ears plugged, no matter what happens."

He nodded, still stunned, then pushed his fingers into his ears. Seabreeze quickly began her song again. She gestured for Thomas to follow her, then snuck to the door. After making sure the hallway outside was empty, she grabbed Thomas' shoulder and yanked him into a run. Her bare feet pounded on the crystalline floors as she raced down the hall. She begged that all of her sisters would still be preoccupied in the ballroom.

Reaching the bottom of the stairs, she spun down the large front hall without pausing. Halfway down, she glanced back and saw Thomas looking toward the ballroom. At first she was terrified that he had been lured in by the music but his fingers were still in his ears.

"Thomas," she called in a whispered shout. He didn't respond. Clenching her teeth, she ran back grabbing his arm. He looked at her. "Thomas, what are you doing?" She spoke louder and toned down her song to a mere whisper.

"My crewmates," he said. "I can't leave them."

"They're dead," she told him. "I watched them die—you were there too."

"There has to be some still alive. I—"

"I am going against everything I have ever known to save you," Seabreeze said. "And honestly, I still have no idea why." There was a grinding sound from behind her. She spun, noticing the ballroom door opening. "Hide!"

They practically dove behind one of the statues in the hall. Holding her breath, Seabreeze listened as a group of her sisters exited the ballroom and made their way down the hall. When they exited through another door, she ran. Thomas stumbled after her as she raced toward the large front doors. Slamming into them, she grunted, trying to push them open. *They're so heavy!*

Thomas collided into the doors next to her and the door began to shift, opening slowly. He was in an awkward position to push while holding his fingers in his ears. Just as they got the door far enough open to slip through, she heard a shout from behind them. Glancing over her shoulder, she gasped. The Queen herself stood farther down the hall, glaring at her, a number of sisters surrounding her.

"Stop her!" the Queen shouted, raising her finger.

Seabreeze bolted out the door. She ran faster than she had ever run before, Thomas right behind her. Careening down the hill, the ground beneath her feet turned from grass to sand. The sudden change made her stumble, her knee hitting the earth. Thomas grabbed her arm, hoisting her to her feet. Then, throwing caution the wind, he pumped his arms, leaving his ears open. Seabreeze's heart caught in her throat as she watched, but whether it was the wind whistling in his ears, or the fear and adrenaline racing through him, the spell did not retake him. Risking a glance behind her, she saw her sisters racing down the hill, a flood of figures, their grace contrasting with the death in their eyes.

Thomas reached the water first and looked out. "The boat," he called back to her. Her sisters had shoved it off of the land, and it was drifting a few hundred feet offshore. He leapt into the water without a second thought, swimming out to sea. Seabreeze jumped into the water as well. As she did, something struck her. Not something physical, but vibrations, powerful vibrations.

Her sisters were singing The Song of the Kill. It was unlike what she had ever heard before. The beats were rapid, the melody fierce. As she submerged, the vibrations increased tenfold, rattling through her bones. It was her own power turned against her.

Screaming underwater, she kicked as hard as she could, rocketing through the waves. She easily caught up to Thomas but she knew that as soon as her sisters reached the sea, she was as good as dead. She surfaced next to him, yelling at him to go faster. Instead his strength seemed to be failing. The song was getting to him.

It's getting to me too. Seabreeze felt a weakness in her limbs. She shouted in defiance, grabbing Thomas and towing him toward the boat. Though their speed was increased, she knew they would barely reach the ship in time. But what then?

She was so concentrated on swimming, that she nearly rammed face first into the ship's wooden hull. Grabbing hold a ladder hanging off the side of the ship, she climbed as fast as she could, Thomas managing to follow. She threw herself onto the deck, rolling over just as the entire ship shuddered. Thomas hit the ground next to her, looking up. Then the entire boat began to spin. They were thrown to the far railing, smacking into the thick wood. The impact seemed to shock Thomas out of his daze, and he leaped to his feet, racing to a strange metal barrel. Seabreeze glanced over the railing behind her and saw the sea roiling, her sisters gripping the boat's hull.

"Help me!" Thomas shouted.

She leaped to her feet, swaying as the ship continued to spin. Forging her way across the deck, she grabbed hold of the metal barrel next to him. He lit a match, then touched it to a string sticking out from the top. Suddenly there was an earth-shattering *bang* and the metal barrel slammed backward, throwing her to the deck again. She heard screams. Scrambling to the railing, she looked over the edge. Her sisters had retreated from the boat, shaking fists and howling. Their harsh, grating song filled the air.

Thomas dragged her over to a stack of black balls, getting her help to carry one over and place it in the front of the metal barrel. Then, he lit it again. This time she was prepared for the jolt, and she watched as the metal ball went flying, smacking into the ranks of her sisters. More screams. Blue-green blood filled the water where it had struck. Seabreeze's eyes widened, and she clasped her hands over her mouth.

"Stop!" She grabbed him as he went for another ball. "Stop hurting them!"

"They killed my crewmates." He jerked out of her grip.

"Please, you've hurt them enough. Let's just go."

Thomas hesitated, glancing over the railing. Seabreeze's sisters seemed unwilling to approach the boat again, their shouts filled with anger and fear. His hair whipped in the breeze, and he looked up at the sails.

"The ship is still ready to sail! Use that rope to lower the sail." He then jogged toward the back of the ship where he grabbed hold of the helm. She followed his orders and soon the sail's were billowing in the wind, the gale's force propelling the ship out into the open sea.

As the last rocky protrusion passed on her left, Seabreeze, leaned against the railing, staring back at her home. Many of her sisters had climbed up on the rocks, watching after the escaping boat. None had dared attack again.

"Goodbye," she whispered. The receding shoreline of her life lay behind her. Even as the island began to disappear beyond the horizon, the morning rays of sunlight struck the crystalline castle, sparkling in the morning light. She felt a tear slide down her cheek. Then she turned and walked over to Thomas.

His jaw was set as he stared forward, his face emotionless. "Thank you."

She simply nodded, sitting on a pile of ropes behind him. Deep in her chest she could still feel it, the gnawing hunger that had been growing for months. She grimaced, hugging herself. She was journeying to a place where no siren had gone before. Taking a deep breath, she squared her shoulders. She would make it work. She had to. With the rising sun at her back, she turned away from the life she had known and looked toward something new.

Captain Abigail Kelley

Abigail knelt by her father's side, straining to hear his last words. "Abigail…" he whispered, barely audible. "Listen to me." His eyes seemed to look straight through her. "This ship will need a captain."

"Papa, no," she said tearfully. "Don't say that. You're going to be just fine. Everything is fine."

"I know." Her father smiled wryly. "But if it's not…will you take care of the ship?"

"Papa, no," Abigail said again. "You're the captain. It's your crew." She choked out a sob. Had she been here just a moment sooner, she could have killed his attacker and saved her father. Papa wouldn't be here, lying on the deck, bleeding to death. Just a moment sooner.

"Abigail." His words were almost nonexistent. She knew these were her last moments with her father. The thought made her feel like she'd been hit in the stomach. She felt helpless. "It's your crew now." His hand shifted gently, his hat clenched in his fingers. It took all the strength left in him to reach upward and place it on top of Abigail's head. The smallest action must have caused excruciating pain. But there was nothing she could do to stop her father's pain and she hated herself for that. "Listen." He placed a hand on her cheek. Tears ran silently down her cheeks as she held his fingers against her face. "Don't let them see you cry. You're their leader. Everything…is going to be all right." His hand fell limp. His eyes lost what little focus they had left. He was dead.

Abigail wiped the tears from her face and remembered his words: *Don't let them see you cry.* How could he expect her not to cry after her entire world had been torn away from her? Any type of physical pain could not be worse than this feeling of this loss.

Abigail had no idea what she was to do now. But she refused to disobey her father's last commands, no matter how much it pained her to bury her grief. *We won the battle. Papa is dead but we won. His killers are in our hands and he would not want mercy.* Abigail rose to her feet. She straightened her spine and adjusted her cap. She slid her sword into its sheath at her hip. *This is the moment that I become captain.* Abigail let the title sink in, feeling the power flow through her veins. The cost of becoming captain had not been worth it. It would never be worth it.

She looked at the men on her ship. Some were tied up as prisoners, while others clutched caps to their chest, standing silently in mourning. She took a deep breath.

"Men!" Abigail yelled. They stood respectfully at attention. "Our captain is dead!" A pang filled her chest as she spoke the words but she continued speaking. "The scum that killed him are tied up on our ship." She slid her sword out of its sheath, still holding the gaze of every man on board. "What should we do with them?"

She strolled toward the closest prisoner. This was her chance to make right the wrong. These men were responsible for her father's death. She raised her sword slowly to the man's throat, looked him dead in the eye, and whispered wickedly, "Should we kill 'em?"

The man whimpered and looked away, closing his eyes tightly. These men deserved to be afraid. They deserved to be punished. Abigail didn't feel guilty for what she was about to do to them.

"One of your men is already dead," she whispered to the man. "I killed him myself with this same sword." She pulled back her sword to examine it, the dried blood caked on its edge. Abigail returned it to her side. "Thing is, I killed him from behind, so I didn't have the *pleasure* of watching his reaction." She felt a wicked smile stretch across her face and a dark rage build in her gut. Abigail felt almost giddy at the prospect of getting revenge. "I am so *very* looking forward to watching you die." With that, she pierced his abdomen in one swift, unbroken movement.

✦

Captain Abigail Kelley stood in a peaceful trance at the bow of the *Bloody Rose*, the wind sweeping through her hair. As her eyes closed, she could smell the salty air. It smelled like they were going the right way. Now seventeen years old, she had been captain for nearly three years. In those years, she had learned to navigate the water on sheer intuition.

"Anthony!" Abigail called to the man steering the ship. "Take us north. We're nearly there."

"Aye, cap'n," Anthony said.

Not ten minutes later, one of her men called, "Land ahead!"

The crew weighed anchor a good half a league away from shore to avoid detection. Abigail took all her crew with her and they would split up once they reached the town. The closest houses were a mile away. Abigail liked her crew a good deal. She liked the respect they gave her. It must not be easy taking commands from her, especially considering many members of the crew were twice her age. Anthony was closest to Abigail's age, so she made a point of spending most of her time with him. Not for matters of romance, Abigail wasn't interested in that sort of thing, she just enjoyed the occasional pleasant conversation. In addition to being younger than her subordinates, Abigail was the only female on board. Although having a woman on a ship was supposedly bad luck, Abigail didn't believe such foolishness.

Abigail and the men planned while they rowed. They paired off to find a place to stay inconspicuously for the night. The small crew should be able to find enough inns and empty barns for seven pairs of men to rest. Once they had reached the shore, Abigail watched as each member of her crew found a partner.

"Now men!" She called. "Listen to me. Today we will scout things out. Any fooling around before we have a solid plan could get us caught. We meet here at four tomorrow morning. Sharp." The crewmembers nodded and started off.

Abigail heard someone clear their throat behind her. "I don't suppose you'd like to team up with me, captain?" Anthony spoke in a very sophisticated, fake accent.

She smiled. "I don't see why not," she answered in an equally false voice. It was tradition for them to take on a fake identity whenever they entered a new city. Anthony gallantly offered her his arm and she allowed him to escort her toward the town.

"How do you feel about becoming *John and Rachel Martin*, the charming pair of siblings visiting their childhood home?" he asked.

Abigail laughed. "You have far too much time on your hands."

"Perhaps," Anthony looked at her sincerely. "But I always make time for you."

Abigail hesitated a moment and pulled her arm away from his. They walked in silence the rest of the way. Abigail hoped she hadn't made him uncomfortable, but she felt awkward whenever he did something like this. When a glance lasted a moment too long or a hand lingered a bit too much, she didn't know how to respond.

By the time they had crested the hill, the silence had become comfortable again. "Do you know what the name of this place is?"

"Westwend. A small town just off the coast of Spain," Anthony responded.

Abigail nodded. In truth, gold was the only reason why they were here, so here could be anywhere. The two walked into the town confidently and quietly. Hundreds of people dwelled in the town, a few inns dotted the main road to accommodate visitors. She scanned every building they passed, trying to find a place to stay.

The pair booked the cheapest room at Smith Lodgings. Abigail figured a small room was all *John and Rachel Martin* could afford. Before they could go upstairs to their room, however, Anthony whispered to her, "We really should scout out the town."

"I'll take the north side, the one with the Manor," Abigail said.

Anthony nodded, and they split ways.

Abigail liked this part. She liked exploring each new city. Knowing that they would ransack the town in just a few short days was an extremely gratifying thought. Though she tried to stay inconspicuous, Abigail was aware that she turned a few heads. How could she not? She was *not* the sort of person you'd see every day. With her long brown hair that she always wore down and a flash of the trousers beneath her petticoat, she stood out in the crowd. She was used to the scattered stares she earned. If anything, it helped her and her men go undetected. When she saw a member of her crew, nods passed between them without notice. Abigail wondered when she would see one of her men. She hoped they had spread out and hidden themselves according to plan. The last time several pairs of men boarded in one inn hadn't ended well. Hopefully, this town was large enough for all of them to escape detection.

There. That was a face she knew. Joseph, one of her men, walked toward her without noticing her. She could only hope he wasn't planning on checking into the same lodgings. Abigail shot him a warning look to tell him that the inn in that direction was *hers*. Her head followed him as he passed, but he didn't glance her way.

She had better find a way—too lost in thought to notice where she was going, Abigail ran straight into a man wearing a cloak with its hood drawn. He was a span taller than her, and Abigail had to look upward to meet his gaze. She was about to mutter an apology when the man raised a silent finger to his lips.

"Wha—" Abigail began, but the man shook his head furiously and grabbed her arm tightly. She yanked her arm away from him, but his grip was firm. "Hey—"

With that, the man swept her up, holding one hand clamped tightly over her mouth. Abigail worried, but not for herself. She pitied anyone who tried to match her strength. She knew she could take this man with ease, but she would prefer to settle this without confrontation.

The hooded man ducked into a nearby alleyway, with Abigail still in his grasp. He set her down, but he faced her away from him and held her tightly from behind, wrapping his arms around her torso.

Abigail took several deep breaths before saying very steadily, "I would like to know who, exactly, you are, and what you think gives you the right to *harass* an innocent woman." The man's grasp did not relent, but Abigail felt him sigh.

"If I let you go, you have to swear to me you won't say a word about this." The voice was that of an educated man. Articulate, crisp.

Abigail could've laughed. "I most certainly *will* be saying quite a few *well-chosen* words. If you don't want them to be the last thing you hear, I suggest you give me some sort of explanation as to *what you are doing.*"

"Listen. I am Lord Thomas of Westwend."

Lord Thomas of Westwend? This man was noble. This man could punish her for her crimes, if he knew what they were. She had to choose her next words very carefully should she like to remain hidden in this town as Rachel Martin. Abigail considered her options, then took a breath. "Nobility, then. Do you think you have the right to kidnap whatever lady you choose?"

"What? No! I just—" As he startled with surprise, Abigail tried to escape the man's hold. His arms tightened around her as she struggled. "Listen to me. I am just trying to enjoy the day without drawing attention to myself. Hence the hood, hence my adamancy that *you must not say anything.* If my uncle knew I was here unsupervised—"

"Your uncle?" Abigail laughed. "You really are something out of a storybook, aren't you?"

"*Listen.*" The Earl said. "I apologize for my actions. I would like to make it up to you, if you'll let me. You seem an amiable enough person."

Make it up to her? That could mean too many things, and too many of those things involved Abigail having to *talk* to this man and let him get to know her. She couldn't risk that. On the other hand, what consequences would there be if she refused him? He knew quite well he couldn't have her going around telling the story of the day *Lord Thomas of Westwend kidnapped her and held her captive in an abandoned alleyway.* If she refused to let him "make it up to her," she was sure it would come back to haunt her. Blackmail, possibly, to keep her quiet. She preferred to not have some nobleman digging around in her business. If she couldn't keep her mouth shut. Abigail had plenty of secrets to hide. The correct choice was clear.

"All right," she said, "I'll let you make it up to me."

"And you won't mention this to anyone?"

"I swear it."

Thomas let her go. When Abigail turned around, she was able to see his face for the first time. He had a kind countenance with soft eyes one could easily trust. Abigail made a mental note to be wary of those eyes. Just looking trustworthy didn't ever make one so. His light hair was cut short, but long enough to fall in front of his eyes in messy pieces. Abigail studied his face a moment more, then nodded and said under her breath, "Not bad."

Thomas laughed. "And the same to you, Miss, uh...?"

Abigail hesitated a moment too long. "Rachel Martin," she dipped into a quick bow. After all, she was addressing an Earl. Although Abigail didn't care much for nobility, Rachel probably did.

"Pleased to meet you, Miss Martin." Thomas returned the bow and then offered her his arm. "Shall we be on our way?"

Abigail took his arm and asked, "Where, exactly?"

Thomas smirked. "You'll see."

Arm-in-arm, the two walked across nearly half the town before they reached their destination. Thomas gallantly held open the door. Abigail didn't know if he was joking with her or if he was always this gentlemanly. As she walked into the building, she saw the smallest of smiles on his lips. Abigail knew, no matter how much she wanted to hate this day, she was going to have one of the best afternoons of her life.

The minute she entered the shop, the warmth and scent overtook her. It was a stark contrast to her life aboard the cold, windy ship. For a moment or two, Abigail closed her eyes and just breathed in the scent of this wonderful bakery.

Thomas walked in beside her. "Here we are! Best pastry shop in all Westwend."

Abigail smiled at Thomas' enthusiasm. "You say that as if you stroll unsupervised through the square on a regular basis."

"Well, just not often enough for people to recognize me." Just as Thomas was finishing his sentence, a plump, amiable looking man walked out from a door behind the storefront.

"Tommy!" the man said brightly.

The Earl returned the baker's smile and walked toward the countertop, placing two coins down on it.

"Two of whatever's freshest, John," Thomas said.

"Coming right up," John said as he headed into the back room. "I've got quite a treat for you!" He came back out with two golden, buttery pastries, oozing with a yellow custard. The baker wrapped them in pieces of brown parchment before handing them to Thomas and taking the coins.

"You and the lady enjoy your day!" John smiled.

"Thank you, sir," Thomas called as he led Abigail out of the shop and handed her one of the rich pastries.

She could feel its warmth through the parchment. The light, chilly wind blowing through her long hair, the pastry warming her hands, and an Earl walking beside her made such a picturesque scene. Abigail followed Thomas to a shaded hill, secluded from the rest of the town. She smiled. It was like with every step she took, she fell farther and farther into this fantasy drawn up for her by an ignorant nobleman. It was all truly, very stupid.

So what if it's stupid? She decided. *I'm going to enjoy this stupid day for as long as I possibly can.*

Thomas and Abigail sat on the hill for quite some time, long after they both finished the pastries. They talked until the sun was setting gently on the horizon, coating them both in an amber light. They talked of all the stupidities of the day and of the world. They talked of ships and nobles and horses and love.

That was the one that worried Abigail the most. That subject on its own was usually enough to make Abigail uncomfortable, but it was easier to discuss this time.

"I've quite enjoyed spending the day with you, Rachel," Thomas said.

"Really? Wasn't everything just a ruse to keep me quiet about what happened?"

"Maybe," Thomas nodded his head from side to side. "That, and an excuse to spend the day with a beautiful girl."

Abigail felt her face grow warm. This was the sort of compliment Anthony gave her often and it made her feel so out of place. Instead of looking at her expectantly like Anthony often did, Thomas just looked at his hands, apparently as uncomfortable as she was. For whatever reason, this seemed to make Abigail less wary. She slid closer to him.

"You think I'm beautiful?" She truly meant the question.

"I mean..." He turned to look at her. "Yes. I do."

Abigail smiled. "Thank you, but I'm not."

Thomas laughed.

"I mean it. Look at me." She gestured to her frayed petticoat and worn-down boots. "The way I dress and act... It's nothing like the beautiful people that you meet."

"Exactly, you're different from them in every way. I know we hardly even know each other, but I can tell." Thomas forced her to meet his gaze. His face was full of kindness and sincerity. "And that's why you are the most beautiful person I've ever met."

His stare was magnetic. She couldn't look away. She didn't *want* to look away. She wanted to stay here with him for as long as possible. Abigail couldn't believe she managed to keep from screaming when Thomas gently cupped her cheek and brought her face closer to his. It was a foreign gesture and the feelings that came along with it were even more so. It felt like a warm fire inside her, beginning to blaze and spread to every inch of her being. Just before their lips touched, the flames overtook her, Abigail caught something out of the corner of her eye.

Anthony.

He was a good hundred feet away, but Abigail could see the pain in his eyes as clearly as if he was standing beside her. Anthony shook his head and walked back into town.

"I have to go," she said.

"Hm?"

Abigail stood suddenly. "I'm sorry, I just..." She kept seeing the betrayal wash over Anthony's countenance. Abigail was a captain and her duty was to her crew. Nothing more. She couldn't waste her time on courtships and noblemen and love. "I have to go." She ran back toward the town.

✦

Abigail barged into her room at Smith Lodgings to find Anthony sitting on the bed.

"Please, let me explain," though she didn't know how she could explain. Abigail messed up, and there was no undoing it.

Anthony stood, prepared to argue. "No! I don't want to hear your explanations. You—"

"Yes, I know, I know. I shouldn't have wasted time talking to him. I should be sticking to the plan, anything else is inexcusable—"

"The crew?" He yelled. "What about me? Did you even think about my feelings?"

Abigail was taken aback. She had expected him to be upset with her, but she hadn't considered that she might have hurt him personally.

"What do you mean?" She asked, quieter now.

Anthony took a step toward her. His voice was softer as well. "Abigail..." He paused, as if considering. "You must have known I loved you."

Before she could say anything, Anthony took her face in his hands and kissed her. It was so unlike what had occurred minutes before with Thomas. Abigail felt none of the thrill or rising panic. Instead, she just felt numb.

How could Anthony do this? She had suspected his affections for a while, but not once had she imagined he would act on it. Abigail was his captain. His *superior*. And just like Abigail, Anthony's duty was to his crew. Nothing more. Abigail touched a hand to her lips and looked away, unable to meet his eyes. The pair sat in uncomfortable silence until Abigail said with finality, "I think you should leave."

Anthony nodded. "I'll see you in the morning."

Abigail shook her head. "No. I don't want to see you again. You're no longer welcome on my crew."

Anthony hardly seemed shocked. Perhaps he predicted this as a possible outcome of his actions. Nonetheless, he nodded solemnly and left without saying another word.

The second the door closed, Abigail fell onto the bed. Hunching on the edge with her head in her hands, Abigail felt defeated. For three years, she had captained her men without fail. There was food to spare, more riches than any of her men could have hoped for, and plenty of fame with no consequences. To lead your crew to glory and to keep them out of danger's path was what it meant to be a captain. Not once had romance entered the picture. A captain didn't waste time over such a trivial matter.

This is not what my father would want me to do.

Abigail felt a heavy pang in her chest when the thought came to her. Her father left her the ship and the crew. He trusted her to make the decisions that were best for *all* the men. She had failed him.

In the corner of the room, she spied a chest of drawers. Silently crossing toward it, she pulled out the drawers one by one. All were empty except for the very last one. Abigail smiled. In the bottom drawer was a half-full bottle of gin and a gun. Anthony must have brought them with him when they left the ship.

Pity he forgot to take them with him. No use letting them go to waste now.

Abigail tucked the gun into her belt and uncorked the bottle. Taking a swig of the drink, she winced a bit at the taste before taking several more sips. Trying not to think too much, she just sat in silence and tried not to cry. Hours later, she fell asleep with the bottle still in her hand.

✦

Abigail awoke with a start and a splitting headache. A thin stream of sunlight spilled through the open window. The brightness of it made her head throb. She groaned and rolled over. She shouldn't have been drinking last night. She needed a clear head today, although she couldn't recall exactly why. Maybe if she slept for another hour or two…

As she let her heavy eyes close, they shot open again with a sharp memory.

She had forgotten.

She was supposed to meet her crew on the shore at four. *Sharp.* She had disregarded her own orders. Abigail felt sour guilt welling up inside her, making her hands shake and her shoulders heavy. Could anyone be less suited to captaincy than herself? She pushed away these negative thoughts. When she promised her father to take care of the ship and crew, she meant every word. Abigail knew she had to try to fix her mistakes.

She rocketed down the stairs, completely ignoring the headache that still resonated within her. Once outside, she realized she didn't have a course of action. Knowing that her crew was well hidden, she didn't know where to begin. If she checked all the inns, she could—

In the distance, Abigail suddenly saw the faint outline of a structure she knew all too well. A structure she had spent most of her time avoiding. The gallows. *They've been arrested. They're all going to be hanged.* The thought came to her suddenly, but she knew it was true. But was there enough time to formulate a plan of escape?

"Lost, are you?"

Abigail's focus centered on the man who had spoken them. "Thomas?" she said vaguely, almost confused. Her eyes returned to the gallows in the distance. "I, uh…"

Thomas only smiled. "Where are you headed at this hour?"

Abigail thought a moment, perhaps a moment too long, before saying, "I was just looking for my brother, but he seems to be… preoccupied."

"So, you're not busy, then?"

Abigail shook her head. "No, I'm not. Well, I mean, I am but, why do you ask?"

"My uncle decided it's time to start taking my position seriously. He wants me to attend an execution."

The words resonated in Abigail's mind. "Execution?"

"Yes, it's wonderful news. We've captured the famed crew of the *Bloody Rose.*"

It took all of Abigail's strength to maintain an expressionless face. All she dared say was, "Oh."

"I was hoping," Thomas's words trailed, but he took Abigail's hand and continued with assurance. "Since I gain my full title in a few months, I'm expected to marry within the year. Would you mind if I announced our courtship?"

"Courtship?" Abigail reeled, unable to uphold her façade. For some reason, this announcement was more surprising than the news about her crew being in custody.

"Of course, if you don't want to… I mean, I know we've just met—"

"Oh!" Abigail resumed her character quickly. "Of course, I would love to."

Thomas smiled, then took her hand and kissed it gently. "Let's be off, then."

Abigail laughed lightly, forcing herself to keep up this disguise until she could get close enough to save her crew.

+

"Ladies and gentlemen!" Thomas stood before a sizable gathering awaiting the execution of the crew from the *Bloody Rose.* The men looked dejected beside the gallows, many of them eyeing Abigail unhappily.

"Let us rejoice in this victory. These men have roamed the seas for years, causing trouble in many innocent towns."

Standing at Thomas' side, Abigail wrung her hands as she scanned the faces of her crew. All the men had been captured and were in custody. Despite the fact that she had deliberately excluded him from lodging with the crew the night before, Anthony was standing with the other men.

Abigail formulated a rescue plan. She had tried to think of every possible outcome or interruption and hoped that failure wasn't an option. All she needed was a weapon. As the fates would have it, Thomas had a large longsword at his hip.

There was one flaw in her plan. While her plan was taking effect, one man would lose his life. The sacrifice had to be made, and there was no way she could avoid it. If she wanted to save at least some of her men, one of them had to hang. Chance determined which man would suffer that fate.

Thomas rambled on, but his words were lost to Abigail. She abandoned her plotting when Thomas pulled the cutlass from its sheath and strode toward the group of criminals. "Your captain will suffer first." He held the sword to Anthony's throat.

Abigail's heart sank. If Anthony revealed her presence, she would have no chance to help any of her men. Even as the blade pressed against his throat, Anthony did not break eye contact. He looked past Thomas to Abigail. "I am the captain. Let me suffer before my men."

Anthony had been her friend for years. She knew they would die for each other. Without a second thought, she would die for any man on her crew. But after her actions of the previous day, it was hard for Abigail to imagine Anthony sacrificing himself to protect her. Anthony, her best friend, was prepared to give his life for her sake and the whole crew. That idea coupled with Abigail's final harsh words made her sick. Still, she had to press through this pain if she wanted to save anyone's life.

Thomas returned to Abigail's side as Anthony was led to the noose. The townspeople were watching expectantly. Abigail couldn't bring herself to watch as the rope slid around her friend's neck. Anthony would die thinking she hated him. But if she wanted her plan to succeed, she had to let him believe it was true.

Thomas slid an arm around Abigail's waist and she leaned into him. She wrapped her arms around his torso, taking the opportunity to grasp the hilt of his sword.

This was her chance.

As Abigail heard the floor beneath Anthony's feet drop, she ignored the sickening pain in her gut and turned away from Thomas. She drew the cutlass out of its sheath and held the blade toward him. His face was indescribably confused and hurt.

"Rachel, what are you doing? This is ridiculous. Give me that sword." He reached out to take it from her, but Abigail skillfully flicked his hand away. Thomas reeled, inspecting his now bleeding hand.

Abigail spun around, wielding the weapon in the direction of anyone who dared oppose her. All the surrounding faces bore the same look of confusion and terror. For the first time, her crew looked hopeful. Turning, she caught a glimpse of Anthony hanging limply from the end of the noose. She would have time to mourn once they were all safe but for now she buried her flaming guilt.

Abigail faced Thomas. "You should know, sir, that my name is not Rachel Martin. It is Abigail Kelley. And if you wish to keep your life, I would suggest staying out of my way." She strode toward the lawmen holding the members of her crew in captivity. "You." She pointed the blade at one of them. "You will let these men go."

The man looked to Thomas for support, but Thomas gave no evident response. "Why should I?" the man asked.

Abigail touched the tip of the sword to his chest. "I will not hesitate to go to extreme measures to ensure the freedom of my crew."

There was a long moment of silence before Thomas replied loudly behind her, "Apprehend her."

At that moment, Abigail drove the blade through the lawman's chest and ran. She hoped her crew would follow suit. She ran for an eternity before she spotted the rowboats on the shore. As she neared them, she slowed and turned around. To her delight, she saw what she believed to be her entire crew running after her. She would have smiled if all her energy had not been wholly devoted to escape.

"Go! Get in, all of you!" she yelled. The men crammed into the little boats. Abigail climbed in last after ensuring that every one of her men was on board. As the group paddled to the safety of the *Bloody Rose*, Abigail saw another empty rowboat, still sitting on the shore. "They're going to follow us," she whispered.

"Pardon, Cap'n?" one of the crewmembers asked.

"Faster!" Abigail yelled to the men on both boats. "They're going to catch up to us!"

The men nodded in understanding and rowed faster. Not half a minute later, the lawmen spotted them and started the chase. Abigail's heart raced as she willed the boat forward. With every stroke of the oars, she felt her breath hitch. What if they didn't get to the ship in time? What if they were all apprehended again? What if more of her men hanged?

She couldn't afford thoughts like these. Not now. Not after what happened to Anthony. Even now, she could picture his lifeless body swinging. She shook her head, ridding her mind of the image. She would welcome those types of thoughts later. Now she had to save her crew.

As the boats drew beside the *Bloody Rose*, Abigail grabbed one of the thick ropes hanging from the side and handed it off to the man closest to her.

"Go! Now!" she said. The men climbed quickly into the ship, and only minutes had passed before everyone was on board. She whipped her head around to check for stragglers. A few voices urged her to get on the ship. Abigail's nerves were tense with urgency as she grasped the rope, preparing to climb onto the *Bloody Rose*.

A hand grasped her skirts tightly, pulling her downward. Abigail saw the third and final boat right up against her own. The unstable floor of the vessel swayed beneath her as a man climbed into her rowboat. Abigail reached for her sword, but nothing was there. She had left the weapon in the body of the lawmen. Abigail scowled.

In the third rowboat, a man stood ready to apprehend her. There was nothing Abigail could do—not even jumping overboard would get her out of this situation.

Abigail took a step toward the lawman and held her hands out to him. He smirked, grabbing her wrist painfully and pinning her hands behind her back. As Abigail turned, she saw one more man stepping into the rowboat.

Thomas looked at her with poison in his gaze. Surely, this wasn't the same man that had made her heart race only yesterday. Abigail glared back at him. She felt no remorse for lying to him. He captured her crew and killed her friend.

"Let go of her hands," Thomas said casually. "She won't run away." He placed a finger patronizingly under her chin. "She wouldn't dare."

The man behind Abigail released her wrists, and she resisted the urge to rub the soreness from them. She pushed Thomas's hand away from herself.

"Audacious, aren't you?" He chuckled.

Abigail's mind raced to find a way out. Anything that would let her get away with her crew. She had gotten too far to fail now. Then, like a gift from the heavens, she felt a forgotten weight around her middle. Last night, she had put Anthony's gun in her waistband before falling asleep. She prayed it was loaded.

"Thomas, I am going to tell you this only once. I am the captain of one of the most infamous ships in the world. You have seen firsthand what I am capable of. I recommend a quiet retreat and let us be on our way."

Thomas smiled condescendingly and patted her cheek. "No. I don't think so."

"Very well, then." Abigail pulled the gun from her waistband and aimed it directly at Thomas's chest.

"Filthy pirate." With hatred blazing in his eyes, Thomas spoke his final words. "I can't believe I ever trusted you."

Abigail pulled the trigger.

Lenicka Lee (signature)

LENICKA LEE

Inconspicuous

"**Y**ou there! How long until shore?" I ask.

"Maybe two more hours, *Captain*," the sailor sneers.

I frown at his tone. "Would you rather I was something else?"

He smirks at me. "No, sir, obviously not. I call you what you are." He turns, whispering something under his breath.

"What did you say, friend?"

"Oh, nothing you need to worry your pretty little ears over, sir," he calls over his shoulder, walking away.

I grind my teeth in frustration. That's been happening more often, the blatant scorn from the crew. Every time I give an order, they sluggishly obey. Every time I ask a question, they mock my authority. I give even a suggestion and they laugh and ignore me. I sigh heavily, hoping a mutiny is not on its way.

I am Josiah Taylor, captain of this ship. I repeat the phrase, reminding myself that technically I am in charge. *I am a pirate. I am captain of the Lonestar. I am the most powerful Mystic on this ship.*

I decide to find Elijah. He usually endures listening to my rants in these moments. I head down below to see if he happens to be organizing the loot from our last raid. I pass pirates who mutter and snarl. Luckily, there are no audible insults yet.

Elijah is expertly counting our resources and writing them down while remaining upright in the swaying ship. He glances at me then turns back to his work. "Ah Josiah? What is it this time?"

"Oh, you know, the usual. Crew being in general dislike of me and such." I pull over a bucket and taking a seat.

He grunts. "Can't say I'm surprised. It's only the millionth time you've complained about it."

"I know. Everything I do seems to make them hate me more."

"If they hate you so much, I don't understand why they rejected your petition the other day. It's not logical."

"Not logical? I'll say! They locked me in my own cabin!"

He laughs good naturedly, green eyes twinkling.

I had petitioned to resign as Captain of the *Lonestar*. Obviously, the crew turned the idea down. The pirates thought it was a dirty joke to keep someone they hate in charge, though I cannot fathom why. Elijah seems to be the only person without their sick sense of humor.

"Josiah?"

"Hmm?"

"I don't have new advice for you and I need to focus at the moment. This chat is making me forget my numbers."

I take the hint. "I'll leave you then. Thank you for being loyal, Elijah."

"My pleasure, Cap'n."

I tromp back up to the captain's cabin on the main deck. Maybe a visit with Evelynn will cheer me up. I knock three times on the door then enter. I find Evelynn pacing, wearing a pair of trousers and one of my shirts, with a leather-bound book in hand. The sun is setting through a port window, casting a crimson glow over her. Suddenly, all my worries about the crew seem meaningless.

"I cannot understand," she says almost immediately after the door closes, "How your famed 'Mirages' work! Show me again."

I roll my eyes. This is a common point of discussion for us. "What is there to understand, Eve? It's magic."

"That is not a good enough explanation! I refuse to be satisfied. Make me an illusion." She lifts her chin imperiously, a playful gleam in her brown eyes.

I chuckle softly. "Fine." I reach deep within and feel the swirling power of the Mirages. Seizing it, I shape it into something visible. A miniature model of the *Lonestar* appears in front of us, hovering in the air. Evelynn jumps when it appears, then leans forward, obviously intrigued. Technically, she is not supposed to be on board, but I was able to sneak her into my cabin by creating an illusion. She swipes a hand through the illusion, the image fuzzing slightly and refocusing.

"I'll never get tired of that," she laughs.

"A part of me wonders if I only make illusions so you can whack them," I smile.

"Today I will discover their secrets!"

"There are no secrets! Magic is a part of me."

"But why can't you make them on land, then? Are they *powered* by the sea? Is that why you can only use them while sailing? Or does the land block the power somehow? Or are you not skilled enough to—"

I cut her off with a kiss, but pull away long before I want to. "No more questions. Especially ones I don't know how to answer." I let the *Lonestar* illusion fade away.

She pouts, hands on her hips. "You can't just kiss me every time you want me to stop talking. It's unfair."

"But it works," I point out. "If only for a few seconds."

"You're impossible," she sighs.

I grin, spreading my arms. "And that's why you love me."

She rolls her eyes, pointedly turning her back on me and walking to the window. I follow slowly, wrapping my arms around her waist and resting my head against hers. The final light from the setting sun glows across the horizon.

"I know a girl," I whisper into her hair. "Who is intelligent and inquisitive. She's incredibly brave and more than a little stubborn." Evelynn snorts at that. "She loves adventure and danger and doesn't care that her boyfriend is a crazy pirate captain. In fact, she barely cares what society thinks of her at all." I find myself smiling. "On top of all of that, she's unimaginably beautiful with gorgeous brown eyes and golden hair. Her name also happens to be Evelynn."

She leans into me. "I know a boy with a ridiculous name. He's most definitely crazy, but he's also charming. He's very handsome and has the darkest hair and the bluest eyes. He always knows just what to say to make his girlfriend blush."

I sigh contentedly. We stand there like that, watching the light fade and simply enjoying each other's presence.

The sky goes dark and someone starts yelling. "Josiah! We need you! We're nearing shore! Where are you?"

I groan, loathing the thought of leaving Evelynn and returning to the hostility of the crew. I pull away. "They need me to put an illusion over the ship before we're recognized as pirates." I grimace. "We'll have to get you ashore as soon as we dock. Wait here."

She nods as I leave. I close the door behind me and nearly bump into Elijah.

"Oh, there you are," he says, unfazed. "We need you to…" He waves his hands in the air. "Do the thing."

I raise an eyebrow. "Yeah, I got that."

He grunts.

I walk past him to the middle of main deck. Closing my eyes, I reach within and find the power of illusions and Mirages. I imagine the *Lonestar* coated with the power, changing to become an inconspicuous merchant ship. The power obeys. I open my eyes to watch the illusion fade into existence, disguising us. A faint tugging sensation reminds me that the illusion is in place.

Laughter echoes behind me. "Hey, Captain! How does it feel, eh? You're only good at making pretty pictures!" More laughter.

I form my hands into fists. *I am Josiah Taylor. I can do things they cannot. I am a Mystic.* Light flashes around my fists. Mists of darkness rise around me. Such power! The imbeciles. They cannot understand this glory. I take a breath, forcing myself to think clearly. The worst thing right now would be to start a fight with Evelynn on board. I release the building tension and the light disappears while the mists cease rising.

The pirates groan. "Aw, c'mon, Cap! We were hoping for a light show!"

I turn. "Not today, friends. Try me tomorrow." With that, I stride back to the captain's cabin and slam the door behind me.

Evelynn turns in surprise. "What's the matter?"

"Just the usual. Don't worry about it." I shake my hands, ridding myself of the excess emotion. "We'll be docking in a few minutes," I say. "You ready?"

"I just need the coat and hat, then I'll be ready to go."

I nod as I dig around and finding the spare clothing. She quickly pulls on the black coat and stuffs her hair up into the hat. The coat is too long while the hat is on crooked, but she only needs to look like me from a distance. I find my own hat and put it on, then we wait in anxious silence. I grab her hand and squeeze, trying to lend her comfort. She smiles weakly. No matter how many times I have brought her on board, the arrival and exit are always the worst parts.

The passage of ships, visible in the port window, become more frequent as we near the harbor. I tap my fingers absently against Evelynn's hand, anticipation growing.

I hear someone calling out orders and sailors scrambling to obey. That should have been my job. I sigh. I am a captain by title only.

We glide in smoothly and are docked within a few minutes. My gaze flicks to Evelynn. Time to go. I create an illusion that makes her nearly invisible, a slight distortion of the air. A mirage in its purest form. We leave the cabin, bee lining for the exit ramp. I am the only one who remains visible and the sailors, for the most part, ignore us. We reach the ramp and travel halfway down. This is the tricky part. My illusions cannot function while on land, so I stay on the ocean side. I create an illusion of invisibility for myself, while Evelynn continues to the landside, pretending to be me. I glance around. The harbor is strangely silent tonight. Watching as she leaves, I hope for no sounds of alarm from the ship. There are none. I let out a soft sigh of relief and step back onto the deck of the *Lonestar,* shedding the illusion.

"Oh, Josiah," calls out a singsong voice from behind me. "I believe you're missing something!"

I whirl around. Elijah is standing twenty yards away, holding a knife to Evelynn's throat. My knees weaken and I stumble forward, tripping when my power is ripped away at the barrier between land and sea. "Evelynn!"

"Stop!" Elijah barks. "Don't come closer. You can guess the consequences." His voice is gruff, almost unfamiliar.

"Please, Elijah. Why? I thought I could trust you! Please don't hurt her!"

Evelynn stares at me with wide eyes, her fear reflecting my own.

"Please? Josiah, are you begging?" He laughs. "I'll tell you why. The crew was getting restless with you as captain long before they started to show it. They could see you had priorities other than our raids, such as this girl here, so naturally they turned to me."

I glance at him, my fear mounting. "Why even keep me as captain, then?"

"Because of your magic. But we've decided that isn't a good enough reason anymore."

"Wha—" I cut off as something hits my head from behind, knocking off my hat. I fall to my knees, pain exploding behind my eyes. I hear Evelynn cry out as rough hands haul me to my feet. I blink rapidly, my vision fuzzy. "Kill—Kill me if you want, but please let Eve go."

"Where's the fun in that?" Elijah calls.

Realization dawns. I strain against the men holding me as my vision finally clears. "Please don't do this!" I make eye contact with Evelynn. Tears run down her cheeks. Time seems to freeze. "I... I know a girl," I whisper, not daring to take my eyes away from her.

"She's innocent and beautiful. She's always so strong. She's a much better person than me. To be without her, forever, would kill me." My voice cracks. "I love you, Evelynn."

She smiles sadly. "I love you too, Josiah."

"Josiah, look at me," Elijah commands.

I numbly obey and he slits Evelynn's throat.

"NO!" I yell, trying in vain to pull away from the men holding me. I watch, helpless, as the light fades from her eyes and she falls to the ground limp. Elijah tosses her to the side as if she were nothing, blood pooling beneath her. Red, so much red.

I hang my head.

Elijah walks toward me and grabs my face in his hand, forcing me to look at him. "Two birds with one stone."

With that, he stabs me in the chest with his knife. I gasp, sagging in the arms holding me upright. They drop me to the ground as the life bleeds out of me. "You... " I cough out. "You can kill me... but never my love."

Elijah frowns down at me, then crouches. He says something but I can no longer hear him. He stabs me again but the pain is fleeting.

I come to you Evelynn.

The knife comes down again.

Everything goes black.

Siamaids

Fourteen was the magic age of courtship and marriage for young women of royal blood. I was no exception. That process should have been completed for me by now but it was a tradition I didn't care for. I shoved Edward from my mind. My marriage would be on my terms and by my choice. Two days was all it took to become the captain of a pirate ship called *The Ocean's Jewel*. The crew didn't like me, yet, I am in command, and they cannot make me leave. This is my home now.

"Ahem." I cleared my throat in the galley doorway, catching the attention of the three pirates lounging there. "Don't you boys have something better to do?"

"I don't know, don't *you* have something better to do, Destiny?" One of them replied, mocking my tone of voice.

"That's *Captain* to you." I pushed the brown locks out of my face. "Now make yourselves useful before I ma—"

"Men, I need you on deck," the ship's quartermaster, Feytan, interrupted as he burst in next to me.

I shifted, allowing them to leave. I was itching to make those three pay for their insolence. I pondered creative possibilities like putting them on ice or doing extra chores for weeks. *They should pay, especially that one who talked back.* It occurred to me that a demonstration would be a perfect solution to remind the crew who was in command. Sooner or later, they would accept my authority.

"Everyone on deck!" I stepped onto the bridge of the three-mast ship. As I leaned against the cold pine railing, I looked at my men. "Listen up because I'm only singing this once."

The wind carried my hum to each crewman. The sound expanded as I opened my mouth to let the notes ring out with strength. Enchanted beyond their will, every soul heeded my tune.

There they are. I spotted the unruly trio from the galley. As my song continued, I extended my hand toward the unlucky boys. I imagined them awaking from their trance. Panic would fill their eyes, realizing their feet were frozen to the deck. *They will be more respectful after this.*

In moments, my attention turned to everyone else. My gaze rose skyward as I thought about what to do with the others. When my song ended, the tune echoed with hypnotic effect, lingering in their minds. I internally groaned as dark clouds loomed overhead. Rain would drench this deck before long. I had to hurry if I wanted to stay dry. On the other hand, the crew would get wet. I decided the entire slothful lot could stand in the rain for a while. I sang a few more notes to bind the men to the deck. "This is what happens when you don't listen to me."

I slid past the stunned pirates with ease, darting into my room as the first drops of rain tapped the pine deck. The Siamaid song would keep them in place.

Foolish men have little understanding of my species. Some think we are two separate creatures. On land, we are known as Sirens with the ability to compel humans to do our will through song. When we get wet, our legs turn into a mermaid-like tail, which makes rain annoying. However, we are not true mermaids. They are a distinct species. Like them, we have the ability to manipulate, move, heat, and freeze water. Unlike them, our kind is peaceful.

Rain pounded the deck mercilessly. I felt a twinge of sympathy for the pirates as I tried to view them through the rivulets of water coursing down my windowpane. Not everyone was deserving of my punishment. However, strength was the way of a leader. My father's example taught me a leader should be fierce. Exact obedience to every command was the only way to maintain security and peace.

✦

My body ached from falling asleep while leaning against the window. Unwillingly, my body responded as I stretched in the darkened room. It must be the middle of the night. The rain clouds dissipated and allowed the light from the moon to shine into the cabin.

I left the crew out in the rain! Suddenly the memory of the evening before returned, and I rubbed my forehead. I left them to freeze in the rain! I did not want to face my crew, but I knew I must. With a deep breath, I walked quietly on deck, careful not to wake the ones who might be sleeping.

Indistinguishable voices came from down below.

I softly descended the stairs, straining to hear. For a brief moment, I considered doing something for my crew but dispelled the thought as I made sense of their conversation.

"Aye, let's boot 'er!" one man yelled.

Feytan, the quartermaster, spoke to little avail. "Listen, let's not make any rash decisions."

"I agree. We need to boot her first chance we get! She's no captain and she wasn't elected 'ither."

"That's true," agreed a third voice. "She just came in, killed our captain, and took over. So what if she's a Siamaid. She's the worst captain I've ever seen!"

Boot me out? Could they do that?

"I agree that circumstances are strange, but we should try to work things out," Feytan tried again.

"Do you think she accidentally killed Captain Peytren? Tonight wasn't the first time we were unjustly punished. I won't stand for it any longer," someone else added.

I took a step back from the shock of their words. The need to escape took over and caused me to race to the top deck. Pausing at the gunwale, or the upper edge of the ship, I looked at the deep-blue waters below. No one understood. Being a captain on a pirate ship was not going to change that.

I was ready to jump, when someone grabbed my hand.

"Wait!" Feytan's voice pleaded.

However, his grip was not tight enough to prevent me from dropping into the water. I heard the sound of him plunging after me.

"Destiny, please wait!" he called.

"Why should I? I don't know how to be a ship's captain." I propelled myself forward. "I'm better off on my own."

"You could be an amazing captain. I know you don't have the respect of the crew yet, but they do listen to you."

I blinked the tears out of my eyes, glad the ocean hid the evidence from Feytan.

"Destiny." His voice was suddenly close.

"Oh my Trident! You're a Siamaid, too!" It was such a shock to see him underwater, breathing and swimming beside me. I couldn't help but laugh. "How does the rain not affect you?"

Feytan gestured to a ledge near the ocean floor. I followed him.

"Let me tell you about my past first." His hand combed through his dirty blonde hair. "Ueria in the Ocearic Sea was my home. I was the second youngest of ten sons to King Perann and Queen Shelica. Until my seventh year, we lived in peace. A battle between pirates took place above our kingdom, which escalated into a great war. Cannibals destroyed and sunk ships at an alarming rate. Wreckage descended into our depths and destroyed part of my home. Our people chose to fight back in order to save our kingdom. I wanted to fight as well, so I followed our soldiers at a distance. If they spotted me, they would have sent me home. I don't know if it was the great storm or the battle waging around me that knocked me unconscious. Slave traders found me around the time I awoke on a beach. They sold me to a pirate captain, and I've spent the last few years working my way up in rank while trying to find a good ship and crew. The Ocean's Jewel is such a ship."

"But that doesn't explain how you keep your tail from appearing when you get wet."

"The thing that keeps me in human form is this blue quartz." He showed me his crystal on a chain hanging around his neck. The stone itself wasn't fancy. "No tail, unless I'm fully submerged in water. But now… I want to hear about you."

"What?" His request caught me off guard.

"I told you about me, now it's your turn to tell me your story."

My defenses were slipping with Feytan. He made me feel safe. "I'm the middle of twenty-one siblings - three brothers and seventeen sisters. I ran away from home because they don't care about me. No one seemed to want me and I was certain no one would notice my absence. It was during my escape that I became entangled in your net. When the captain took me to his quarters, he tried to kill me. I told him I wasn't a mermaid but he wouldn't listen so I defended myself against his attack."

A moment of silence passed. "You would make a good captain, you know."

"What are you talking about? I make a horrible captain, and you know it."

"I can teach you about the ship. And the crew can teach you about being a pirate," he said. "I'll talk to the others and I'm sure they'll give you a second chance."

"They won't go for it. They'll just assume you're under my spell."

"Siamaids can't control others of their kind," he said. "And they know I'm a Siamaid."

"They know about you?" I could feel my eyebrows collapse in wonder. The crew knew Feytan was a Siamaid and still allowed him to be their quartermaster. "And they know I can't control you?"

He nodded. "As for the blue quartz, I think I have an extra piece aboard the ship. You can wear it until we get you an actual necklace."

As nice as he seemed, I still didn't trust his motives. "Why do you want me back? You would be captain if I left."

He seemed to find that funny. "I don't want to be captain. I'm not confident being in the spotlight. I lack the drive and forcefulness that you possess. Those qualities make you a great leader, and a good captain."

"I don't know the first thing about being captain," the guilt-ridden words fell from my mouth.

"The crew and I can shape you into the best pirate around," he said.

I avoided his gaze, unsure of how to reply.

Again, he adjusted his position to meet my eyes.

"All right," I blurted out. "I'll come back."

"Come on then." He grabbed my hand, and we shot off into the water. I was barely able to keep up with him.

+

It was almost two months before my captain duties became enjoyable. There was so much to do. I spent time getting to know each member of the crew. Feytan taught me the rules of piracy, the roles of each crewmember, sea terms, and ship terms. It was hard work but I learned fast. The crew was hard to read, but they seemed more friendly and open. Most of them had a similar background, many had run away from different things and like me, they found a home here on board. For once, I was glad to have been caught in their net. Maybe things could be different.

"Captain, we received a message from *The Crystal Dagger*." Feytan walked toward me with a familiar seabird on his shoulder and a message in his hand. My mind flashed to a few months ago when we came across a sinking pirate ship. After rescuing their boat, towing them to shore, and aiding in the repairs, we formed an alliance. Messenger birds flew letters of communication between our vessels.

"What does it say?" I sat down on a crate.

"Three merchant vessels are under attack by two pirate ships in the Seryon Sea. Requesting assistance," he read.

I smiled and called out to the crew, "Well. It seems we've been invited to a party!" To Feytan, I replied, "Inform them we are on our way."

As I began helping the crew ready the sails, I turned to our navigator. "Jackson! I want the quickest route to Seryon." After a smooth trip, we arrived swiftly to join the fight already in progress. I formed water into a blunt sword of ice and used it to knock people out since I would rather have as little bloodshed as possible. Once the battle ended, Feytan and I collected the riffraff using water to pull them all into a bubble where we could move them down to the cells. We created an ice lock that would melt in about four hours. The crew pillaged for any valuables. They returned the stolen merchandise and the rest would be ours to keep, sell, or trade in the next town we came across.

After rummaging through the captain's quarters, I grabbed some paper and ink. They needed a small warning:

Next time, think twice before attacking innocent ships! ~ The Oceans Jewel

"Where to next, Captain?" Jack asked. "You wanted to check something out?"

"Let's go southwest, down to the Norestian Sea, toward Bermuda." I pointed to an area on the map in his hands. "There are decent trading posts in this area," I pointed to some small islands.

"Sounds like a good plan. I'll get the crew ready. By the way, it's been brought to my attention that we're almost out of drinking water."

"I got it," Feytan and I spoke in unison.

"You always do it," he complained.

I smiled. "I like to stay busy."

"Then let me help you." He rushed down the stairs, disappearing below deck.

Staying behind, I drew a portion of ocean water up, holding it mid-air. Turning my palm up, the water heated to a boil. The process created steam, which allowed me to do two things simultaneously. First, I withdrew the moisture and moved this freshwater into another contained sphere. At the same time, the separated salt grew heavy and fell back into the ocean.

Feytan arrived next to me, setting a barrel down. As we finished filling up the bucket with the freshwater I'd created, Feytan hefted the container.

"I'm holding one end." I gripped the bottom of the barrel and together, we hauled it downstairs.

"Are you sure you aren't going to Bermuda for *other* reasons than the trading posts?"

Of course, he can see right through me.

"Destiny, you should see this," someone interrupted, peeking into the galley. Due to the urgency in his voice, I followed swiftly behind him. Arriving above deck, I froze.

No! I rushed to the side of the ship. Ship wreckage was everywhere. "What happened here?" Looking at Feytan, I felt panic rise in my chest. *What if the same thing that had happened to his home happened to mine? What if my family was gone, and I couldn't save them? What if I could have prevented it?*

"Hey! It'll be okay." Feytan put his hand on my shoulder. "Whatever happens, you have us."

I nodded, but could not shake my worry. *What if—*

A sudden flash came from the water. When I looked in I could feel something large coming toward us very fast. I knew Feytan could feel it, too.

"Go! Find *The Crystal Dagger*, or one of our other allies," I ordered. "Everet! Get the cannons ready. Aim for right above the water, but don't fire. All able-bodied men grab your weapons. Use every firearm in our possession, but no one fires until I give the order."

"What's happening, Captain?" someone asked.

"I don't know." I closed my eyes as the energy grew closer and the pull enhanced.

Then, it stopped. At once, my eyes snapped open. The ocean was still.

Like popcorn popping, one by one, the people whose presence I detected, surfaced.

"Mermaids!" one of my panic-stricken crewmembers called.

The despise that mermaids held for humans would completely explain the wreckage but this was Siamaid territory. I checked for a bluish tint to their skin but found none. "They aren't mermaids!"

A shot rang. A bullet entered the water five feet in front of the nearest Siamaid.

"You squid-headed idiot." I took the gun from him, but it was too late.

A fight broke out between my crew and the Siamaids. I forced a wave to form, pushing the Siamaids away from *The Ocean's Jewel*. The wave crashed down keeping their attention momentarily diverted. "We don't want to fight you."

The Crystal Dagger appeared with Feytan on board. He shot three rounds into the sky, alerting everyone to his presence.

"Your actions show otherwise!" a Siamaid replied.

I quickly scanned the crowd. I knew that voice. In the congregation of Siamaids, I spotted my mother. Next to her was all of my family, my younger sisters and even my older ones who had kingdoms of their own. Everyone was alive, but I felt a sudden weight in my chest that I had not felt before. I rubbed my forehead. "Feytan!" I snapped. "Get over here!"

He grabbed a rope and swung over, landing next to me.

My attention turned again to the Siamaids. However, before I could explain, a giant ball of ice had been formed collectively by them. I had to do something, but I could not stop it alone. That ice cannonball would obliterate the ship and everyone onboard. I lunged off the gunwale and straight into the line of fire.

I do not actually remember the moment of impact, except the pain. Everything hurt. Breathing hurt. Still, I forced my eyes to open. Feytan was cradling me in his arms, keeping me almost fully submerged in the water. I sat up to take in my surroundings. Both ships looked damage free, for the most part. Chunks of ice were floating everywhere atop the water.

Turning to my family, and my people, I opened my mouth to speak. "Why would you attack without thinking twice about the consequences? You could have *killed* all the people on my ship! Did you cause all this destruction to all of these ships? Did you think about the effects this would have on the kingdom and our *people*?" I ignored the pain that was shooting through my whole body.

"Destiny, is that you?" one of my sisters asked.

"What Kessla?" I growled at her.

Suddenly, everyone rushed forward arms wide, but I backed away.

"Careful, she's hurt," Feytan warned, keeping them back.

"What happened? You just disappeared. Were you captured by pirates? Are you okay? Where have you been?" A sea of questions bombarded me from every direction, all at once, and my head started to spin. I squeezed Feyton's hand.

"I didn't get captured. I ran away."

"You ran away?" my mother asked.

"Yes, I ran away. I felt forgotten and ignored. I just wanted to be a part of the family but you were always so busy. No one in the family understands me. No one even tries. I've been aboard this ship for just over two months, and I am closer to my crew than I ever was with you." I was furious and just a little hopeful. Maybe they would understand now.

"Why didn't you come to us before? We cannot read your mind," my father explained. "You're a part of our family and we love you, Destiny. However, you can't expect to be the center of attention if you never even try to be a part of the family."

"You still don't get it!" I swam to my ship, pulling myself out of the ocean, and climbing up the side of my ship, Feytan behind me. I turned to my crew. "Set sail for anywhere but here."

"Are you sure this is what you want?" Feytan put a hand on my shoulder.

"Don't." I brushed his hand off and walked to my room. *It was stupid of me to have come here.*

+

"Please tell me we should turn around because I'm acting rash."

"No. It's been a year, Destiny." Feytan swam ahead of me, in case there would be trouble. The guards opened the door to the throne room without a fight.

"Destiny?" My mom and some of my younger sisters were playing with a Kelp Ball. "Ariala, go get your fath—"

My father entered the room without Ariala's announcement. A series of emotions flashed in his eyes when he spotted me. His face remained neutral. "What is the meaning of this?"

"I've come to apologize—about what happened." I swam forward then lowered myself into a deep curtsy.

"If you think you can just swim in here and resume your life, then—"

"I'm not staying," I interrupted.

My siblings had left the room, but they were listening through the doors.

"I am still captain of *The Ocean's Jewel* and I'm not abandoning my crew. I came for a short visit, if you'll have me."

"And who is this?" My father nodded toward Feytan. "We lacked an introduction at our first meeting."

"I am Prince Feytan of the Oceraic Sea, Your Majesty." He bowed, in a dignified manner. "I am most pleased to make your acquaintance. I am the quartermaster of *The Ocean's Jewel*."

"Another runaway?"

"No, Sire. The slave trade sold me into piracy during an attack on my kingdom years ago," he explained.

"I'm so sorry for your loss," said my mother. "Ueria was in ruins before word regarding the invasion reached us. No one survived."

Feytan paused, taking a sharp breath almost as if he hadn't known.

"May we visit for a few days?" I quickly changed the subject.

"Of course," my mother answered before my father could. "Follow me."

As we swam down the familiar halls, we unexpectedly stopped by my favorite guest room. "Aren't I sleeping in my room?" I asked.

My mother looked back and forth from me to Feytan, confused. "Is he not courting you?"

I could feel the heat rise in my cheeks. "Mom! No, we're just friends."

Feytan was clearly withholding a chuckle. "I'm afraid not, your majesty."

"Then Destiny will stay in her room and you can take this one." She opened the door to our largest guest room.

Once his belongings landed on the bed, I grabbed Feytan's hand. "Come on, I'll show you around." We swam off before my mother could make another completely embarrassing assumption. "I am really sorry about that," I said.

"It's all right. I miss having a family like this. I can't wait to meet your siblings."

"Let's go to the gardens first. Siblings can be last."

+

"Did we really have to leave so early?" he complained.

Exhausted myself, I shouldered my bag and continued swimming. "Yes." Leaving later would mean saying good-bye. I would miss them enough without the added farewells.

The ship was not far away, still in the same cove we had left it three days ago. I crawled on board and set my bag down, feeling a little uneasy on legs again.

"Welcome back!" The whole crew cheered, everyone was on deck. They parted and a banquet of my favorite dishes lay before my eyes.

"This is so sweet!" My stomach churning. "How did you know we were coming back this morning?"

No one said anything but I caught their gaze on Feytan. I rolled my eyes and nudged him hard.

"Oh, come on, you love it!" he said.

Despite wanting to argue, he was right. I did love it. Walking to the table, I grabbed some grilled octopus, putting the whole thing in my mouth to chew.

"You know, I've been thinking about this for a while," Feytan said. "May I have your permission to court you?"

Some friendly advice: Swallowing octopus when your friend is asking to court you will result in it being lodged in your throat. I couldn't breathe.

"Is she all right?" a crewman asked.

My body jerked as someone smacked my back. After several blows, my throat released its hold. I coughed and coughed, making sure my throat was clear. "Are you trying to kill me?"

"That wasn't the intention." Feytan's face was red with embarrassment. Still, he seemed to be waiting for an answer.

Although courtship was a part of aristocratic life, it was never on my agenda. Thinking about it, the answer was clear to me. "Ask me in a few years. I want to be a pirate for now. I'm not ready to be courted and I don't want to lose your friendship. Is that all right?"

"Of course," though his eyes looked disappointed. "At least it's not a no."

"And if you stop acting like a pirate, you're walking the plank."

"I understand," his eyes glistened in amusement.

Together, we joined the crew in partaking of the feast.

✦

Three years sped by faster than a sailfish being chased by a dolphin fish. We were quite busy with pirating activities: stealing, plundering, trading wares, and rescuing people.

"Where now?" Feytan asked. "We've seen every square inch of the known surface of these waters."

"Well, I like the idea of going home again. What do you think?"

"Jackson! Chart a course to the Norestian Sea," Feytan called.

I smiled and left the crew to the expedition. In my quarters, I retrieved a special kelp-paper journal and my squid ink from beneath my bed. I opened it and started to write on the last pages of my fourth journal.

I'm headed home again. Today has been pretty relaxed. The battle with the mermaids, lasted for a week and barely ended yesterday. Now we deserve rest. Everything has been amazing. Feytan has been really active and helpful, despite how exhausted I know he is. However, that is Feytan for you—always the hard worker. He has been spending a lot of time in the ocean lately, leaving every chance he has. On his numerous trips, he is gone for long periods of time. I wonder what he is doing? I worry he is seeing someone, yet he has every right to court another Siamaid. I did turn him down three years ago. I wish I could tell what is going on in his head.

Someone knocked on my door. I stored everything quickly before opening it.

"We have arrived at the Norestian Sea," said Jack.

"Thank you." I stretched as I exited my quarters. Despite my sleepy feeling, I had things to do. Rest could wait.

"All right, everyone! It's A-B shifts. Switch off every hour and no back-to-back shifts. We need everyone at their best, in case of anything unexpected. Now move."

They shuffled around, getting to their stations. I was not surprised when Feytan jumped into the ocean since he had B watch. Nonetheless, my body tensed as I pondered the what-ifs.

Being on A-watch, I worked first. It was pretty uneventful, like usual. My watch ended before Feytan returned, so I jumped into the ocean, letting myself drift to the bottom. I found a nice warm, soft place to lie down. Napping was not a common past time for me. Nevertheless, my eyes longed to be closed and I allowed the rolling current to lull me into a dream.

✦

I indulged in sleep for far too long. It was time for A-shift again. I raced along Jackson's charted route. Concern blossomed when there was no ship in sight. *Even at top speed, they wouldn't have made it this far. Where could they be? I've lost my ship!*

Closing my eyes, I called to the ocean, hoping to feel for the general direction of my ship. Following my instincts, I swam near the surface, letting out a breath of relief when I found it only slightly off course. Curious what had happened, I climbed aboard, double-checking that it was indeed my ship. This was *The Ocean's Jewel*. However, this was *not* my crew. "Who's in command and where's my crew?"

They all came at me. I worked to fend off as many as I could. During the struggle, a man who looked like a captain walked out of my quarters. I froze. A large burly man grabbed my arms, pinning them behind my back.

"Destiny, it's been a long time," the captain said. His light chestnut hair and auburn eyes were as I remembered from my childhood. Only, I could never look at him the way I once had. "It should have stayed that way, Edward. You had a better chance of living when you *stayed away.*"

He laughed at my warning. "You still like me and you know it. Why else would you surface? Well, your hunt has come to an end."

"Hunt? For you?" I scoffed. "I have not been hunting for you, Edward. You stole my ship!" Clenching my fists, I caused the ocean to stir.

"You became a pirate to find me," he said.

"No, I became a pirate to run away from my family. *You* became a pirate to escape from me. I have no intention of ever resuming a relationship with you. Now, where is my crew?"

The man holding me, kicked the back of my legs. I collapsed to my knees. "No one speaks to Captain Blackbeard like that," the man growled.

"Blackbeard? Funny name, given your appearance." I glared up at Edward. This conversation was getting nowhere. No one was giving any indication to my crew's location. I'd have to deal with this my way. I opened my hands. Water sprang from the ocean, knocking everyone off their feet and gathered them into an ice cage. Everyone, that is, except Edward, the so called 'Blackbeard.' "I'm going to ask *one* more time, Edward." I froze his legs to prevent him from moving. "Where is my crew?"

"I took care of them." He touched the ice with his finger. It cracked, then shattered, sending ice crystals everywhere.

"How? Everyone said you gave up being Siamaid to be human!"

"I'm not crazy. I'd never dream of giving up such power." He armed himself with an ice sword, sinking into a fighting stance.

I created two swords as well. My only hope was to trap his entire body in ice. Edward would survive the cold but, theoretically, he shouldn't be able to break free.

Using my swords, I swung and dodged, then dodged and swung again, trying to find an opening. Minutes passed and I could tell my chance would never come with my hands occupied. Swinging my swords, I came in close enough to kick him. The swords fell from my grasp and with both hands I commanded the water to encompass him then freeze. Solid ice engulfed him. I turned and started to walk toward the stairs that led below deck.

A sickening crack filled the air.

"No!" The blast this time was stronger and the ice, sharper. I worked swiftly to prevent the shards from doing any damage to me.

"You *will* love me again, Destiny," he growled.

Then, he crumpled to the ground. I looked at Edward lying there. Standing above him was another man. "Feytan?" He held a huge chunk of ice that he'd employed to knock Blackbeard out.

"You're okay!" There was relief in his voice. "When I saw *Queen Anne's Revenge* come into view and you weren't back, I knew I had to find and warn you. It looks like you handled the situation pretty well without warning."

"We need to take care of his crew and find our men."

"Our crew is down in the brig and I know where Blackbeard's vessel is too. We can return them and pillage it, if you like."

"I'll free the crew. Start sailing us East toward their ship."

He nodded, walking to the helm as I headed to the brig.

Arriving back on deck, Feytan called me over. "Destiny, we have a situation."

"What?" I asked.

"We're in line with their ship but I think you should swim ahead and scout out the waters. This is a dangerous zone—mermaid territory."

"All right." I jumped off the side of the boat. As I neared *Queen Anne's Revenge*, the water got murky. It became hard to see very far ahead. Pivoting to return to my ship, three mermaids confronted me.

"You are in the wrong waters, *Siamaid*. This ship is under our protection. You are an invader," she smirked.

"I mean no harm," I said. "We're returning the captain and crew safely to their ship and then we will be on our way."

"Unharmed," another said. "One cut on the captain and we'll find and destroy you and your entire crew."

The last one spoke. "You have ten minutes to deliver them and leave, or else we will eliminate you all."

"Thank you." They parted enough for me to swim between them and head toward my ship. We didn't have much time.

+

Five minutes remained. We locked up the enemy crew, then froze Edward's hands so he couldn't escape when we woke him. With an ice dagger pressed against his neck, I hissed, "Don't even think about coming into my waters or near my crew again. I won't spare your life twice."

He moved just slightly, causing a tiny rivulet of blood to stream down his neck.

"Made a deal with the mermaids, did you?"

Biting back a curse, I stood up and crushed the knife to ice dust. "We need to go," I told Feytan.

He nodded understanding and together we gathered my crew. Trying not to tip the mermaids off, we left as calmly as possible. Even when there was no sight of the mermaids after reaching our ship, despite the ever-growing distance between us, relief did not come. "It won't take long before they come for us. If we can make it to an island, we can run the ship aground. Jackson, any idea where we could go?"

"Yeah." He scanned the map with a grin.

✛

Secured on the beach, I covered the ship's hull in ice to protect it from the sand. The mermaids were nowhere in sight and neither was Edward and his crew. We were safe.

"Relax, Destiny." Feytan left the campfire and the crew to join me by the ship, where I stood, gazing at the ocean.

"What are you doing all those times you go out to sea? You disappear often."

Feytan was hesitant but I couldn't determine why. "I wanted to keep it a secret," he started, "but I'm trying to rebuild my kingdom… for someone special."

Is he talking about me? Or has he found someone else? Gathering courage, I tried to share my feelings. "Well, if you still want to," I stumbled over my words, "I wouldn't mind being courted now."

"You saved me the worry of asking." He smiled. "Thank you for that."

"Really?"

His head bowed once.

"No awkward stuff though," I warned. "We're still pirates."

"I understand."

I hugged him and he swept me off my feet, spinning me around.

"Come on. Let's go join the party."

The adventures were barely beginning but with Feytan and the crew by my side, nothing could stand in our way.

SEQUOIA BRIGHTON

Whitewaters

Amelia Whitewaters found it ironic that a family whose name literally ended with the word 'water' had become involved with the shipping industry. Perhaps fate had forced the job upon them. The *Sea Spray* was due to enter the Sandren Isles carrying over five thousand precious tomes, all carefully treated with an alchemical substance and wrapped in wax paper to protect against the rough sea voyage. Each book was roughly worth five crissons, and a small fortune in paper. But that was not the ship's only cargo.

Amelia and her sister Isabell, two highborn nobles of house Whitewater, had also been placed aboard by their father. Amelia rolled her eyes skyward. Whatever power dwelt in the heavens was surely laughing at her now.

Isabell was the perfect daughter. Pretty, intelligent, and moldable as potter's clay. She did exactly what was expected of her for no other reason than gaining the approval of others. If it weren't for her older shrew of a sister, Isabell would already be married to some rich tosh with dimpled cheeks and golden blond hair that waved in the breeze. She rolled her eyes at the image. Life amounted to more than sitting quietly, tatting lace and striving to make some man happy. Life should be full of adventure and excitement. You should live it the way you want. Not the way someone else deemed fit. At least, that's how it seemed to her.

A flicker of motion caught her eye. She half-turned to catch a young sailor staring at her. His eyes met hers. His face reddened. He hurriedly turned away while she turned back to the water smiling. She shifted in order to emphasize the trousers she wasn't supposed to be wearing. As a noble woman it was extremely scandalous for one of her stature to dress like a common tavern wench. Her movement also emphasized the long saber at her hip.

The boy's footsteps thudded across the deck as he fled. Amelia felt a wide grin spreading across her face and had to stifle a laugh. *Oh, if Father could have seen that!* Her smile faded as she remembered her argument with him.

"Amelia!" he'd said as she walked into the room. "What in heaven's name are you wearing?" He had a high, shrill voice when he got upset.

"Trousers, father." She gave a small twirl. "Do you like them?" He spluttered. Her father was a good man and usually so confident, but he was never sure how to put up with his strong-willed eldest daughter.

"It's… it's not proper," he spluttered.

She rolled her eyes.

"They're practical. You could never move this way in a dress." She put her hands on her hips ready to argue the point. "Besides, I can hardly carry around my saber in that prison of lace and ribbon."

"You shouldn't be carrying it at all! You should be focusing on your studies or on courting. Goodness child, don't you want to get married?"

She sighed in exasperation.

"Would you prefer I cover my face in powder and dye each day? Put on dresses and titter about like every other half-baked noble in the city?"

He started to respond but she cut him off.

"No, Father. I don't intend to put on a show just to gain a man's approval. If I am to marry, it will be because he accepts me as I am, good and bad or not at all."

He rubbed his face with both hands. Then, as she expected, he drooped. "Then at least wear a long shirt or tunic over the top of the things."

She smiled. "All right, Father, for you." He chuckled and put both hands on either side of her face placing a kiss atop her red brown curls.

"My daughter," he sighed. "What am I going to do with you?"

Pulling herself from that memory, Amelia looked out to the open ocean. *Ship me away apparently.* That was his answer.

⚓

Jack Riddley, the least appreciated crewmember of the *Wave Walker* stared through the lens of the telescope at a ship in the distance. The *Sea Spray* was about four knots away. As a small ship, it had a mast and a crew of more than a dozen. Yet, it lacked the gravity of a bigger vessel such as the *Wave Walker*. He shook his head, sliding the telescope back into a compact disk and shoving it into his pants pocket.

"Well?" the first mate asked. "What do you see, boy?"

"They're not moving very fast and the wind is against them. The ship itself is too small to put up much of a fight. They'll be faster than us though, able to move quickly if they catch the right breeze. We'd have to sneak in close to grab them before they can run."

The first mate grunted. He was a large boned man, not overly tall with salt and pepper hair and several weeks' worth of stubble on his face that hadn't yet grown into a proper beard. His name was Dale, but almost everyone just called him First Mate or sir. He scratched his chin as he squinted at the distant ship. "This one might be tricky." He clapped a hand on Jack's shoulder. "Good work Jacky boy, go tell the crew to be ready."

Jack didn't say anything. As he left, a few men lingered and cat-called to him as he passed. He didn't need to tell the crew to be ready. It was the whole reason they were here. The men knew it. He knew it. What was the point of wasting time? He thought about the many meaningless tasks he preformed to keep himself out of the way. He was far from respected or even liked among the crew, despite twelve years of eating, sleeping, and working beside them. He listened with half an ear as Dale and the captain discussed strategies. Eventually the men made a decision and the ship banked to the side as they turned. They were going to try to catch the smaller ship. Jack wasn't terribly surprised. The captain almost always made a race of it.

Jack filled the passing time by running up and down the rigging to check small jobs that needed his attention. Finally, the time came. The *Sea Spray* was trying to speed desperately away but had noticed the larger ship too late. Cannon range was not yet possible so they would need to wait until the smaller ship was closer. The little ship was fast, but the *Wave Walker* had a better captain.

Captain Aldridge always played things just right, the smaller ship would be forced to surrender without a fight. He pulled out his collapsible telescope and focused it on the ship, adjusting the focus to watch the crew.

On board the other ship, the men were running around in a panic as one man shouted orders. They clamored about this way and that, pulling the sails and—was that a woman aboard the ship? A woman wearing trousers? It was bad luck to have a woman aboard a ship. What was she doing there? She stood at the front of the vessel facing he larger ship. She wore a blue tunic tied with a belt around her waist over a pair of men's trousers. Clutching a saber, she faced them with her feet braced. Her auburn hair whirled around her in the gusty wind. He focused the telescope on her. She stared back with grim determination, her blue eyes narrowed. Without the face paint or powder that most women preferred, she was lovely. She looked furious, and he could tell that this one was not easily willing to back down before a challenge.

+

Amelia watched steadily as the huge ship approached. It was a massive beast of a vessel fully twice as large as *Sea Spray*. The men around her were yelling in panic. Captain Talm was shouting orders. The captain spared her a glance before he bellowed more orders at his men. Isabell stood next to him shifting anxiously back and forth. Amelia gave her a small smile.

"It will be all right Isabell."

Her younger sister bit her lip. With brown curled hair, blue eyes, straight posture and immaculate dress, she was the perfect model of what a highborn lady should be. She was a sharp contrast to Amelia's own auburn locks, pale blue eyes, and trousers. Amelia felt rather shabby in comparison.

Finally, the captain gathered all the men and was attempting to decide what to do. "First, do we fight or surrender? We can't outrun them so it'll have to be one or the other." Pirates were sometimes known to leave survivors if they surrendered willingly. Sometimes.

"What kind of a question is that?" asked a man with a strong Scottish accent. "If we don't surrender they'll gut us. We stand down, but if they're looking for a fight I say we give it to 'em. I won't sit cowering while some soulless pirate cuts me down."

A few men muttered in agreement. The captain nodded and ordered the men to drop anchor.

Amelia felt sick. They wouldn't survive a fight. If the men aboard the *Wave Walker* decided to attack, everyone would be killed.

Her eyes hardened into frozen chips of ice and she glared defiantly up at the other ship. Whatever happened, she wouldn't back down without a fight.

The larger ship slowed beside the *Sea Spray* and men started to board. There were thirty of them. With so many aboard, the ship felt crowded. The two crews stood facing each other, silent and grim as a hangman fitting a noose.

The captain of the *Wave Walker* spoke first. "Throw down your weapons."

The men looked to their captain, unsure of what to do.

"This is your last warning. Throw down your weapons." The men stirred, looking from their captain to the enemy surrounding them. A few dropped their swords, most simply waited. Captain Talm hesitated.

The other captain's eyes flashed with a cold fury. "Kill them!"

The crew of the *Sea Spray* screamed as they were cut down. Men lunged for fallen weapons. Some fell to their knees and begged for their lives. Several stared with hollow eyes as the pirates ran them through.

Amelia drew her blade and shoved Isabell in front of her as she ran for the cabin door. Several of the pirates chased her as she ran, but she was quicker. She made it to the cabin door and shoved Isabell through.

"Lock it!"

"But—"

"Now, Isabell!"

Her sister squealed as the door slammed shut behind her. She heard a thud as the lock clicked into place. The three men after Amelia came to a slow stop. They wore hard, hungry grins, much like their captain. One of the men chuckled. He was a broad chested man with blunt, ugly features and thick-knotted muscles. By contrast, the man on his right was short and fat with a potbelly hanging several inches over his belt. The one on the left was whipcord thin and younger than the other two. His hair was a dark black and had deep-gray, intelligent eyes. He held back watching the other to, keeping most of his attention on the fighting around them.

Blunt spoke first. "Drop the sword girl and no one gets hurt."

Letting a snarl bubble up in her chest, she carefully shifted her feet to jump back should he charge. "That's what your captain said before he ordered you to kill me."

The man's face reddened. He opened his mouth but before he could speak, Amelia charged. He tried to get his blade up in time to block but she was already moving. She slashed at the thick meat of his forearm with her blade, cutting a deep gash into his flesh. He howled, swinging wildly in pain. She was already scrambling back, and the blade sliced only open air. Blunt lunged for her. She rolled to the side and he kept after her.

Gray Eyes whipped his head around in surprise. Meanwhile Pudgy drew a chain to defend himself. Amelia cursed. He swung and she managed to dodge the chain, mostly. Striking her lower leg, she cried out in pain and fell. Blunt tripped over her, still snarling. She squirmed back and grabbed her fallen blade. She thrust at Pudgy and drove the tip into his gut before he could reel in his chain. He gasped, eyes going wide, but didn't scream. She jerked the blade free, then felt cold steel press against her back.

"Don't move." The voice was soft and calm. Gray Eyes had been biding his time, picking his moment.

She didn't move.

"Drop the sword."

Amelia let it clatter to the ground. The blade prodded her and she obediently moved in the direction indicated. His hand was on her shoulder, guiding her. Her stomach roiled at being caught so easily. She wanted to spin and defend herself even if it killed her. But rebelling now wouldn't help Isabell. She felt like laughing. How could she possibly help anyone now? She had been a fool.

Numbly she realized the fighting had stopped around them. Most of the men lay in pools of their own blood. Captain Talm's head lay in a pool of scarlet several feet from his body. The survivors of the *Sea Spray* knelt on the deck of the ship, heads down. The *Wave Walker*'s captain surveyed the deck, eyes scanning the ship until they came to rest on her. He cocked his head to the side like a curious bird.

"What is this?" The captain made his way over to Amelia, slowly stepping over the bodies of the dead, his boots leaving a trail of red behind him. His eyes scanned Amelia as if studying an interesting bug he hadn't seen before. "A woman." His eyes roamed up and down her body, taking in every part of her.

She straightened and lifted her chin in proud defiance, her blue eyes glittering. If this was her last moment, she would not cower.

"A woman who dresses like a man and carries a blade." He glared at her. "Why?"

Amelia gritted her teeth, saying nothing. The dagger pressed hard into her spine. She let out a strangled cry and arched her back, gasping as a trickle of hot blood began to soak through her shirt. The pressure on the knife relented slightly.

"She was trying to protect her sister, Captain." It was Gray Eyes who spoke. "The girl shoved her into the cabin and told her to lock the door, then stayed to fight."

The captain gave him a disapproving look before turning back to Amelia. "Is this true?"

When she didn't say anything, the man's eyebrows shot up. "You have spirit." He hesitated a moment, seeming to consider something before his shark eyes focused back on her. "Break down the door, find the girl."

Two of the men behind him responded immediately. There was a short sharp scream from inside and the two men emerged, dragging Isabell between them. She was crying.

The captain cocked his head in that curious bird-like gesture again. "This one is not as strong, she lacks the fire in your eyes." He spoke like a man commenting on the taste of a meal, his eyes never wavered from hers. "I am going to give you a chance to save her. But not only her, them as well." He gestured to the four lone men huddling on the deck.

She eyed him steadily. "What do you want from me?"

"You." He smiled. "I want you to join my crew."

She nearly laughed at him. "And what would you do with them if I were to come with you?"

"Spare them. Your sister boards the ship with my men, you lead me to the cargo, and we leave. The others remain here alive, free of harm."

It was worse than murder. The men would die a slow death of dehydration and starvation with no hope of manning the ship back to shore alone. Even worse, they would be forced to throw the dead into the water, which would attract sharks. Lifeboats would be useless in those circumstances.

The captain seemed to sense her thoughts. "There's a port not nine days from here. There's a chance they'd be spotted by another boat and rescued."

"A small one." He shrugged as she thought about it. There was a chance the men would live. It wasn't a very good chance, but it was possible. If she went with him, it could save their lives. It didn't really matter. He held her sister's life in his hands. They both knew she would agree.

"I have two requests."

"You are hardly in a position to make demands."

She continued as if she hadn't heard him. "Leave a gun with four bullets in it." It was an old custom—an act of mercy for her crew should the worst come.

He shrugged. "A small enough favor. And the second?"

"Isabell remains untouched."

The man's eyes flickered to Isabell. They traveled up and down her slender frame like a butcher sizing up a side of beef. His eyes sparkled with an ugly sort of interest. "For the time being, I swear to you that none of mine will harm her."

Amelia gritted her teeth and nodded. "All right; I agree."

The captain motioned for Gray Eyes to release her. He did so hesitantly.

"Captain!" The man's eyes narrowed.

"Jack?"

"Don't bring her aboard, sir. This one's trouble. I can tell." The youth watched her with narrow, untrusting eyes. Cautious eyes.

A few of the men sniggered. A smile tugged at the corner of the captain's mouth. "Is she now?"

Jack didn't back down at the men's jeers. "Yes, sir."

Amelia narrowed her eyes at the man. He didn't break her gaze. He was taller than she by several inches, thin and well muscled.

The captain looked back and forth between them, obviously amused. "Are you afraid of her, Jack?"

"No, sir. I'm not afraid." His tone implied that he wasn't afraid of anything.

"Then you should be able to handle her."

Jack's head snapped up to face the captain.

"From now on, the girl is your responsibility."

Jack's face tightened but he didn't protest. "Yes sir."

"Good." He turned back to Amelia, "Jack will be showing you the ropes. He'll tell you how things are done aboard my ship and keep you out of trouble. You will take orders from him and from me. He'll also be teaching you to use that sword you carry. You are to do what he says when he says it, am I clear?"

Her eyes flashed. "I know my way around a blade."

"Perhaps if you learned from a book, but combat training is different. You need practical experience."

She said nothing.

"I expect you to heed my orders, girl."

She dipped her head in acknowledgement, though it felt like driving a knife into her gut.

"All right!" The captain yelled, "Back to work! Throw the dead over and start hauling cargo off this piece of driftwood!" He motioned for Amelia to lead the way. Behind them, Isabell started to cry.

✦

Life aboard the *Wave Walker* was not at all what Amelia had expected. The sailors seemed to accept her as a crewmember. They didn't treat her like cargo and didn't view her presence as bad luck. She worked hard, but not overly so. Isabell had been put to work in the kitchen as an assistant cook. Basically, she passed out rations and cleaned dishes, or rather scraped the leftovers off and put the dishes back in the cupboard. Fresh water was too precious to waste on silly things like cleanliness.

Amelia spent the first day aboard the ship following a list of chores from Jack, while he did something he deemed worth his time. The second day, however, he was waiting for her on the main deck looking sullen, a dark bruise blossoming on one side of his face. He tossed her a long wooden practice blade.

She eyed it distastefully. "I've handled steel blades before."

"Not well."

"Well enough to handle those two thugs."

He snorted. "Believe me, girly, if you thought that was a real fight, you might as well slit your wrists and jump over the side. It'd save me a lot of time and frustration."

"But—"

He cut her off.

"You got lucky, Princess. Now stop whining or go bother some-one else."

"Don't," she said slowly, "call me that."

He smirked at her. "I'll call you what I want."

That self-righteous little—Amelia snatched up the practice blade. If he wanted a demonstration, she would give him one. Preferably in the form of bruises across his body. She started with a basic fencer's stance.

They both stood frozen for several seconds, then he charged her. His blade came in, low and hard. She bent at the waist and knees to compensate for his superior strength and caught the blade. Not hesitating, he spun the blade to the side, forcing her to go high. She wobbled and retreated a step, only for him to pull back before the blades could touch. He spun to the side, and slapped her on the rump with the flat of his blade. She yelped as the heavy oak practice sword connected causing her to lose her balance. Before she could compensate he planted a boot squarely in the center of her back and kicked hard enough to shove her down to the deck. He tapped his sword lightly on the back of her neck.

"Dead," he said without emphasis.

She spluttered in irritation. "You—you cheated!"

He stepped off her and pulled back his blade. "In the real world, there is no cheating. It's kill or be killed. Do you honestly think your opponents are going to fight fair?" He snorted in disgust. "They'll do what they have to do to win. If you don't do the same, I'd advise you to cut your throat now to deny others the pleasure."

She stared at him for a minute in shocked silence.

He regarded her with cold, grey eyes. "Now either shut up and learn what I have to teach you, or tell the captain you've changed your mind."

She stood slowly and picked up her blade.

His eyebrows shot up in surprise and he smiled faintly. "All right then."

"Riddley?" Amelia spotted a newcomer with a calm wariness.

Jack turned toward his approaching crewmate.

"The girl and I have some business to deal with. Leave." The man's hand rested lightly atop his sword.

Amelia's heart beat faster in her chest. If this man meant to kill her, there was little she would be able to do to stop him.

Jack's posture didn't change but he moved his hand to the belt of his pants several inches closer to the hilt of his sword. "Back down Taggard, I'm working."

The man let out a snarl. "Get out of my way, now."

Jack regarded him with his calm, steely eyes. "No. You heard the captain. The girl is my responsibility. So, you'll leave her alone, or I'll make you regret it."

"You—"

Jack drew his blade. He held it with one hand between himself and Taggard. His voice was calm. "We both know I'm the better swordsman, Tag. Back off."

There was a tense silence, then Taggard cursed and stomped off down the deck.

Amelia let out a soft sigh of relief. She wasn't good enough to beat Taggard in a real fight. In all likelihood, Jack had just saved her life. "Thank you."

He shrugged. "It's nothing." He held out a hand to her.

She hesitated, took it, and he hauled her to her feet.

"All right," he said. "You obviously know the basics, but your technique's sloppy. We should start there. Now place your feet like this... Good. This time, when you draw your sword, you will have much better balance."

They drilled for hours before finally stopping to take a break.

"So...Jack?"

"Yes?" He didn't look up from his food.

"How did you come to be part of this crew? I've seen the way the men treat you, the way the captain looks at you. They hate you. Why do you stay?"

"I don't like to talk about it."

She waited.

Finally, he let out an annoyed huff. "You're not going to let this go, are you?"

"Nope."

He gave a faint smile. "All right, fine. My father was a sailor. He died when I was about six. Aldridge is my uncle. He considers it a favor to my father to keep me around. I'm nothing but a nuisance to him."

"Why stay?"

He looked at her as if she were simple. "Because no one else will take me, that's why. I have no great love for my uncle but I have a place here and I'm lucky for it. I owe him everything for that." He took a calming breath and his voice softened. "Eventually, I'll earn enough for my own boat and I'll leave."

"And do what? Start your own crew of thugs?"

He shrugged. "I was born to sail. It's all I know." He gave that half shrug again. "As long as I keep sailing, I don't care what I do."

She was quiet, thinking about that for a time.

"So, what are you doing here?"

She narrowed her eyes at him and he held up both hands in mock surrender.

"All right, all right, what are you doing here if you would care to tell me my most esteemed noble women?" His mouth turned up in a smirk, and the way he tilted his head made his gray eyes shine even brighter.

She found herself smiling a little. "Careful. If you keep instructing me in sword play, I'll make you pay for that remark."

He gave her that grin again and she couldn't help but smile back at him. "I was headed for the isles."

"Monastery? You don't seem the type."

"Father sent me to *further my education*."

278 · BAND OF MISFITS

"Ah." He got it. "Too much of a handful at home, I take it?"

She snorted. "You have no idea."

"Then tell me about it."

She smiled. "All right."

They talked for hours while Jack taught her sailors' knots. When the sun began to set, they joined the rest of the crew in the mess hall for dinner. Isabell joined her once everyone had been served. Jack was somewhere down the table in a large group of men and Amelia caught herself looking for him. She scowled and turned back to Isabell.

"You all right?" asked Isabell.

Amelia nodded.

"Here." Isabell passed her another chunk of the hard, flat bread. "Eat this."

Jack came over and sat down across from them. "Meet me on the starboard side of the ship by the rail in ten minutes."

Amelia nodded before he stood then walked away.

Isabell's eyes flickered back and forth between them. As soon as he was gone, Isabell turned to face her sister, her pale face screwed up in consternation. "Amelia, you can't!"

"Can't what?"

Isabell's voice was a low hiss. "You can't possibly like him!"

Amelia felt her face go blank as she straightened her back. "I don't."

"Liar," Isabell sighed. "I'm not a complete fool, you know."

"I know."

"Whatever," she said petulantly. "That isn't the point, Amy. How could you even consider it? He's a pirate. He wanted the captain to kill us!"

"No, he just wanted to leave us behind."

"In this case, it's the same thing. How long have you known him anyway? Two days? Three?"

Amelia set the rest of her bread aside not feeling hungry anymore.

Isabell crossed her arms. "He's using you."

Amelia stood up. "I'm leaving."

Isabell watched her go.

✦

She met Jack at the designated spot. "What?"

He frowned at her. "Is everything all right?"

She felt something inside her snap. "No, everything's not all right. I like you, Jack. I like you a lot, and the fact that no one would approve of us just makes me want it that much more, but—"

He kissed her.

She stiffened, then melted into the kiss. He leaned into her and she pressed herself against him. Angels above, she wanted this. Wanted it so much that it ached inside of her. She let herself stay there for a minute, just feeling the warmth of him. Then, she pulled away. Those gorgeous gray eyes regarded her calmly, that attractive half-smirk on his face.

He could tell she'd liked it. "What is it?"

"I…I don't know you, Jack. Don't know anything about you. For heaven's sake, I've only been here two days and here I am kissing you!" She bit her lip. "And I like it, I really like it. I like you, but—"

A high-pitched scream broke out somewhere nearby and a man bellowed in rage.

Isabell.

Before Amelia realized she was moving, she reached down and yanked the knife from Jack's belt, then ran across the deck toward the source of the sound.

"Amelia!" Heavy footsteps pounded the deck behind her.

She reached the stairs down to the hold just as Isabell stumbled out onto the deck. Her sister was sobbing and a bruise was starting to purple on one cheek. A dark shadow rose out of the darkness behind her. Taggard. Amelia shoved Isabell behind her with a snarl, holding the knife out in front of her. She might be able to stick him with the small blade if she was fast enough. An iron grip squeezed her shoulder.

"Amelia stand down!" It was Jack.

She tried to shove his hand away but he was too strong. More and more men were piling onto the deck behind Taggard, staring with confusion at the scene before them. Even through the ruckus, she heard the captain's door creak open. She didn't break eye contact with Taggard, but the men around them went silent and still. The captain's heavy boots thudded to a stop.

"Explain." His voice was calm but laced with anger.

Isabell stood, sobbing uncontrollably.

Jack spoke up. "Amelia and I where on the deck when we heard Isabell scream. We saw her fall to the deck. Taggard arrived seconds later. Amelia defended the girl with my belt knife."

"Taggard?" The captain's voice was calm, but hinted at a rage boiling inside him.

Taggard's lie was smooth and fast. "I came to see if the girl was all right after I heard her screams. She must have slipped on the steps."

"Liar!" Amelia lunged at Taggard but Jack's sturdy arms held her back.

Captain Aldridge gave her a pointed look before turning to Isabell. His voice softened as he spoke to her. "Tell me child, what happened?"

Isabell hadn't stopped crying. "H-he a-a-attacked me. He said he w-would kill me if I s-s-screamed." She started to cry harder.

The captain's hard eyes narrowed on Taggard. "I gave my word that the girl was to remain untouched." His voice lowered. "I am willing to overlook one mistake, Taggard. Just one. You disobey a direct order again and I will cut off your hands and throw you overboard. Do you understand me?"

Taggard didn't speak, just nodded once.

Then the captain turned to her. "You are a part of my crew now. I promised your sister you would be safe but if you ensue another riot like this aboard my ship, I will let you hang from the ship's mast three days before I kill you. You have been here two days. I have sailed for twenty-five years. Don't think that I won't hesitate to kill you should you cause me more trouble." His eyes traveled around to the rest of the men. "Off my deck all of you!"

The men scattered like startled cockroaches. Taggard gave Amelia a venomous glare before following. Amelia glared back, guiding Isabell toward their cabin. Jack trailed behind. The captain watched them go, his predatory eyes tracking their movements. Amelia could see the wheels turning in his head as he watched them, calculating her worth. Jack followed her into their cabin. He watched as she tucked Isabell into bed. She stroked her sister's hair until she quieted, finally having cried herself to sleep. Jack pushed himself to his feet and jerked his head toward the door. Amelia followed him into his own cabin.

He sat down on one corner of the bed and waited for her to face him, his gray eyes serious. "You can't stay here."

"I know that."

"No, you don't understand. We have to get you off this ship right now."

"What? Why?"

He let out a frustrated puff of air. "Right now, you're a curiosity. A vague amusement, something to entertain the captain and the men. But you've been causing trouble. He might think it best to just kill you now to prevent further mishaps. We have to get you out of here. To-night."

She frowned. "How?"

"The lifeboats. We sneak you and Isabell into one with enough food to last a few days. We're close enough to port that someone should find you."

"I—"

He cut her off with a sharp glare. His knuckles were white, hands clenched into fists. "Listen. Taggard will to try to kill you."

She stiffened.

"Listen!" He grabbed her by both wrists dragging her closer to him, staring into her eyes. His eyes went cold. There was no light in them now. "Stay with Isabell. I'll get what you need and meet you at the boat, then I'll lower you into the water."

She jerked her hands free of his grip. "And you?"

He said nothing.

"You'll come with us?"

He shook his head. "I can't. My life is here, the ship is here…"

"But—"

Jack walked out of the cabin. He moved silently down the hold of the ship. The room he needed was about six doors down from the mess hall. He would need to get in, get the food, and get out again without being spotted. It wouldn't be easy, but if he was careful he should be able to manage it. Someone grabbed him by the collar and slammed him hard against the wall. Taggard.

"What do you think you're up to boy?"

Jack reached for his knife, but a blade pressed hard against his ribs.

"Don't try it. You may be something of a swordsman but I have the advantage here."

Jack let his hand slip back to his side.

Taggard smiled. "Now, I'll ask again, what are you doing down here?"

"That's none of your affair."

"Oh, but it is." More men moved in the shadows behind Taggard. "I'm tired of being pushed around. Tired of listening to that fool Aldridge giving me orders. He has the whole crew scared of 'im. Except for me. I'll rid this ship of 'im once and for all."

A chill ran up Jack's spine.

"You mean—"

"I'm here to offer you a choice. You can side with us, or we'll cut you down same as the rest." He let go of Jack and shoved him back. Jack stumbled briefly before finding his balance.

"Gavin, you watch him. If he tries to raise the alarm, kill him. The rest of us are going to deal with the captain, and after that," his eyes glittered with eagerness, "I have unfinished business with the girl."

✢

Amelia knew something was wrong when Jack didn't come back to the cabin. What had happened? Where was he? Had he been caught? She had picked a lifeboat at random and shoved the meager blankets from both her bed and Jack's inside. He may not know it yet, but he was coming with them. The cover was off the lifeboat and Isabell huddled inside wrapped in a blanket shivering. Amelia had lowered it enough that it wasn't visible form the deck. She planned to jump over the side and cut the ropes as soon as Jack arrived. But where was he?

On the stairs leading up to the deck, a board creaked. It was followed by a muffled curse. There was a tense stillness, then the footsteps continued up the stairs. The lifeboats were suspended by ropes. Between them and the deck was a small gap just a few inches high. Making a snap decision, Amelia dropped to the deck and squirmed underneath the nearest lifeboat. She was barely out of sight when the men emerged from the hold of the ship. There were eight of them, Taggard at the front of the group. She felt herself tense up and prayed they wouldn't notice the missing lifeboat, dangling just a few feet down from where they stood.

They didn't. She watched them as they moved down toward the captain's cabin. Mutiny. She watched the men, a sick feeling in her stomach. She could call out a warning to the captain, give him a chance. But if she did, she would be condemning herself and Isabell to death.

More footsteps sounded as Jack emerged from the hull. He was alone, thank the heavens. He had a long smear of blood along the left side of his face and he was limping. A furious bellow split the air from inside the cabin followed by the sound of steel on steel and shattering glass. Jack's eyes snapped up as he ran to the place where the missing boat had been. Amelia was already squirming her way out from hiding.

"Amelia?"

"Here," she gasped.

Jack looked down at her. A fierce grin spread across his face. From the crew's bunks far below men started shouting and the clash of steel grew louder. His smile died. "Back in the boat. We don't have much time. Taggard has already started his attack." He tossed the sack over the side, into a corner of the boat, and drew his sword.

Amelia didn't move though footsteps pounded up the stairs.

"Well? What are you waiting for?" he asked.

"Come with me."

More clanging of steel could be heard as the first men emerged up onto deck.

His eyes were wild. "I can't get in the boat."

"Come with me," she said again.

"I told you, I can't. My life is here. The ship is here."

"I'll buy you your own ship! Just get in the boat!" she begged.

His eyes widened. He lunged and shoved her overboard. Amelia let out a panicked scream as she hit the cold water hard. She gasped and sputtered to the surface. The lifeboat swung halfway up the side of the ship.

Jack jumped back from another sword swinging at his head. He dodged nimbly to the side and swung, slicing through one of the ropes holding the lifeboat. Isabell screamed as she clung to one of the wooden seats inside, as the whole boat swung from side to side. The bag of food snagged on a loose nail and tore open, spilling half of its precious contents into the sea.

Jack dodged another swing as more men poured onto the deck. Taggard emerged from the captain's cabin holding the man's head aloft by the hair. A lantern had shattered, spilling oil across the deck. Soon, parts of the ship were aflame. Men loyal to their captain bellowed in rage and attached the rebel mutineers. Swords clashed and men died spilling their precious lifeblood across the ship's deck. There was no honor in the deaths. One man stabbed another through the back. Another man shoved his comrade in front of him in a desperate attempt to block a falling blade. There was no way to tell loyalist from rebel.

Through the chaos, Jack managed to dodge the swing of a second opponent as he sliced through the final rope holding the lifeboat. The vessel fell with a splash into the waves. Jack turned and jumped onto the railing, facing his opponent but paid dearly for his effort. A blade slashed across his chest.

Amelia screamed as he wobbled, then tumbled over the edge into the water. She gasped in a breath and dove beneath the waves. She kicked her legs as hard as she could to reach him. She got ahold of one of his arms and started struggling back to the surface, her lungs burned in her chest. She kicked desperately trying to reach the surface.

They broke through with a gasp. Isabell was waiting, reaching her arms toward them. Slowly and painstakingly, she dragged him toward the boat. Isabell hauled him over the side, then took hold of Amelia and did the same for her. Amelia coughed and crawled to Jack.

"Jack? Jack can you hear me? Jack!"

He groaned. He was alive. There was a ripping sound, then Isabell pushed past Amelia to wrap the ends of her torn dress around his chest. She was shivering with cold. Her hands trembled.

"Isabell?"

"I'm okay." She clearly wasn't. Her lips were pale blue, her skin ashen. For the first time Amelia noticed that her clothing was as wet as theirs. "You're soaking wet."

"A lot of the food went into the water. I couldn't do much but I managed to save the canteens at least. We're going to need that water."

"You're shaking."

"I'm fine, Amy! We need to leave now before they notice us." With that, she made her way over to one of the enormous oars and took it with both hands.

Jack groaned and sat up. "Wh-what happened?" He glanced blearily up at the ship.

Amelia steadied him. "Just sit for the time being."

Isabell watched the deck of the ship with worried eyes. "How long until they come after us?"

Jack shook his head. "They won't for a day or two at least, at least, I don't think they will. It'll take some time for Taggard to clean up this mess." His eyes met Amelia's. He gave that little half-smirk of his. "I guess I'm coming with you after all."

She felt a laugh boiling up inside her from somewhere deep down in her chest. She couldn't help but smile back. They were only a few days from port. They would contact her father, then she and Isabell would return home, with a young pirate no less. She felt her smile broaden.

Her father was not going to be pleased.

KENZIE KOEHLE

A Mermaid, A Human, and a Siren

The waves jumped and rolled past Nova as her body cut through the water at breakneck speed. Her tail flipped impatiently behind her, propelling her closer to her target. Despite the endless blue around her, her thoughts were channeled solely in one direction. Somewhere beyond these waves sat a vessel that was carrying her best friend, Matthew, and there was nothing, not the distance nor her own fear, that would stop her.

She thought back to Matthew's surprising capture. After borrowing his dad's sailboat, Matthew and Nova were just enjoying a day on the ocean in an environment where they could both be in their respective element; Nova, seeing as she was half fish, in the water, and Matthew on a somewhat stable landing for his human legs to hold him. However, while they were distracted, they didn't notice the pirate ship approaching until it was too late. Nova tried to help Matthew escape, but the sailboat was important to his father, so he had Nova promise him she would return it. Before she could protest, Matthew threw Nova in the ship, tied one of the ropes around her tail, and threw the rest over her.

By the time she had untangled herself, Matthew and the ship were gone. She had only glimpsed the name of the ship, the *Lorelei*. Begrudgingly, Nova discretely returned the sailboat to his parents before turning around and beginning her search for her friend.

She was aware of the danger posed by pirates. It was said that they stole mermaids' scales in exchange for gold and healed injured humans with some secret power they apparently possessed. But no mermaid, not even Nova, knew what that was. These pirates would keep any captive mermaids in tiny pools of water and not release them until the mermaid's every use had been exploited. Those who made it back alive barely escaped with some scales still on their tail and never really recovered from the horror.

But Matthew was worth the danger, Nova thought loyally. What would a pirate do to the son of a fisherman? Hopefully it wasn't as bad as what they do to mermaids. *Regardless, I've got to get him out of there before they harm him.*

A few days passed while she searched for the pirate ship that had captured her friend. She prayed to anything or anyone that was listening that the pirates hadn't killed him in her absence.

Finally, without even realizing how much time had passed, she spotted the *Lorelei*. The ship swayed in the distance, its white flag emblazoned with a skull looming overhead. On this pirate ship, she knew that she was about to attempt the scariest thing she'd ever do in her life.

She swam closer, trying to keep just out of sight under the waves. Nova tried to swim up to the surface, but realized it was too bright outside for her to go undetected. Frustrated and impatient, she waited under the ship for the next few hours until the waters, as well as the sky, transitioned to a black-blue.

Finally, when Nova felt comfortable that she wouldn't be spotted from the water, she silently swam up and searched the giant wooden hull. Straining her arm muscles, she started climbing up the wall, using holes in the wood as handholds.

This is all worth it. Nova reassured herself. *I'm going to get Matthew back and return him safely home to his family.*

As she approached the deck, she noticed lights that illuminated the ship, making the wood glow like a searchlight. Nova felt the stomping of feet while loud music was being played. She gripped the floor, immediately hiding herself in the shadows.

After a few minutes where she allowed her heartbeat to calm, she dared to peek around the ship, trying to find the face of her friend. She imagined the fear that would cloud those enchanting brown eyes. *He must be terrified,* she thought, worrying herself even more.

A shout erupted from the crowd, making Nova almost lose her grip on the deck. The music and the stomping slowed as everyone seemed to pay attention to what ever was about to be said.

"Hostages! Don't you wish to celebrate with us? See how much fun we are having? If you join us, you can live your wildest dreams while roaming the seas in search of adventure and treasure!" A couple voices cheered, the tips of swords being seen above the railing. Nova stole a peek to see a large crowd of men standing around together, their backs toward her and the man they were listening to out of sight.

Nova dared to look deeper into the ship and saw that the hostages were all tied up just a few feet away from her. She quickly searched the faces of the unfortunate souls, but fear took hold of her heart when Matthew's brown eyes and sharp features weren't among them.

Then, one of the hostages spoke up. "All right, fine! I'll join you! Untie me!"

It was a middle-aged man with fierce silver-blue eyes that burned in the darkness. Despite his arms being tied behind his back, his large stature and stern face made him seem less vulnerable and more rebellious, like flames flicking underneath a closed door, about to be unleashed. One of the pirates walked up to him, hand on his hip and a smirk covering his face.

"You think you want to be a part of our crew? Do you really think you have what it takes?"

The hostage's face pinched up in delight as he nodded his head while the other hostages looked at him with disdain and dismay.

The pirate shrugged and pulled the man to his feet. He shoved him to the middle of the ship, where the other pirates had all settled down and were now watching intently.

Another pirate emerged out of the crowd. He had a wide, black trifold hat that looked like it had been submerged in water, shredded, and then rolled in the dirt. His red coat swayed behind him, and his trimmed beard twitched with every muscle that moved along his jaw. As he moved closer to the hostage, the other pirates quieted until there was nothing to be heard but his footsteps across the wooden floor. The pirate stopped in front of the hostage, and the two men observed the other skeptically.

Finally, the pirate spoke. "What's your name, man?" Nova recognized his voice as the pirate who had called the hostages to join them.

The hostage lifted his chin, the picture of confidence. "Johnathan Powers."

The pirate chuckled and held his hands behind his back. "Well, Johnathan Powers. Do you know who I am?"

Johnathan's appearance seemed to falter slightly, and he stuttered, "C-Captain Luke Whistler, otherwise known as the White Whistle. Your flute can play such high-pitched notes that-"

"Good, good." The pirate cut him off, his tone warm, yet strangely foreboding. "Seems my reputation proceeds me." He gave an amused look to some of his crewmates, and the all snickered.

Captain? White Whistle? Nova thought to herself. As he started circling around the hostage, she was able to get a better look at his face. *He was handsome too... a dangerous kind of beautiful.*

He continued. "Here on my ship, we only accept those that are willing to die for our cause. Will you do whatever it takes to bring this crew its wants and desires?" The captain's voice chilled at the words, yet the tone hardly affected Johnathan.

"Yes. I wish to join your crew and to fight beside you until I die by the sword." Johnathan said the words with determination. The words almost sounded recited. Had other people already joined this captain's crew?

Captain Whistler took one more look at him, then turned around, flipping his hand dismissively. "Welcome aboard, Johnathan Powers. You may go join the other new recruits."

Johnathan smirked as another pirate cut his ropes, and he sauntered over to a group of people that looked like the pirates, but some didn't seem as enthusiastic to be standing there.

Suddenly, it was if Nova was awoken from a dream.

Her heart stopped when she recognized one of the new recruits. Among the big, strong men, there was Matthew, who was at least half a head shorter than the rest of the men, his arms tight at his side as he wore a nervous smile and a new sword strapped around his waist.

It was all Nova could do not to yell at Matthew.

Did he decide to join their ranks, like Johnathan?

It can't be possible. Matthew is too sweet and too shy to join such rowdy characters.

Yet there he was, standing awkwardly among the other men, looking unsure and remorseful.

Nova knew she had to get him to notice her. She looked around the deck, trying to find something to get his attention. Remembering her purse full of sand dollars strapped across a shoulder, she reached into her bag.

A line of sand dollars on the beach, a red and orange sunset. Heavy breathing, tiny feet squishing wet sand.

Nova thought back to the first time she met Matthew. Years ago, he saved her life when she washed ashore next to his house. He had nursed her back to health, and they had been best friends ever since. Her sand dollar collection had spilled on the beach, and he followed the shells until he had found her.

Moving to the other side of the ship, she chose a new position that was only a few feet away from him. Then, she started throwing sand dollars in his direction.

At first, he didn't notice them. As more and more sand dollars toppled to the floor, Matthew realized what was happening. Nova watched as he bent down, hands shaking as he started to fiddle with his shoes. After a few moments, he picked up one of the sand dollars, much to Nova's relief.

As his eyes grew in alarm, his gaze drifted over in Nova's direction. Her heart leaped in her throat, and she smiled at him, then tried to voice her confusion and concern through her eyes.

Matthew's eyes drifted around a bit, and he mouthed, "I'll explain later. Come back when it's quiet." Quickly, he stood up again, laughing anxiously at something one of the recruits said.

Nova slipped down into the water and followed behind the boat for the next few hours. As she stared at the stars above her, she reminisced about her past adventures with Matthew.

She saw clips of them, first as children, splashing each other with the ocean water, collecting sand dollars and giggling together. Then there was a few years later, the first time Matthew was strong enough to pick Nova up and they explored some of the pools away from the ocean. Then, they were teenagers, both on Matthew's father's sail boat, just learning how to sail it, venturing farther away from the shore.

A few days ago, when Matthew was captured, they had gone out the farthest distance. Matthew's parents thought that he was with some friends, and Nova's parents figured she was just exploring the ocean.

If only they hadn't gone out that day, or if they hadn't wandered so far, or...

Nova's thoughts were interrupted by a head poking out from the railing of the ship. She quickly recognized Matthew's messy, windswept hair, and they smiled at each other. She climbed up the hull, quietly and slowly.

Matthew barely gave her enough time to land on deck before he pulled her into a tight, desperate hug. Alarmed at first, Nova quickly returned the hug affectionately.

In her hair, Matthew whispered, "What in the holy heavens are you doing here?"

The fear in his voice surprised Nova, and she pulled back. "Are you serious? I'm here to get you!"

Matthew quickly looked around and then sighed with relief when he saw nobody around. Matthew moved his hands to her shoulders, shaking her a little.

"You shouldn't have come back for me. We both know what these pirates will do to you if they catch you!"

"Then why would you become one?" Nova couldn't hide the hurt in her voice, as she gasped for breath.

Matthew searched her face, before pulling her in for another hug. "If I didn't join them, they'd sell me off as a slave. I would never see you or my parents again. This way, I can join them until I get the chance to escape.

Nova sighed and turned her face closer to his neck. "But what if that doesn't work out? What if you get killed before you can return? Or what if you never return? What about your parents? You know I can't let them see me; they don't know we exist. They don't even know what's happened to you."

Matthew pulled away, and he held Nova's cheek with one of his hands. "I don't know, but it'll work out. I promise. I'll return back to you somehow." The intensity in his eyes made her cheeks grow warm involuntary, and she smiled sadly as she leaned into his hand.

"You can't promise something like that." As much as she wished it were true, Matthew didn't have the power to predict his own return.

Moving closer to his face, Nova felt his breath on her skin. His soft brown eyes bore into hers so deeply, that she saw nothing else.

"Believe me when I swear to you that I will always return." His eyes quickly looked down at her mouth and he leaned in closer until...

A sharp grip latched onto Nova's arm, and she cried out in pain.

"Well, well, well. Looks like little Matthew has a secret. How very lucky for us."

To Nova's horror, she was now being lifted by a strong arm that was certainly not Matthew's. His brown eyes followed her, watching her in terror. Slowly, she was brought face to face with a young man with rough, sunburnt skin, and bottomless eyes. He lifted her so that her head was straight above his, and she had no choice but to stare at him.

"C-Captain Whistler! I—" Matthew stood quickly, holding his hands against his chest as if to stop himself from wrenching Nova from the captain's strong grip.

The captain? Nova's blood ran cold. *Why didn't she jump in the water with Matthew when she had the chance?* A series of mer-tales flitted through her memory, each one more terrible than last.

"Thank you, Matthew. I'm glad you decided to join our crew. We'll take special care of her." The captain's tone turned Nova's blood to ice, and her face froze in terror. The rest of her body grew limp, the only thing keeping her up being Captain Whistler's grip on her. Her mouth dropped in a silent scream, and she saw that Matthew's face mirrored her own.

"Please sir, if you could return her to the ocean..." Matthew's choked out.

"No, I don't think so. Instead, we're going to put her to good use." The captain stroked Nova's hair, before plucking a long silver strand. "Hmm, want to guess how much this single hair will go for? I'd figure a hundred gold pieces, give or take." He wrapped the strand around his fist before bringing more of her hair to his nose. "Smells like money." He purred, a grin playing on his lips.

"M-M-Matthew..." Nova whispered, but like her, he was frozen, left to do nothing but watch as the captain started stroking her scales.

"And these beauties could easily go for a thousand each." Captain Whistler murmured.

Suddenly, Nova felt a sharp pain, making her whimper quietly. As she tried to understand where the pain was coming from, the captain brought one of her shimmering blue scales to his face, rubbing his beard with it.

Quick as lightning, Matthew leaped onto the captain, crashing him to the floor and letting Nova free of his grip. She immediately crawled toward the edge of the boat and just as she was about to leap, her torso already hanging over the edge, some force yanked her back.

Nova turned around to see that Captain Whistler's black boot was standing on the end of her tail, the heel of it grinding into her fin. When she looked up at him, she saw that he had an arm around Matthew's neck, holding a metal object to his head. All at once she recognized the item as a gun, making her freeze as she pulled herself back onto the deck.

"That's a good girl." Captain Whistler's low and melodic voice hypnotized her. "Now, crawl over to the center of the ship and don't try and escape again. Only then will I release little Matty here."

Nova's body shook with fear as she followed his command, crawling backward so that she was always watching the captain and Matthew.

"Nova, what are you doing? I got you into this mess. Don't worry about me, get out of here!" Matthew hissed between his teeth. Hearing this, the captain pressed the pistol deeper into Matthew's hair, causing Nova to crawl faster.

Once the captain felt sure that Nova was far enough away from the edge of the ship, he shoved Matthew toward her.

For a few short, beautiful seconds, there was nothing but Matthew and Nova, and he held her face eagerly. Before Nova knew what was happening, she felt a pair of lips meet hers, and she willingly relished the taste of her best friend's lips on her own.

The splendid moment was over too soon, and she was yanked from Matthew. His hand followed her, but in the captain's grip she was far too gone. Just as Matthew was about to stand up, Nova felt the cold kiss of steel next to her temple, and a sob escaped her mouth. Captain Whistler knew he didn't need to say anything to get his point across.

Nova watched Matthew's eyes grow wide as he bit his lip, obviously trying to not say anything that could get either of them killed. As the captain walked backward, Nova and Matthew watched each other as one was about to enter a dark torture and the other descended into a guilty sorrow. There were so many words they wanted to say to each other, but their closed lips were creating a dam that was the only thing keeping them safe from the captain and his gun.

Before Nova was ready, Matthew disappeared behind a door.

"Well, little lady. Let's start making a profit, shall we?" Captain Whistler hissed, making Nova's blood run colder than it already was. He tucked his gun away and adjusted Nova so he was now carrying her fully in his arms instead of dragging her half on the floor. His footsteps echoed in a dark hallway, filling her with fear.

"I've heard mermaid scales look better when they've been hydrated for over half a day. Shall we test that theory?" He opened a door, revealing a tub full of water.

"I was going to take a bath myself, but I figure I can wait a while." Something about the way the captain said that sent more chills down Nova's spine, and she wished he would just say nothing. The quiet might put her at ease. Or maybe that's the last thing the captain wanted for her—to feel comfortable. He didn't have to do much for her to become uneasy.

He threw her in the tub without another word. The freezing water immediately startled her, and Nova's teeth started chattering involuntary.

"Well, dear, see you in a few hours." Captain Whistler said in the doorway, his voice dipped with poison. Before he closed the door, he brought a flute to his lips and played a few notes.

Nova blinked, and he was gone.

How did he...? She looked at the door to see that there was light spilling beneath it. Wasn't she in a dark hallway just moments before? She heard a couple of voices go past before it was quiet again.

In the corner of her eye, she saw her scales glimmering brightly under the water. Had her tail always glowed so bright in the water? Or was there something about the captain's water? She searched for the chink in her tail where one of her scales used to be, the one that Captain Whistler had taken. There it was, nothing but pink flesh beneath it.

Suddenly, the door was flung open to present Captain Whistler, a strange smirk on his face and a bright light shining behind him.

"Your time is up little lady."

Alarmed, Nova's tail twitched slightly. "What do you mean? You were just here a minute ago." Nova's voice surprised herself. How did she talk so easily to him?

The captain closed the door and chuckled to himself. "Ah, so you don't know?" He lifted his hand to reveal his flute. "I'm named the White Whistler for a reason. My music is said to put anyone or any-*thing*," he gave Nova a pointed look, "to sleep. With my strange white flag, all who come near my ship are given full warning to stay away. Obviously little Matty didn't take a hint." He smirked at Nova, and she scowled.

"My ship is even named after Lorelei, the home of the sirens. It is believed that their songs will put you in an eternal slumber, whereas my tune is only temporary."

Nova didn't have to be reminded of her terrifying cousins. All mermaid kind had learned to avoid those creatures, as they brought nothing but bad luck to those that dared go near them.

Captain Whistler stepped closer, twirling some of Nova's hair with his flute. "Now, you will give me some of those scales."

Before Nova could protest, he reached into the water, grasping for Nova's tail. She wriggled away from him. After a few seconds, he stretched to his full height and glared at her. "So, you want to do this the hard way?" He cocked an eyebrow and brought his flute to his lips to play a few notes. Nova closed eyes, but immediately opened them to a sudden pain.

In front of her, she saw Captain Whistler holding two of her scales triumphantly. "Oh sorry, did that hurt? Did I fail to mention that

294 · BAND OF MISFITS

it hurts more to have scales pulled out when they're shining like this? My apologizes." He grinned wickedly, and before she knew what was happening, he'd pulled out two more. The water surrounding her turned a faint pink as he stuffed the scales in a pocket.

Next, he turned his attention to her face, specifically, her hair. "Apparently, mermaid hair is a rarity too. They can be sold for money, but they also say that if you stitch up any wound with your kind of hair, it heals in a matter of minutes. Though it's not as special as scales, seeing as hair grows back the same way every time. Scales take longer to grow back, and they never look as extraordinary as they do the first time." The captain then proceeded to pluck out a couple of Nova's hairs, interchanging between her blue and silver strands. Any time he thought she was wigging too much, he played his flute, making the whole ordeal completely out of her power.

Finally, he took a step back from her. "That should be enough for today. No need to make you ugly right from the start." The captain grinned before turning his back on Nova and slamming the door.

Instead of putting her to sleep, he forced her to wait for hours, with nothing but her thoughts and her surroundings to occupy her. The room was the size of a tiny closet, only big enough to fit the bathtub and a soap bar. There was nothing else to help her escape.

So, Nova sat back, weak and hopeless, dreaming of better times, dreaming of Matthew.

She was awakened by a quiet rapping at the door. Her first thought was that it was the captain, but seeing as he didn't knock last time, she let herself hope for a moment that it was someone to help her.

But nobody appeared. Instead, to her surprise and delight, a sand dollar slipped under the door. A sign of hope and her connection to Matthew. A huge burden is lifted off Nova's shoulders, and she smiles.

✢

A few days passed with the captain's torture, leaving Nova's head spinning and her tail feeling numb. She stopped fighting at some point; the Captain always got his way regardless of what she did. Sometimes, a sand dollar appeared under the door, occasionally with a small message on it, letting Nova know that Matthew is doing everything he can to figure out a way for her to be freed.

But Nova knew there was not much he could do.

A few weeks have passed, and Captain Whistler continued torturing her with his sleeping spells and cruel words, even though the fight in her had died long ago. Now missing many of her scales and her head constantly feeling lightheaded, Nova was feeling her hope dying more and more every day. She knew her scales would grow back, as a few of them had already started to reappear, but they were growing different colors and sizes, each piece a reminder of her pain and loneliness. She couldn't tell as well when it was light or dark out, and which direction they were going. Though mermaids don't need to eat much to survive, she was feeling weak in body and in spirit. Her voice was hoarse from not being used to being deprived of food.

Early one morning, Nova was awakened by a strange melodic song. Dread filled her as she recognized the sound of a siren's song. Were they near the Lorelei Cave?

Nova reached for the door handle, but unsurprisingly, it wouldn't budge. She banged on the door, raising her aching voice.

"Don't listen to the song of the sirens!"

But, naturally, her voice didn't seemed to reach anybody on the ship, and she was left wondering if she would ever escape this ship, or if she would be stuck forever in this room, with nobody to let her out.

The time and the silence both stretched slowly. She heard a few, faint splashes that sounded like bodies hitting the ocean, and she lied to herself that it was just her mind playing tricks on her.

But then, she could hear footsteps in the hallway. The door handle jiggled.

At first, she was terrified to think it might be Captain Whistler. But at this point, she didn't care who rescued her, as long as he had gotten away from the sirens.

Immediately, her world mended when she saw Mathew's glowing face in the doorway.

After being in the cold presence of the captain for so long, with horror being her constant companion, tears filled her eyes and her heart began to swell in her chest. As she reached out to him, no words needed to be exchanged as he scooped her in his arms, hugging her tightly.

As much as she wanted to stay in this moment forever, she knew that they had to leave. As Matthew sprinted out of the dark hallway, Nova was alarmed by the sudden light of the sun. She squinted and shrank as her body adjusted to the outside world. All other sounds were muted except for that of Matthew's breathing. With one slight tilt of her head, she could feel his breathing as well, and finally, she knew she was safe.

Matthew spoke first. "Do you think you can swim us out of here?" He whispered to her, and she nodded her head against his chest. Matthew walked to the side of the boat, and just like that, Nova left the same way she entered, this with what she was there for.

As the salt water slowly seeped into her skin, refreshing her in body and in mind, she realized that the water tasted like iron. She looked around, trying to find the source, when she froze at the sight of a red cloud around Matthew. His face was pale as he pulled a pained smile, and his eyes start to lull to the back of his head.

Alarmed, she wrapped her arms around him, and with a flick of her tail, she swam as quick as her cramped body would take her. The water around her seemed to make way for her and Matthew as she tried to find a safe place to put Matthew on dry land.

Nova swam to the nearest island and set Matthew on the sand, the waves washing up behind them and breaking against their bodies. She tried to find where he was hurt and found that he had a deep cut on his arm with blood spilling everywhere. At a loss for words, Nova covered her mouth, and trying to think of any solutions.

"The captain…" Matthew starts.

"Shh… Don't talk right now. I need to get you fixed up." Nova's own voice sounded strange to her, so strained and dry, but she ignored it.

She thought back to how the captain said that mermaid hair could heal any injury. Now that she thought about it, maybe that was the secret mermaid healing power humans always talked about, but she never knew how it was done until the captain talked about it. She found a nearby sand dollar on the beach, broke it, and got one of the teeth from inside. It wasn't exactly a needle like the ones humans use, but it would suffice.

She took one of her own hairs, at this point her scalp beyond used to the pain, and started stitching Matthew's arm together.

To her astonishment, it seemed to be working. Maybe that captain was useful for at least one thing. The skin around the cut immediately merged together, leaving only a bad bruise behind.

Matthew opens his eyes and smiled faintly at Nova. He sits up with a groan, rubbing his palm over his face.

Nova tested her voice a little. "Wha-what happened, Matthew?"

Matthew grinned, and Nova's heart just about stops.

"Well, the captain had threatened me that if I tried to come visit you," and just like that, Matthew's smile disappeared, "he said that if I tried to come visit you, he would have us both killed." Matthew looked down before continuing. "So, I knew I had to get a plan together. I told him that I knew where the mermaids were hiding."

Nova gave him a strange look, and he smiled again. "Of course, I don't actually know about your hiding place. I was bluffing." She smiled in turn and let him continue.

"I led them to what they thought were more mermaids. In reality, I had remembered wandering near Lorelei Cave with you, but you told me it was where the sirens were, how if I were to ever encounter one, I should fill my ears with something. I told the pirates that's where the mermaids lived, and when we stared heading toward the cave, I put beeswax in my ears, so that I was the only one that survived." He paused, and Nova put a hand on his arm. She understood that even if they were pirates, that must have been hard to watch.

"Just as the captain was about to walk over the edge to his death, I think he realized he got caught under the siren's sleep spell, and that I had tricked him. He aimed his pistol at me, but he missed, only grazing my shoulder." He gestured to his arm that Nova had just fixed up. "Once the whole ship was...cleaned out, I steered the ship to safety, and now here we are." He smiled at Nova sheepishly.

Nova smiled back, and whispered, "Thank you."

Matthew noticed her strange quietness, and frowned slightly. "I am so sorry for putting you through this." He grasped her hands, looking at them. "This is all my fault. If I had just been more cautious..."

Nova shook her head determinedly, gripping Matthew's hands tighter. "It was a horrible experience, but it's not your fault. I'm just glad you were there for me and I'm glad we're both safe now."

Matthew's eyes fell on Nova's tail, and his face became even more ashen. "But your tail. I can't believe he would do that to something so beautiful." His voice came out almost like a terrified whisper, and Nova touched his face lightly. But when her eyes bet his, no words came to her, and she didn't know what to say.

But it seemed she didn't need to say anything anyway. He understood.

Matthew dropped her hand and reached into his jacket pocket. "Before we left the ship, I grabbed some of these." He pulled out a small bag and dumped the contents into Nova's hands.

She gasped audibly as she saw what now lay in her hands.

"Obviously, I couldn't get all of the scales, seeing as he had already sold some of them. But I grabbed as many as I could." Matthew murmured sheepishly.

Nova played with the scales in her hands, turning them over and stroking the shape.

But eventually, she looked up at Matthew, and reached her hands out back to him. "You keep these. I have no use for them."

Matthew was taken aback; he tilted his head in confusion. "No, we can try and put them back in, or do something. You have so many missing from your tail, you should keep some of them."

Nova shook her head. "Keep them. That way, even when we're apart, you'll think of me, and the experiences we have gone through together. When they grow back differently, I'll think of them too."

Matthew seemed to hesitate, so Nova placed the scales back in his bag and wrapped his fingers over the small package. Matthew squeezed his eyes shut, then took a deep breath. He grabbed Nova's hand, making her turn to him. "I can't believe you would want to re-member this experience. I put you in danger, and the White Whistle, well, he seemed like a siren himself the way he—"

Nova put a hand over Matthew's, stopping him. "I'll remember as the experience where everything changed. We've journeyed the farthest from home, we met some of the darkness of our world, and because, well..." Nova looked down, feeling her cheeks warm a little, "because it was the first time you kissed me."

Matthew didn't say anything for a moment before he lifted her head with a finger under her chin. His eyes, which shined with pride and love, where hidden in the folds of his smile, and his joy spread warmth through her. She returned his smile, and after a quick glance at her lips, he brought her in for a kiss. Unlike their first kiss, this one wasn't desperate or scared; this one was warm, content, patient.

After a few moments, Matthew pulled away slowly. "Shall we continue our adventures? Hopefully we won't have to go through as many scary things." He said jokingly, cracking another smile.

Nova smiled back, before saying, "Well, kissing you is pretty scary." As if to prove a point, she acted out on a sudden burst of con-fidence and placed a quick kiss on his lips before leaping back in the ocean. When Matthew followed her deep enough, his laughter deep and vibrating through the waves, she grabbed his arm and at break-neck speed, jetted him back home so he could grab his sailboat. The boat was their connecting piece to each other, so obviously they were now ready for their next voyage through the sea of their future.

LEXI ROGERS

Song of the Seals

Where I come from, stories are precious jewels and guarded like secrets. I live on a tiny island where myth and legend hang so thick in the air, that I am dripping with tales of exotic creatures and words filled with mystery.

I barely remember my life as a small child far from the sea in a village. My mother died of sickness and my father died of heartbreak not long after. I moved to my grandfather's cottage on the ocean's edge with nothing but a memory of gentle hands and soft red hair. My life began on the day that I arrived at my grandfather's. The smell of salt and fish was unbearably strong, and I had wanted to curl up in a dark corner and hide from my pain. My grandfather said nothing to me on that first day. Instead, he took my hand and led me down to the ocean. I remember staring at the blue water that stretched on forever. For hours, I listened to the seagulls cry overhead. Slowly, my sadness melted away into the foam of the tide.

Soon, I learned my grandfather only talked when it was necessary. Not long after, I understood the reason for his silence. As the village Storyteller, my grandfather shared many stories but telling them was exhausting. The village would crowd around him as he spoke, his voice demanding attention and inviting imagination. When he began his stories, a magic flowed from his mouth and vibrated in the air.

My beloved grandfather raised me on the words of these mighty tales. The first one he told was about a mermaid. A week after moving in with him, I felt overwhelmed and too scared to live in a world without my parents. Sitting me on his lap, my grandfather described the green-silver scales of a mermaid with such detail that my heart eased from the pain. I vividly remember the way he talked about the mermaid's long brown hair and mischievous eyes. I have never forgotten how I felt when I was listening to his voice.

He told me fascinating stories of his life as a sailor, but my favorite stories were about mythical creatures. My grandfather did not divulge these types of stories too often since they were his most prized possessions. On a day when the clouds reached toward the boiling waves of an angry ocean, he told me a tale about a sea serpent. We made hot tea together and sat by the window. In between sips of tea and pauses to stare at the storm, he told me his story.

"Many years ago, on my ship, *The Red Dolphin*, I faced a storm that reminded me of this one. My crewmates and I were trying to tie down deck items in the blowing wind. Running to a water barrel, I saved it from flying off the ship. I grabbed it and moved it below deck. Running downstairs, I felt the ship sway in an odd way. Shaking my head, I convinced myself that the waves were just getting higher. Back on deck, I couldn't see clearly through the sea spray and fog. As I felt the ship rock again, I saw silhouettes of men stumble to the ground. After a third massive tilt, a head rose from the foamy water amidst a streak of silver. The strange head had fins on both sides with fangs as long as the ship itself. The creature was covered with silver scales that were dull against the gray, rumbling sky. It struck the side of the ship with a shriek, and I have never felt more afraid. I saw grown men fall to their knees, crying and praying for relief. I yelled over the screaming wind. 'FIGHT BACK!!'

"Somehow, my cry reached the ears of the panicked sailors and we scrambled to grab weapons to defend ourselves. I threw a piece of broken mast at the monster. Nothing happened. Our attack did not make a dent in the serpent's tough scales. After struggling for ages, someone struck the serpent in the eye with a harpoon. After writhing in agony for several minutes, the sea serpent slunk back into the water, turning the foam red and leaving a shrieking echo in the air."

Silence settled over our little house as the final words lingered. I could almost hear the scream of the serpent if I strained my ears, and I tasted salt on my tongue. The master Storyteller leaned forward and whispered, "And we came home a little worse for wear but with a great story to tell…"

Eyes wide, I memorized every word and clutched the story to my heart. His voice had transformed the story into life right before my eyes. My grandfather's eyes twinkled, and he smiled knowingly at my wonder.

As time passed, he told me stories about giant crabs, kraken, nereids, and monstrous squids. These tales instilled in me a desire to uncover the mysteries of the ocean. I guarded each treasured tale he told like they were pirate's loot.

Years later, we sat on the porch cleaning fish. Salt permeated the air around us. A breeze ruffled my hair as I looked up at my grandfather. He had been quieter than usual.

"Would you like to hear a story, Rowan?" He had said. I nodded eagerly and waited for him to start. For many minutes, he didn't say a word.

"Grandpa? Are you gonna tell the story?"

He smiled and said, "Little one, this is the most precious story of all. It is different than the others I have shared with you."

I nodded like I understood. He looked out to the horizon and began slowly. "Many years ago, a legend was told about the protectors of the sea, the seals. They have compassion in their hearts and protect all creatures. When you see a seal, you must grant them a low bow, for they created the ocean and the creatures living in its depths. After a time, the seals realized that no one protected the animals on land, so they created Man. Man's sacred duty was to watch over all living creatures—including each other. Hate and revenge entered the world, so only a few people remember this responsibility. The seals are saddened by this, but not surprised. Every so often, a seal will have a heart so big that they learn to shed their skin. These seals are honored and exalted. They walk on land as humans to ease pain, solve disputes, bring joy and comfort, and to make sure that Man has not completely forgotten their duty and purpose.

"On long nights, they will shed their sleek seal coats and dance for hours on the sand. They have deep, rough laughter that ripples over the waves. When they sing songs of the sea with their warbling voices, one can imagine they hold the magic of the ocean. Their surpassing beauty and grace is hard to imagine, my child.

"It is rumored that you can marry these seal creatures when they have shed their coats. Their loving hearts make them great partners in life. However, you must capture their skin, so they cannot slip away and return to the waves." My grandfather's eyes were thoughtful as he said this. "Son, the seals are the masters of the sea, just as I am the master of stories. To take their skin would be very disrespectful, no matter how tempting it may be."

He looked right at me to make sure that I understood this point. I nodded, eager for him to continue.

"I have never seen these creatures in person. Every night I've walked the shores, but I have heard joyful laughter carried by the breeze and hidden by shadow only a few times."

Silence stretched between us as I stared at my grandfather. I knew it was true. I could feel it in my bones.

The moment felt sacred, so I whispered, "Can I look for them too?"

My grandfather grinned. "I thought you'd never ask."

We walked the dark shores together every night as thousands of stars blinked into existence. We talked about many things, and my mind grew strong and full, as I grew into adulthood.

After many years, my grandfather could no longer walk with me on the beach. When I returned from my own walk, I told him how the salt spray felt on my face and how I had strained my ears for music. He would smile and close his eyes.

The last thing my beloved grandfather said to me was, "Keep listening for the song of the seals, little one." His rattling breaths released the magic in his soul a little at a time. When the last breath shook his frail body, it floated into the air and dissipated on the wind, cooling my tears.

I did not go to the beach for many weeks. I had too many memories of a man who loved the sea with his whole soul. I had a hard time doing anything, including remembering his stories.

Slowly, the pain of my grandfather's passing subsided. As I walk the shores late at night, I see him in the twinkling stars and in the foam of the waves. I became a fisherman so that I could be surrounded by the water. I had also been appointed the village Storyteller not long after my grandfather's death. A long time passed before I took up the responsibility, for I knew that I could never be as good as he was.

Finally, one night, I knew I had to make an appearance. I took a deep breath and walked into the village square. I perched on the edge of a water fountain, praying that no one would come. I sat silently for many minutes before a boy and a girl walked over to me.

"Are you The Storyteller?"

I nodded. They grinned and eagerly awaited a story. Taken aback, I stared at them for a couple minutes. The poor kids grew uncomfortable and fidgety. They stood up to leave.

"Many years ago, there was a legend," I heard myself say. My breath caught in my throat, I had heard my grandfather's rough voice in the familiar words. The two kids quickly sat back down.

I cleared my throat in discomfort and looked down at my hands. "Many years ago, there was a legend of the mermaids. Mermaids are wondrous, mischievous creatures with green and silver scales and flowing hair." My words were tumbling out different than my grandfather had told them. I was about to give up and go home before I disappointed anyone. As I looked up, I was surprised to see at least half the village crowded around to listen. Whispers floated through the crowd and I wanted to run away. I could not remember my grandfather's version of the story anymore. I was not the real Storyteller. I closed my eyes and pictured my grandfather's wrinkled hands and twinkling eyes. Taking a deep breath, I knew what to say.

Without opening my eyes, I began to speak. "Mermaids are full of revenge. They are the women thrown off a ship for being bad luck. Fellow mermaids rescue them from drowning. They surround these women as they sink and begin to chant. Crying tears on the soft female skin and spilling blood on her legs, magic seeps into the water and the woman's legs fuse together. The human women become green and silver, covered with scales. Her eyes become bigger and her teeth become sharper. It is not hard for these women to seek revenge, so they are taught how to spend their lives making mischief and singing beautiful songs to sailors. These songs are irresistible, and once you hear them you cannot break away. Images burst into your mind of joy and happiness and maybe a little bit of fear. If you keep listening, you lean over the side of the boat. In the water, you will find big eyes and a smile full of hate and revenge. For many sailors this is the last thing they will ever see."

I paused here and opened my eyes. I looked out at the crowd and fought a grin from spreading across my face. You could have heard a pin drop. I do not think a single one of them was breathing.

"Mermaids are dangerous, but beautiful creatures. When you pass through these deadly waters, you must stuff your ears full of wax so you will not fall under the spell. If you're lucky, one day you will see a mermaid and live to tell the tale."

The village square was silent. All you could hear was the crashing of waves.

The silence was broken when a soft voice whispered, "The Storyteller is back."

The crowd erupted in cheers and chants as my grin finally broke through. I had done it. I had told my story, even though it was a short one.

Since that first story, I have learned ways to work the crowd. My words flow and I am figuring out how to put magic in my voice like my grandfather.

Since I am often alone as a fisherman, I have plenty of time to think and to imagine. Dropping my hand into the ocean, I run my fingers through the water. It's time to bring my boat to shore, but I don't want to leave the wide expanse of blue just yet. Slowly, I head home and pull my small fisherman's dinghy up on the sand. I named it *The Red Dolphin,* as a constant reminder of my grandfather's teachings. Spotting two seals sunbathing on the dock, I respectfully lowered my head in a bow.

"Rowan!"

I turned toward the sound of my name. "Oh, h'llo, Ian," I said pleasantly.

"My wife will be very pleased with the catch today. Why don't you come over for dinner? We'll cook up some fish and then maybe you can tell us a story."

"I'd love to Ian, but I already have plans tonight."

Ian looked at me in complete shock, "You do? You never have plans."

"Ah, yes, but tonight is different. I must go. Thank you for the invitation." I sidled away and walked toward the little cottage by the sea. If you count walking on the beach, completely alone, I had plans. Ian asks me to dinner every night and every night I have a different but very believable excuse. Being The Storyteller has its perks, I know how to talk my way out of something.

At home, I made myself some tea. I rarely eat dinner, because I like to be out on the beach as the sun sets. I downed the scalding liquid and shrugged on a coat. I wandered aimlessly down the beach, lost in my thoughts. Liquid gold peered over the side of my shoe and began to run down the rest of my body. Sunset was here. I turned to face the water and grinned. I would never get tired of how beautiful the sky looked as the last rays of sun touched the waves and set the world on fire in blazing flames of gold and pink. I closed my eyes and let the last bits of warmth rest on my face. The crisp air cleared my mind and a peaceful nothingness filled my soul.

When I opened my eyes again, the sky was a dusky blue. I shivered as the sea air grew cold without the sun, and I pulled my coat tighter around me. As stars burst into view, I headed home. By the time I got there, the sky was littered with stars. I sat on the rickety porch and stared at them. There had to be a story hiding behind those winking, mischievous stars, and I wanted to figure it out. After years of searching for it, the sky does not want to give it up.

Feeling cold, I went inside and made myself another cup of tea. I fell asleep listening to the tantalizing song of the stars.

The next morning, I noticed the air was unusually warm. It was rarely warm this early in the morning next to the ocean. As I stepped out of my hut, I noticed another unusual thing. No wind stirred, not even a breeze. You cannot live next to the water without experiencing its cold whispers. Perplexed, I walked down to the docks, where everything made sense. Fifteen seals lay stretched out in a pile at the water's edge. No wonder the weather was so perfect.

I stopped walking and knelt on one knee. I have never seen so many seals in one place. I lowered my head as I bowed to the seals, and I felt all their eyes on me. Glancing up, I saw the seals staring at me with wide intelligent eyes. Unnerved, I walked to my little boat, determined not to look at the seals again.

As I headed out onto the water, I glanced back to shore and noticed that the seals were all looking away. I shrugged and let my glance fall. I felt eyes on my back. I turned around. They all looked away. This went on for a couple minutes when I finally sighed and continued to go out farther on the waves until I couldn't see the seals anymore.

As the day went on, quiet and warm, I tried to shake the seals from my mind. There was no way they were watching me. These rulers of the sea spend their time watching all sorts of people. I tried to forget the way that they looked in my direction. Their intense stares had implied that they wanted something from me. Absentmindedly, I stared at the clear blue water.

With a start, I almost fell out of my boat. There were blue eyes in the water that blended into the sea. As I looked closer, I realized they were attached to the body of a seal. My heartbeat returned to normal and confusion entered my thoughts. Seals don't have blue eyes.

The eyes disappeared, and I watched ripples head to shore. Were the seals watching me everywhere?

I was on edge for the rest of the day and didn't pay too much attention to my fishing. When I pulled my dinghy to the docks, I averted my gaze from the pack of seals, which had grown significantly.

"Rowan!"

I jumped. My nerves were strung tight. "Yes, Ian?"

"Look at all these seals!"

I cleared my throat in discomfort. "Yeah, there are a few."

"A few! Are you daft, lad?"

I laughed nervously. "I *am* The Storyteller. I can be quite daft."

Ian chuckled and I mumbled something about seals and stories and walked away, leaving Ian puzzled. I needed to find out what was going on. Could it be that after all these years the seal people wanted to dance on our shores? My grandfather's voice burst into my mind, and I heard him tell the legend of the seals once more.

"...but I've walked the shores every night and a few times I've heard joyful laughter carried by the breeze and hidden by shadow." My heartbeat sped up and my breath grew fast. I had to find the seals tonight.

The night would not come quick enough. I made myself eat a small dinner as I waited for the sky to be covered in black velvet. I was too nervous to watch the sun set.

Finally, the lights in the sky dimmed and I bolted out the door, pulling on a coat as I ran. As I passed the docks, my suspicion was confirmed. There were no more seals piled on top of each other, watching me with clear eyes.

I stumbled to the beach, tripping over my feet

I strained my ears until I thought they would burst, listening for the music. Thoughts whirled around in my head and I knew I shouldn't get my hopes up. Pushing away disappointment, my insides were a mix of nervousness, skepticism, and excitement.

The sound of music carried over the crashing of the waves. I laughed out loud for joy. My walk turned into a run and I hurried through the sand, beyond eager to find where the music was coming from. I ran for a long time, but I could not find the seals. Dawn was starting to poke her weak rays over the sea, so I began my long walk home.

When I got back to the docks, I was shocked to see a pile of seals crowded on top of each other. All of them were looking at me. My heart leaped for joy. I had one more night to find them.

The rest of the day seemed to take thousands of years and I didn't catch a single fish. I brushed off Ian's invitation to dinner and I strode off down the beach. I would find them tonight.

Hours passed before I heard the faint sound of music again. I walked faster and faster, racing to the source as the music grew louder. I could almost hear the words to the song. I ran until the flickering light of a flame burst into view.

I forgot how to breathe. My grandfather's voice ricocheted through my head, repeating the story of the seals. I don't remember falling, but I was suddenly on my knees in the sand with tears running down my face.

"I found them, Grandfather. I found them for you." I whispered to the air. Even the air was tight with magic. The seals were magnificent. Their graceful bodies moved with time itself, and their skin shone with the magic and mystery of creation. I looked at the unusually bright stars and knew my beloved grandfather could see them too.

The seals from the docks turned into the most joyous creatures you could ever imagine. Dancing around a fire, they sang songs of the sea with their rough, natural voices. Tears flowed down my cheeks as I watched the creatures with awe.

The men and women had large, dark eyes and small bodies. Despite their size, they were well built and exuded power. The women had long dark hair that flowed down their backs in waves. Each had a loud and clear laugh. I grinned. You could not help but be happy when you looked at them. I remembered that only the seals with the biggest hearts could become human and walk on land. Happiness filled every seam of their bodies.

I glanced to a pile of seal skins—black as night. Running my hand over them, they felt wet and as smooth as silk.

Although I was hidden in the shadows, the seals must have noticed me. Silently, I slipped away from the beautiful sight. I wasn't about to push my luck, and I needed to get back to my cottage.

With a skip in my step and a light heart, I ran home. I laughed into the night air in my happiness. When I got back to the docks, dawn approached, so I went inside to make breakfast.

After I finished eating, I went to the water's edge. The seals were there yet again. I giggled like a schoolboy when I saw that the seals were still there. I would get to see them one more night.

I caught more fish that day than I had in a very long time, and I could not hide the grin that was plastered onto my face.

"Rowan, what is the matter with you?" Ian asked me that evening.

"It was a good haul of fish today," I responded giddily.

That night, I sat watching the seal people dance and sing again. My heart expanded with the beauty of it and I wrapped the scene carefully into my soul. I would never forget this moment. Someday I would tell the story to the villagers, but that would not be for a long time.

I closed my eyes and soaked in the images that floated through the seal's songs. They were vivid and beautiful.

I felt a tap on my shoulder and I jumped about three feet into the air. My heartbeat quickened as I looked to a seal woman. Wearing a gentle smile, her long black hair flowed in a nonexistent breeze.

"Blue eyes," I said stupidly. "You have blue eyes."

"Aye, I do." The woman replied. Her voice was the most beautiful thing I had ever heard. It sounded like the song of the seals.

"Seals don't have blue eyes," I blundered on.

"Aye."

"Was it you under my boat?"

"Aye, that was me." Her eyes twinkled with mischief.

"Why were you watching me?"

"You are The Storyteller," she said simply.

"Why does that matter?"

"You hold the magic."

"The magic?"

"Aye. Seal magic was given to the first Storyteller and passed on through generations. That is how you are able to capture a crowd's attention with your words."

"I have seal magic?" I said, eyes wide.

"Aye, you do. It was given to The Storyteller as a way of helping mankind."

"How do you choose The Storytellers?"

"The Storytellers have always been the kindest and most loving people. They inspire other people to do good."

"I don't do that."

"Aye. You do."

I gaped at the woman.

The woman continued, "I am The Storyteller for the seals and that is why I have blue eyes."

I nodded, pretending that I understood. "So, do you tell stories about us, as we tell stories of you?"

"Aye. They are grand stories. I have always wanted to meet one of your kind."

As she said this, I noticed how youthful she was. The other seals possessed an air of self-control and grace. This woman was brimming with life. She couldn't sit still and her eyes flashed with a hundred thousand thoughts.

"I have waited my whole life to meet a seal," I said in return.

She grinned. "Will you take my skin?"

I was taken aback. "Will I...what?"

"I want to learn to live on land, but I cannot do that if you do not take my skin."

"But that's the most disrespectful thing a person can do."

"Aye. Not when I ask you, however. Please."

I was wary. "Where will you go?"

She looked confused. "Go?"

"Yes, you have to live somewhere."

"Oh. I'll just live with you."

My face burned red. "Oh, well, that would be improper."

"Why?"

I cleared my throat in discomfort, "Here on land, men and women do not live together unless they are married."

The seal woman burst out laughing. "I am a Storyteller for a reason. I know about marriage. I was trying to make you uncomfortable."

I grinned in spite of myself. "You're going to need a name if you live on land."

She snorted. "I have a name."

My face flushed again. "Forgive me."

"It's Ren."

"Ren. I'm Rowan."

She grinned her wide, perfect smile and I found myself grinning back.

"What if I married you, Rowan?"

"What if you...what?" I said.

"What if I married you? Then I could live with you."

"I don't want to make you unhappy, Ren. You would not like it on land."

She scoffed at me. "Of course I will like it on land. And I would like to be with *you* on land."

I grinned. I had just met this girl, this seal. I should not be grinning. But I didn't stop grinning and I heard myself say, "Well, we better get started."

Ren whooped as she fetched her skin from the pile. She dropped it into my shaking hands. "See you soon."

She ran back to her fellow seals and began to dance. My eyes watched only her, as her sealskin ran through my fingers. She glowed as she danced with joyfulness. None of the other seals seemed to have her vivacity.

As the sun began to rise, all the seals grabbed their skins and jumped into the water. All the seals except one. One woman stood alone on the beach, facing me. She grinned and put a finger to her lips.

"Don't let go of the skin, Rowan," she whispered. I shook my head and gestured for her to follow me.

"All right, we can talk now," Ren said abruptly.

"Why couldn't we before?"

"My people might have thought I was being taken forcefully if they heard a fight. All through out history, people have stolen our skins and we are forced to follow them. We try to prevent that from happening. It's best for them to know I went willingly."

I nodded my understanding. "Welcome to your new home, Ren."

Standing in front of my humble cottage by the sea, she gasped. "Oh, it's so beautiful."

My eyes shone with pride at her recognition of its simple beauty. Inside, she began exploring, breathlessly. I was breathless for an entirely different reason.

I found an old dress that my grandfather had kept after my grandmother had passed away. I presented it to Ren, but she wrinkled her nose.

"How am I supposed to do anything in this?" She asked in confusion.

I laughed heartily and said, "I have no idea. I'll find you something else."

She nodded, and I quickly found a pair of pants and a shirt that had grown too small for me. She put them on and still looked like a goddess.

"That's much better," she said.

Ren was different than any girl I had ever met. I put her skin in a chest and locked it tight.

The next few days, I explained lots of new ideas to her and showed her around the village. When people asked where she had come from, I said I had found her on the shore. Everybody assumed she was the victim of a shipwreck. It was easier that way.

It took Ren many weeks to learn how to fish the human way since she was used to fishing with her mouth.

Before long, she learned our traditions and customs and aided me in my storytelling. On more than one occasion, she added an element that I hadn't even known was lacking.

She was very curious and loved to learn. With her strong mind, we shared many intelligent conversations. Always full of energy, she brought out the best in me and I was happy and playful. She was funny, kind, and beautiful inside and out.

Over the next four months, we fell in love. I asked her to marry me on the beach as the sun set behind us.

We lived in playful harmony for a year before she was with child. She gave birth to a beautiful, healthy little girl. We named her Mira, after the ocean. She had her mother's blue eyes and my red hair. She was the perfect addition to our happiness.

Late one night, Ren and I sat on the porch, after Mira had fallen asleep.

"Do you know the story of the stars?" she asked me.

"I have almost figured it out, but the stars keep the details from me."

She smiled. "I know it."

"You do? Ren! How have you not told me this before?"

She laughed, "Well, I'm telling you now."

I rolled my eyes as I laughed. "Will you please tell me?"

She nodded and looked up toward the sky. "Before the world had cooled, there was only ocean. The seals made many creatures for the shallows, but there was no light. These new creations could not see into the depths of the ocean. The seals thought about this problem for many months before they came up with a solution. They created a swift and tiny animal with a long, sharp beak—the first hummingbird. The hummingbird poked holes in the blanket of sky. It took many weeks worth of trips and many rests until her job was complete. After resting on a small patch of land made by the seals, she fell, exhausted, into the ocean. The seals transformed her shiny feathers into stars. That hummingbird was the first constellation, and she rests among her creations."

My soul sighed in relief and satisfaction. Finally, I knew the story of the stars. I looked up at the little white dots that winked merrily at me. My body relaxed for I no longer strained to hear the stars.

I looked at Ren. "Thank you."

She nodded. She knew my heart and was content.

As the days bled into years, Mira became a toddler who loved the stories about the sea. Ren took her on walks and waved to me on my fishing boat. We were the happiest family on the island for a long time.

Paradise doesn't last long. Ours came crashing down the day that I found Ren sobbing on the floor of our room.

"Ren!" I cried. I knelt next to her and tilted her chin. Her eyes were sad.

"Go away, Rowan."

"No. I won't. What's wrong?"

"It doesn't matter."

"Ren, darling, of course it matters."

She sobbed as she spoke the words that would change our lives forever. "I am being called back home."

"Your home is here, Ren."

"Aye, it is, but the seals need their Storyteller back. They are calling me home."

"How do you know?"

She touched a hand to her heart. "It is a pain that grips my heart and tugs me toward the water. If I resist, it will destroy me."

My thoughts scattered. "Why do they need you so badly?"

"You know that storytellers bring balance. Without me, our seal kingdom might be destroyed. They cannot choose another Storyteller until I am dead, so I must either return or be ripped apart by the strain."

I could not bear the thought of her in pain, and losing her would break my heart. Ren was my everything.

"Ren," I whispered, tears brimming in my eyes.

"I love you, Rowan." She whispered back. We fell into each other's arms and embraced until Mira came looking for us.

The next morning was a somber occasion. I held Ren's sealskin in my hands as we walked down to the water with Mira skipping along beside us.

"Don't let go of the skin, Rowan. If you do, I will grab it and run."

"I won't let it go. I won't let *you* go," I replied.

"You must. You *must* let me go." Her voice cracked. "If you don't, I don't think I can leave on my own."

I nodded. "I understand that I have to let you go, but I will always love you."

"I love you, Rowan. You are a part of my soul that will never unravel. I will never forget you."

"I love you so much, Ren. All the way to the stars and back."

She laughed softly. "Aye, you are my hummingbird."

"To the very end," I said with a sad smile.

Ren bent down and smiled at her daughter. "I love you, Mira. You are the light of my life. Listen to your father and know that I am watching over you." She kissed her daughter's head.

She looked at me with eyes full of love mixed with sadness. "When you look at the ocean, think of me." Ren leaned forward and kissed me for the last time. I tasted salty tears.

"Give me the skin." I put it in her hands, but I didn't let go. I couldn't.

"Ren, I love you. Go tell your stories."

Ren grinned her perfect smile that was full of life and winked at me. "You are my greatest story."

I grinned back and let go of the skin. Seized by the magic of the seals, she slipped into her skin and dove into the waves.

Years passed, and Mira grew into a lovely young woman. She was my light. When she sang, her soft voice was the most beautiful sound in the world.

Ren watched over us in her own special way. One day, I sat in my little dinghy and stared out to sea, as a slosh of water sounded behind me. When I turned to look, my boat flipped upside down. A single seal swam beside the boat, staring at me with unusually blue eyes. *Ren.*

I felt a flipper on my face and a nuzzle on my nose. The salt water washed my tears away as I stared at her. She didn't stay for more than a few minutes before she swam away into the darkness.

Often, a silhouette catches my attention in the distance—at the end of a road, on a hill, or in the shadows. I know the small silhouette is her. I lift my hand in a wave. She never waves back when she watches from afar. My Ren watched Mira grow up and have kids of her own, even if she could not be there herself.

When they were old enough, I told my grandkids magnificent stories of mermaids and sea serpents. One story about a beautiful, young seal dancing in the moonlight long ago was perfectly true. They would stare open mouthed and beg to go searching for the selkies.

Laughing, I would take their little hands and we would spend many late nights walking along the dark water. I would tell them to keep searching because the song of the seals is unforgettable.

I looked out at the vast ocean and thought of Ren.

"I love you," I whisper to the salty air.

LILIANA SMITH

....

The Journey of Captain Swift

Hugh grunted as he rolled a barrel up the ramp. "All right, Captain. That's the last one."

Swift nodded and put his hand out for the man to shake. "Thank you, Hugh. Good doing business with you again." Both of them know that he's one of the only merchants who *will* do business with the captain of the *Gannet's Flight*. Everyone else scoffs, telling Swift he's "Still wet behind the ears, son."

"When your father got sick, a lot of the crewmembers hoped he'd leave the ship to one of them. To leave the ship to his young son like he did...you weren't even fifteen!" Hugh chuckled and shook his head.

Swift glared at the older man who saw that he had crossed a line. Swift hated being reminded that he had earned his position because of his father. "That was more than three years ago. How many times do I have to prove myself to people?" He turned without another word and boarded his ship, making final preparations before casting off.

✦

"Adlai! STOP!" The boy slowed to a stop and looked guiltily at Swift, who had grabbed one of his wrists. "Open your hands. Now."

Adlai opened his hands, revealing a giant handful of dried fruit. "But, Skipper! Why can't I have some? I'm hungry!"

Swift had to work hard to keep himself from hitting his crew-member. Not only was the insolent fool stealing things *again,* he called Swift "Skipper," which was one of the things he hated more than anything. *Keep calm, Swift. If you lose your temper here it will make the situation worse.* All the same, Adlai wasn't helping the situation either. The recruitment workers had promised that he would be very helpful on-deck, but he was not living up to Swift's expectations.

Adlai pouted, scrunching up his rodent-like face. "I'm hungry! It's not even meat or anything, just some fruit."

Swift glared and took the fruit away from Adlai, scooping it into his own hands. He forced his voice to sound calm and informative, instead of angry and extremely annoyed like he felt. "Adlai, I'm very sorry that you're hungry, but the rest of us are too! We're rationing the food, *especially* the fruit. We'll only make it to port if we don't die of scurvy, and that means not letting one hungry person eat it all. Okay? If I catch you sneaking food one more time there will be *serious consequences.* Now, let's take this food back to Pepper." He nodded to Adlai and they moved to get below deck.

As if summoned by the mention of his name, Pepper's head appeared, quickly followed by the rest of him, squinting in the bright light as he clambered up the steps. "Er... Captain, we've gotta talk." He beckoned for the captain to follow him and retreated. Swift followed after the cook, leaving Adlai with a look that said, *get to work.*

+

"All right, Pepper. What is it?" Swift ran his fingers through his hair.

"Well, we got a problem. This journey started a bit rough, since your merchant friend wasn't able to supply us with the same amount of food as usual. But then the ship got caught in calm waters. For a *long* time. You know as well as I do that we're runnin' low on food. Well, even wiv' the rationing, we're down to one week's worth of meals. We'll 'ave to start fishin' or shootin' down seabirds."

"We aren't traveling quickly even now," Swift replied, furiously. "We've got a very weak tailwind and that's it. Even if we get insanely lucky with fish and birds, we're not likely to get to the Colonies." He paused, letting out a breath. "Our crew is more likely to starve than to survive this voyage, huh?"

"Don't be so 'ard on yourself. Just bad luck is all." Pepper patted Swift on the back.

"Ha. Luck or fate. Maybe destiny?"

Pepper grinned at that. "It's strange enough for a sailor to be without superstition, but a captain? That's downright crazy." Just then, the first mate Quincy clomped down the stairs. He brushed his long, unkempt hair away from his ruddy face and frowned.

"Hey, Captain. Pepper. Sorry to bust in. Food may be a problem, but we've got another thing to deal with." He stared at Swift. "In case you haven't noticed, your crew is getting a bit restless. You can't blame them, of course. But it's getting out of hand. They're talking about how you're apparently foolish and how you got them into this situation on purpose. They call you weak-minded. Dissent is spreading."

Swift groaned and covered his face with his hands. "Why...? Everything else is going so poorly, I don't need mutineers to top it off. What should I do, Quince? You're better at dealing with people."

Quincy shrugged. "In my experience, directness is the best course of action." Swift stiffened, uncertain. "So...go up and talk to them, Captain!"

Swift sighed and headed above-decks. Quincy followed, then Pepper, rubbing his eyes, trying to adjust to the light. Pepper had weak eyes that couldn't see well when it was bright, and he was very near-sighted. Cooking was one of the only jobs he could do successfully, not that he let that bother him.

Swift walked to the helm and shouted for his crew to gather. Quincy went back below-decks to round up anyone who was down there. "Okay, well," Swift said once everyone was gathered. He clapped once and straightened his posture, trying to look serious. "It's come to my attention that many of you consider my choices on this trip to be poor or misguided, and that the misfortunes we've faced have been my fault. So, rather than having tensions continue to rise, let's talk. What should I have done differently? And can I do something to help?"

The whole crew was silent. Looking around the deck, there was guilt and shame present on most of the crewmembers' faces. Dissent had run its course, but now they realized that there wasn't a lot for the captain to answer for. Then one spoke up. "You should have noticed the warning signs that the *Gannet's Flight* would end up in becalmed water. You should've been prepared for all these problems. Instead, you're careless, just like your father!" That was Hermon Drake, a capable sailor with a fierce temper, whose father had worked for Swift's father and had long hoped that Swift's father would give him the ship.

Ed, the boy next to him, shouted out, "Yeah! Careless, like your father," readily agreeing with Drake, as always.

Swift shook his head. "How could I have known? The seas on the day we left looked like the seas on any good sailing day. Any of you could confirm that! It was just poor luck that we ran into bad weather." But his protests were drowned out by angry remarks from his crew. *That's one problem with having your crew be around your age. They may not challenge your authority because of your age, but they're so unreasonable and pouty sometimes!* He waited for the cacophony of voices to die down, trying not to clench his fists, then. "I couldn't have known. It was just poor luck."

Fenton, who was very superstitious, even compared to other sailors, pointed up at him accusingly. "Not luck, Swift! What have you done to curse us all?"

Quincy, appearing suddenly beside Swift, gently nudged him to the side, whispering, "I'll take it from here." He then looked out to the crew beseechingly. *He sure knows how to talk to a crowd.* "Surely you know he would never do anything to land us with a curse. A few of you—" He looked at Adlai, Fenton and a few others. "—a few of you are on your first voyage under Captain Swift. Those of you who have sailed with him before know him to be knowledgeable and wise. He doesn't make foolish choices. Any captain on the sea could have been stuck in the calm. We were just unfortunate. Now, instead of quarrelling, let's do something to help our situation. I believe our good friend Pepper has something to say, if you would be kind enough to listen." Quincy beckoned the surprised cook forward.

"Er, well… I'll cut straight to the point, yeah? We're runnin' out of food. Big time." Some of the crew had already figured that out, but others were still surprised. "I've got a bit of a plan to 'elp us out. Along wiv' your normal on-deck jobs, you'll be responsible to hunt for seabirds an' fish. I can rig up some crossbows to shoot harpoons, since I really don't wanna deal with cleanin' bullet wounds. As for which people 'ave to be the ones huntin', we'll set up a rotation."

Swift took over again. "Do we have any volunteers to hunt today?" Thankfully, there were a few raised hands. *Above all else, they're good souls.* He called on some of the crew: "Today's fishers and bird hunters will be Fergus, Garridan, Jarvis and Lark."

Fergus was twenty-one, the oldest man on the ship. Garridan was sixteen, and renowned for his successes in fishing as a youth. Jarvis was a weak, pale boy who constantly seemed to be sick, and had a snotty nose now. Lark, the only girl onboard, was seventeen and handy with knives. Two were kept on her belt, ready to gut anyone who suggested women on board were bad luck. She was skilled with a crossbow as well. All four nodded and went to talk to Pepper.

Swift sighed with relief and turned to Quincy. "Well, it would seem that we managed to avert disaster."

Quincy looked around as the crew dispersed, then looked Swift in the eye and murmured, "For now, at least."

+

The first two days of taking food from the sea had gone fairly well. That first day, Lark had spotted an albatross flying near the ship. She had left it alone, being a little superstitious herself. She and the other three brought in a good catch of five fish and three unfortunate sea-birds. It was a lot, but not enough to fill the stomachs of a full crew. However, it could help take the edge off of their hunger. The second day had brought in a rather large pelican and two fish.

On the third day of hunting, Swift leaned against the railing on the starboard side of the ship, watching the sea. Today Pepper joined the hunt, to show the crew that he wasn't too proud to help. No one had the heart to tell him that he wouldn't be much help.

The sky was just a bit cloudy and the waves were small, but there was a brisk wind blowing behind them. The *Gannet's Flight* was moving much more quickly than it had the past week. The albatross cried out with a sound somewhere between a tweet and a screech, and Swift looked up at it, deep in thought. *The albatross. One of the bigger seabirds, and a big part of superstition too. Most sailors believe it to be either sacred or cursed. Well, it's been bringing us luck, either way.* He smiled.

Swift looked over at the hunters. Quincy and Fenton were fishing, and Mervin and Pepper were going to shoot down birds. He saw Pepper raise his crossbow, squinting. *Wait, he's aiming at...?*

"Pepper! Stop!" He rushed to Pepper's side and sure enough, his target was the albatross.

"I get it, Swift. I can't see clearly, and that's a problem, yeah? But I can see a bit of a blur, so I'm shootin' at that." His finger reached to press the trigger. Swift pushed the crossbow to the left just as Pepper shot. Swift watched in horror as the harpoon flew, the rope trailing behind, and hit the albatross right in the chest. He dropped to his knees, unable to speak. Pepper drew the rope back, pulling his catch in. "See, Swift? What did I tell ya? This bird is really somethin'. It's a big one." Then, pulling it closer, he saw what the bird looked like and his grin fell. "Oh. That's what was wrong." *Cursed or sacred, either way... Shooting it down is* not *a good thing. Maybe I am super-stitious after all.* "Captain? What should we do?"

Swift looked at the corpse in despair. "What a cruel joke. You would have missed if I hadn't tried to push the crossbow away. That means I'm responsible for its death." Swift picked the bird up, mar-veling at how heavy it was. Its giant wings flopped.

"No, Captain. It's my fault. I was the one tryin' to shoot it down, so I'll be the one to carry it." Swift nodded reluctantly, knowing the burden that Pepper would have to carry. If a sailor shoots down an albatross, he has to wear it around his neck, or else the bird's spirit will cause awful things to happen to the sailor's ship. Pepper picked up the bird and removed the harpoon as gently as he could. He then tied the rope around the bird and then around his neck, making a heavy necklace.

"Let's put this behind us. Curses don't exist," Swift said to reas-sure himself along with Pepper. "You should head back to the kitchen. We'll get someone else to hunt." Pepper headed below-decks, hunched forward from the weight of the bird. Swift called for Ed to take the crossbow.

✦

They didn't catch anything that day, and one of the fishing lines snapped, leaving the hook inside a fish. "We were able to save most of our rationed food thanks to good huntin' yesterday and the day be-fore," Pepper said to Swift, "But we won't 'ave enough to last us the rest of the way to the Colonies if we don't catch anything else. I'm thinkin' it was the albatross that brought us luck, and now we're not goin' to catch anything else." Swift nodded morosely. Pepper looked sorrowfully into the kitchen. "It's 'ard to cook wiv a bird around the neck, I'll tell ya." The crew were all sneaking glances toward the alba-tross but said nothing.

✦

The next day they had a strong headwind. *I wish Father gave the* Gannet's Flight *oars to row. We're not making any progress with this wind,* Swift thought in frustration. Quincy was giving directions to Fergus and Garridan to roll up the sails. Pepper raced up to Swift. "Captain," he said quietly, looking to make sure no one was watching. "We 'ave another problem." Swift cursed, then followed Pepper into the storage space that held the food as well as the ship's cargo.

Pepper pointed silently to something lying on the ground. On closer inspection, Swift could see that it was Mouser, the ship's mousing cat. The cat lay on its side with its many claws out and a terrified expression on its face. Its once-beautiful pelt was covered in rat bites.

"This had better be a nightmare. If Mouser is dead..." Swift shook his head angrily. "Have you checked the food and cargo?"

"Sure thing. The rats didn't get into the cargo boxes at all, just the food. Last night we 'ad five days' worth of food. Now we 'ave one day's worth, at most. There must 'ave been a lot of rodents, because they ate a lot."

Swift heard shouts coming from above-decks. He and Pepper pushed their way through the crew to where Adlai was curled up on the ground crying and moaning, his face an awful green color. Samien, the ship's medic, kneeled over Adlai. Drake turned to face Swift. "This is your fault, *Skipper*. He's probably got scurvy."

Samien looked up sharply at Drake and shook his head. "It is *definitely* not scurvy. I don't know what it is, though."

Drake continued to glare at Swift. "Not even our medic knows the nature of this disease. It was given to him by the albatross! If you hadn't shot it down, Adlai would be okay!"

Drake was clearly angry, and as he looked around, Swift saw other crewmembers getting mad. Pepper butted in. "You can see that the albatross is around my neck. That means I shot it. Now I'm makin' up for it. The albatross has nothin' to do with this." Pepper's words did little to help break the mounting tension.

Quincy cleared his throat. "If you lot would pay attention, you'd realize the wind has shifted. Let's put the sails out and take advantage of it, okay?" The crew scurried away to their positions, leaving Samien, Quincy, Pepper and Swift leaning over Adlai.

"Captain, we're losing control of our crew," Quincy sighed.

"Yes, I could kind of tell," Swift replied, pulling at his hair. *That's a habit I'll have to break.* "What am I supposed to *do* about it?"

Pepper shrugged. "We were kind of handlin' it until the albatross got shot down. Then our mouser got killed, our food was eaten by rats, and our luck with huntin' dropped."

Quincy took a deep breath, clearly confused about the business with the mouser. "You'd better hope nothing else bad happens on this voyage, Captain."

✦

The afternoon was rather uneventful. One of the crew, Aldred, caught a rather scrawny gull and proudly carried it in to Pepper.

Pepper kept Aldred in the kitchen and called for Fergus. "You two are goin' to be the chefs today. I need to step away, because this bird is startin' to smell bad an' get all rotten. I don't want to accidentally get rotten meat in the food, so I'll tell you two what to do an' you can do it." Swift stood by, thinking. *Fergus is one of the level-headed ones... Good choice to have him help out.*

+

That evening, in the middle of a meager dinner (But well-cooked, to the new chefs' merit), the winds picked up. Lark, who was on watch above-deck, rushed down. "Storm! There's a storm!"

Swift raced upstairs, followed by most of the crew—some more reluctant than others to leave their meal. Swift looked around, then cursed. The sky was an ominous deep purple, full of dark clouds. The wind was howling. It began to batter the sails. Waves were breaking over the sides of the ship, covering the deck and sweeping away pretty much everything that wasn't tied down. He pulled at his hair in frustration. "Why wasn't I warned before we were *in the middle of the storm?*"

Lark came up behind him with the others who had been on watch. "We barely had time to spot it before it was right on us, Captain. Even for a sea storm, it moved quickly."

Swift let out a long, exaggerated breath, then calmed down some. "All right. Regardless, the waves have already swept away half of what we had on board, so tie down anything left that you'd like to keep. Fergus, gather some of the others and take care of the sails, we don't want the mast to be damaged."

Swift ran to the helm of the ship to replace Garridan, who looked relieved. He was training to be a helmsman, but he still wasn't as confident as Swift. As soon as the wheel traded hands, it jerked left. *Hard.* Swift winced as the ship let out a groan. He shouted directions over the gale-force wind to an unsure Garridan. *"Go help Fergus with the sails!"*

Garridan turned to leave, then turned back again. *"Captain, they've already taken care of the sails! What now?"*

"Tie yourself down and tell the others to do the same!" Garridan blinked in confusion and yelled something in return, but Swift couldn't hear it because the wind had picked up a lot. He repeated his

instructions again, practically screaming to be heard. Garridan nodded and moved, staggering against the wind, toward Lark and Fergus.

Swift's vision became blurry and he realized the wind was making his eyes water. *This is by far the worst storm I've ever been in.* He reached up with one of his hands and quickly wiped the water from his eyes, flicking it away. The wheel tugged again and threw Swift to the ground. Someone from behind quickly helped him get up again. He turned around to thank them, then saw who was standing there. "Drake!" He jumped back, surprised.

Drake grinned and held up a length of rope. "You know the rules, *Skipper.*"

Swift did. In the case of a bad storm, the crew were tied to anything solid. In an even worse storm, the captain was tied to the wheel. He sighed, resigned to his fate. "Please," he whispered, looking up at the sky, "please let this storm blow over soon. The crew won't take much more of this." Then he turned to the wheel and held still as Drake secured both hands tightly.

"Good luck to you, Cap." Drake stepped away.

Swift's hands stung from the rope, which rubbed against him every time he turned the wheel. From behind him there came a loud *crack*, and he cried out in pain as a piece of wood—presumably from a crate that hadn't been tied down—hit him in the back of the knee. His leg buckled under the impact and he fell. His hands, still attached to the wheel, dragged it to the right and the ship struggled to stay balanced.

He heard a commotion behind him. It lasted for a while as he tried in vain to get back up, unable to prop his legs underneath himself. Then Ed and Drake came up behind him, along with Pepper and Quincy. Quincy helped Swift stand up again, grabbing him under the arms and all but hoisting him upward. Swift nodded quickly in gratitude, then he looked back expectantly at the small group. *"Well?"* He shouted, *"What is it?"*

Ed sneered, "We know you were responsible for the death of the albatross. But, being the captain and believing in your own importance, you made Pepper take the blame for your actions." *Wow,* thought Swift, *I had no clue he was able to say anything that Drake hadn't said right before*

Pepper spluttered, indignant. "Now, you look 'ere! Swift didn't make me do nothin'. It was my fault an' you know it! That's why *I* 'ave the bird on my neck—"

Drake cut him off. "Most of the crew believes us. And we agreed that the only way to fix this situation is to get rid of the one who brought it upon us. You were bad luck from the beginning, and things only got worse after the albatross. We're throwing you overboard!"

Fergus came up then. "Most. Not all."

"What?" Swift asked.

"Not all of the crew want you dead, but not enough want you alive. So we've decided to compromise by sending you off in a dinghy." Swift was cut free and led to the port side of the ship, where a depressingly small boat was tied up, holding about an inch of water.

"How…how many of you stood up for me?"

Only a handful stepped forward. Quincy, of course, followed by Pepper, Fergus, Garridan, and most surprisingly, Adlai, who still looked sick and green. "Well, thank you." Swift nodded in respect and clambered into the dinghy, assisted by Fergus.

Quincy and Pepper clambered down right after him. "What? No! You two… you have to save yourselves. Stay on the ship!" *My chances of survival are practically nonexistent, and I won't let my two closest friends share my fate.*

"No, Swift. It's my fault you're in this mess." Pepper held up his grotesque bird necklace. Quince smiled, trying to mask the fear in his eyes, and clapped Swift on the shoulder.

Swift held onto the two oars and nodded to Fergus, who started undoing the ropes. "I'll do my best to take care of this ship," the man said. "I owe it to you. I hope… I hope you make it back to shore alive." Then, as the ropes slipped, the knots undone, Fergus snapped his hand up in a salute, and the small boat plunged toward the giant waves below.

MARIA YATES

Atlantic Angel

O nce upon a time...I guess that's how most good stories start, isn't it? My story starts a bit differently, maybe something like this. Angel Tourmaline, my unique name, is not the weirdest thing about me. I am a quiet kind of person, which can come in handy when you spend your life around ghosts.

✦

Staring at the ground, I try to block out the noise. I've heard enough crying today to drive me insane. Visiting the graves of unknown family members with flowers and tears is a big deal for my family. If I really cared to mourn, I'd go off by myself and think. Instead, I turn to leave. I spot my cousin Blair , inching away from the mob. Maybe we are both unfeeling, and tired of our family. She jabs a thumb toward the beach a few feet away. We escape amidst the sound of the wails of our family.

We run all the way to the blue waves that lap the golden sand. Kicking off our shoes, we sit together quietly for a moment.

"Some vacay."

I shake my head with a sigh.

"I was hoping Florida would be fun," she groans. "I have been here for a week and have not seen a single sight."

"Well, let's go explore, unless you'd rather go back and visit aunt-so-and-so or great-cousin-what's-his-face."

"As fun as that sounds, I think I'll pass." Dusting herself off, we laugh in unison. she helps me to my feet and we head down the beach, stopping occasionally to skip rocks or wade into the water.

After a few minutes, I stop to cool off and Blair goes exploring. Closing my eyes, I lean back to rest on my hands. The sun warms my arms and face. Listening to the sound of the ocean, I decide that, despite its flaws, I like Florida. A second later, Blair runs back, her bare feet sliding on the sand and her hair damp with sweat.

She grabs my wrist and drags me after him. "You've got to see this!"

Pulling me behind her, we climb the ridge to find an isolated tree. A feeling of depression lingers around its leafless, twisted branches. All the grass is dead in a six-foot circle around the tree. Stepping into the foreboding ring, I feel a tangible coldness almost in the air.

"What is this place?" I ask anxiously, not wanting to linger.

"Come see." She gestures around the back of the tree, so I cross to her side. A silver painted wooden cross stuck out of the ground at an angle. One word in faded turquoise paint adorned the cross: *AN-GEL*

"Cool, let's go." They'll miss us if we don't hurry back."

Finding my name on a creepy beach grave is the opposite of cool. If I pretend to not care, we can leave this cursed place. My bare feet miss the hot sand. I grab her wrist and brace myself to drag her away. As I give a sharp tug, she tumbles over the grave and knocks it over. We race out of the circlet.

Welcoming the sun on my skin, I half listen to Blair's theories of a widow lost at sea or a dog suffocated by an alligator. "Her ghost still haunts the beach," she says.

We make it back to the beach house in time to help with dinner. After supper, the adults chat in the living room. The cousins congregate in the communal room up stairs. The little ones sprawl on the floor while the teens lounge in the loft. We smuggle up a bag of Doritos, humus, and a few cans of Sprite. After a round of truth-or-dare, the topic turns to ghosts. When a few pirate stories end with the giggles, Blair takes the lantern. She holds it beneath her face, casting an eerie shadow on the wall behind her.

"Your stories are lame. Today, Angel and I encountered a widowed spirit lady, also named Angel." When no one replies, she gasps and clutches her chest dramatically. "Well, I'm sure you've heard of her."

Everyone shakes their heads, playing along. Putting her head in her hand, she shakes it sadly "You, my dear family, are jeopardizing your safety," she continues. "This tale will rattle your very soul! You have been warned! From now on, every creaking door and every thud in the dark will drive you mad! This is not an ordinary widow. If she wants you, she will track you down and drag you away in chains of her own creation."

Pausing for theatrical effect, she continued the story. "Many years ago, a girl of 18 ran away from home to be married. Her parents tried to warn her that a man of questionable character would only bring her grief. Soon after the wedding, her new husband abandoned her. Theories arose about what happened to him. Some say he died, but others insisted that he was pirate. Or a pirate by nature, since he was untrustworthy and had a deep love of the sea. He stole a boat and sailed away from his wife. The universe did not approve of this decision and urged him to turn back. When he refused, his boat was destroyed in a storm."

"After news came of his death, his wife would walk the beach searching in vain for a sign of her husband. Pushing everyone away, she blamed the world for his betrayal. When she found she was pregnant, she wanted nothing to do with the baby and sent the child away. After waiting for him every night of her life, she withered away to die a lonely woman. Legend says she appears on the shore every night to wail at the loss. That baby is our great, great, great, great, great, grandfather."

Below us, the door opens, making the girls scream and the boys laugh. My dad knocks on the sideboard. "Curfew! Anyone still out of bed in ten seconds sleeps on the beach." We jump as Dad starts the countdown.

✦

On the trundle in our room, I think about our "ghost encounter." I recall an ancestor that shares my name that is buried in the family plot. My bare feet slap against the hardwood floor as I walk down the dark hallway. When I reach the living room, I turn on the light over the fireplace. Running my hand over the thick volumes of family history on the dust bookshelf, I grab one at random and start thumbing through boring life stories. After skimming a few pages, I become engrossed in my reading. Our ancestors were pirates, and I find a multitude of stories about ghost ships and krakens. For hours, I relish each story until I stumble upon a familiar name. A journal entry by Emma Eve Tourmaline.

April 13, 1654.

I wish with all my heart to see land again. I miss everyone at home and the sea is unbearable. Each new day is worse than the previous ones. I tried staying below deck for a while but it was unbearably stuffy, and the smell is revolting. I will try to look for the good in this trip but today has been especially difficult. There is nothing worse than being pregnant on a rocking boat full of vile smells! I'll muster through it, if it means that I can be here with Ben. I don't understand what he loves about the ocean, but I can only bear it for his sake.

Nick, another of my cousins, clears his throat. I look up to find him leaning against the doorjamb in loose clothes and mussed hair. "Light reading?"

I nod.

He sits next to me and lifts the edge of the book to check the title. "Family history? Really, girl? It's two in the morning!"

I look at the clock over the mantle. "Sorry to wake you; I didn't realize how late it is." As I put the book back on the bookshelf, he turns off the light and we head to bed.

+

The sunlight slants through the window and wakes me up. I roll over lazily and slip out of the trundle onto the cold floor. I yank on my high tops, letting the laces drag behind me. I dress and rush down the stairs for breakfast crepes. I inhale one and grab a novel off the mantel. My mom stops me when I'm halfway out the door.

"Hey. A bunch of the cousins are going to the beach later. You wanna go?"

I nod. "Yeah. Sounds great!"

She smiles. "Okay. See you around lunch time."

I step outside and enjoy the sun's warm greeting. The sun is making the beach glitter like gold. I walk up the hill toward the trees with the novel from the living room under my arm. I am lost in thought and am enjoying the scenery when my surroundings change. I've stumbled into the dead circle from the sandy embankment. I feel a tangible coldness spread through me.

How did I get here? I was walking in the opposite direction. Turning in a circle, I catch a glimpse of a small girl at the base of the tree. When I double check, no one is there. As I turn to leave, she is standing in front of me. She is around seven years old, and she looks pure white. After the ghost stories last night, I think she is a ghost. I try to convince that she is albino. I smile at her, but her expression remains blank. She looks me up and down before her gaze settles on my face. Her eyes are completely white—pupil and all. I've never seen eyes like that before. I'm trying to figure it out when she walks through me. My blood turns cold like someone has dumped a bucket of ice water over my head. When I turn around, she is a few feet away. As she walks, she becomes shimmery and transparent until she just disappears.

+

Six hours later, everyone is back from the beach but me. No matter which way I walk when I leave, I end up at the creepy grave. In fact, I couldn't leave at all until my cousin, Blair, finds me and helps me home.

Instead of researching apparitions and hallucinations, I am assigned cooking duty. When I am released, I try the internet. *Casper the Friendly Ghost* is about all I can find.

+

Later that night, I sneak downstairs to do more reading. I flip to the next entree by Emma Eve:

June ninth , 1654.

Ben is being stubborn. Last night, we ran into a storm that damaged a mast but he refuses to turn around. He won't tell me why we are on this crazy expedition in the first place. I long for home more than ever. Our little Angel cries every night. She is sea sick and afraid of the vast ocean. I try to sooth her. Comforting someone that shares my own fears is no easy feat. I want to turn the ship around myself, but I trust him.

I shut the book and slide it back on the shelf. When I turn around, the white girl is in front of me, staring at me with milky eyes. Walking away, I pretend not to see her, but she is in front of me in the hall. I close my eyes and walk through her, but she is in front of me again when I open my eyes. When she takes my hand, I pull away and rush down the hall to my room. When I get there, she is sitting on the windowsill watching me curiously.

+

I wake to undisturbed silence slipping through the house. It is still dark outside so everyone is still asleep. Looking out the window, I pray she has left. When I don't see her, I grab my things and head out the door. Waiting on the porch, she stares me down icily. She grabs my hand again and pulls me to the grave. Then, she urges me to sit next to her on the ground.

"Help me!"

"How can I help you?" I imagine describing my trip to everyone back home. "I relaxed at this gorgeous beach, camped in our family cabin, and, oh yeah, there was a dead 5 year old girl. The "ghost" girl liked to follow me around at night, teleported, walked through solid objects and asked me to be her mental health counselor." Um, I don't think anyone would believe me.

"Help me!" she cries out again, near tears.

I nod in agreement and prod her to tell her problems. She cries quietly but says nothing. Then, she disappears, leaving me shivering on the ground. I wander back to the cabin in an exhausted daze, ignoring the feeling that I'm missing something. Is she the "Angel" from the grave? Are we related? If she is dead, why is she a kid? No matter what it is going on, I'm going to figure out what is tormenting her. I am hesitant to help her. As sad as it is, she is a dead child that watches me in my sleep. Tomorrow, I will read the journal and look for more clues. I'll memorize it if will help. I'll start first thing in the morning.

July 1, 1654

This storm rocks the boat and may tear us apart. Ben won't tell me anything except our position in the ocean. Our compass stopped working days ago, but he won't turn around for home. I'd leave in a life raft if it weren't for the fear of being dashed to pieces in the process. Everyday, Angel becomes more afraid. Her behavior is starting to scare me since she continuously asks non-living objects to return her home.

July 31, 1654

Angel nearly passed away last night. Now that the situation is dire, my husband agrees to turn around for a brief burial. When he will sail away again, I will not be going with him. Instead, I will bury my daughter with a view of the beach. Though she fears riding a boat upon the storm tossed sea, watching the sun set over the water is her favorite pastime. I pray a doctor can save her, but I fear it will be too late by the time we get home.

August 12, 1654

She is gone.

Closing the journal, I looked around the beach and pondered the sad story of Angel's death. No wonder her spirit lingers on earth. The only way a spirit can stay on earth is if they have unfinished business. She died naturally but under terrible circumstances. I think about all the heartbreak in her story, until something pushes my arms out from under me. I fall back and land in somebody's lap. I look into the deep brown eyes of an attractive boy around my same age. He has tawny, curly hair that nearly brushes his shoulders. He cradles me for a second before his expression changes.

"Oh, I'm so sorry. I thought you were someone else." He helps me sit up.

I brush the sand off my clothes. "No problem. I'm visiting my family's cabin on the cliff." I point in the right direction and blush. *Wow, that was dumb.*

"Ah, the old Tourmaline place?"

I nod happily, letting him accept my blunder.

"Well, cool. Sorry again. See ya around."

I nod and wave goodbye. "Maybe I'll see you later." *Ugh, why did I have to sound so desperate?*

"Soooo, who was that?"

Rolling my eyes, I force on a smile before looking at my annoying younger cousin. "Hi, Britt."

Only two hours younger than me, she is boy crazy and rude. She is the evil half of a set of twins. Sometimes, I wonder how they split the good and the bad so evenly between two people. Blair, my older cousin by four minutes, got all the goodness and treats me like an equal. On the other hand, Britt is rude to everyone, especially me. I can't help it that I'm closer to her own twin sister than she is. When we were younger, people called us triplets. Her mom even bought us matching dresses. Becoming enraged, Britt cut off chunks of my hair in my sleep and ruined my dress. For her punishment, she had to give me her version of the matching dress.

Matching her sister and going to the same school did not help our relationship. I shared Blair's group of friends. After a while, Britt replaced us with a new friend, Constance. She didn't talk to us much after that. Soon, she told everyone that Constance was her cousin. No matter how often we apologized, she stayed angry with us. I figured that this conversation wasn't going to end well. Things never ended well with Britt.

"Angel, who was that?" She glared at me.

"No one." I dust off and head back to the cabin. Sadly, she follows.

"Didn't seem like nothing," she says persistently.

I roll my eyes and ignore her. Blaire, my darling cousin, rushes me and wraps me in a tight hug. "Hey Britt." She waves to her sister politely. The twins haven't hugged since Brittany rubbed super glue in her hair during their last one.

"You wanna go for a swim?" She directs the question to me, then she links her arm with mine. Throwing a glance at her sister, she begins to saunter off.

"Brittany, you can come, too. If you want." I add.

Blair raises an eyebrow.

"I don't need your consent. I'll come when I feel like it." Britt races away from us toward the beach.

We run to the water. "I saw you talking to that cute boy. Who was it?" Blair asks.

"Honestly, I don't even know his name. He thought I was someone else."

"Oh, okay. Whatever you say," she says playfully. I roll my eyes and we laugh.

+

After everybody is asleep, I sneak into the living room, hoping to find answers about Angel in one of the other volumes. When I get there, a light is already on and Brittany is sitting in the armchair by the empty fireplace. She is reading out of *my* family history book. I step into the shadows, but she has already seen me.

"Hey, Britt," I say, stepping into the light.

"Hey, Angel," she answers almost too sweetly, slamming the book.

After I watch her leave, I fling open the front door and race to the grave. Rather than looking in books, I'll ask her in person. Angel is sitting in the tree that guards her resting place. She climbs down when she sees me approach.

"Can you help me now?" she asks sadly.

I nod. "I'll need *your* help."

She hesitates a minute before nodding slowly. I crouch to meet her eyes. "Ghosts have unfinished business on earth. Do you know why you are still here?"

She shakes her head slowly. "Mummy and Daddy moved on to the next life. I feel like I am finished here, but I don't know what to do."

An entire sentence! This is the most she has said to me. "Do you know what happened to your dad after you died? I can't find any records about it."

"I guess he died too."

"Do you have any idea what he was doing on that boat? Was he looking for something?"

"He never said."

"Well, I'll see you tomorrow. We can talk about it more."

A huge smile crosses her face and she fades into her grave. Expecting her to return any moment, I step away slowly. A few paces away, I run into a group of teenage boys.

When I look closer, I recognize the boy from the beach. I stand there awkwardly, waiting for someone to say something.

"Hey! What are you doing out here this late?" I direct my question to the boy that spent a few moments with me in his lap this afternoon.

"What are *you* doing?" he asks anxiously, deflecting my question. I raise an eyebrow. He rubs his hands on his pants nervously and I notice their gear. They are all in black pants and hoodies. Each of them carries a different piece of equipment—one has a video camera around his neck, another carries a black bag, and the last boy holds a laptop and shovel. Beach-boy is the only one not holding anything. They all wear the same expression of guilt, their eyes downcast.

"Treasure hunting?" I ask with a laugh. None of them answer. "Seriously? I know for a fact that this is private property and I can have you arrested for trespassing."

The group of boys look to beach-boy to explain. He takes me aside. "We are, um, ghost hunting." Dylan whispers, looking embarrassed.

"Really? Can I come?"

He looks up suddenly. "Are you serious?"

I nod and reply, "Well, you are on my property. That means I should be able to come by default. What ghost are you looking for?"

"Angel Tourmaline."

I smile. "I've been reading family journals about her. She's my namesake. And I know exactly where she's buried. Follow me."

"Hey guys! We found a guide." He motions for the boys to join us. "Lead the way."

Of course, I will never reveal Angel to them. Admiring their interest and knowledge about her life, they may be able to tell me more about her than the book. Learning a little about ghosts in the process will probably help as well. When we get to the grave, they gawk at the simple wooden planks serving as her marker.

"We always knew it was somewhere around the property but we could never find it." They pull all kinds of instruments from the black bag to take "readings". There was even a thermometer in there. The boys seemed to enjoy their midnight trips to graves on other people's property.

I need them to help me find something to help Angel. I wonder how they know so much. "Where did you learn all this stuff about the ghost? Is there a book or something?"

"Actually, my mom studies local history. She is always at the town library and even got some information from your family. Well that and the stories."

"Stories?"

"You haven't heard it?" He says, sounding genuinely surprised. "I have told it a hundred times. I'm so excited to share my favorite story with you."

With a glimmer in his eye, he begins the story. "Long ago, a lonely sea captain was abandoned by his wife and daughter. His daughter was his pride and joy. He loved her and nurtured her dreams and wishes. His daughter wanted them to be a family again, but his wife wouldn't take him back due to his poor finances. So, he set off on a journey to find a great treasure. He hoped that if he found treasure, he could support his family and everything would work out.

Unfortunately, he was lost at sea and his 16-year-old daughter was desperate for his return. Every night, she waited on this ridge overlooking the sea, waiting for him to come home. She died there still waiting for his return. Every night, she seeks revenge for her father demise and waits on the beach for him. She blames her mother for the loss. As a tormented soul, she can't find happiness or move on. Her parents have passed onto the next life, so she will never gain satisfaction from a revenge. In order to finish her work on earth, she must forgive her mother and let her father go. Until then, she remains unhappy and unsatisfied."

"Is there any way I could read those stories myself?" I was shocked by the heartbreaking tale.

"Sure. It *is* a story about your family."

"I have a few journal entries by Angel's mom that I could lend you." He readily agreed and gave me the address of the location of the records. I helped them pack up. Before we went our separate ways, I remembered to ask his name.

"Dylan," he replied. "I'll see you tomorrow, Angel."

"Goodnight, Dylan."

+

The next morning, I walk to the library archives bright and early. Entering town, it's easy to spot the ancient building towering over the newer buildings that line the rest of the street. I head straight for the archives and start digging through records. A few minutes into my search, Dylan walks in.

"Sorry I'm late." He grins sheepishly.

"I just wanted to get a head start."

Bending on one knee, he opens a drawer. "What have you found?"

"Not much. I brought you those entries as promised." I pull the book out of my backpack and hand him the thick volume. He skims the marked pages before putting it in his own bag. Slowly, we move around the room, reading different documents.

Suddenly, Dylan looks at his watch. "I'm really sorry, but I have to go. Do you have time to meet again tomorrow?"

"Sure. See you then."

+

Secretly, I hide something in my bag and sneak it out of the building. I race to Angel's ridge to look at them in private. When I open my bag, nothing is there.

"Looking for these?"

"Dylan." I wince and turn.

"Wanna tell me what this is about?"

I shake my head.

"How about part of the story?"

I shrug and pat the ground next to me, so he can sit beside me. "I'm not sure how much of your story I believe. All the journal entries that mention Angel do not portray her mom as the villain. In fact, the journals hint that the dad caused the problem by making them go on the ocean in the first place."

He hands me the journal and I flip to the entries. As I try to make connections between the two stories, he reads the journal. Pulling out a laptop, he brings up a picture of the Bermuda Triangle. "Emma was in the Bermuda Triangle when she recorded the last set of coordinates written in the margins." He hands this tidbit over with a smug look on his face.

"How would she have known their exact location with broken equipment?" I ask.

"Ben must have known the treasure was nearby. Maybe, he told her they were close."

"Do you still believe in the whole treasure angle?"

"It makes sense doesn't it? Think about the story. That had to have come from somewhere. Maybe when Ben died, he passed his obsession on to his daughter. That could explain why she is stuck here," Dylan says with a huff.

"Maybe. I don't know. Would treasure be a good enough reason to not pass on to the next life?"

"I bet that if she finds the treasure, she will finally find peace." His face is animated. "I'm going to take a boat into the Bermuda Triangle tonight to look for answers."

"Not without me. I'm coming with you," I add with excitement.

"All right. Be packed and ready to go by 10. Meet me at the grave." He went to his house to pack.

If anyone would understand this situation, it was Blair. I cornered her and shared the entire story from the beginning. When I finish, she sits for a while to process the whole account. After agreeing to help, we plan to meet in the front room at 9:30. As we open the front door to sneak out, the light came on behind us. Fearing the worst possible scenario, we see Britt at the top of the stairs. I was wrong, this is much worse. Maybe it would be better for us to join Angel and become ghosts right now.

"Why are you going out so late?"

"Brittany," Blair says with disgust.

"What would happen if I screamed and woke the parents up right now? I bet that would ruin your plans, and that boy of yours would think you chickened out." Britt cackles with glee.

"How'd you know all that?" I ask weakly.

"I overheard everything. You need to take me with you or I'm sounding the alarm right now." Britt crosses her arms over her chest.

We all look at each other. I jerk my head to the door and we rush to the grave to meet Dylan.

"Who are they?" he asks in shock.

"They are here to help. At least one of them."

Britt rolls her eyes.

Picking up the tension, he grunts and does not ask any more questions.

✦

I cannot get over the sound of disappointment in his voice. It would have been nice to go with him, just the two of us. There is nothing that I can do about it now. We walk quietly ocean's edge and follow if to the boathouse. After locating his boat in the dark, we load up and set off.

"Bermuda Triangle, here we come," Britt shrieks into the night.

Dylan mutters under his breath. For three hours, we steer our boat through dense fog. All around us the air turns cold. While the weather is frustrating, it means we are getting close. Soon after, the engine dies.

The whole situation would be easier to bear if Brittany did not spend every second complaining. "Why would you drag me out here in the middle of the night? I knew this was a bad idea, but no one ever listens to me. Brrr. Couldn't someone warn me that it was going to be freezing?"

Dylan growled, "It is literally impossible to ignore someone that didn't pause to draw a breath." He scooted back on the seat next to me. "No offense, but why was she invited?"

"She wasn't. Unless you count the fact that she invited herself." He smiles at me before addressing everyone else.

"We are so close to our destination. Find something to use as a makeshift oar and we will press forward." Using two of Blair's textbooks, we begin rowing again. Twenty minutes later, we have barely moved.

Putting his mouth by my ear, Dylan whisper. "You've seen her, haven't you?"

I whisper "yes" and notice how close we are sitting.

"That makes you a host?" He is still whispering. "It means ghosts are comfortable around you."

I nod in agreement.

"Maybe you should try talking to her. I bet she would listen. Maybe she will join us in the search for her father's treasure."

"Why would she be able to come on the water now," I ask in confusion.

"She might need a living host on the water. Please give it a try."

I wedge myself into the far end of the boat, feeling stupid. If there is a slight chance he's right, I guess it's worth a try. "Angel, I need to talk to you. Do you have a minute?"

"Of course, she has a minute! Command her! She is not even alive. You are the one in charge!" Dylan whispers behind me. I can feel his breath on my neck.

"I really need your help." I try again.

"Be assertive!"

"Angel, come to me now or we refuse to help."

"By we, she means them. I am so over this." Brittany whines behind us.

Dylan puts his hand on my shoulder. "Keep going and just ignore her. You can do this."

I turn back to the water. "Angel, we are here to help you. But we can't do it without *your* presence. Please give us a chance to make things better for you. Isn't that what you want?"

"I told you she's crazy. Now she is talking to the water." Britt exclaims. Dylan shoots her a look to tell her to stop talking but she doesn't get the memo. "Oh, excuse me, dead person in the water. I wasn't carried of in the middle of the night to listen to ghost stories. I—" She stopped mid-sentence as Angel appeared in her ghostly form.

Angel was walking on top of the water, smiling broadly. Everyone else leapt to the back of the boat. Dylan and I were standing alone.

"There is no treasure," she whispers. "My only desire has been to follow my father's other passion and love the sea. With a host on the water, I can use the energy from your body to fulfill my work here. Thank you, Angel."

"Thank *you*, Angel."

"Good bye." I wave to her. She smiles and fades into mist as she walks further away from the boat.

"What is wrong with me? I didn't even take a picture!" Dylan pounds the side of the boat in frustration.

After the encounter, our boat works starts up with no problems. The time passes quickly as we all ponder what happened to us that night. Before I know it, we are making our way up the beach toward home. Before I turn toward my house, Dylan grabs my hand. Before letting myself completely overreact, I decide to enjoy myself. After a few moments of bliss, my thoughts begin to churn. *Who did he think I was that day on the beach? Did he have someone else? Was he messing with me?*

I look over at him in the dark. "Do you like someone?"

Slowly he nods. "Yeah. Yeah, I do."

I pull away in disgust and run home.

The next day, we pack to leave Florida. Blair and Nick walk with their heads together, full of secret triumph. I don't tell them about what happened with Dylan, even if it makes me a little sulky.

Dylan comes by later to say goodbye. Blair must have mentioned to him that we were leaving.

"I came to say goodbye. And to ask why you ran away last night? I was going to tell you I liked you. Maybe it was too fast. I'm sorry."

"I like you, too. But, I won't let myself if you already have a girl-friend."

"Wait! What?"

"Remember that day we met on the beach? I thought you were meeting someone else when you bumped into me. And you thought I was her?"

"You mean, my sister? There is nobody else. I like only you." He hugs me tight. "Have a nice trip."

We talk and joke for a few minutes. I make sure to hug him back in farewell when he leans in one more time.

On the flight home, I think about everything that happened. I know things will be better with Brittany. I left the faded "twin" dress in her suitcase with an apology pinned to the sleeve.

In six months, I'll be able to see Dylan again when my family returns to Florida. He left a note with his phone number and a heart around his name in my hand as he left. I feel a happy sense of peace when I think about Angel finally reuniting with her family after all this time.

Calypso

My story begins with a mutiny.

A ship full of smelly, filthy men fed up with an insufficient captain, led by one with a rebellious spirit. Shouting, rallying, stomping. It is not my first mutiny, and far from my last. As I look at the waves below me I wonder if I'll ever get tired of this life.

The point of a sword digs into my back.

Did I mention that I am the captain?

"As is custom, you get a gun with a single shot."

Well, I *was* the captain. I gaze at the island in front of me. It's perfectly fine but rather small and not especially interesting compared to other islands where I have been marooned.

"Do you fools know what becomes of mutineers like your-selves?" I ask.

"They sail away and never look back!" cries Beasley Blythe, the new captain. The crew all cheer and rally with him.

"They never make it past the horizon. May Davy Jones have mercy on their souls," I look Beasley in the eye, "A captain always goes down with his ship."

There is a certain unease that silences the traitorous crew and I see a flicker of doubt in Beasley's eyes, but it's too late for them. I hop off the end of the plank, hearing many words from my former crew.

"Wait!"

"Stop!"

"We didn't mean it!"

"Serves us right for trusting a woman as our captain."

Unfortunately for them, I don't give second chances. Under the water, one of my friends cuts the rope that binds my hands. I swim ashore to my new home. Looking back to my ship feels like a stalemate staring contest. I expect them to leave; they expect me to come back. Instead, I raise the gun and shoot a single shot into the air, then drop it to the ground.

"Are you gonna off 'em?" A voice asks from the foliage.

"Well, did they maroon me?"

"Yeah."

"Then, of course."

"What are you waiting for?"

"Naomi, they were a wonderful crew," I sigh, "but traitors are traitors."

I thrust a hand forward and summon a storm. Dark clouds full of thunder and lightning close in on the boat. I hear shouts of calamity as the boat sways back and forth in the fierce winds. Beasley attempts to control the frenzied crew, but I witness a second mutiny barely a minute after the first. The boat desperately tries to escape the storm, but, as I promised, it goes down before it passes the horizon.

Naomi runs from the bushes and grabs my hand, pulling me straight to the sea.

"Do I have to come? Some of those guys were really young..."

"At least make an appearance so they know."

Naomi dives into the deeper water and swims out. I swim next to her all the way to the shipwreck, still sinking.

"Tonight, we feast!" the leader of the clan, Accordia, announces, holding up my hand. I blush. Former members of my crew look at me with horror as they drown.

Mutinies are always a whirlpool of emotions. Despite my anger at the crew for their betrayal, I mourn them as mermaids kill them. Despite their faults, every crew becomes a deep seeded part of my life.

"Leave no survivors."

I swim back to the island to start constructing a monument to the crew. I use sticks, grass, rocks and whatever else I can find to create a makeshift model of each crewmember. I do this to busy myself while the mermaids finish off the crewmembers. One by one, they bring the clothing ashore to dress the models. Now, my warning is complete as I dress each model and scribble a note on a nearby tree.

*These men led a mutiny against their captain on
the fair ship* Andromeda. *They now sail under Davy
Jones' command.*

We feast in the dining hall of the sunken ship. I get all the rations
from all the mermaids who are full from devouring my crew.

On land, mermaids have legs and are called sirens. They can only
stay on land for about a week before dying. I'm not a mermaid, myself, which is why I can be on a pirate ship for months without
needing to go back to the water.

I'm adopted.

The mermaids found me when I was and infant after my father
tossed me off of his ship in the middle of the sea. They had pity on me
and gave me gills for underwater breathing along with the ability to
summon sea storms at will.

They've raised me as their own since that time.

"You know, it's funny," Naomi says. "When we named you Calypso, we didn't know how many islands you would end up stranded
on."

We dine in the tattered quarters of the shipwreck, as we always
do after a mutiny.

"Are you going to look for a new crew today?" Accordia asks.

Dark ink fills the water around us as Davy Jones appears. I dive
under the table while the blackness conceals me. While hidden, I hear
a conversation between Accordia and Davy Jones.

"This lad has escaped my grasp no less than ten times…"

The mermaids have kept me hidden from Captain Jones because
they know that he wouldn't be pleased that my life was spared. Had I
died at sea, Davy Jones would have collected my soul and sold it to
the devil for gold. But because I was thrown into the water as an infant, I slipped by the notice of his crew. If he should see me with the
mermaids, he would know that I was a human. Unfortunately, it's hard
to stay hidden from him. When mermaids kill humans, Davy Jones
collects their souls and sells them to the devil. The mermaids get a cut
of whatever gold he gets from the souls they kill. Disguised as sirens,
the mermaids purchase luxuries at human markets that they can't get
underwater. In exchange for riches, they wreck ships and are the best
suppliers of souls for Davy Jones.

Once Davy Jones departs, I head to the tattered captain's quarters
on the sunken ship. Accordia brings me my share of gold, along with
wanted posters of Davy Jones' latest targets.

"Watch for these folk at Tortuga when you go recruiting."

I promise that I will before I go to bed.

Davy Jones is always on the lookout for the worst of the worst. The sinners so rotten that the devil himself is shocked. These vile humans have murdered innocent people and betrayed those that were loyal to them. The devil pays more for wickeder souls. In order to get these vile humans, Captain Jones puts their faces on the wanted posters to hand out to different mermaid clans so that they know who to target. When a crew maroons me and I sink their ship, our little mermaid clan gets lots of money for the souls of my crew. In turn, the mermaids cut me in on the gold that I assist them with.

Rarely do I find a man from the posters. Many of them are sailors, not pirates, but the payment is worth my while when I manage to find one.

Before I go to breakfast, I sift through the list of targets. Most of them are loosely classified by what they've done, or where they're located. None of the posters have all the information. Sometimes, there may be pictures and no names. In this batch, one man seems to have caught the Sea Demon's eye.

Eris Pratton.

The poster lists his misdeeds and his status as a pirate. A detailed sketch jumps off the page. The most useful bit of information is his exact location.

Nassau.

At breakfast, I show the poster to Accordia. I explain that I won't be recruiting a new crew at Tortuga. Later that afternoon, the mermaids recover the ship from the bottom of the ocean.

"What shall we call it this time?" Accordia asks.

"Sinann."

With the wave of her hand, Accordia changes the name from *The Andromeda,* to *The Sinann.*

"I presume this name has some importance?"

"She is the goddess of the Shannon River in Ireland."

"You're far too sentimental."

"Perhaps. Tell the ladies to set a course for Nassau. We sail at dawn."

The mermaids have become quite the crew after all my years spent as a pirate. If they could remain out of the water for long periods of time, I would keep them as my permanent crew. We would pillage the world together. Alas, that isn't possible.

After a week of sailing, the mermaids are weak and must return to the water. I have to sail the final stretch to Nassau alone. Sailing alone is a challenge. It's hard to maintain the massive ship on my own, but for brief moments I feel like I control the whole sea by myself. As freeing as it is, I prefer a crew when possible, especially when going to pillage towns.

A short walk from the docks in Nassau lies a tavern. That's where I go to look for my crew. I order a pint at the bar. It's hard to find men willing to work under a female captain, especially with my dark skin tone, but I've been doing it for years. Most will agree to anything when drunk enough.

"What is a pretty lass like yerself doin' in a place like this?" A young man takes the stool next to me. He has brown hair, fair skin, and eyes that sparkle like emeralds. He looks familiar, but I can't place him in my memory.

"I'm looking for a crew."

"Ah, well Nassau won't have what yer lookin' fer. These fools couldn't crew a rowboat, much less a ship." His accent is an odd combination of places. I can't quite pin it down, but his voice is smooth and cool.

"I usually recruit at Tortuga, but I heard of a man called Eris Pratton who lingers in these parts."

"Ah, so ye've heard of the one-man-wonder."

"Aye, you know him?"

"Perhaps…for the right price."

I slip him a small bag of gold and sip my drink. He raises his eyebrows as he takes it.

"Easier than I thought…" he mutters.

"Gold is meaningless when you're as rich as I have become. Now, do you know Eris Pratton or not?"

"I can do you one better—" He finishes his drink. "—I *am* Eris Pratton."

I sigh. *Of course.*

"May I ask how ye've heard of me?"

"You may," I say, "but I never reveal my sources."

"Fair enough, then may I ask *what* ye've heard of me?"

"I've heard you're quite the master at cheating death."

"Ha. I wouldn't call it cheating death so much as refusing to accept it." He orders another pint.

"Nevertheless, I've come to offer you the position of first mate."

"Hm," he shrugs, "What's in it for me?"

"I have far more riches than you could ever dream of. I will make you rich."

"If ye be so rich, then why not settle on land someplace?"

"I don't sail for gold, I never have. I sail for a love of the sea and the freedom it brings. I sail for the wind on my face and the salt on my skin. When I am on the sea, I am home."

Perhaps that isn't the entire truth. In the beginning I sailed to get revenge on my father. I sailed so that I could find him and kill him for what he did to me and my mother. As I started to sail with the mermaids, I discovered the joy of living on the sea, controlling a ship and commanding a crew. I fell in love with the life, and I never looked back.

"I don't quite believe ye, but I believe I've had just enough rum to accept yer offer."

I spend the rest of the night finding other unemployed sailors who've gotten themselves drunk enough to agree to sail with a woman. Many of them are wary until I bribe them with gold. By the end of the night, I have added thirty-five men to my crew. In the morning, I sail the ship out in deep waters.

Once the men wake up, I give them the speech that I give to every new crew.

"Welcome aboard!" Most of the men are dazed. "I am your captain, and all of you have agreed to be a part of my crew. If you don't remember that exchange, you probably should consider having less rum."

"What if some of us don't remember and we'd rather not be sailin' with the likes of ye?"

"Feel free to walk the plank. It's always open."

No one seemed ready to chance drowning to escape the ship. I hear Eris chuckle beside me.

"Are there any other questions?"

Everyone remains silent, giving mutinous looks to each other.

I bring out a map scavenged from a shipwreck. Eris looks over my shoulder

"Quite the map ye got there."

"I won it in a bet."

Eris watches in silence as I plan a route.

"Would ye like any help, Captain?"

"Have you nothing better to do?" I ask.

He flashes a smile. "Perhaps, but I find you more interesting."

I roll my eyes. He is quite the romantic. I wish he would use his idyllic sentiments elsewhere. There is nothing he needs to know about me, unless he wants to use it to stab me in the back.

"Why did ye start sailing? I know many a lady who wouldn't dream of leaving the land."

My ears burn at the question, though I know he's right.

"My father was a captain."

"Did he teach you to sail?"

"I never met him. I became a captain to find him."

Eris doesn't ask any more questions until later that night, when he joins me for dinner.

"So ye sail in search of your father. Ye want to meet him, yes? To know where you came from?"

"No."

"Ye want him to come back to yer mother?"

"No."

"What is it then?"

"Who wants to know?"

"I do."

"Why?"

Eris puts down his fork.

"There's something about ye, Calypso. I need to know ye."

I scoff. "There's not much to know about me."

"Ye mean not much ye want me to know."

"Nevertheless, I'm afraid you won't be getting to know me."

"As ye wish, Calypso."

He pours more wine into my glass. I see what he's trying to do.

"You're not going to get me drunk." I pick up the glass anyways.

"Not trying to. Let's talk of something else, shall we?" He pours some wine for himself.

"I feel that you have something in mind."

"The map. How did you come across it?" He drinks.

"I told you, it was a bet." I drink.

"But who did ye win it from?"

"A ruthless captain who went by the name of Edward Teach."

"Am I supposed to be impressed?

"I said he was ruthless, not that he was well known."

Eris laughs.

"Indeed. Now I'd like to ask about your life."

"Go ahead."

"How have you cheated death so many times?"

"It's rather simple." He finishes off his wine. "If you don't buy into superstitions, it's easy to circumvent them. I simply refuse to accept the notion that I am fated to die at any one moment. I'm a man of science. I fight death with potions. If I can survive, I will."

"Do you not believe in any myths? Mermaids, the Flying Dutchman, Davy Jones?"

"People who claim to have seen such things have been months at sea and are either starving, dehydrated or drunk. They're delirious and probably hallucinating."

"That's an interesting thought."

"What? Do you believe the stories?"

"The Flying Dutchman isn't real in my experience," I say, "but mermaids and Davy Jones are no joke."

"Ye've seen them?"

I look down at my drink and smile, seeing my reflection in what little wine remains there. He was a rare breed. I figured I'd have some fun with him while he was still around.

"I told you that I never met my father, yes?"

"Ye did."

"I've also never met my mother. She died when I was born." Eris smirks at his wine.

"You're far more interesting than I imagined." A warm feeling enters my heart, but I push it away. I can't get attached to him knowing that he's going to die.

"I was raised by mermaids."

Eris laughs. "No, you've had too much wine."

"You don't believe me?"

"No."

"How do you think I was raised?"

"I suppose in an orphanage."

"You think an orphanage would take me? Look at me, they would have sold me to a sugar plantation."

"That's no proof that ye were raised by mermaids."

"I'm not going to force you to believe me." I sit back in my chair and set my glass down, "Tell me more about your science. I've heard it described as witchcraft."

"Ha, far from it. I make medicines and potions—"

"Sounds like witchcraft."

"—and test them in order to prove their efficacy."

"A more advanced version of witchcraft?"

"If ye insist on seeing it that way…"

"Well what sorts of things do your potions do?"

"I have one that allows anyone to breathe underwater."

That would make him harder to kill in a mutiny.

"Have you cheated death using that one before?"

"Indeed, I have. I swam to safety in a shipwreck," he chuckles, "Of course safety meant a deserted island with a shrine to a mutinous crew."

I smile knowing that I had made the shrine.

Over time, I grow quite fond of Eris. He teaches me about his work, and he eventually starts to listen to me when I talk about myths.

"Ye say ye've survived a mutiny before?"

"Oh lots, my crew always regrets it."

"How?"

"I told you Eris, I was raised by mermaids. A little water is no problem."

"Ah yes, the mermaids."

"You still don't believe me, Pratton?"

"I'd love to believe you, Calypso, but it simply doesn't make sense."

"What part?"

"Ye know too much about yer father and yer mother. If ye were raised by mermaids, they wouldn't know those details. Either yer lying or they are."

I consider that. I know I'm not lying.

"I don't know *that* much about my father. I just know he was a pirate captain."

"And you want to kill him."

"He threw me into the ocean moments after my birth."

"It's more than that."

I sigh. "My mother was his prisoner. He raped her to conceive me. He threw me out because I wasn't a boy."

"Who told ye that?"

"The mermaids."

"How could they know everything happening on his ship?"

"Well...I don't know."

"I want to tell ye a story from the island I grew up on.

"When I was a mere infant, there was a man who fell in love with a slave woman. Others couldn't see past her lowly status, but he saw that she was a rare, enchanting creature.

"They wed in secret, and he hid her away from her master and the town for months. During that time, she became pregnant, and the couple was overjoyed. However, tragedy struck the night she gave birth.

"Complications arose, and the man's wife was dying. He sent for help, but the doctor refused to help her. She died, but the child survived.

"By then, the whole town knew about the forbidden marriage and disgraced child. They demanded justice. The man tried to flee on a simple rowboat, but he didn't get far before something in the water caught his attention. He dove in, and he was never heard from again."

I was silent. Something inside of me whispered that the story was about me.

"It sounds like he was attacked by mermaids. What happened to the child?"

"Everyone assumed she went down with her father."

"Are you suggesting…"

"That the story could be about ye? I am."

I let the implications from the story sink in for a minute. Eris has forced me to look at the situation from new angles. Everything I've ever been told seems wrong. I can't tell if I believe him. There's only one way for me to find out.

"Eris, you're in charge until I get back." Without another word, I run out of my quarters and dive off the edge of the boat.

"Accordia!" I shout. Right away, she appears with a few other mermaids.

"Is it a mutiny?"

"No. I need you to be honest with me."

"What are you talking about, Calypso?"

"I'm talking about my father. Did you kill him?"

Accordia lets out a nervous laugh, "Where would you get an idea like that?"

"You didn't answer my question."

"Calypso, sweetheart, we told you about your father."

"Are you sure you didn't just tell me that to control me? So that I would keep sailing and sending you crews to make you rich?"

"Your father didn't care about you! He abandoned you in a shoddy rowboat to die. All for a pretty face."

"No, you tempted him with your pretty voice. You used your magic to kill him. When you heard my cries, you felt guilty. Am I wrong?"

Accordia reaches out and touches my face, "You know I love you."

I smack her away. "I used to know that, but now I'm not so sure."

"I've given you a good life, better than any human would give you. You know what they would have done with you."

I turn away from her. "My father wouldn't have sold me. If you hadn't killed him, I would have had a fine life."

"Are you sure? Were you worth more than his status? At best, you would have been a house servant. At worst, he could have sold you. The only ship you would have sailed on was a cargo ship with others like you."

My heart crumbles. Accordia is right. Eris is right. All I know for sure is that I'm hopelessly lost. I swim back to the ship and climb up to the deck.

"Calypso…" Eris tries to comfort me, but I push him away.

"You're still in charge until further notice."

I lock myself in the captain's quarters and open a bottle of wine. I drink half of it over several hours of swirling thoughts.

Knock. Knock.

"Calypso?"

"Go away, Pratton. I don't want you seeing me like this."

"Please open the door." When I refuse to respond, he jokes with me. "You know I can pick locks."

He breaks into my room, but I refuse to look at him.

"Calypso, it was never my intention to hurt ye."

"You didn't hurt me. *They're* the ones who lied to me." I pick up the wine bottle, but Eris snatches it from me.

"I think ye've had quite enough of this." He pours himself a glass.

"I haven't felt so… emotional since I was a young girl."

"There's no shame in being human," he gulps down his wine in a matter of seconds.

"I don't know what I am anymore."

"I know that yer the most beautiful creature I've ever had the pleasure to know."

"Pratton, don't…"

"I'm not lying. I thought it was the rum the first time I saw ye, but I found that my feelings hadn't changed the next morning."

He strokes my face.

"Nobody's ever felt that way about me before."

My heart swells and I realize I might feel the same way about him. Eris leans over the table, slowly. I find myself leaning in too. It's a long first kiss.

"I should go to bed." I mutter. Eris tucks me in before leaving. When I wake up, my head is spinning. I see a plate on the table next to my bed. The memory of my kiss with Eris almost counters the hangover I'm suffering.

I sit up to eat. After a few minutes, Eris comes in to check on me.

"Are ye feelin' better this morning?"

"Not much, but I appreciate ye…you asking." Eris chuckles at my slip up. I laugh at myself, too.

A presence enters the room. It's a presence I know well.

It speaks, *"Ah, two cheaters have fallen in love. How fitting."*

I realize that Eris can't hear Davy Jones' whispers.

"The mermaids told me about you."

"How do ye feel about last night?"

I grin.

"Send him to me, Calypso, and I will give you anything you desire."

"I think I liked it."

I lean in and we kiss again.

"Calypso...I'm making you the offer of a lifetime. I can give you anything."

I grab Eris' head and pull him closer. I kiss him until I feel Davy Jones' presence leave.

"Pratton, Davy Jones is after you."

"What?"

"That's why I recruited you in the first place. He told the mermaids you'd cheated him, and he offered a reward for your death," his eyes grow wide. "The mermaids and I have been trapping sailors for years. All my past crews have marooned me. Once on shore, I sink the ship, and the mermaids profit from the sunken vessel."

"What does that have to do with me?"

"Davy Jones will give me anything I want for your death."

Eris sighs. "Will you make it quick?"

My heart stalls.

"I'm not going to kill you, Eris."

"Sounds like he was making ye quite the offer."

"He was, but the price was too steep."

He smiles.

The ship sways.

"No..."

Rain hammers the deck. Wind tears the sails. Waves rock the boat.

In all my years, I've never had a problem with storms. I can summon and dismiss them at will. This huge storm cannot be natural, and I realize that I must have angered Davy Jones.

I rush up to the wheel. I know our location and steer the ship straight toward the nearest landmass.

"Pratton, keep us on a straight course!"

Eris takes the wheel. I use all of my focus to try and dispel the storm. After several minutes, the rain thins out and we're on a steady course toward safety.

"Are ye all right, Calypso?"

I'm too exhausted to reply as I continue to fight the power of Davy Jones himself. "J-just get us to land," I mutter. I sit on the deck. My head pounds. My stomach spins. My breath is light. With no energy left, my body compensates by slowly shutting down.

"Calypso..."

"Land, Pratton! That's an order!" I bark.

He sighs as he steers us to land. The journey feels like an eternity, but I manage to hold the storm at a light rain. When we make port, Eris scoops me up and carries me into town with a small bag of gold.

"What's the name for the ship?"

"Calypso."

"Surname?"

"Uh...Pratton. Is there a hospital here?"

"Yes, down this street until the third left."

Eris moves as fast as he can to get me there.

"I'm really fine."

"No, yer not."

"Can't you make a medicine?"

"I can, but not out of nothing."

The hospital refuses to help me.

"Is she your slave?" A nurse questions us in the entryway.

"If I say yes, will you help her?" He begs.

"There is a slave hospital that way." The nurse points.

"Slave hospitals are not hospitals."

In the middle of a loud argument that is obviously going nowhere, I shoot the nurse.

"Just put me down somewhere and go find what you need. I'll be okay."

"I'll at least find ye a bed."

"No, you won't."

The inn won't admit me either.

"We don't serve her kind here."

"Why in hell not?"

The innkeeper just rolls her eyes and shuts the door.

"I told you, Pratton, nobody wants me. If you insist I have a bed, take me back to the ship."

He brushes a lock of my hair out of my face. The rain starts to pour.

"Please hurry and make a decision."

After laying me down in a dry spot, he leaves to find a general store. By the time he comes back, the intensity of the storm has increased. He starts a small fire with nothing more than a rock, a knife, and some dry grass.

"I knew you were a witch."

He barely flashes a smile as he quickly mixes ingredients in a small bowl and heats them.

"Some of the elements are mixed in with other stuff, so it won't be perfect."

"Don't talk to me about 'elements' just..." I feel myself getting weaker.

"Is that done?"

"It just needs to cool—"

"Give it to me."

"I'm not letting ye burn yerself like that."

He guards the bowl from me until it's cooled to a suitable temperature for me to drink. By then, the wind is picking up and I'm too weak to hold the bowl. Eris helps me drink the mixture.

"It'll be a slow process, but you should be feeling a little better."

I nod. Hours pass. It takes far longer for me to feel better than it did to get sick. By midnight, I'm well enough to head back to the ship and to command the crew away from this place.

"Ransack the town. Kill the innkeeper. Bring back supplies. Any money you find is yours."

Eris makes me stay in bed. Through the stained glass window, I can see smoke from the burning town. Soon after, everyone boards the ship.

"Get ready to sail. Is someone manning the cannons?"

"Aye. Always."

Eris gives me a quick kiss on the head before leading the crew to escape. Once we're safely away from the island and sailing smoothly, Eris comes back to me.

"Ye know, I thought once ye knew the truth about yer father, perhaps ye would want to settle on land," he says. "I'm beginning to believe that yer father wasn't the only thing keeping ye on the sea."

I sigh, "There's no life for me within society. Pirates are a more forgiving bunch. They're a band of rejects, just as I am rejected."

"I could build ye a house, and we could live there together. Nobody would bother us."

"Aye, just as nobody bothered my parents," Eris keeps quiet, "I told you Pratton, the sea is my home."

"But what if Davy Jones comes for us again? What if the sea is too dangerous?"

I press my head back into my pillow. If Davy Jones pursues me further, there will be nowhere on this earth for me. "Then I'll find an empty island and maroon myself."

He strokes my hair, tracing his fingers around my ear and down my neck. "I'd like to say that's a bad option, but..." he sighs, "it may well be yer best."

He tells me to get some rest. I awake after sunrise, feeling restored. I find Eris barking orders at the crew.

"Are ye sure yer well enough to be up here, Captain?"

"No, but here I am nevertheless."

I gaze at the cloud filled horizon. "I don't like this."

"We'll have to tread carefully."

I spend the following days rummaging through maps and searching for an island that would be safe, but I find nothing.

"We could go somewhere else entirely. We have the whole world to explore."

"No, we don't. Europe has claim to all of it already."

On my sixth day of map hunting, a storm hits. Once again, I steer the ship toward land before fighting the storm. This time, I have a vial of Eris' medicine ready.

"Take that the moment you need it."

I nod.

I take it once we get to a port. Eris takes me ashore, determined to find me a place to stay. Like the last port we visited, not a single place lets me inside. Even the tavern is forbidden to me.

"Perhaps we could sail to Tortuga to settle down." Eris smiles a little.

"Maybe."

Once we set off again, we head in the direction of Tortuga. Davy Jones is ruthless. He sends storm after storm with increasing frequency and intensity.

"Do you have a potion to help you breathe underwater?"

"Aye, why?"

"I don't know if I can fight off many more of these attacks. If the ship goes down, I don't want to lose you."

Closing in on Tortuga, the biggest storm hits.

"There is an island closer to our current location. Tortuga could take hours," Eris says, "What do you think, captain?"

"Tortuga, I never want to do this again."

I drink a vial of medicine before fighting the storm.

"Calypso. Let them die; let them all die. My offer is still on the table."

"No…"

"Calypso, Are ye all right?" Eris looks panicked.

Davy Jones appears next to me.

"*There is nowhere for you to live on land, they'll never accept you. You will never have the life of your dreams. You know that. You have doubts about Tortuga even now.*"

"Calypso." Eris is right in front of me.

"Steer the ship, Pratton!" I point to the wheel. He knows better than to argue with me.

Davy Jones leans down and grabs my face. "*You can't stay on the sea as long as the human is alive, and you can't be with him on land.*"

"I can and I will!"

"Calypso!"

"*You're living in a fantasy if you believe that.*"

"Go away."

"*You can't change the truth.*" He disappears.

I approach Eris.

"I'd like an explanation."

"You deserve one." I sniff and take a shaky breath. "Davy Jones was here. He wants me to kill you. He says it's the only way." I want to believe that Davy Jones is wrong, but I have lost all my hope.

My head spins. My heart aches.

"Calypso, there is another way, there has to be." His words, though simple, spark the last kindle of hope in my heart.

"Tortuga."

"Tortuga."

I draw closer to him, putting one hand on the wheel and the other around his waist. He takes his hand off the wheel and puts it around me.

"How are ye feeling?"

"Better than I usually do at this point."

He nods and looks at the sky. The clouds are thinning with the rain. Eris looks quite dashing with his hair stuck to his face and raindrops streaking down his cheeks. I hug his soaked form close to me.

"I love you, Eris."

He smiles, "I love ye too."

I realize that's the first time I've called him by his first name.

I take a shaky breath.

"Are ye all right?"

"Y-yeah, just… you know…"

He pets my wet hair.

"If ye need to sit down—"

I nod.

"We're almost there."

"Don't lie to me Pratton, I know where we are."

Lightning flashes, I'm losing control. I gasp for air before sitting down and leaning on Eris' legs.

"Ye know where the medicine is, right?"

"You ask every time."

"Sorry, I just worry about ye is all."

"I know."

After a few more minutes, I go back to my room to get another dose of the potion. Even after I take it, I'm too weak to go back on deck. Instead, I lie in my bed until we reach Tortuga. Too weak to cry for help, I sink into a stupor.

"Calypso!"

Eris rushes to my side and fumbles with a vial that he pours into my mouth.

"Calypso?"

"Eris…"

He strokes my hair and face.

"I'm sorry, Eris."

"What do ye have to be sorry for?"

"I laid down and I didn't realize…" I choke on my words and start coughing.

"Shh. Don't talk. You're okay. Just rest. The storm is gone."

I nod, "Did we make it?"

"Yes, but we can begin the search for our future when you're well."

It doesn't take long for me to drift off to sleep. When I awake, Eris is curled up next to me. I shake him a little and his eyelids flutter.

"I swear I was only asleep for a second," he mumbles. As he starts to get up, I pull him back by his shirt collar and kiss him.

"Let's go find our future."

⚜

Eris is the one who inevitably has to buy the land and hire the builders. Although he's the legal owner, I never let him forget whose money he's using. We elope by holding the priest hostage. After a year of building, our home is complete. Everything falls into place perfectly, except one thing.

"Alas, ye can only be the Lady Pratton within these walls." He dances me around the parlor.

"Aye, but I can be the Captain Calypso in town."

He sighs. "Perhaps, but with only old tales to tell."

"I can always make up new ones."

Eris laughs and pulls me into a hug.

"We've arrived, Calypso. This is our future."

And I don't regret a moment of it.

SYDNEY BEAL

Case 264

WMPO (Worldwide Magic Protection Organization)
Case 264: Perspective of Agent Stevie Johnson, age 16.

"Are you kidding me?" I smack the handlebars of the Jet Ski with my palms in frustration.

"Stephanie, it's okay." Dad reassures me.

"It's Stevie, Dad. And how is this okay? We've been tracking this vampire for months and we miss him because of a freaking half tank of gas!" I watch the criminal fade into the distance and become nothing more than a speck on the horizon. We were so close!

Seated behind me, Dad begins shuffling around. I turn to see what he's doing but the sudden shift in balance makes the Jet Ski wobble, so I stop. He's probably just checking his phone for contacts in the area who know about the WMPO and are willing to help out. "We've got a contact in the area, heading this way." Nailed it. "The vamp's bound to run out of gas sometime soon and there's nowhere else for him to go. We'll be able to grab him."

I nod. I'm just so tense. This is my first case with a vampire since I officially started doing fieldwork as an agent of WMPO and I want to prove that I'm capable. Sure, I've helped out in the office since I was eight but that was just paperwork. I barely got out in the field last year. I don't want to screw this up.

"Sounds good. Have you contacted them yet?" I ask.

"Calling him right now," Dad says.

Despite the setback, I can't help but notice how beautiful the ocean is today. Sunlight glints off the blue waves that carelessly roll past us. I lift up my ponytail, letting the sea salt breeze cool my sweaty neck. The adrenaline pumping through me slows, letting my muscles relax.

"Hey, John?" Dad says. "We just ran out of gas on a chase. Do you think you could give us a lift?" Dad pauses. "Yeah, I get that it's really funny." Another pause. "You can stop laughing. It's not *that* funny. Uh huh. See you soon then." Dad hangs up. "Hmmm." He makes a worried kind of sound.

"What's up?" Everything sounded great from this end. This John we called must know my Dad well or there's no way he'd be laughing at us. Not with Dad's 6'3" height and a build like a bull. He's really stern if you don't know him well, with this kind of bodyguard vibe.

I try to turn to face him again out of habit before the wobble of the Jet Ski stops me. I hate not being able to read body language while I talk with someone. Something I picked up from my dad over the years. "Can he not pick us up or something?"

"No, he said he'd be happy to give us a ride," he says. "But he sounded off. I'm not sure what, but something's definitely up."

"Well, how long have you known him? Maybe you were just reading him wrong," I offer.

"I've known him for nearly five years. And he's usually an easy read," he responds. I wish I was at my dad's level of reading people. If we'd been face-to-face, my dad would've been able to figure out why John was so off. He's just not so good with only voice inflections.

"Do you think we should grab a ride with him then?" I ask. "If something's up, maybe it would be better to wait for someone else."

"There's no one else close enough. This is our only shot to catch that last vampire."

I look up when I hear shouting. A ship is bearing down on us.

"That was quick," Dad says. I nod slowly, watching the boat suspiciously. He's right. They found us way too fast. "We're gonna want to stick together while we're on the ship. Keep your gun handy."

I nod again as a rope is thrown down to us. Slipping a leg over the seat, I grab hold of the rope, deftly pulling myself up the side of the boat. Once aboard, I swing over the railing, landing lightly on my feet. I glance around cautiously but it looks like a pretty standard crew. I see only a couple men on deck cleaning and fishing but I assume there's more on the floor below or in the cabin. Most of the men glance up at me before returning to work. One man studiously stares at the ground, refusing to meet my gaze.

"Welcome aboard." It looks like the captain—neatly trimmed beard with thick eyebrows, dressed in a well-worn blue T-shirt and a pair of khaki shorts. The only thing that makes him stand out is a jagged set of four scars starting just below his left eye and ending at his jawline, along with scars across his bulky arms. "You must be Stevie," he says with a smile. "I'm John Black." John grabs one of my dad's thick hands with both of his, shaking it heartily. "Travis!" he exclaims. "It's been too long! How's the WMPO treating you?"

"Same as always." Dad shrugs. "How's retirement?"

John shrugs in return. "Can't complain. Still have to work to get that little bit extra to make ends meet. Half of a retirement fund doesn't quite cut it. But it's fine work. Missed that salty smell of the ocean and the wind in my face anyway."

"Why'd you retire?" I hope it's not a delicate subject. He looks way younger than the normal retirement age. Of course, WMPO is an organization dedicated to catching mythical and magical creatures that break the law—mostly the laws dealing with staying under the radar of regular humans—so it can get dangerous. I can't even name how many times my dad has come home with some kind of injury that I've had to fix up. Dad says I would make a good nurse with all the practice I've had on him, but that's not my kind of thing.

Ever since I was little, I've watched my dad and wanted to be just like him, hunting down the bad guys and saving people. It's not quite that simple to me anymore, now that I know about all the procedures and paperwork, as well as the bloodier side of the job, but I still love it. The blood-pumping chase, the thrill of the catch, even just interacting with the creatures interests me. I mean, come on, what other sixteen year old girl can say she met a werewolf (who, for the record, was actually a decent guy) last weekend?

John points to the scars across his face. "Werewolf." He lowers his voice dramatically. "Your dad and I had been tracking him through the woods for days. On day nine, we set a trap. We camped out, waiting for him to walk into the trap, but he'd already seen us. He acted as bait while his mate circled us from behind. We caught him under a net and, while we neared to get in the killing strike, she leapt at us, transforming mid-air. I spun around and caught her, throwing her into a tree. I sprinted to stab her, but she dove at me again, catching me off guard. I landed on my back, pinned underneath her. She snarled and tried to turn me with a bite, but I grabbed her jaws and held her back. She clawed me and nearly knocked me out. But I held on, my chest soaked with blood, holding her back with all the strength I had left. Just when I was about to give up, she froze and fell over with a weak whimper, a spear protruding from her back from where Travis pierced her heart. I pulled myself up with your father's hand, and we walked triumphantly back."

I raise an eyebrow. "And left the bodies?"

"No, of course not," he says. "We threw them in the back of the truck."

"And you landed and broke no bones? From a werewolf hit?" I ask, smirking a little. "I don't believe that for a second."

My dad laughs proudly. "John likes to be dramatic."

"I just like to make it a little more exciting, that's all," he protests.

I look at my dad. "So what really happened?"

"We'd been tracking him for a day or two and he got the jump on us. John was so beat up and bloody, to this day, I still don't know how he made it out alive."

John shakes his head. "Fine, spoil it all for her," he says good-naturedly. "That's impressive though. You've trained her well."

Dad nods in agreement and gives me a small smile. I return the smile, trying not to show how proud the comment makes me feel. He's not one to throw out compliments.

"Would you like something to eat? It'll be a while before we catch up with the vamp." My stomach growls just as I'm about to politely refuse, and John laughs. "I'll take that as a yes. Hey, Ryan!" He calls to a sailor with sandy hair.

The sailor sets down his fishing pole and heads toward us. As Ryan gets closer, I notice his movements are stiff and his muscles are tense.

"Show these two to the galley," John says.

Ryan nods, turning to us with a smile and waving in the direction I assume to be the kitchen. "It's this way. You'll love the food." Ryan keeps talking, but I've already stopped paying attention. I look up at the corners of his blue eyes, noticing that there aren't any wrinkles. It isn't a real smile. He's just putting on a show. But why? I look over at my dad, who's scanning the deck with squinted eyes. Does he know what's up yet? Ryan leads us downstairs to a small kitchen area, where a couple sailors are eating lunch and a woman stands peering into a fridge.

"Here we are," he says. "Hey, Cook!"

The woman by the fridge turns to face us. She looks to be around mid to late 30's, with her auburn hair pulled up in a bun. A dusting of flour covers her left cheek and blue apron.

"Yeah?" she says, glancing at us and giving us a quick smile before returning her gaze to Ryan. "What's up?"

"You wanna get these two some grub? They're the ones hitching a ride with us for the next couple hours."

"'Course." She waves us over with a smile.

"Sorry to ditch you but I've gotta get back. Jen here will take care of you though." Ryan apologizes as he cracks his knuckles. We turn as he hurries up the stairs.

"What are you guys in the mood for? I've got turkey sandwiches or some chicken noodle soup in bread bowls." A smile is plastered on her face. Again, fake smile. I guess it makes more sense here, because she doesn't know us and has to put on a smile to save face, but with all the other sketchy stuff that's going on…definitely suspicious.

"I'll take the sandwich. And could I get some water?" I ask.

"Sure thing. What about you?"

"Same here." My dad analyzes her body language. Her smile gets more genuine when she sees him looking her over.

"I'll be right back with that." She gives Dad a flirtatious wink. I roll my eyes as she walks to the drink machine in the back to get our water.

"Come on, Dad!" I complain quietly.

"What?" he asks, confused.

"Can't you be a little more…discreet when you're analyzing women?" I whisper.

"Why? They always assume I'm just checking them out."

"Exactly! Do you have any idea how awkward it is?"

He smiles, about to say something, but is cut off by the cook's return.

"Here's those sandwiches and two cups of water." She hands us our food. "Enjoy."

"Thanks." Dad gives her a blinding smile as he takes his lunch, lingering slightly when their hands touch before pulling away. I turn around before I have to see more of it. Dad follows me to a table, and I can hear him chuckling behind me.

"You flirted back just because of what I said, didn't you?" We sit down at a small metal table. It might have seemed pretty tame to anyone else, but for my dad, that was practically a proposal. He never flirts with a woman, except when he wants to tease me. I take a sip of water, letting out a content sigh as the cool water slides down my throat.

"Well, when you give me an opportunity like that..." He laughs as I let out a huff.

"Okay, but seriously, what's up with this?" I lower my voice. "Everyone's on edge."

"They're just on edge when we're around." He lowers his voice as well. "What else did you see?"

"Well, I saw..." I trail off. "Are you trying to use this as a teaching moment? Don't you realize that..."

"Shh!" He looks around. One of the guys glances over at us but quickly returns to his conversation when he sees us looking back. "Just think of it as a training exercise. I can't have my eyes everywhere. What did you see?"

"No one has real smiles. They're all tensed up. And they're all..." I pause, trying to think of the word.

"Overly enthusiastic about everything?" he finishes.

I nod.

"It's all fake because they're hiding something. And John mentioned that we were chasing a vamp but I never said what we were chasing. It's a trap. We've got to get out of here."

"And go where, Dad?" I blink, trying to clear my vision. How come it seems like the room is spinning? Maybe it's just because I'm dehydrated and on a moving boat. I guzzle some water, hoping it'll get rid of the dizziness. "The Jet Ski is out of gas and I didn't see any other boats upstairs."

"Yeah, and none of my other contacts are nearby." He absentmindedly scratches his scruff. My vision starts getting dark around the edges as Dad keeps talking. I waver in my chair, trying to keep my balance. "Well, we have our weaponry, so—"

+

I jerk up, frantically looking around in confusion. The room is dark, but the light streaming through a small window on the door is enough for me to assume this is some kind of storage room. Large crates and barrels are stacked neatly against the walls, labeled with things like "nets" and "life jackets." I try to reach up to brush some hair out of my face, but realize my hands are tied around a wooden post behind me with a piece of rough rope.

"Dad?" I whisper raspily. "Dad?"

"I'm here."

I gasp when I see his face. His eye is starting to swell and darken, and his jaw is starting to bruise. A trail of blood lines his face, starting from the top of his head and ending at his jaw. I hope all his damage is only on the outside. We really don't need any internal damage right now. "What happened? Are you okay?"

"I'll be fine. They slipped some kind of drug in your water."

I roll my eyes at myself, smacking my head against the post. I'm such an idiot! First rule of being in enemy territory: never eat or drink anything. I didn't even think about drinking the water. I was so thirsty.

"Well, if it makes you feel any better, they got me without any drugs." He winces as he straightens. "They had to resort to more violent methods."

"What do they want?" I try to work out the knots.

Dad shrugs. "I just woke up a couple minutes earlier than you. I have no idea. It's not like they made demands while they were trying to knock me out."

"Can you get your wrists untied?" I'm still working on mine.

He squints at me quizzically. "Are you kidding? They're sailors. Knots are their specialty."

I stop working at them. He's right. There's probably no way I could get them undone, even if I could see them. I look up when the door squeaks open, blinding us with the light.

"Grab them," a voice says reluctantly.

I hear someone walking around me and a pair of hands unties me as I blink rapidly, trying to adjust to the light. They finish and tie my hands back together behind me, pulling me up to my feet. I stumble as they pull me forward. I can hear them doing the same to my dad. My eyes adjust enough that I can see that John is the one ordering his men. My stomach drops. I hoped one of his sailors had gone behind his back to get us. No such luck.

"Travis Johnson!" Someone calls Dad's name when we reach the main deck.

The vamp we'd been chasing is now strutting toward us, his head tilted cockily to one side. His name is Drake Stevens. We've had a file for him since he'd been a suspect for a murder case. He's part of one of those weird cults that look forward to becoming vampires. They wait to become vamps until they're twenty-three and have at least one kid, so they can continue the tradition. "Nice to finally meet you when you're not chasing me all over town," Drake says.

Dad straightens and pulls his shoulders up, glaring down at him.

"What, no comeback?" he sneers.

Dad just keeps glaring until Drake punches him, sending him sprawling out of his guards' hands and face-first onto the deck.

"Just got a fresh batch of blood so I'm feeling nice and strong. AB positive, my favorite."

Dad groans as the guards—probably some of Drake's men—pull him back up to his feet. I look around as he continues to taunt my dad. John stands off to one side, not meeting my eyes. He's ashamed, as he should be. So why did he do this? Will he help us get out?

I try to get a read on the other sailors. Two of the men (probably half vamps, judging by their single elongated canine and their ability to stand in the sun) are new and obviously on Drake's side, but the rest...I can't tell. Most don't seem too happy about what's going on, but they don't look too motivated to stop it, either.

In their defense, they probably haven't worked with creatures like this before. But, they don't look scared, so they must have been told about magical creatures at least. I can't judge them too harshly for not wanting to help, though. If I hadn't been so well trained to take down animals like these, there's no way I'd voluntarily put myself in the middle of a fight like this. We're on our own.

I look around for some kind of escape. Drake's Jet Ski is pulled next to ours, on the side of John's ship and tied to the railing with rope. If we can get away from our guards, we could probably get away on that. Assuming there's enough gas in the tank to get us to land.

All my plans involving any kind of swimming go out the window when one of the men holding me attaches a large metal weight to my feet. There's no way I'll be able to get away now. At least they want us alive for some reason, or we'd already be dead. Maybe we'll get a chance later.

"—and then you took away my family!" Drake lands another punch in Dad's stomach.

I wince as Dad wheezes, the wind knocked out of him. I've just remembered the other major thing on Drake's file. There were some complications with his transformation, so now he has some...issues. Things like a fiery temper, a tendency to obsess, and dramatic mood swings.

Suddenly, it all becomes clear. Why he's doing this. Why he's got such a grudge against my dad. "Your...brother." He turns to me, and I immediately regret my outburst, but I meet his gaze steadily as he stalks toward me. "Your brother was the one that died."

I hadn't been with my dad on that case, but I'd read the report. Drake's brother had been pulling something out of his pocket—a vial of blood to hand off as a way of disarming—but my dad thought he was pulling out some kind of weapon and shot.

"Yeah, he just *died*," he says, making air quotes with his fingers. "That's a nice way of putting his murder! And then you took my sister! And I know how your justice system works," he rants, spittle flying from his lips.

I fight the urge to use my shoulder to wipe the spit from my cheek.

"There isn't any justice in it! Because you guys don't believe in anything that isn't human! She was only fourteen!"

I just raise an eyebrow. "Fourteen with a death sentence at twenty-three."

I see Dad roll his eyes right before Drake slaps me. I gasp, but straighten, spitting blood on the deck. Hostage rule #8: don't speak to the kidnapper unless it's absolutely necessary. And apparently you shouldn't sass them when you talk to them either.

"It's not a death sentence! It's a rebirth! A new way of life!" He takes a deep breath before considering me closely. "Get rid of her. We just need one of them."

His two henchmen holding me exchange glances. "You mean...?"

Drake spins around. "What do you think, you moron? Throw her overboard!"

Panicked, I look over at Dad. He always has a way out. He's always got a plan. But my anxiety grows into panic when I see the same terror I feel mirrored on his face.

"But...sir..." one of them stutters.

"It's murder," the other finishes.

Drake rolls his eyes. "And what do you think sucking people's blood is? A friendly kiss?"

"But we need that blood to survive. This is cold-blooded murder. And she's just a girl," the second one replies.

Drake sighs before grabbing me by my throat, lifting me up in the air. I desperately strain against the rope around my wrists, trying to get air. Drake pulls my face close to his, his breath warm on my face. His stench of blood intensifies.

"And just like my sister's life ended when she went into your justice system, so will yours."

My eyes widen, begging silently for mercy. I can't die now! There's so much I haven't done!

"Drake!" John shouts.

I look over at him, unable to move anything but my eyes. My struggling gets weaker, the air running out quickly.

"You said you just wanted Travis and then you'd let my family go! You said nothing about the girl!"

Drake rolls his eyes. "That's because we didn't know she'd be here. But here she is, so we get to improvise. She's one of them. She's got to go."

John shakes his head. "No. I won't let you!"

He lunges toward me but Drake swiftly lifts me higher in the air, throwing me overboard with one hand.

I scream hoarsely as I fly backward, plummeting to my death.

Every sound around me mutes when I hit the shockingly cold water, the temperature difference feeling like an abrupt punch to the stomach. I try to hold my breath but I can't stop gasping for air after just being strangled. I try to swim to the surface, try to fight for survival, but the weight is too heavy, and the movements are too awkward with my hands tied.

I drift down into the deep, my lungs burning as the surface slowly fades farther and farther away from me. My eyes grow heavy, everything slowing down until the movement of the waves feels as slow as sliding molasses. I close my eyes, waiting, just waiting for death to inevitably come. There's nothing left that I can do. I'm going to die down here, and my dad's going to die up there, and no one will know what happened.

Something grabs me by the waist, yanking me up. I blearily try to look around. Who grabbed me? Is it an angel? Are angels even real? I'd never spent much time thinking about where I'll go after I die. It never seemed important until now, when I'm actually faced with it.

We race upward, going as fast as when Dad and I were in a high-speed chase to catch a dragon. I close my eyes again, about to give in to the fogginess and bursting lungs, when my head breaks the surface. My eyes fly open as I gasp for air, coughing up water, blinking quickly to clear my vision.

"It's okay!" someone calls from behind as they keep pulling me.

I whirl around, trying to free myself from whatever is holding me, still choking on water.

They stop, trying to calm my thrashing. "Stop! You're safe! Stop wriggling around!"

I pause for a second, trying to turn and see what's going on. Something is shoved into my mouth. I try to spit it out, but a hand is pressed over my lips, stopping me.

"Just swallow it, for Triton's sake!"

I unwillingly swallow whatever it is and immediately cough up the rest of the water in my lungs. I take a deep breath, unconsciously smiling as the air fills my body. I turn to see who saved me.

"Gwen?" I ask in confusion when I see her face. Gwen is a mermaid we helped a while back when a dark mermaid had been using sorcery against some of the higher ups, and Gwen, as the crown princess, needed to put a stop to it. But, since they aren't allowed to have dungeons anymore because of WMPO laws, she asked us to come in. We ended up saving her life when the dark mermaid came after her.

The mermaid holding me up laughs. "Close. I'm Gwen's younger sister, Sierra. I'd shake your hand, but then I'd have to drop you." She laughs again.

I nod then remember Dad. He's still on the boat! Who knows what Drake could be doing to him? "My dad," I panic. "He's on that boat, and he's in trouble. You've got to take me back there!"

She shakes her head. "No way! They'll just kill you some other way where I won't be able to save you."

I look down and realize she got the weight off and untied my hands, probably while I was almost unconscious. I jump out of her hold, pushing off her tail to swim to the boat.

"Okay, just stop it." She grabs me again.

I fight against her but her grip is relentless.

"I meant I'm not taking you there alone. I'll send out a call and see who shows up. There's bound to be some mers around that are willing to help someone who helped save the queen. Can you tread water?" I nod. "All right. I'm going to dive under and send out a call. Don't do anything stupid while I'm gone."

She dives under, sending a spray of water into my face with her purple tail. I hear some kind of vibration go through the water before she comes back up, flipping her blue hair out of her face. "All right. Now we wait."

"For how long? He needs our help now!"

She holds up her hands defensively. "Three minutes. Give them three minutes."

I frown but reluctantly nod in agreement.

"And while we're waiting..." she closes her eyes and holds her amulet. The amulets help mers channel their power. The water beneath me solidifies into some kind of gel like substance. "Now I won't have to hold you until the others get here."

I let myself fall into the seat of goo behind me. It's surprisingly comfortable, like one of those chairs that you sink into and it sort of envelops you. My head and shoulders rest above the surface, the waves occasionally splashing my face. My thoughts spin anxiously as the seconds tick by slowly, each minute passing like a century. What's happening to my dad? Is he even still alive? How many mers will show up? Will it be enough?

"It's got to have been three minutes by now." I start to climb out of my chair. "Let's go."

She holds up a finger. "Wait. Here they come."

Waves start to build, and I feel movement under the water. I look around frantically, trying to see what's going on beneath me. A head pops up next to me, and I jump in surprise, nearly falling off my seat. It's a teenage boy, with a mop of bright red hair. He grins at my surprise.

"Did I scare you?" he asks, an impish look on his face.

Sierra swats his arm. "Come on, Quentin, quit messing around. Where's everyone else? I felt more people come."

"They wanted me to come see what was going on before they join us. You know how they are about going above water."

Sierra and I both nod. A lot of the older merpeople have a horrible fear of going above the water, but the younger generation doesn't really see a problem with it.

Sierra gestures toward me. "This is… I never got your name, did I?"

Quentin bursts out laughing. "No wonder Aunt Merideth thinks you still need manner lessons!"

"Wait, aunt?" I ask, raising an eyebrow.

Sierra rolls her eyes. "Yeah, Quentin's my cousin."

"Technically, second cousin…" he says.

Sierra gives me a patronizing, look-what-I-have-to-deal-with look. "Right. Second cousins," she says. "And I didn't get her name because I was too busy trying to save her life and then stop her from getting herself killed again, for your information."

Quentin looks at me questioningly. "Is she just being dramatic, or were you actually—"

"It's my dad. He's in trouble." I point toward the boat. "I don't have time right now to give any other details. "They threw me overboard and I have no idea what they're doing with him."

Quentin nods. "All right. I'm sure the others will be happy to help. Just knock the boat over, right?" he asks.

I shake my head. "Most of the people on that boat are innocent, even if they aren't doing anything to help. It sounds like the captain was blackmailed into catching us. And then what if something happens to my dad?" I take a deep breath. "What if you guys use that fountain spell of yours to get up to their level, then take them out from there?"

Sierra and Quentin nod slowly. "Sounds more risky, but you're right. We can't risk killing anyone besides the vamps," Sierra says.

Quentin nods in agreement. "I'll go tell the others."

He dives under and returns a few seconds later with two mers. One is a woman with sleek green hair who looks to be in her early thirties but is probably much older, based on the slowing of the aging process once they get into their twenties. The other is a man with navy blue, almost black hair, with thick biceps and an amulet that shows at least fifty years of experience, though he barely looks to be in his forties.

"Everyone good on the plan?" Sierra asks.

Everyone nods.

"I'll carry, um…" Quentin stumbles.

"Stevie," I smile a little. For all his teasing about not knowing my name, he didn't even get it.

He gives a sheepish smile. "Right. I'll carry Stevie."

He offers me his hand. I take it and step off my chair. He cradles me in his arms, making sure I'm secure before nodding to Sierra.

"Let's go." She waves them onward.

We take off, heading toward the boat. Sierra took me a lot farther than I thought. The boat is a good quarter of a mile away. If I weren't so focused on saving my dad, Quentin would have been very distracting, his muscles tight against my back, his breath warm against my cheek…but, of course, I'm focused.

When we get close enough for the people on the boat to see us, Quentin tells me to hold my breath. I barely have time to inhale before he dives under to travel the rest of the way to the boat. We surface quietly next to the hull and I take a deep breath, trying to be as silent as possible.

"Ready?" Sierra asks. The rest of our team nods. "Then let's go."

Each of the mermaids and mermen gather the water beneath them before lifting up their arms, shooting them upward. I jump onto the boat when Quentin and I are high enough, and land on the deck, looking for my dad.

The vampires immediately turn, charging toward us. I dodge out of the way of one vamp, spinning around him before jumping up and knocking him down with a kick to the back. Another vamp comes at me and I pull out a silver knife. He looks at me with fear in his eyes, but he jumps forward anyway. I spin to the side, slashing his back as he passes. He screams as the silver burns him, collapsing on the deck.

He continues to groan as I turn to look for my dad. I notice John laying unconscious on the ground, blood streaming from his nose. Glad he decided to not be a coward anymore and fight.

"Dad!"

He's kneeling in a patch of shade. Drake is pointing a gun to his head while holding him up by the back of his shirt. I pull out my gun, pointing it at him, hoping he won't see through my bluff. There's no way my gun will work after it went in the ocean with me. But I can't take him on in a fight. Not when he's hyped up on blood.

Drake steps to the side, using my dad as a shield. "Don't take another step—"

I stop, hardly breathing. Dad's face is bloody and swollen. He barely looks conscious. Drake won't actually shoot, will he? I try to think rationally but I'm too emotional.

"—or I'll shoot," Drake continues. "Let me get back to my Jet Ski, and I'll…"

A burst of water hits him from behind, knocking him on the ground. Dad falls limply beside him with a thud. The vampire tries to stand back up, but John, who apparently regained consciousness while I was distracted, has already cuffed him, planting a foot on his back to keep him down. I race to my dad's side, rolling him on his back to see the damage.

"Dad?" I shake his shoulder gently. "Dad!" I look up at Quentin who was the one to knock Drake down. "He's not waking up!" There's a gunshot wound in his stomach. That must have happened when I was under the water. He's bleeding out, not to mention possible brain damage from hitting his head. "Quentin, can you pull him overboard? I need to call someone and figure out what to do."

He nods as I grab my dad's phone. Quentin creates a pool of water under Dad and slides him and the water over the side of the boat while I dial my dad's best friend on the force.

"Mike! My dad's hurt. He got shot in the stomach and probably has a concussion and a lot of other injuries. I'm going to ask a merman to drop him off on the shore but I need you to get him to a hospital. I've got to stay behind and get this case figured out."

"Slow down, Stevie," he says. "What happened?"

"The vampire we were chasing? It was a trap."

"Okay, you've got to stay with him," Mike says. "He needs you, and you need to stay with him for your peace of mind."

"But what about the vampire?" I ask. "I've got to make sure he doesn't go anywhere."

"I'll watch him," John offers.

I glare back. "You think I'd trust you after what you just pulled?"

"We'll watch him, too," Sierra says.

I look at her gratefully. "Thank you."

I run to the side where the vamp's Jet Ski waits. Quentin creates a fountain to gently lower me to my dad's limp body. "You won't go fast enough," he says.

"Thanks for the encouragement," I snap.

"That's not what I meant. I meant, I can help you. I can swim him to the shore while you use the vehicle. I'd carry you both if I could."

"Please... get him there fast."

Quentin nods, giving me a salute with a smile before putting some kind of bubble over my dad's head to prevent water from getting into his lungs and taking off. I watch them go for a second to make sure my dad's secure before hopping on the Jet Ski. I sigh with relief when I see that there's enough gas to get me to shore. I start it and take off, but Quentin was right. He's much faster than I am. Regardless, I push the Jet Ski as hard as I can, the engine screaming beneath me.

By the time I make it to shore, the ambulance is already there, crowds surrounding them. I slide off the Jet Ski and race down the boardwalk.

"Let me through!" I yell at the crowds, throwing elbows to get past. "That's my dad. Let me through!" I make it to the front, but the ambulance is already taking off, sirens screeching.

"Whoa, where do you think you're going?"

"That's my dad in there!" I point to the ambulance. "I have to be with him. I have to make sure he's okay."

The police officer glances at his partner. He waves him on. "Go. Get her to her dad. But come back and pick me up, will ya?"

The officer nods and we bolt toward his car. We jump in, and he pulls out with a sharp twist of the wheel, flicking on his lights. The siren screams, but I hardly notice it with my racing thoughts. He's hurt badly. But he has to make it. He just has to.

+

I pace impatiently in the waiting room. It seems like it's been days since he went in, though it's really only been a few hours. A surgeon comes out and I turn abruptly to face him.

He gives me a small smile. "Your dad pulled through."

I breathe a sigh of relief.

"He's not out of the woods yet, but in all likelihood, he'll survive. We'll keep him here and monitor his progress."

I nod and he leaves as Mike comes running in, giving me a giant bear hug before pulling away and looking at me.

"I just missed you," he pants. "You were pulling out of the parking lot in that police car as I was pulling in, but then I had to go take care of the vamp. How's your dad?"

I smile in response. "They said he pulled through, that he's still at risk, but he should make it."

"That's the best news I've heard all day." He smiles as he hands me a small shell. "Sierra was worried about you. She sent this so you could talk to her and let her know how things turned out. And, ah, Quentin also wanted to hear from you."

I examine it, turning it on both sides. "How do I use it?"

"I'll show you in a bit. Right now you need to be with your dad."

I nod. He's right. I can worry about that later.

"Excuse me," Mike says to a short nurse with a blond bob. "We're looking for her dad. He just came in with a gunshot wound and a concussion a couple hours ago and he just got out of surgery. Could you let us know where he is?"

"Yes, of course. Travis Johnson, right?"

Mike and I nod.

"Right this way." She leads us to a small room where my dad's lying in a bed with white blankets, hooked up to machines, still unconscious.

"Let me know if you need any more help," she says. I nod and she leaves us.

"I'll give you guys a second. Just let me know when it's okay for me to come in," Mike turns and leaves as well.

I pull up a chair and sit, my leg bouncing nervously. After a couple minutes, my dad's eyes open blearily. He looks around, trying to make sense of where he is.

"You're in the hospital," I say.

He turns to me, a smile coming to his lips when he sees me. "Stevie, what happened?"

"I came in and took out the vamps with the help of some mermaids and mermen. One of the mermen got you to shore, and I rode the Jet Ski."

"And left the vamps? That's against protocol," he says with raised eyebrows.

I gape at him. "You were hurt, Dad! I know protocol but Mike said that..." I trail off when I see him smiling. "You're joking."

"Of course, I am." He lets out a laugh, then winces, grabbing his chest. "You really think I'd be mad about you saving my life? I'm proud of you, sweetheart."

A swell of pride fills my chest and I smile. "Well, I better let you rest."

Dad nods. "Sounds good. I'll see you soon."

I start to leave but then turn. "By the way, the police are asking what happened. I told them I wasn't there for it, I just found you later, so have fun figuring that out."

He groans. "So you throw the guy doped up on drugs under the bus?"

"Pretty much." I walk out, a smile ghosting my lips.

Author Bios

ALLIE STAFFIERY, AGE 16, is passionate about writing and has been intensively learning her craft since age eleven. She's completed more than twenty poems and fifteen short stories, but most of her writing work has gone into drafts of twenty-nine novels that are in various stages. Her fascination with psychology plays out in the characters she brings to life. Allie is also an avid reader, especially with her Pitbull puppy, Mac, by her side.

ARIANA HARRISON, AGE 15, is a dedicated writer who adores her craft. She's been writing since she was five, which was when she decided she wanted to be an author. Since then, she's written numerous poems, multitudes of short stories, and worked on 8 novels, the majority of which she'd like to eventually publish. Ariana is a self-proclaimed "hardcore" Alaskan who enjoys dancing in thunderstorms, singing at the top of her lungs, and spending time with loved ones.

CHEYENNE INGALLS, AGE 17, lives in Utah. She writes every second she has a chance...even in class. She loves to create worlds and characters. Sharing those characters and worlds with others brings her great joy. She also likes reading and being outdoors. One of her favorite outdoor activities is dancing in the rain. She loves spending time with her family, her friends, and her adorable cat, Peaches.

DAEYANG DRAGONE, AGE 17, the preferred name of James Kim, is a lore nut. Often reading all they can on the lore of any story or universe. They, in their writings, attempt to infuse the seeds of further growth of lore past the story itself. Daeyang is also very political and often tries to infuse that into their writings as well.

EMILY CARLISLE, AGE 15, is an LDS teen author that spends nearly all of her time geeking out about the latest astronomy news, obsessing over fictional characters, and cheating death-AKA, surviving high school. Lover of sci-fi, the unknown, and making her readers sob in anger. Whenever Emily does have free time ("I can't remember the last time I had free time," she says, hidden behind mounds of homework), she spends it reading, writing, or watching BBC.

EMMA PERRY, AGE 16, when she isn't choreographing pirate ships and rambling in a Scottish accent, can be found rocking overalls, asking bizarre hypotheticals, and dancing shamelessly to her playlist. Although she calls herself "half-homeschooled," the truth is she's a senior at Liberty University Online and graduates with her bachelor's degree this summer after turning 17. When asked what the most important word is, Emma responds with *swashbuckling,* although *sushi* is a close second.

HAILEY CLEMENT, AGE 17, is a full-time High School student who is fluent in both English and Sarcasm. She has a mild addiction to pizza and video games. When she isn't stressing over homework or writing, she is probably waiting for her Hogwarts letter or hanging out with her muggle friends.

HEATHER DRABANT, AGE 17, loves daring adventures and impossible odds, preferably fictional ones to real ones. She spends her time weaving and reading grand tales in the outskirts of Spokane, Washington with her family and Labrador.

JACOB WILLDEN, AGE 18, is a student and an unabashed geek who is attending Utah Valley University. When not writing, he experiments with programing software, reads, cycles, sings, enjoys time with family, and most of all, does homework. He developed a small holiday light show display, complete with synchronized music, from scratch. He currently lives in Pleasant Grove with his family and dog.

JAMIE PERONA, AGE 16, is a teenage writer from Washington state who spends most of her time falling in love with fictional characters, admiring the mountains behind her house (which are totally straight out of Middle-earth), and attempting to make good art. A three-time NaNoWriMo winner, Jamie loves her pets, the Oxford comma, and coincidences. Oh, and she's a Ravenclaw.

KALEAH JACKSON, AGE 18, has been an avid reader and writer from a young age, enthralled by the worlds of fantasy and sci-fi. She also loves to travel and explore the world around her, drawing much inspiration from the places she has visited. She is currently studying computer science and animation.

KELLY LUNDGREN, AGE 18, is a perfectionist who knows that the quickest path to perfection is failure. She's an artist, actor, and oldest sibling. You might not think that would be important to her writing; but if you looked in on her, you'd see her acting out her writing, and even doing the voices! Her desk is crowded with doodles of characters, and her siblings give her the best writing prompts anyone could ever ask for.

KENZIE KOEHLE, AGE 18, has been an aspiring writer since her debut book in Kindergarten, "Angry Flower and Heart Flower." When she's not reading or writing, she's either playing tennis, trying to understand Calculus, dreaming of her favorite books, or coming up with new ideas. She's got two adorable dogs and a cat, as well as three brothers who aren't as adorable, but just as lovable.

KYLIE "KJ" HALLET, AGE 14, lives in Riverton, Utah. Aside from writing, she loves to sing and be onstage. She has been in nearly 20 productions, and aspires to one day perform on Broadway. Kylie would like to thank her parents, her siblings, her friends (hi guys), and her cat Romeo. "People who are different, their time is coming!" —Tracy Turnblad, *Hairspray*

LENICKA LEE, AGE 15, is entirely too skilled at stumbling over her words, which is why she writes. When not dreaming up new stories, she is beating her friends at board games, singing in choirs, and frantically finishing homework. She often wonders what happened to the days when a healthy amount of sleep was actually possible.

LEXI ROGERS, AGE 16, is a junior in high school. She's the oldest child in a family who loves the outdoors. She's passionate about the beach, the stars, and telling stories. She has a tiny dog that takes up too much room in the bed. She loves music, people, and musical people. She can't wait to travel the world someday.

LILIANA SMITH, AGE 14, when not writing stories, spends her time reading books (when she really should be going to bed...), working on seemingly endless amounts of homework, singing along to her favorite songs (poorly), playing video games, hanging out with her pet cat, or contemplating the mysteries of the universe (also known as: staring blankly at the wall for no apparent reason). This is her first published story and hopefully not her last.

MADISON PETERSON, AGE 18, has lived in Utah most of her life, except for an awkwardly-placed five years in Arizona, which reflects the early teenage years she spent there. She likes to write fantastical stories and angsty poetry, which reflects her grasp on reality. She also likes mirrors, which don't reflect anything, because she is a vampire. She loves Harry Potter, her family, and her handsome boyfriend.

MARIA YATES, AGE 13, is imaginative and enjoys sports and just about any kind of art. She loves school (except math!) and is a hardcore daredevil. She has a talent for exaggeration and inventing far-fetched stories that usually end up getting her what she wants. She has even been nicknamed "Tom Sawyer" for her mischievous nature and uncanny ability of persuasion. Her favorite pastimes are reading, acting, singing, writing, and finding loopholes.

MERLIN BLANCHARD, AGE 18, is a writer named after his great-grandfather (an Idahoan farmer). Merlin enjoys worldbuilding when he should be writing, letting his mind wander when he practices sword-work, and using his knowledge of Latin to sound cool. Despite being a long-time native of urban Utah, this half-wizard misses the forests of rural Virginia.

NATHAN SCHAFFER, AGE 17, is a junior in high school. He is a big fan of fishing, nature, art projects, and creating stories. Born in California, Nathan has lived in Utah since he was three. He loves spending time with his friends and family and has an older and younger brother. A Black Belt in Taekwondo, he likes to stay active and is currently on his high school baseball team.

SARAH STANLEY, AGE 15, is a teen who does teenager-y stuff (like doing homework responsibly and avoiding social media). For time to write, she must battle assignments, chores, and an incredibly persistent cat. When Sarah can steal away a few moments, she prefers to write sci-fi. She is a famous and universally acclaimed author among all her imaginary friends. Sarah lives in her house with her family, multiple pets, and a typewriter named Shawn.

SEQUOIA BRIGHTON, AGE 18, lives in Utah with an amazing family and very spoiled pets. She enjoys acting in school plays, spending time with her friends, and reading amazing books. She also spends a fair amount of time wandering through the world inside her own head and discovering the stories that live there. Her favorite author is Patrick Rothfuss who taught her to "love the feel of good words."

SHION COOK, AGE 14, has a creative passion for the arts that has existed since she was a child. That passion drives her desire to continuously improve her writing, drawing, singing, and acting skills. She also plays four musical instruments and aspires to become a renowned musician and actress. Pineapples and the color blue happen to be slight obsessions of hers. However, Shion's vivacious personality does not prevent her from caring for and serving others.

SOPHIE NICHOLSON, AGE 17, is a creative girl with a big heart. She has a passion for stories, both reading and writing them. She is an editor for her school's literary magazine and loves to help others improve their work.

SYDNEY BEAL, AGE 18, was born in Tulsa, Oklahoma, but raised in Spanish Fork, Utah. She plans to go to school at Southern Utah University following her graduation from Maple Mountain High School in May 2018. She likes shooting rifles and handguns, reading, fangirling, and hanging out with her family, which consists of her parents, brother, sister, and a chubby guinea pig.

Editor Bios

HANNAH STILES SMITH is an educator, has a BA in History, and has worked for years as an editor, helping bring fabulous books to their full potential. She spends her spare time escaping between the pages of a book, and a foray into publishing seemed like the best way to channel that energy. She lives in rural Virginia with her husband and four rambunctious children.

NICOLE BROUWER was born and raised in Georgia by a family of Southern storytellers. In kindergarten, she wrote a story about a misjudged bush that won first prize in the MOSAIC creative writing competition and she's been hooked on writing ever since. Nicole graduated from BYU-Hawaii with a degree in Social Work, married a great guy from Holland, and is the happy mama of three busy children. She loves to travel and excels in people-watching and daydreaming. Nicole recently completed her debut novel, *The Lotus Ladies of London*, and is currently working with her dream agent, Jenny Bent of the Bent Agency, to prepare for submission.

For more information and to discover other books by Owl Hollow Press, find us here:

Website: owlhollowpress.com
Twitter: @owlhollowpress
Facebook: Owl Hollow Press
Instagram: owlhollowpress

OWL HOLLOW PRESS

WORLD-ALTERING STORIES, REAL AND IMAGINED

73823777R00234

Made in the USA
San Bernardino, CA
09 April 2018